Fox

THE SHAAR PRESS

THE JUDAICA IMPRINT
FOR THOUGHTFUL PEOPLE

INTERRUPTED

A
SHAAR
PRESS
PUBLICATION

JOURNEY

A NOVEL BY RACHEL SCHORR
TRANSLATED BY ZVI BEN BARUCH

Published by **SHAAR PRESS**
Distributed by MESORAH PUBLICATIONS, LTD.
4401 Second Avenue / Brooklyn, N.Y 11232 / (718) 921-9000 / www.artscroll.com

Distributed in Israel by SIFRIATI / A. GITLER
6 Hayarkon Street / Bnei Brak 51127

Distributed in Europe by LEHMANNS
Unit E, Viking Business Park, Rolling Mill Road / Jarrow, Tyne and Wear, NE32 3DP/ England

Distributed in Australia and New Zealand by GOLDS WORLD OF JUDAICA
3-13 William Street / Balaclava, Melbourne 3183 / Victoria Australia

Distributed in South Africa by KOLLEL BOOKSHOP
Shop 8A Norwood Hypermarket / Norwood 2196, Johannesburg, South Africa

ISBN: 1-4226-0040-8 Hard Cover
ISBN: 1-4226-0041-6 Paperback

Printed in the United States of America by Noble Book Press
Custom bound by Sefercraft, Inc. / 4401 Second Avenue / Brooklyn N.Y. 11232

CHAPTER ONE

Road to Tel Aviv, July 1966

Yaakov and Sarah Binder sped down the road with 3-week-old Elchanan nestled in his carrier in the car's back seat. The happy family was traveling to Tel Aviv to finalize their plans for *aliyah*. Sarah carried all their French papers in her handbag, to submit everything needed for naturalization and Israeli citizenship.

They stopped at the side of the road to take pictures of each other holding Choni, and quickly finished the roll of film already in their camera. "I can't wait to get home so we can have these pictures developed," said Sarah. "I want to put all of Choni's photos in an album right away!"

Yaakov smiled at the obvious happiness in her voice. He added, "Don't forget to have copies made, so we can send them to our families in France. Your parents haven't seen Choni since they flew in for his *bris*, and he's changed so much in the past two weeks! My parents are constantly asking for pictures. So is our sister-in-law Dinah. She's so happy for us, and she's so impressed that we made *aliyah* so close to your due date."

They got back into the car and Yaakov continued driving. Suddenly, the steering wheel locked. The car skidded toward the side of the road, crashing into the guardrail. The sound of *Shema* filled the air as the car flipped over. There was a screech of tortured metal, then silence broken by the newborn's cry.

ھچھۑ

Responding to a radio call, the Israeli policeman drove up to the wrecked vehicle at the accident scene. The driver and his wife had both been killed, but their 3-week-old son had survived. Officer Ron Green followed the ambulance that carried the baby from the scene of the accident to Tel HaShomer Hospital, on the outskirts of Tel Aviv.

The nurse showed Officer Green the chart confirming that Elchanan Binder had been born at the hospital three weeks earlier. Feeling sorry for the infant and not wanting to leave him alone, Green asked for a phone at the nurses' station. He called the French embassy to apprise them of the deaths of "Jacques and Alice Binder," the names he found on the papers in the dead woman's handbag. He was given the phone number of Alice's parents in France, and was told to call them himself. Her parents, religious Jews who called their daughter "Sarah," spoke fluent, French-accented Hebrew, and the phone call to deliver the painful news was brief. The Kahns were overwhelmingly distraught to hear of the deaths, but relieved that their grandson, at least, had survived with only minor injuries.

Several religious Jews soon arrived at the hospital to claim the baby on his grandmother's behalf. Officer Green watched as they left the hospital with the infant. They took him to the home of an Orthodox family, where the wife would watch the baby until his grandparents arrived for the funeral.

⧈⧈

Dinah Binder finished packing her husband's suitcase. "You go to your brother's funeral in Eretz Yisrael; I'll stay here with the kids," she said, looking at the family portrait on her dresser. Eight smiling faces shone up at her.

"Dinah, how will you manage with six kids by yourself?" protested Chaim.

"I will, don't worry about me. Worry about your orphaned nephew, instead. What will happen to Choni?" asked Dinah.

"I'm sure Sarah's siblings will take him, or her parents will," Chaim answered.

"They're too old and already have houses full of much older kids. They won't want him. Let's bring him here, to France. We can raise him. Pinchas is already a year old, and Yoav is 14."

"Are you serious? Do you really want — " Chaim couldn't finish his question.

With eyes brimming with tears, Dinah said, "Yes. I think we should adopt Choni and raise him as our own."

CHAPTER TWO

Jerusalem, 5736 (1976)

Pinchas burst into the house calling, "Ima, where are you? We got back our Gemara tests!"

"I'm here," called Dinah, momentarily abandoning her lunch preparations. "What did you get?"

Choni, the youngest in the family, also approached his older brother and waited to hear the grade.

"Ninety-six!" said Pinchas triumphantly. "I didn't believe it myself!"

Dinah hugged the child warmly. "You're going to be quite a *talmid chacham*, aren't you?" she said excitedly. Her French accent was very pronounced. It was most apparent when she was very excited or angry.

"Yesterday I got 100 on a test," said Choni from the side.

"Hey, Elchanan, we were excited for you, too, yesterday, and we even showed the test to Abba," Dinah reminded him.

"That's right."

Choni left the living room and went into the kitchen. "What happened to my lunch?" he whined. "It's burned! You only think about Pinchas, not about me!"

"Ridiculous!" said Dinah.

"It's true. You even left my food to go hug him." The jealousy was clear in every word. It ate up Dinah, who did not know how to react.

She sent Pinchas to his room to get ready for dinner.

"Why are you so angry? I'll make you more food."

"I'll have to wait again," Choni complained.

"In two minutes you'll have a hot meal."

Dinah quickly prepared the food. When Pinchas walked into the kitchen, she practically ignored him. "Choni and I are eating together now," she said. "Soon I'll prepare a cutlet for you, too. You can take some soup in the meantime." There was a note of pleading in Dinah's voice, and Pinchas was mature enough to grasp it and follow her lead.

"If you're tired, Ima, I can wash the dishes," Choni volunteered.

"And I can wash the floor," added Pinchas.

Dinah gazed at her children lovingly. "You two are the greatest," she said, and lightly pinched Pinchas' cheek. "You're both *tzaddikim*, but I have enough strength to take care of the house myself. You go learn."

"You always get excited about him," Choni whined as he ruined the pleasant moment. "You don't love me at all, you only love Pinchas. I made the first offer, and even so...."

Dinah Binder paled. "Why, Choni, what's the matter?"

The child left the table and stood beside her. He spoke with anger. "You think I don't notice it? Why do you hug Pinchas when he gets a good mark, while all I get is a smile? It's always Pinchas, Pinchas, Pinchas. I can't take it!"

The younger boy retreated to his room, leaving his mother astonished and almost in tears.

"Choni is a bit upset. We'll give him time to calm down," she told Pinchas quietly. Then she collected the dirty dishes and put them into the sink.

"I'm going to a friend's house to learn," said Pinchas. "In the afternoon, I'll go straight to *cheider* with him."

"Fine."

When Pinchas left the house, Dinah went to rest. Two minutes later, she ran to the door to make sure Pinchas had closed it. He had. She passed by Choni's room. The music was on high volume, and Dinah knew that he was still angry. She did not want to speak to Choni while he was feeling that way. Actually, she was afraid to speak to him at all. His arguments were valid, but her reasoning was also valid. Who was right here?

She had tried speaking to her husband about the matter, but he felt strongly that there was a simple solution to the problem. He claimed that the child needed to know the truth, but Dinah adamantly refused to tell Choni his history. She did not want to expose his young heart to such pain. *At least let him have a serene childhood*, she thought.

"You wanted to take him in, and now there's no turning back," her husband Chaim had said impatiently when she complained about her difficulties.

"He is your nephew," Dinah reminded him.

"True. And I'm happy that you wanted to take him. But we knew there would be difficulties. Now there is no choice but to find a way to manage."

Chaim's voice softened. Actually, from the moment his real estate office had begun to flourish, he was almost never home, and that is where they all felt the greatest pressure. Success had smiled upon the head of the family after nine years of hard work. The turning point had come in the past year. Without waiting, as soon as he had the money, Chaim had hurried to buy a larger apartment.

He had invested a fortune in it, but Dinah thought it was a waste of money. She had loved the quiet evening hours, when she would prepare tasty suppers and she and Chaim would eat together. Now that the office was so successful, Chaim had to spend many more hours there. True, she no longer had to go out to work as a saleswoman. Now she could allow herself an entirely different lifestyle, one that somewhat resembled the light-hearted days of her youth in Paris. But Chaim's busier schedule was hard for Dinah to adjust to.

When they had moved to Israel, Chaim reminded her that this was actually her decision, and she could still change her mind. But she could not bring herself to back out, and so they packed up all their belongings, took their young children, and flew to Israel.

Dinah's afternoon nap was filled with discomfort. After half an hour of misery, she took the phone and quickly dialed a familiar number.

"Yoav, are you busy now?"

"Not at all. How are you, Ima? You sound upset."

"I am."

They conversed in French, so that Dinah could speak without worry. Yoav was her firstborn. When she needed advice or a listening ear, she did not hesitate to call him.

"I need your help, Yoav," she said.

"I noticed that lately you've been very tense."

"Very much so. Yoav, I hope that you have some time for me, because there's a lot I want to say."

"My *chavrusah* will be coming late today. Take your time," Yoav said while holding an infant in one hand and helping his oldest daughter assemble a puzzle with the other.

"I don't know what to do, Yoav. Abba is very insistent, but I'm hesitant."

"About what?"

"Abba says the time has come to tell Choni the truth, but I'm very worried. This arrangement is far from ideal. Pinchas is so jealous. Look, Pinchas is my youngest son. He's older than Choni, but unfortunately, his learning capabilities lag behind Choni's. Not only is Choni gifted intellectually, but he has wonderful *middos* as well. I try to encourage Pinchas, but every time I do, Choni becomes angry and argues about my discriminating against him. I feel compassion for him and I love him, but I must help Pinchas. He looks at Choni's test scores and you can see the jealousy in his eyes.

"As they grow older, Choni notices more and more clearly how I try to protect Pinchas. You know, he once told me that he notices how different he is from the rest of the family. They are all — without exception — light skinned and blue eyed. Only he is dark, with curly black hair. More than once he asked me if perhaps he was adopted — "

"I thought there were no problems with it," murmured Yoav.

"There are many, Yoav. The child is eating himself up. Look, I don't want to cause Pinchas to be jealous of Choni's academic success, but on the other hand, I want to encourage Choni. It gets more complicated. Choni is aware of what happens around him. He's a very clever child. I'm very concerned."

"Is Choni home now?"

"Yes, he's in his room."

"So that's why you're speaking French."

"Of course. Today he complained that I don't love him. I'm afraid that even though we love him like we do all of you, he senses that there is a difference."

"And perhaps you are feeling pangs of conscience for no reason?" suggested Yoav.

"Perhaps." Dinah's delicate voice sounded helpless. "So what do you think we should do, Yoav?"

Yoav's answer was short and to the point. "To tell you the truth, Ima, I think you should ask a Rav. Perhaps it is best to tell him the truth."

"Impossible!"

"Look, Ima, you called to hear my opinion. This time, I agree completely with Abba. Choni has a right to know the truth. He can't be kept in the dark forever. This is his life."

"Tell him at such an early age?"

"Why should this be dragged out into adolescence, when everything becomes harder to accept?"

"Maybe you're right."

As if on cue, the baby in Yoav's arms started crying, and his big sister asked for a different puzzle.

Dinah hung up the phone and tried to nap, but Choni's words pounded in her head. "You don't love me ... You don't love me ..."

She did fall asleep for a short time and awoke like a bolt when she heard knocking on the door.

"I'm going to *cheider*, Ima. It's 4 o'clock already. I'm nearly late."

"You're right. I overslept and forgot to wake you," Dina replied.

He stared at her half serious, half in anger. "You wouldn't have forgotten to wake Pinchas. You'd be afraid the rebbi would be angry with him."

"Choni, I want you, once and for all, to stop these comparisons," Dina insisted.

He became quiet for a moment. Then he blurted out, "It doesn't matter. One of Pinchas' friends said it was impossible for us to be brothers. We don't look or act similar. I'm different from the whole family. I know. You love me the least of all."

Dina interrupted, "That's not true. You know that I love you. Come on, Choni, get moving before you really are late for *cheider*. Have a great afternoon."

She walked him to the door and waited until she saw him reach the end of the street. Then she shut the door behind her.

No doubt about it, life was full of doubts and difficulties. It was impossible to go on living this way. Sensitive as she was, Dinah knew that the truth would come out and it was better to tell him before someone else did.

She went back to bed and closed her eyes. As if in a dream, she saw Choni as an infant. She had met him here, in Israel. His cheeks were red, flushed from crying. She had gone over to him, picked him up, and hugged him.

"He's like my own son," she had declared, and had taken the child to their home in Paris.

Choni had been a dark-eyed baby with a pure soul that had shone on his delicate face. His helplessness and the reality of his life had caused Dinah to undertake the responsibility. Chaim, who was more realistic, had been opposed to the idea. Those were hard times. Israel was practically a war zone. He didn't want to move to Israel, but Dinah insisted on raising the child there, where no one would know that he was not her own. She was adamant, and in the end, Chaim agreed to move to Israel.

"Why?" Chaim would ask repeatedly.

"Because your brother wanted to raise the child in Israel. He wanted to take advantage of the stronger level of *chinuch* and *Yiddishkeit*."

Chaim had always wanted to change his brother's mind about where to raise his son. But since that was impossible, Chaim had to abandon his comfortable life in Paris for the sake of his nephew. More than once, when he encountered difficulties in Israel, he felt he had sacrificed his life for his nephew.

Whenever he looked at Choni's face, he saw his younger brother Yaakov. Little Choni was the spitting image of his father. The child resembled his father in personality as well. Choni's questions were like Yaakov's had been. They contained the same curiosity, deep investigation, unusual goodness of heart, and feeling for others. He was also sensitive to details.

Choni had inherited all of Yaakov's good qualities, which would invoke Chaim's memories of his brother, who had also been a good friend. The memory of it all pained Chaim, and Dinah knew it. She tried to compensate for the confusing relationship Choni had with his adoptive father.

But now, as the child was growing up, things were changing. In the first place, Choni was a bright child. He was looking around and noticing the physical differences between himself and the other members of the family. Secondly, the very fact that she was always protective of Pinchas, accentuating his successes, was sending Choni a message that he was somehow different from Pinchas.

In reality the situation was no different from that of other households where there are two siblings who are close in age but vastly different in personalities and scholastic ability. To Choni school was a breeze, while Pinchus struggled through his day. It was only natural that Dinah paid greater attention to Pinchas' needs, but she still felt guilty. It pained her that maybe she wasn't being fair to Choni — but what should she do? Every mother knows that different children have different needs. She could only pray for *Siyata DiShmaya* to do her best for both Choni and Pinchus. She felt as if she were caught in quicksand — the more she struggled, the deeper she sank.

But that evening she received a surprise phone call from Paris that left her little choice.

CHAPTER THREE

A fluorescent light glowed in the small kitchen. It was 1 o'clock in the morning. Paris was asleep, but the elderly couple was wide awake and alert as ever.

"How did you remember him all of a sudden, Moishe?" asked Rivkah as she put up the water to boil.

"He's our grandson. You don't understand. He is the *Kaddish* of our Sarah, *aleha hashalom*." Although the old man's voice was steady, the tears glistening in his eyes betrayed his emotions.

Rivkah did not like to speak about Sarah. She preferred to vent her feelings with her head buried in her feather pillow. Who would have believed that her Sarah, her sweet youngest child, would meet such a fate? All that remained of her was this one child.

"I, too, would like her son to know about her. The same way you do," she tried to calm Moishe. "I, too, would like to know him, Moishe. But we have to consider what is good for the child."

Rivkah poured the boiling water into a large mug.

Moishe stood up and leaned on the table. "The boy is getting older. Soon he will be bar mitzvah. Why did we give him up? Why did we give him to Yaakov's side? Why?"

Rivkah closed her eyes and sipped the hot tea. In her mind, she returned to that terrible summer day, ten years earlier.

ֿ♥♥ֿ

The police officer, Ron, had spoken to her before Moishe picked up the phone extension. After that, many tears flowed in their little house. They had traveled from France to the funeral of Sarah and Yaakov. They were joined by their children — Gitty and her husband, and Pessiah, Shimon, and Baruch—while their spouses had remained behind to take care of the little children. The stewardesses on the flight were surprised to see adults sitting and quietly weeping. Many puzzled passengers eyed them, but the family did not pay attention.

Yaakov's brother, Chaim, was on that flight as well. The parents of Chaim and Yaakov were living in a home for the aged. They were very old, and Chaim felt there was no reason to inform them of their son's death. They had bid Yaakov farewell when he had left for Israel. Let them think he was still alive and well. As the only representative of Yaakov's family, Chaim had felt alone on the plane until Sarah's relatives drew him into their sorrowful group.

The funeral was small but heartrending. Yaakov and Sarah were buried in the land that they loved so much. After the funeral, they all went to see little Elchanan. The woman who had been temporarily caring for him did so with devotion, putting her whole heart into him. He seemed blissful in his ignorance of all that had transpired.

"What are your plans for the child?" Chaim had asked.

Everyone looked at everyone else. The master of the house, the baby-sitter's husband, ushered them into his living room and closed the door so that they could discuss the situation.

Moishe suggested that the child come to live with them, but everyone disagreed.

"Mama does not have the strength to raise a child. Someone — one of us — will have to take him."

Gitty, the oldest daughter, voiced her hesitation aloud. She was trying to find a shidduch for her fourth son. It was not easy to take an infant who would require so much of her attention into a household of grown-ups.

Pessiah had fifteen children of her own. She did not have room for another crib in her house.

Shimon volunteered, but everyone rejected his offer. He had a 2-month-old daughter, and his wife would not be able to take care of the orphaned baby.

Who was left? Baruch.

Baruch cleared his throat, in an obvious state of discomfort. "Chayah said that if there is no one else, then... but... that is... can someone else volunteer? Please understand. Parnassah is a bit difficult, and she works very hard," he stammered in his wife's defense.

No one pressured him. There was no point in placing a helpless infant in a house that would not welcome him with open arms.

"I'll take Elchanan."

Six pairs of disbelieving eyes turned their riveting glace to Chaim. "You're from the father's family. Doesn't the mother's family have more of an obligation?" said Shimon.

"No problem. My wife very much wants to take the child. I hesitated at first because I felt you all had first rights. But I see that you are having difficulty working it out. My youngest is already 1 year old, and Elchanan will fit in well."

"Are you sure it won't disturb your family?" asked Shimon. He felt ill at ease.

"Not at all. I'll tell my wife to come to Israel, and then we will take him to live with us in France."

Moishe said firmly, "I don't want my grandson to leave my family."

Chaim looked him straight in the eye. "I don't see any alternative, Mr. Kahn."

Everyone understood full well that if none of the families would take him, the baby would have to be given up for adoption — which was out of the question.

"Papa, please don't be so stubborn," pleaded Gitty, the oldest. "They will simply raise the child; they are not kidnapping him. This is the best environment for him now. The time will come when you will see your grandson."

"Promise us that we will be able to see the child whenever we wish," insisted Rivkah.

"Very well, I promise, b'li neder," Chaim announced unwillingly.

"As long as he is a baby, there will be no problem seeing him. When he gets older we will figure out what to do," said Moishe, consenting to the unwritten agreement.

Dinah arrived from France and treated Elchanan as if he were her own child.

"She will raise him like a mother would," Rivkah comforted Moishe. "The child will not run away from us. Don't worry."

A few days later, when they were all back in Paris, they saw that Chaim and Dinah treated the child as if he were their own son — too much like another son and too little like the only child of their beloved youngest daughter.

One day Chaim and Dinah came to them with little Elchanan, and the grandparents were delighted to see the 2-month-old who already smiled at everyone and showed signs of affection. "This is the last visit for the near future," said Chaim. "We've decided to move to Israel."

The elderly couple protested vehemently. But Chaim and Dinah were adamant. "The child's parents wanted to raise him in Israel. We will do what they could not. This was their wish and we want to fulfill it," said Dinah resolutely.

Later, she was inundated with phone calls from various Kahn family members who tried to pressure her into reconsidering their decision. First Sarah was snatched from them, and now their precious grandson Elchanan.

Her husband's entire family joined the fracas, which was resolved in the Binders' favor.

≈❁❁≈

The passage of ten years left the stamp of age on Moishe and Rivkah Kahn. Lately, Moishe had been complaining of some physical ailments and diminished functioning. This past week, he had brought up Chaim Binder's decade-old promise.

Now, at 1 o'clock in the morning, Moishe woke up from a nightmare. "Rivkah, I want to see Sarah's son, Elchanan. I want to know that all is well with him. I feel uneasy about him."

Rivkah served him another glass of tea. "Drink, Moishe, it's good for you. I don't understand why you remembered him suddenly now."

Moishe looked at her through squinting eyes. "You don't understand? I'll tell you." He lowered his voice. "I am not a youngster. Perhaps it's not so pleasant to hear me say it. Perhaps it's also not right to speak this way. But I'm not getting any younger, Rivkah, and I want to see my grandson. I have a right."

"Don't talk that way," said Rivkah, frightened.

"Very well. Let's say I feel fine, and let's say that I'm 100 percent healthy and a good few years younger. I still want to see my grandson."

"You will disrupt his peaceful, happy life. Why do you want to befuddle the child with the past?"

"Because that past will be his future. He must say *Kaddish* for his parents. He must know what happened to them years ago. We must not let him ignore the matter!" Moishe's voice was pleading. "The best thing is for the child to live in the real world, to know the truth. I'm sure it's also hard for the Binders to live this way."

"I don't think it's so hard for them," she replied. "They have only one young child at home, Pinchas, who gets along well with Elchanan. I call them once in a while to hear how he is, and they tell me everything is fine."

"Let's invite the child to us. We'll sit him down and tell him the truth, the whole story, in a way that it will be easy for him to hear. It pains me that he calls his aunt Ima, and that he thinks that she is his real mother."

Moishe sobbed into his handkerchief, and Rivkah did not know what to do. She hoped that a good night's sleep would help him forget about his preposterous idea, but she was sorely mistaken. In the morning, Moishe phoned each of his children and told them of his desire to see his grandson, reminding them of Chaim's promise to him.

"I'm sure they won't keep him from you, Papa, but why do

it? Why don't you just leave well enough alone?" Gitty tried to convince him.

"I am not young anymore. Elchanan must know the truth," he said in an obstinate tone of voice.

☙❦❦☙

While Dinah was in the kitchen washing the supper dishes, she thought about the tranquility that had finally settled over the family. At last, Choni appeared calm. Pinchas was sitting and learning in the living room. Her married children were busy at their homes, getting their children ready for bed. Chaim was in his office. True, it was a bit hard that he was always so busy in the office, but ultimately it was to her advantage.

Life had been difficult of late, but even such challenging periods pass, she thought with satisfaction as she began to dry the dishes.

The phone rang, breaking into her thoughts.

She lifted the receiver and then cast a quick glance around. Choni was in his room, playing with the new computer. Pinchas was in the living room. She could speak freely.

"How are you, Mr. Kahn? How is your wife?" She spoke in a warm, friendly tone, but the old man was in no mood for small talk. He got straight to the point and Dinah was taken aback.

"I will have to speak to my husband about that."

The older man's reaction was somewhat angry, and Dinah's tone immediately softened. "Of course you're right, Mr. Kahn, we will not stop you from seeing the child. It's your right and privilege as his grandfather. I only said I can't give you an answer without first talking to my husband."

There was a brief silence. Then Dinah spoke again. "Look. If he promised, I'm sure it will be no problem. We will be in touch. Of course, we have your phone number. Goodbye."

She hung up and sat down on a nearby chair. Her hands trembled.

"Ima, do you feel all right?" Choni came out of his room and ran to her, frightened by her appearance.

"I'm fine, Choni," she said. "Go back to your room."

"Do you want something to drink?" Choni continued. "Maybe I should call Abba. One time, a rebbi fainted in *cheider*. He looked just like you do now, Ima."

"Everything is fine, Choni, go back to your room," she told him. She wanted to phone Chaim.

"I'll stay with you and watch you," the child volunteered. "Anyway, I finished my homework and I have nothing to do now. After all, Pinchas doesn't want to play with me. He never wants to."

Not wanting to start this discussion right now, and feeling a growing need to speak with Chaim privately, Dinah tried again to get Choni to go to his room. He resisted her coaxing, and Dinah became impatient.

"Choni, go to your room immediately," she said.

Choni felt snubbed. He walked slowly to his room. Just before entering, he turned and called out, "You never used to treat me like this. Now you're always getting angry at me."

He went into his room and closed the door.

Dinah bit her lip. Suppose the aging grandparents *do* meet Choni. Would he tell them that she was a bad mother?

Dinah wanted to sit with him, to comfort him before they were forced to give him the disturbing news, but she couldn't move. After a moment of silence, she got up and went to the phone. With her hand on the receiver she suddenly changed her mind. Instead she took her pocketbook and told the boys she was going out for a short time.

Chaim would be surprised to see her.

CHAPTER FOUR

The receptionist sitting in the waiting room pressed a button on the telephone.

"Mr. Binder, there's someone here to see you," she announced in a soft voice. Chaim responded quickly, "I'm busy. The only reason we're here this late is because I'm busy. Tell them that I see people by appointment only."

Dinah bit her lip. You could count on one hand the number of times she had visited her husband's office. Why should she have to explain to some employee that she was the boss's wife?

"Mr. Binder is busy. Would you like me to set up an appointment?" the receptionist asked politely.

"No, I just want to know where his new office is located." She did not have this information either, and was quite embarrassed to admit that she was none other than Mrs. Binder.

"It's the office all the way on the right," the receptionist indicated with a wave of her hand. But when she saw the woman set out in that direction, she cried out, "Excuse me, ma'am, you can't — "

But the woman had already disappeared into the room. The receptionist shrugged her shoulders in resignation. She was sure to be reprimanded by her boss, an occupational hazard.

Chaim Binder was heavily preoccupied when Dinah entered his office.

"I said I was not accepting any appointments now," Chaim said, his face buried in his paperwork.

"This is an exception," she said. The familiar voice surprised him and he raised his head in disbelief.

"Dinah, what are you doing here? Have you come for a visit?" His expression immediately changed to one of deep pleasure. He was always urging his wife to visit his office. It was important for him that she know what a success he was, how large the office had grown, and how much his employees respected him.

Dinah's expression, however, was subdued, which Chaim found frustrating. He lit an expensive cigar and moved toward the window. There was a brief silence in the room, short enough for Dinah to wipe away a small tear.

"What's the matter?" asked Chaim gently.

"They called."

"Who are they?"

"They — the Kahns, if you remember — "

The Kahns, Chaim muttered to himself, blowing out small white smoke rings. Dinah did not look in his direction but sat in the chair, seeming withdrawn. "Aah, I recall. You mean my brother's in-laws. What do they want?"

"They are interested in their grandson."

"Why now, all of a sudden?" Chaim left the window and stared at his wife with growing discomfort. "You don't have to cry anymore. Whatever happens, don't cry over them. You've performed a great *chesed* for them."

"But they yelled at me. You should have heard how hostile they sounded."

"What did they want?" asked Chaim patiently, handing his wife a tissue.

"They want us to send Choni to France," answered Dinah. "They want to tell him who his parents were. They want to bring him back into their family."

"Is that what they want? Did I hear you correctly?" Chaim was overwrought. While continuing to listen to his wife, he moved to close the door of his office. One of his secretaries buzzed, and he replied with some impatience that he should not be disturbed for the next few minutes.

As usual, when Dinah became excited, she usually reverted to her mother tongue — French. "Well, they've decided the boy is old enough to learn the truth. They also want to see him before they die. Go argue with them about death. I told them that this would be detrimental for the boy. They started screaming that we stole Choni. They're talking like we kidnapped him. That's ridiculous. We have always treated him with the utmost kindness."

Chaim replied, "You're right, although I do agree with them that the boy needs to know about his family and his past. You yourself see how the entire business casts a shadow over our lives. Nevertheless, they are not connected to us. They have no right to make decisions regarding the child. We were the ones who accepted Choni. I know the Kahns wanted to keep him in their family, but their children vetoed their suggestion on the grounds that it was difficult for elderly parents to raise an infant!" Chaim recalled with indignation. "We raised him since he was a baby, and now that he's almost grown up, they want him back on a silver platter. After we have grown attached to the boy, I will not allow this. I will deal with them today about it," Chaim promised.

"Be gentle with them; they are sensitive people."

"We'll see."

Chaim abruptly changed the topic. "I'm pleased that you came here. Would you like to see the other rooms in the office? You haven't been here since the renovations."

"Chaim!" Dinah scolded. "How can you think about such things at a time like this?"

He shrugged his shoulders. "If you'd rather not, it's okay. We'll leave it for some other time."

She left with a serious look on her face, and Chaim accompanied her out of his office. The confused receptionist stared at them.

"I told her she couldn't go in, but she didn't listen," the girl muttered.

"So I see you met my wife without me. Too bad, I wanted to make the introductions myself," Chaim announced.

The surprised expression on the secretary's face was a classic. *This was Mrs. Binder? But she seemed so unpretentious!*

When Chaim and Dinah took leave of each other at the elevator, Chaim remarked, "It would be a good idea to start preparing Choni for the truth."

"Does that mean you're ready to give in to them?" She deliberately stated it in an inflammatory manner. Although Chaim seemed to agree with their viewpoint, she was convinced that he could not tolerate others telling him what to do.

"I'm not giving up. I believe that it's important that he hear the truth, but only from us, and not from anyone else," Chaim explained. "You know what? Hold off on that for the moment. Let's first see how things develop."

The elevator arrived, and Dinah pressed Hold. "Are you willing to send Choni to them now?" She looked straight at him and waited for his response.

Chaim was disconcerted. "Under no circumstances. Choni is my son, just like my other children. Choni is ours, and we're not going to give him to anyone. We will be the ones to determine his fate."

The elevator door closed, and Dinah felt some satisfaction from Chaim's last statement. She had achieved her goal. He admitted that he loves his nephew very much, and will not give up Choni so easily. It was just too bad that he did not bother demonstrating his love to Choni once in a while.

⋙✤✤⋘

"Have I reached the Kahn family?" asked Chaim. He had called the French phone number after he had returned home after Dinah's visit.

"Yes, Chaim, it's Moishe Kahn, how are you? How is Choni?" The affability was noticeably artificial. Even Rivkah sensed a lack of sincerity. She came to stand next to her husband to help reinforce his words. Sarah's child was so important to her.

"He's fine, *baruch Hashem*, growing all the time. You spoke with my wife, who told me briefly about your call. I'd like to hear more details."

Moishe sat down in a chair near the telephone. "We'd like to see the boy. Not to take him — just to see him."

"No problem." Chaim's response surprised Dinah, who was listening on the other extension. She nearly fainted when she heard Chaim agree to their request without even discussing it first with her.

"Reb Moishe, you are invited to visit our house at any time. Of course, you understand that we are under no obligation to inform the boy that you are his grandparents. We might tell him instead you are an aunt and uncle. We can settle on a day that would be convenient for you."

"Just a moment, Chaim. What do you mean 'settle on a day'?" The old man became agitated.

"What's the matter?" Chaim said innocently.

"What do you mean 'what's the matter?'" yelled Moishe. "We cannot travel to Israel. At our age, we can't fly! We are the boy's grandparents. We'd like him to know that we exist."

"I thought you said you were interested in just seeing him," said Chaim.

Moishe groaned. "You and your brother — both the same," he concluded. "He, too, was very sharp, that Yaakov. He always knew how to turn things around to his advantage. You both inherited the quick wits from your father, the community Rav. Just one thing, Chaim Binder: You won't be able to take advantage of me. Although I'm an old man, I still have some brains in my head. And I'm telling you something that had better be clear to you. This boy is my daughter's son. We want to be sure he's happy in your home. We want him to know that he has grandparents who love and care about him. We want him to become acquainted with his mother's family. My wife wants to tell him stories about his mother's past. That's what we want. Anyway, today he's a grown boy, so — "

"So you are demanding that I decide where he should live?"

The question was phrased to taunt, but Moishe was not perturbed. "Like I said, you are very clever, so I don't have to explain too much for you to understand me. That's precisely what I meant. Maybe the boy wants to live with us in France. He is now old enough for us to offer him a choice."

"Why? How could you even dream of cutting off the boy from his home?" The pain and anger were just below the surface.

Moishe became silent. He had erred, and his mistake would cost him dearly. He tried to backtrack. "You're right, Chaim. I'm not planning to take the boy away. I just wanted you to know how much we worry about him. We worry so much, that we are willing to clear out a room in our house for him, to make him as happy as possible here."

Fortunately, Chaim Binder was a very astute man. He signaled to Dinah not to interrupt their conversation, and to restrain her tears and hold back any angry remarks. He continued speaking calmly in French, as if he were in his house in Paris.

"Reb Moishe, let's not get into an argument. We are, after all, partners in this tragedy. We are not interested in telling the boy right now about his past. Let the boy live in peace."

"You won't succeed in duping me," mumbled Moishe into the mouthpiece, with Rivkah nodding in assent, supporting her husband. "We want to tell the child the truth. You don't have to be the people to do it. Just send the boy to us."

"And if we don't?" Chaim chose his words with care. He wanted to see in which direction the old man was heading, and how serious he was.

Moishe's frightening response came immediately. "You don't want to get involved with lawyers, do you? Let's resolve this by mutual consent."

"Let me think it over. We'll talk tomorrow."

"*S'il vous plaît*, but don't take too long," the old man said politely.

Chaim Binder replaced the receiver, after which a thunderous silence reigned. Two minutes later, he turned to Dinah. "They are more serious than I imagined. They aren't a helpless elderly couple. It could be very difficult to deal with them. The old man is determined, and he has the means to entangle us in serious legal problems."

"What should we do?"

"We'll have to compromise. There's no choice."

"Tell Choni he's adopted? Never!" shouted Dinah resolutely, her fists clenched, a reaction Chaim had never seen in his life.

Chaim looked at her with disbelief.

"What?" asked Dinah in a frightened voice. "What happened?"

Chaim stared at the floor. "You should know that if I were in their place, I too would demand this, and wouldn't give up my rights. Between you and me, they're right. We are just an uncle and aunt. They are the grandparents."

Dinah wanted to shout at the top of her lungs, "We are not an aunt and uncle! We are his parents!" but she restrained herself. Perhaps because she was choked up by her tears — or perhaps because Chaim continued talking, and his words confused her.

"This child, Choni, is simply a copy of Yaakov. You can't imagine how much I miss Yaakov. And here, Choni constantly reminds me of what's missing in my life. If only I had parents who could help me get over this trauma — My immediate family is gone, deceased, and Choni was left behind as a deposit. Sometimes, sometimes — the deposit is too large for me to handle."

When he saw the look on Dinah's face, he became flustered and uncomfortable.

"Don't pay any attention to my ramblings. It's probably a good idea to start getting Choni ready to meet his grandparents."

"No," Dinah cried. She then added, "You tell him; I will not be the one to speak to him about this subject."

CHAPTER FIVE

Dinah was suffused with emotion, but she also possessed a fine sensitivity and an acute sense of understanding. She knew that Chaim's willingness to tell Choni the secrets of his past was partially because Chaim would give her the unwelcome task of telling the boy about his parents' death. Dinah hoped that if Chaim would have to deal with this issue himself, he would decide not to involve the boy in the very unpleasant argument between him and his grandparents. Dinah did not know which way was best. Should they take it to court, or was it better to meet with the old folks themselves and hash it out with them? She decided that she would not hesitate to fly to France if necessary. Choni was her son, and she would protect him from any darkness that threatened to enter his life.

When Chaim heard his wife's request, he immediately understood her intentions. Was it easy to tell a child the circumstances of his adoption? Surely not. But Chaim decided not to retreat from confrontation. He knew that the boy's grandparents would not rest until they met him. So he decided to take control of the matter.

The following day, when he arose, he told his wife, "Dinah, tell Choni that he's not going to *cheider* this morning. I want to speak with him."

Dinah was in control of her voice when she said, "You decided it should be today? I hope it'll be — all right. I'll tell him."

"Tell him to wait for me till I get back from *davening*," he added. He knew what he had to *daven* for, in addition to the usual requests.

"As far as I'm concerned — it's fine. By the way, Chaim, I'm going shopping today."

"Today of all days?"

"I planned this days ago," Dinah apologized.

The conversation was clear to both sides. Chaim thought that Dinah would eventually come to his assistance by speaking with Choni and calming him down. At the same time, Dinah knew that Chaim wouldn't dream of trying to manage without her, that she had to be present when the information was presented. She knew how to extricate herself from the terrible confrontation by very incisive means.

Chaim moaned. "Okay, Dinah, I get the hint. I'll tell him myself."

It was only 6 o'clock in the morning, but it was already late in the day for Dinah. True, she did not have a job that she had to get to, but she was an energetic housewife who had much to do to keep her household functioning like clockwork.

The pleasant scent of fresh coffee had already filled the kitchen as Chaim entered. "I'm going to *shul*," he said. "Please inform Choni of my request."

He's more stubborn than I thought, the notion flitted momentarily through Dinah's mind. His comment left a bitter taste in her mouth, but she was filled with compassion for Choni.

As Dinah entered the boys' room, Pinchas rolled over in his bed, thoroughly entangling himself in his blanket. Choni, however, jumped up.

"It's late," he said as he swiftly washed his hands.

"You don't have to rush," Dinah told him, putting his clothes into his hands. She prayed he wouldn't notice that her own hands were shaking.

"But I have to study today for the quiz. I haven't started yet."

"Whatever the case, take your time, sweetie. Today — today, you're not going to *cheider*," she said finally.

"Why not?" Choni asked.

"Because Abba wants to speak with you."

Don't cry, Dinah, she scolded herself as she bit her lip hard.

"What does he want to talk to me about?" Choni tensed in anticipation of her answer, but Dinah didn't volunteer any information. She was concentrating instead on dealing with the second battle, being waged against her from under the second blanket.

"If Choni isn't going to *cheider*, then I don't have to either." Pinchas refused to get out of bed. "Why does Abba want to speak only to him? I'm going to join in their conversation, too."

"No, you're not, Pinchas. Come to the kitchen and see what I've prepared for you for breakfast."

Pinchas stuck his nose out from under the blanket and looked at her. "Abba never talks to me so much. When did he ever let me skip *cheider*?"

Dinah had had enough. She turned to leave the room without saying another word, the pain plainly evident on her face.

Pinchas realized he had overplayed his hand. He mumbled a word of apology and got out of his bed.

"Abba will speak with me tomorrow morning. I'll make sure he asks to see me. What do you think, how should I ask him?"

"Ask what?" Choni stammered.

"Ask that he should speak to me. Do you realize that Abba is missing work because of you?"

Choni was feeling intensely jealous of Pinchas, who went off to *cheider* as usual. Choni sensed that something was strange about the entire situation, but he did not try to fathom what it was.

At 7:30, Choni returned from *davening*. His father had not yet arrived, and his mother stood in the kitchen with some groceries in her hand.

"Abba will be here any minute," Dinah said, and walked out of the house.

"Are you feeling all right?" Choni stopped her.

"Sure I am. I just — I have to go."

Choni thought his mother was on the verge of crying. *Nonsense,* he mused. *Mothers don't cry. Why should they cry? They don't have problems with their friends, they don't have homework, they're adults, and they don't get insulted.*

He's the one who had reason to be crying now. He realized that his rebbi from *cheider* must have called his father to tell him about Choni's constant bickering with Srulik Schwartz. *The rebbi thinks I'm the guilty one. Well, in that case, it's not so bad, because Abba will understand and will explain to the rebbi why he's wrong. Maybe Schwartz will finally stop picking on me.*

As Choni waited for his father to come home he read a book. A quarter of an hour passed before he heard the familiar jingling of keys.

"Abba?" He moved toward the door and met his father, who flashed a smile at him, which was unusual. The boy returned the smile, and could not understand why sudden goose bumps chilled him.

Chaim Binder stared at his nephew with increasing discomfort. "How is it going, Choni?" At that moment, he felt a sudden need to be somewhere else, anywhere but here having a serious discussion with Choni. Dinah was smart enough to clear out in time.

He decided finally not to give in. Even though he identified with Dinah's point of view, he understood the problem of having the boy learn of his adopted status from comparative strangers. He realized that it could happen, if the obstinate grandparents showed up at the boy's school and irresponsibly unleashed the shocking revelation to him. Such a scenario could have very serious repercussions for Choni.

"*Baruch Hashem*, Abba, what is it you want?"

Chaim took a deep breath. "I just wanted to talk to you. It's been a while since we had a chat."

"That's because you are so busy in the office. Your head is always there."

Chaim was taken aback by the expression the boy used. "Who told you my head is always in the office?" he asked, visibly amused.

Choni answered dispassionately, "Ima. She didn't say it to me; I heard her say it to someone on the telephone. She said that your head is there, and you are not around the house very much and that's why you are so successful."

The smile slowly faded from Chaim's face as he wiped the sweat from his brow with a handkerchief. Whenever he was excited, he would perspire, but the fact that the room was cool made it seem even more unusual.

"Abba, what is it you wanted to tell me?" nudged Choni.

"You're nervous," claimed Chaim.

"Me? What do you mean? It's not me at all. I have nothing to worry about," protested Choni.

"What are you talking about?" Chaim was befuddled.

"What happened is not my fault. I know that you'll understand me, so there's no reason for me to be nervous," said Choni.

It's not his fault — , Chaim wondered to himself. *What? That he is an orphan? "I'll understand him"? Well, his father is my brother. "There's no reason to be nervous." What's going on here? Could Dinah have already told him? Maybe she decided to assume the difficult task of revealing the truth to Choni.*

Choni continued talking in a forceful voice. "I realize that everything is *min haShamayim*. If it is decreed that they will speak about me in such a manner, I will speak the truth and end this business honestly."

By now, Chaim Binder was relieved. *See? Choni knows the situation and calmly accepts it. He's not upset. I was so worried, but for no reason. It appears that Choni knows how to accept a Heavenly Decree.*

Chaim exclaimed, "I'm pleased to see that you are mature enough to understand things from a Torah perspective! Moreover, you will speak only the truth. You will say that you want to remain with us, and that things are good for you here and — "

The confused expression on Choni's face stopped Chaim from continuing. "What are you talking about, Abba?" cried out Choni in bewilderment.

"What — what do you mean — just a minute, what were *you* talking about?"

"I was talking about Srulik Schwartz, a boy who has been

picking on me. The rebbi must have contacted you to complain about it, right?"

Chaim collapsed onto the couch. This was much more difficult than he had imagined.

"No, he didn't contact me," Chaim said in a raspy voice.

"So why did you agree with me?" Choni was bewildered.

"I didn't agree. I thought you were discussing something else."

"What? Did someone else complain about me?" Choni was thoroughly mystified.

Chaim put his arm around Choni's shoulder. "No, Choni, no one complained about you. I kept you home today to speak to you about something else altogether."

Choni sat in a chair facing his father. He fidgeted innocently as he waited. "So what did you want to tell me? I thought I was in deep trouble," Choni said, somewhat relieved.

Chaim thought he was going to lose his mind. *You are in trouble, Choni,* screamed a voice inside of him. *It is so good that you can ignore those troubles.*

The boy's brown eyes, so painfully identical to Yaakov's, were looking straight at him. They appeared so innocent, so childlike. What could he do to minimize the shock and pain that the child would experience? Chaim suddenly realized that Dinah was right.

"You know, Choni, let's have a glass of hot chocolate, and then we'll talk," he decided. He went to boil water and looked at his watch. It was already 9:15. Too much time had been wasted on empty talk, but he had not yet found the courage to speak.

"Why isn't the water boiling yet?" He looked impatiently at the kettle. It took another minute or two for the water to boil. Chaim busied himself with preparing Choni's hot chocolate.

He stalled for time but eventually had to hand Choni the steaming mug.

"Thanks, Abba," Choni said with a huge smile. "I don't know what you want to talk to me about, but it was really worth it to stay home. Pinchas was very jealous. You should keep him home tomorrow and make a cup of hot chocolate for him too.

"You know, Abba, lately you really have been very busy. In my class, many fathers study with their children, yet you barely have time for it even on Shabbos afternoon. Maybe we should learn a little together? Because lately, it's been hard for me to pay attention because — " Choni continued talking and Chaim, making one last attempt, interrupted: "Wait, Choni, all I wanted to say to you was — was — "

Choni stared at him with anticipation. "Say it already, Abba," he urged.

Chaim Binder was very confused. "I wanted to tell you that the rebbi informed me that you've been doing excellent work in school. I'm also very pleased that you are making such a big effort to study. That's all, Choni. Go to *cheider* please. Go quickly."

"Why quickly?" Choni's face glowed radiantly. Chaim, however, felt a twinge of remorse. Why couldn't he tell him once and for all?

A moment after Choni stepped out of the house in high spirits Chaim knew that Dinah was absolutely right.

But this did not answer the looming question: What next?

CHAPTER SIX

Choni ran up the stairs and exuberantly opened the door.

"Ima, look at this letter," he yelled to his mother.

"Choni, hello — this is not the way to enter your house. Tell me first how you are," Dinah tried to calm the excited boy. He refused to settle down.

"Look! A letter from the court." He handed her the envelope.

Dinah silently took the letter and looked it over. It had an official stamp. She inspected the envelope and studied the name. It was addressed to them.

Since Choni was staring at her with questioning eyes, she quickly replied, "It must be a mistake. They must have meant this for someone else. In any case, you don't have permission to read Abba's or Ima's mail."

Whenever she felt pressured, she made mistakes. Speaking

harshly to her child, trying to protect him, she always ended up attacking him instead.

"I'm a bit stressed now, Choni. Please put your knapsack away and go eat lunch," she tried to appease him.

"Because of the letter?" He did not appear to be insulted; he was merely his usual curious self.

"No, for other reasons. Now do as I ask."

He left the room, and Dinah tore open the envelope. She never opened envelopes like that. She always exercised phenomenal patience, carefully using a knife or another sharp object to slit the envelope neatly. Chaim would laugh at her, reminding her that envelopes are discarded right after they are opened. Dinah, however, maintained that a certain amount of respect was due the person who had sent the letter.

Now she dispensed with decorum and consideration. Could it be just a mistake? She tried to convince herself, but the senders' names stood out in black and white: Moishe and Rivkah Kahn. That was enough. She did not have to read any more. It was them.

They want Choni. They want to take him, and were willing to fight for him.

⇛❧❧⇚

Two weeks had gone by since Chaim had called the Kahns' and explained the seriousness of the situation. He told them that he had tried talking to Choni about his past, but he was always overcome with emotion, even though he was not an emotional person.

It had seemed as though Moishe understood and nearly agreed to compromise. Rivkah, however, created some problems.

"What do you mean by not telling him? How long will you keep the truth from him?" she asked angrily. Then she said to

Chaim, "Perhaps the boy is unhappy? Maybe he needs help?"

Dinah would never forget Chaim's reaction to these suggestions. Red in the face, he quickly and loudly answered in French. Dinah reminded him to lower his voice, to relax a bit.

"Who took in your grandchild when he had nowhere to go? Am I the type of person who is capable of withholding food from a child?" countered Chaim.

"To starve — no, of course not," Rivka answered. "But there are things that are worse than physically starving someone—emotional starvation, for example."

At this point Chaim felt it was inappropriate to continue speaking. He could feel the Kahns' determination to achieve their goal. They would want what they wanted, whatever the price, even at the price of the child himself.

Moishe Kahn, who detested all this wrangling, put an end to the conversation. "Look, we'll think it over and we'll decide how to respond. We'll be in touch."

They had parted on relatively friendly terms, so it was terrible to now receive this envelope. How could they do this so suddenly, without any warning?

Dinah hid the envelope in a drawer in her bedroom.

"It must be a mistake," she told Choni, who had come back into the kitchen and was staring at her with big, round eyes. He had such a humorous, curious look on his face that she couldn't keep from smiling.

"What's so funny?" asked Choni.

"You're funny. I can see curiosity written on your face," she told him affectionately while pouring soup for both Choni and Pinchas, who had just returned from school full of exciting stories.

Dinah sat down opposite them at the table and ate lunch too. The envelope was relegated to the back of her mind, as if Choni was about to disappear, and she wanted to revel in his cute stories.

She listened as Choni told Pinchas, in great detail, the *sugya* he had learned that day. She watched the two of them help each other with their homework. She looked at them as they talked and played. She felt that Choni — so much hers — was about to disappear.

"You're dreaming all day today," Choni commented to Dinah before returning to *cheider* for his afternoon studies.

"You're right." She did not see any point in denying it. After the two children left, panic slowly began to set in. She called Chaim's office and told him he must come home immediately.

"I'm coming." He did not question her. Her tense tone of voice told him he had better come, and without any arguments.

When he arrived, the envelope was waiting for him on the table.

"This came today," she told him dryly.

"Did Choni see it?" he asked.

"Just the envelope, not the letter."

With obvious distaste, Chaim read the concisely written letter. "I told you those old folks had lots of money saved up."

"Is that all you have to say?" Dinah, very troubled, stood up. "What are we going to do now?"

"We'll send Choni to them, of course. Do you want to involve lawyers in this?"

He spoke like it was the obvious course of action. There was no indication of hesitation in his voice. He was completely convinced, and nothing at all could change his mind.

"I will not get entangled with the Kahns. I'm sorry. There's a limit to what I'm able to do for Choni. He's been a son to us, but to get involved in custody fights involving lawyers, and against his grandparents, is just not part of my plans."

"Chaim, think it through again." Dinah was nearly in tears.

Chaim turned away, unable to witness her pain. "Listen, there is no other choice, do you understand?" He spelled out the pros and the cons of each possibility, showing her why none was viable.

"Dinah, I'm convinced that Choni will ultimately return to us. But for now, they want to take the child from us and transfer him to their custody. What can I do? Fight them?"

"Why not?"

"Remember, they are Sarah's parents. It would be as if we are fighting her."

Dinah strongly disagreed with his approach, but he seemed to have already made up his mind, so she kept quiet.

"Perhaps we're too hard on them. Look, whatever happens, we will definitely withdraw our claim, no matter what the price," Chaim continued.

"Even if the price is Choni?" Dinah asked.

"Yes. Do you know why? Because, if we give in, Choni is the victim. However, if we go the legal route, all of us, including our children, will pay the price, financially and emotionally. You don't want to add any more victims to the list, right?"

His logic nearly wiped out her position. She nodded in agreement. Chaim told her he planned to be in touch with the Kahns later that day, and would try to reach an agreement with them.

"Will you make things hard for them?" she asked as she stopped him at the doorway before he left for the office.

"We'll see. I will get some advice from other people. I'll be back a bit late tonight; I've got to catch up on the work I missed this morning."

As soon as Dinah was alone, she grabbed the telephone and dialed.

"Yoav, it's Ima again," she said briskly. She then told him all the latest news.

"Just like that, behind your back? Without even bothering to tell you anything?" Yoav was appalled when he heard the details.

"Look, Ima, if you're asking my opinion, I agree completely with Abba. You must not get into legal entanglements with these people. Because, first of all, they are at least partially in the right. He is, after all, their grandson. Secondly, they are very unpredictable, as you've just learned. Thirdly, I'm not underestimating them, but they are probably retirees with time on their hands and not much to do. For them, this is an adventure. I think that they themselves are not taking it as seriously as you are."

"On the last point, you are not entirely correct, Yoav. They are Sarah's parents, and Choni is their grandchild. I don't think people of such an advanced age are seeking thrills, and certainly not at their grandson's expense. He is, after all, the only child of their daughter who was killed in a car accident."

"I won't argue with you on that point." For some reason, Yoav's voice sounded far away, and it sent goose bumps running up and down Dinah's back. "But of one thing you can be sure. They will win this fight. So it makes sense to surrender at the outset."

Dinah finished her conversation with Yoav and debated whether to call Brachi, one of her married daughters. One look at the clock told her this was not the ideal time to call. Her young children probably needed Brachi's attention, and between preparing lunch and supper and helping with homework, it was not a good time to disturb her.

Dinah Binder held back her tears. She felt she had to be strong, for her own sake as well. She went into the bedroom, searched in the closet, and finally pulled out a picture album wrapped in an old French-language newspaper. She unwrapped the album and leafed through its pages.

Yaakov and Sarah smiled at her, holding little Choni in their arms. They looked so young, carefree, and full of hope for the future. Yaakov smiled reservedly like a *ben Torah*, whereas Sarah smiled with the contentment of a young woman who had just become a mother. Little Choni was swaddled in Sarah's loving arms, and his face was not clearly visible. It was easy to see how happy the mother was, holding her baby wrapped in a light blanket and wearing a thin cap.

They'd developed these pictures only after the couple's death. How painful it had been to discover them. Her husband Chaim was the one who had found the film in the Israeli apartment during the *shivah*. Later, when Choni was already living in their house, Chaim had had the film developed. The pictures remained in their house, and the Binders didn't mention them to Sarah's parents.

Dinah had tried to persuade Chaim to give the pictures to Sarah's parents, but he had insisted on keeping them. You couldn't know what the future would bring, and those photographs might be useful one day. If the child would be with them, then his memories would also be with them. That was his decision, and there was no changing his mind. Chaim knew that the Kahns had had to give him the baby. Looking to the future, he decided that he did not want anyone showing Choni any family pictures without his supervision.

Now, Dinah studied those photographs, page after page, until she reached the end of the album. There, at the end, they had added a few more pictures: Choni and Dinah at the beach in Netanya. Choni was laughing, and she was holding him just as any mother would hold her baby in her arms. Another picture of Choni, at age 2, holding her hand tightly. Another of

Choni and Pinchas playing together. Further on, a photograph of Chaim and Dinah and all the children, including Choni.

The children had no inkling that he was adopted. They were little then, and their parents had merely told them that there was a new baby in the family. The children accepted Choni with open arms, and Dinah really felt he was like a younger brother to them. Only later on, when the children were grown, did she tell the older ones about Choni's past. Their attitude toward him did not change. On the contrary, she noticed that her children had a special relationship with Choni. He was more than a brother to them. He was indeed of their flesh and blood. They protected him even more than they did Pinchas. Pinchas had reason to occasionally feel sidelined. For the older children, Choni, as the youngest, was the one to spoil, to play and have fun with. Dinah tried to compensate Pinchas from time to time, but she was proud that her children were able to show their cousin so much kindness.

Dinah could not yet accept the idea that Choni would travel abroad. True, she was disappointed by her son Yoav's opinion. But she knew that as soon as she told her other children the news, they would try to fight her war by somehow preventing Choni's journey. They would not allow the Kahns to do whatever they wished with Choni. They would fight as a family, and, if Chaim was correct, the aged grandparents would also eventually come to the same conclusion.

Feeling encouraged, Dinah closed the album. When Chaim arrived home, she would again try to convince him to fight. She would not be alone. Later that day, she would call Brachi, and then Ayala and Shira. Michael was also on the list.

Nevertheless, Dinah heard her mind's voice repeat constantly, "Choni will go — he will go — "

CHAPTER SEVEN

"**W**e do not want to fight with you. We want to go according to the law," the elderly couple said when they heard Yoav's young and energetic voice. Their words and tone of voice sounded sanctimonious to him.

"If you want a fight, you'll get one. My parents don't know that I called, but I want you to know that we will fight for Choni until the end, with the last ounce of our strength. And we will win, of course." He emphasized the last sentence.

The Kahns were not expecting this sort of confrontation. They wanted to prove to the boy's adoptive parents that they were not just old folks in their dotage, but were very serious about their intentions. They'd anticipated receiving an urgent phone call begging them to rescind the court order. The call did come, but in an unexpected style, from an unexpected source.

"What is your name?" Moishe tried to mollify the angry young man.

"Yoav, if you recall."

"Yoavi, of course we remember you. You were then about 13 or 14 years old," Rivkah interjected. She also wanted to soften the tone of the conversation, but Yoav would not be dragged into her deliberate attempts at nostalgia.

"Mrs. Kahn, my age then or now is irrelevant. What does matter is that you not cause my parents any aggravation. It's one thing not to display gratitude toward them — but to show such ungratefulness," he stated abruptly.

The old man became incensed. "Don't talk so much, young man. All we want is to see our grandson. Why is that ingratitude?"

"I see my parents' anguish. That's enough."

"What about *our* suffering? Where does that fit into this story?" hissed Rivkah.

Yoav felt he was just going in circles. He had not received permission to call the Kahns. In fact, he had specific instructions not to contact them. What could he do? His pain at witnessing his parents' suffering had practically caused his fingers to dial the French phone number on their own.

Yoav decided to take the "friendly bear hug" approach.

"Look, I suggest that you call my parents and work it out with them. We do not want to quarrel at Choni's expense. Don't bother making threats, because we have more resources at our disposal than you do. Don't try to upstage or embarrass us; I suggest you simply behave fairly and try to solve the problem in a sensible way."

There was a brief silence, and Yoav did not know if it signified agreement or was the prelude to a turbulent reaction.

Moishe's hoarse voice was suddenly clear on the line. "We'll see — we'll see what we do."

Yoav cleared his throat before ending the conversation. "I

only called to clarify matters. Let's say that I'd prefer that my parents don't find out about our little talk."

"Let's say that we will inform them." Rivkah was thrilled at this bargaining chip.

"O.K., if you insist." Yoav didn't show any anxiety, although he knew he would be reprimanded for interfering.

"I'm trying to make it easy for my parents and your grandson. You can oppose me, or you can cooperate with me. Consider what your daughter Sarah, *a"h*, would have wanted."

This last sentence was the final bombshell. He ended the phone call.

It had been a difficult conversation, he decided. He would not be surprised if it did not produce any results, but he felt his words had made an impression. Even the Kahns realized they were going too far by turning to the court.

Three hours later, he learned that he was right.

"Yoav, your mother is on the phone," his wife said as she handed him the phone, gazing at him with questioning eyes. "She seems very excited. What's going on?"

Yoav took the phone while a thousand and one thoughts raced through his mind. Were the Kahns maintaining their discretion, or had they decided to retaliate for his audacious conversation with them?

"Yoav, they called and apologized!" His mother's euphoria made it worth all the unpleasantness he had endured on the phone.

"Really? That's great. What did they say?" He could feel her joy as if it were his own.

"They canceled the court order, admitting it was excessive and foolish on their part. But, don't get too excited." As she cooled his elation, suspicion instead began filling his mind. *Here it comes, the big rebuke. How did you dare…*

"They did say that they're not giving in, and they're determined that we bring Choni to them," his mother continued in a sad tone of voice.

"Really?" Yoav was excited. The Kahns were human after all.

"Why are you happy?" asked Dinah.

"Because now we know that we are not dealing with heartless people. See how they were able to admit their error? I think you should be relieved. They are people who will not go overboard the next time. So now it is possible to bring Choni to them."

The unrestrained cry burst from Dinah's lips, "No, no, under no circumstances!" She quieted down, but after a moment she exclaimed, "You're so much like your father."

"I can't help it if we have similar ideas." Yoav wrung his hands. "They have it coming. They are Sarah's parents, they — "

"They're not thinking about Choni. They're thinking about themselves," Dinah wailed, more to herself than to Yoav. "They'll take Choni, and cry with him over his mother's fate. This will drive the boy crazy. They'll tell him stories and cry, and Choni will cry with them. Of course he'll cry over the mother he never knew. He'll be angry at us for not having told him anything. Even if he comes back to us, he'll have nightmares. Wait, there could be serious *chinuch* problems too. It's not uncommon for adopted children to declare, 'You're not my real parents, so why are you telling me what to do?' So we'll have to explain that the Torah requires him to honor and obey us. Then we'll have to undo the detrimental feelings of self-pity they nurture in him while he is in France. Because there they'll feel sorry for him, and there won't be anyone to discipline him. Yoav, I just don't see it working."

Dinah alternated between speaking and crying, and Yoav

could not calm her down. She did not even hear him.

"Choni is such a sweet child who's been growing up in a healthy family environment. Why? Why ruin everything we've been striving to create? Sarah would have understood and agreed with us."

She spoke for an hour into the handset. When she finished, she suddenly discovered Yoav standing in front of her. The shock halted her tears. "Yoav, I'm talking to you on the phone."

Yoav smiled at his mother. "Not any more. You weren't listening to me, Ima, and I was worried about you. So I handed the phone to Nechamah." He was apologetic when he noticed the scolding look in his mother's eyes. "I didn't want you to go on talking to yourself. So I called a taxi and in five minutes I was here. Are you feeling better now?"

Moved for her son's concern for her but feeling exhausted, Dinah replaced the handset after saying goodbye to her daughter-in-law, Nechamah "I guess so. What should we do, Yoav?"

Before he had a chance to answer, the front door opened and his sisters Brachi and Ayala came in. "We're here with you, Ima. We've come to offer our support. You have nothing to fear; we will not allow Choni to leave."

Yoav stared at them with a combination of shock and anger. "Who asked you to come over?" he demanded.

"Nechamah, if you must know. She told us Ima was not coping well, and why. We support Ima with all our hearts. Choni must not be told the truth," Brachi said ardently.

Yoav almost exploded with anger. "What are you talking about? Do you know what the grandparents will do?"

"Let them do as they please; we will stand up to them."

"This then is a fight over Choni, Ima?" Although the question was directed to their mother, Ayala meant the remark for Yoav.

"Just wait until Abba finds out about all this unsolicited advice," Yoav said.

"We are merely expressing our opinion," the two sisters defended themselves. Ayala went to prepare a cup of tea. At the same time, Brachi phoned Shira to invite her to attend this important meeting at their parents' home, where everyone was freely expressing opinions.

Yoav felt a rush of adrenaline. "What are you thinking? If you invite Shira, I'll invite Michael. What is this separation of forces?"

"Michael agrees with us. We already spoke to him."

"He'll come around to Abba's opinion soon enough. Just a minute: Why don't we invite Pinchas to this fight too?" asked Yoav sarcastically. The group of his siblings assembled in their mother's living room was as combative as ever.

"Invite whoever you think can help you. You cannot ask Ima to give up her child," replied his sister.

"We are talking about an adopted nephew who was raised as our brother; we are not giving him away. We just want to allow him to visit his relatives," Yoav protested.

"Sure, but a little visit is just the beginning. We'll never hear the end of it," said Ayala, setting down a cup of tea in front of her mother.

The only one who was not taking part in this discussion was Dinah. She felt her head starting to hurt and become heavy, and instead of taking charge, she found herself losing control. Her children were arguing vehemently in front of her, and she was not responding at all. She heard Yoav explain the severity of the situation. How had he become so involved?

In the interim, Michael and Shira arrived and Dinah greeted them with a wide, friendly smile.

Dinah's married children made themselves at home in her

house. They brought out some of her specialty cookies and passed them around. There they sat, consuming huge quantities of food and arguing their particular point of view. They were in their childhood home without their spouses, and that reminded Dinah of the earlier good old times. She glanced around the room, encompassing them all in a loving look. How many years had it been since they were all in her house, a group of sweet, laughing young children? A broad smile lit up her face.

"Ima, what's going on?" Brachi exclaimed. "We're all dealing with something so momentous, and you're standing here laughing."

They all stared at Dinah with surprise, and no small amount of concern.

"I'm happy that you all are worried about us. Thank you very much for coming over. I'd be pleased for you all to come visit but not just to solve problems," she said. "You all must realize that this decision is in Abba's and my hands, not yours, so there is no reason for all this squabbling."

"O.K., so we'll argue humorously," announced Michael, the youngest of those present, and the rest of them smiled. They continued with some more small talk until Chaim came home. When he walked in, he was surprised to see his living room, which was usually sparkling and polished and empty, filled with his adult children.

"Is this a private meeting or what?"

"We are discussing something of the utmost importance, Abba."

"Yes, it's about Choni."

These brief comments confused Chaim, and they did not understand why he was so surprised.

"You are discussing? I'm sorry to disappoint you, but the decision has already been made." He directed the statement to

Dinah, who nodded in agreement, her face devoid of any expression.

"It was very difficult for your mother to accept this decision. Believe me, it wasn't easy for me either. But sometimes there are obligations, do you understand?"

"You don't have to fulfill all your obligations toward them. After all, they did not fulfill theirs," Brachi tried to object.

Chaim did not argue with her. "The resolution is final. It's possible, however, that the Kahns will regret their actions when they find out what limitations we have placed on their seeing Choni. Nevertheless, for the moment, Choni will travel to France. Is that clear?"

They understood. All except one of them, who had just arrived. He did not understand, and wanted an explanation.

Choni entered the spacious living room, looking perplexed and overcome with fear. Dinah restrained a cry of anguish when she saw him, and the rest of them were silent.

Choni, suspicious of the goings-on, looked at each face in the room. He turned to his father and asked, "What is everyone doing here? And why am I going to France?"

CHAPTER EIGHT

Choni took a step forward, staring at everyone in the room. Then he continued his questioning.

"What's everyone doing here? What do they want from me? Why are they talking about me? What did I do? Why — why do you want to send me to France?" The final question ended with a slight cry that quickly became a fountain of tears.

Chaim Binder stood up. He decided to clarify the entire incident so as not to leave any doubts about the future.

"Choni, I don't understand why you are crying," he said sharply, ignoring the shocked expressions on everyone's face. "We've decided you will go on a little trip. So what's all the excitement, I really don't understand — "

"Me? A trip? What for?"

Choni was too wary and too clever to be fooled so easily. Chaim, nevertheless, continued talking nonchalantly. He ordered all the stunned observers out of the living room. "Come on, all of you, move on out of here. I want to speak with Choni privately."

"But don't leave," Choni implored. "Till we finally get you all here together — " Choni wanted to continue, but he saw that his mother was also about to leave the living room. She spun around, and before Choni had a chance to say anything, she said, "Excuse me, Choni, I have to take care of your siblings."

"They can find their own food," begged Choni. Chaim's eyes also reflected a silent request for her presence. Dinah, however, was unable to face the unpleasant chore, and left Chaim to reveal the news of the upcoming trip to the boy.

Dinah glanced at the clock. It was 7:15 in the evening. *Pinchas would be home in another quarter of an hour. How do we get out of this predicament?*

Through her tears she saw Chaim helplessly opening and closing his mouth, trying to utter words that refused to come out.

Now it became final — even if she wailed to the heavens and cried oceans of tears — from this point on, Choni did not belong to her. His heart would belong to his deceased parents and their family, who eagerly awaited his arrival.

"Sit down, Choni," Chaim said, indicating a place on the sofa. He sat down opposite him and took the boy's face in his hands. He looked straight into Choni's big brown eyes, eyes that so reminded him of his brother Yaakov, *a"h*.

"We really all came together here to surprise you. But it's over now, because you discovered the surprise before we could spring it on you."

"Why aren't you surprising Pinchas too?" Choni's eyes were questioning. He did not yet believe what he was hearing.

Chaim disregarded the question and continued talking to

Choni. From outside came the excited voices of children enjoying a ball game. How he wished he could send the boy out there to play.

"Choni, remember I once told you that we used to live in France? We even have some relatives there. Remember?"

"Of course, you and Ima speak French."

"Now you're not going to believe what happened to us this week." Chaim raised his voice in false anticipation. He tried to pull Choni into the imaginary excitement, hoping that Choni would adjust to the idea of traveling.

"This week, relatives whom we almost forgot about, but who didn't forget us, contacted us. They want us to send one of you to them in France, because they miss us. They don't even know how you and Pinchas look.

"So we thought a lot about it." Chaim scratched his head and silently reproached himself for lying to the boy. "Yes, we thought a great deal about whom to send. We decided it wasn't good for Pinchas to miss so much material in school, especially before the acceptance exams to the yeshivos. So we chose you. Isn't that exciting?"

"You are hiding something from me!" came Choni's emotional and unexpected reply. Chaim thought his nerves could not take any more tension. He had expected Choni to jump up, embrace him, and thank him. He had just offered to send the boy on an overseas trip. What could be more thrilling? He was sure that he would hear the child's exuberant chatter along the lines of, "Aren't I lucky ..."

Instead, all he heard was a question that made him shudder and caused him to hate himself for confronting Choni without Dinah's help.

He got up from the chair, lit a cigarette, and took a long puff on it. "Why do you think we are hiding things from you? It's a trip. You know, Ayala also traveled to France five years ago."

"No, I don't remember, because I was too young then. But I need to know why you are sending me."

Chaim turned toward Choni and explained, "A trip. That's the only reason. We'll send Pinchas some other time. We want to send you to a very pleasant aunt and uncle. We want them to meet you and to show you where we used to live, and who our relatives are. You know, just to see the country from where we came. Is there anything wrong with that?"

"I wasn't born in France."

Out of sheer exhaustion, Chaim closed his eyes. "True, you were born here in Eretz Yisrael."

"So that means I should remain in Eretz Yisrael," exulted Choni.

"No, you have to take this trip. But just a moment, Choni: If I have to persuade you, I mean if you really don't want to go, we can rethink the whole thing." Chaim began to deliberately backpedal, hoping that Choni would realize that he might be missing out on the exciting prospect of taking a trip abroad.

"Just give me the word if you don't want to go, Choni, and I'll cancel your reservation. It's no problem at all. Your aunt and uncle can continue waiting. True, they are a bit old and alone. And they do want to see you very much. I'll just tell them that you weren't interested in fulfilling the mitzvah of honoring your elders and easing their loneliness. I'll call them right now if you'd like, Choni."

Choni straightened up on the couch. "Don't call. Wait a minute. Who said I didn't want to go? I just asked. I really don't want to miss out."

Chaim Binder smiled to himself. It was a victory smile. Choni now thought that there was an exciting adventure awaiting him.

Afterward, when they both left the living room, Choni was smiling and effusive. His father told him to thank his mother for the trip, and he intended to do so with all due respect. He enjoyed schmoozing with his siblings, and even though a warning light flashed in his head, he ignored it.

"I'm so glad you came. But how did you have the nerve not to bring my nephews?" complained Choni in a spoiled-child tone of voice. "Make a list; I'm going to buy them all presents in France."

Choni continued jabbering, but everyone could see that the issue was settled. His two older brothers stood to one side, conversing in whispers. Their father moved in their direction. "I want you all to please stop the quarreling right now. I don't want Choni to hear one word of this."

"But the Kahns surely will reveal that he is adopted!"

"They won't do anything. It's you I have to worry about," replied Chaim, a little irritated. He had expected the married children to be supportive and was disappointed to discover their conflicting opinions.

Before the older children left for home, they talked with Choni, telling him that they would stay in touch until his flight. After everyone left, the house became quiet. Choni and Pinchas ate dinner in their room while their parents ate in the now-tranquil kitchen. As Pinchas took his plate from the kitchen, a fleeting glance at his eyes burning with jealousy told the Binders that they had erred in not informing him about the plan in advance. But Pinchas' jealousy increased Choni's desire to fly and made him forget those worrisome thoughts about the strangeness of it all. Chaim, however, was ambivalent and pained by the thought that his son felt ignored and discriminated against.

"Don't worry. We will take you on a trip next year. Choni is going now because the aunt and uncle are especially asking for him."

"But why can't I also fly in a plane?" Pinchas couldn't forgive them.

"Because next year you have to be tested for acceptance into *yeshivah ketanah,* and it's not worth missing so much school. Otherwise, how will you know how to learn? Do you know how hard it is to be accepted into a good yeshivah? It would be a shame to lose out just because of an unnecessary trip," Dinah tried to convince him.

"But why should Choni get to go?"

Pinchas could not know the reason behind this trip, and his parents realized it was useless to continue trying to persuade him with calming words. They decided to compensate him after Choni's trip, but right now, every additional word inflamed Pinchas' anger and jealousy. His wrath was not directed at his younger brother, but at his parents.

Sitting in the kitchen alone with Dinah, Chaim refused to taste the hot soup. "I cannot swallow. Believe me, my heart is still pounding."

"I believe you." Dinah placed the bowl to the side, giving Chaim the option of deciding when to try the soup. She poured her own soup into a cup. "So what did you actually say to him? We should be saying the same thing."

Chaim leaned back in his chair. "I told him that an elderly aunt and uncle want some company. At the outset, he was quite suspicious. But finally, he decided he would not call off the planned trip. I made sure not to allow him to dwell in that direction. In other words, you could say that Hashem gave me the strength to convey the idea of traveling to France in the cleverest way possible."

Chaim turned to take a spoonful of the cooled soup.

They finished their meal. Dinah cleared the table, placing the dishes in the sink. "What's next? What are you planning to say to the Kahns?"

"They are not supposed to tell him that they are his grandparents," said Chaim.

"And you trust them?" Her reprimand was abrasive and unreserved. "Chaim Binder said not to tell, so the Kahns will obey him without question, even though they are far away in a foreign country, alone with the child. And if they don't adhere to Chaim Binder's instructions? What is he going to do about it?"

Dinah's words came out in a shaky voice, but Chaim did not lose his composure. "I think the Kahns are honest people. If we have compromised on what was important to us, they too will behave in a reasonable manner toward us."

"I don't trust them." The anger emanated from her.

"You don't have too many options, Dinah. You know that very well. They are — "

"I know what they are."

"So then that's it. I can't think of a more cordial way of solving this."

Dinah became silent. She had a different idea, a somewhat feminine solution to the problem. Rivkah was also a woman, a mother, and a grandmother. Dinah would travel alone to her, to speak straight from a mother's heart to a mother's heart. To cry with her over Choni's tragic circumstances, and to plead… How could she not heed a mother's tears?

Outside, twilight became a dark night. In the Binder home, they had not yet gone to sleep. The parents tried to contact the Kahns in France, but apparently they were not at home. No one answered the phone. In the children's room, the light was still on, and the two children were fantasizing about the upcoming overseas trip.

"I'll convince Abba that you should also come," Choni encouraged his older brother. Pinchas was bitter but felt that something was fishy, something that Choni did not realize.

"This time it's not going to work, Choni. There's no point in trying," Pinchas said in an angry voice. "Wait a minute, for how long are you going?"

"Abba didn't say. Tell me, Pinchas: Do you know why Abba and Ima aren't traveling with me? Isn't it kind of scary to fly alone on a plane?"

At this point, Pinchas became the devoted brother who wants to keep things running smoothly. He understood that he was helping his parents by calming Choni's fears. "Do you know how many people fly all over the world every day? What do you mean you're afraid? And anyway, you're a big boy. Why would Abba or Ima have to go with you?"

"I'm not so big," Choni said sadly. "I feel very small, and it seems as if Abba and Ima are forcing me to do this. It must be very important for the aunt and uncle. Pinchas, I don't even know them. What am I going to do in their house anyway?"

"You'll get to see France, all those beautiful places. I think the Twin Towers are there — "

"No, the Eiffel Tower is there. I read about it in a book."

"Okay, so it's the Eiffel Tower," Pinchas agreed. "But I don't think you should give up on touring the place."

Choni puckered his lips and stood up. "That doesn't interest me. I'm telling Abba and Ima that I'm not traveling without you," he said with determination.

He went to make his announcement, but when he got to the kitchen, he saw his father on the telephone, speaking in French. His mother silenced him with a finger to her lips. "Shh, Choni. Abba is talking to the uncle in France. What do you want?" she asked in a low voice with noticeable impatient undertones.

At that moment, Choni decided Pinchas must come with him. His parents' changed behavior frightened him, distanced him. It also drove him even closer to his older brother, who stood resolute with him in facing an inexplicable mystery.

CHAPTER NINE

Wednesday evening, Choni started packing for his trip, scheduled for the coming Sunday. He and his mother went through his clothes, deciding what to take. He packed a tape recorder as a present for the uncle and aunt in France. He also planned to give them several tapes featuring the latest Jewish music.

The entire time he kept on grumbling, "I still want Pinchas to come along, too."

"He can't come." Dinah refused to get into a discussion on the matter. But the boy was stubborn. So stubborn, in fact, that Dinah found herself speaking very harshly to Choni about Pinchas. "I want you to stop bothering me about this. Sometimes you get something extra, and sometimes Pinchas does."

"I don't want to fly alone." Choni pushed the heavy suitcase toward his bed. He sat on it while he laced his shoelaces. "I'm afraid. What's the matter, am I not allowed to be afraid?"

Dinah got up and stood next to him. She wanted to reach out to him, to protect him from the future. She stared at Choni whom she loved him like a biological child.

"You are not flying alone. Did you think that we would send you traveling alone?"

"I'm not?" Her revelation shocked him.

"Of course not. We found people to take you. You will be with them the entire flight."

"Who are they?"

"They are an elderly French couple, Yehudah and Freida Schick. They are very nice people. You'll enjoy traveling with them."

"Why do I need a baby-sitter?" Choni wrinkled his nose.

Dinah restrained herself from lecturing. Choni did not get her angry. She felt for him. He was confused and would be flying to visit relatives he did not know. She marveled at his fortitude in agreeing to take this trip. Dinah herself was such a shy, reserved person. She assumed that Choni had inherited his dynamic energy from his mother. Dinah could never forget how Sarah had encouraged Yaakov to leave France and move to Eretz Yisrael. Choni obviously inherited that strength of character from her.

"Look, Choni, I'm packing your overcoat."

"O.K., but that's enough now. I'm tired of packing."

"So let's finish tomorrow. You're flying in four days," Dinah told him in a calm voice while pushing the suitcase to the wall and calling Pinchas in from the kitchen.

She then straightened Choni's bed, bid them both goodnight, and left the room. Choni lay in bed with eyes open. The thought of the trip excited him, and for the past few nights he had had trouble falling asleep. In the mornings, he wondered which heavenly angel forced his eyes closed, affording him a decent night's sleep. Tonight, as usual, he fell asleep amid stormy thoughts about his upcoming journey.

In the morning, Dinah awoke from a nightmare. In a low voice in the kitchen, she described her dream to Chaim. Despite their assurances, she said that the Kahns had no intention of keeping their secret. "Even if for the moment their intentions are pure, the moment Choni is in their hands, they will not keep silent. They will tell him the truth about his parents. How will he react to the news? Who will be there to comfort him at such a traumatic moment?"

"You are on edge, Dinah, so your mind is filled with nightmares. I really believe that they will keep their promise. After all, we compromised with them," claimed Chaim with a visible lack of patience. "I don't understand why you agonize about it all day. Choni will fly to France, enjoy himself, and return to us afterward. They will show him a good time. They want what is best for the child."

"But I have a bad feeling about this," she whispered.

Chaim gave up trying to understand his wife. "I don't understand why you insist on making a such a big deal out of every little thing."

Dinah buried her face in her handkerchief and wiped the tears from her eyes. "Well, we don't know what will happen. I'm just afraid."

"You told me you wanted to sign up for a course." Chaim tried to steer the conversation in a different direction. It was already 8 o'clock, and he had not yet *davened*. His office, his customers, and new revenues all awaited him. Why did Dinah not understand?

"Yes I did. We'll see. Chaim, I want to ask you just one question."

"O.K." He appreciated her dedication to Choni, so he crossed his legs and listened. Her question, however, shocked him.

"Chaim, let's imagine a reverse scenario. Choni is our child, and we would not be raising him. Yaakov and Sarah would have raised him instead. Would we want them to send our one and only child on a plane flight, alone? Would we want to risk our child's physical and emotional welfare?"

Chaim became confused. He did not know how to answer. "Your question is utterly impossible," he decided as he moved toward his briefcase. "How can I imagine that Choni is our son and that you and I are no longer alive? But I have an answer for you." He found the right response and was pleased with himself. "Look, Yaakov and Sarah can see from *Shamayim* how much effort we are expending on their son's behalf. I think that they understand that we don't have much choice but to continue as we've been doing up to now. Do you think that they don't understand our dilemma? They do and they want us to decide wisely. Since we've already settled this, I consider the matter closed."

Chaim Binder stood in the doorway and said goodbye to his wife, then hurried out to the car.

Dinah moved slowly to the living room with her thoughts dancing wildly in her mind. *If the Kahns reveal the truth to Choni, how will this affect his emotional stability?* She did not have too many opportunities to affect change, but she still was capable of shielding Choni from such a trauma.

The following night she had an idea that she decided to implement before was too late. Dinah took a sheet of paper and sharpened a pencil. She wanted to use a pencil in case she changed her mind about some words. She closed the window and made sure that the front door was locked. Only then did she start writing. After some initial hesitation, the words flowed onto the paper, along with her tears. She wrote in French, but not just because it was her mother tongue and these words flowed from her heart. She did not want Choni to read what she had written.

When she finished, she wiped away her tears and read the letter. She did not change anything she had written; she merely nodded in satisfaction at her words. The letter accurately expressed what she felt.

> *To the Kahns — parents of Sarah, a"h,*
>
> *Do not be surprised by this letter. I intend to speak to you by phone, but there are some things I can better express in writing.*
>
> *I send you my youngest son. Yes, my son; please don't shake your heads. Choni is my son, even if I'm not his biological mother. I feel that I have accepted a mandate, a sacred trust from Yaakov and Sarah to raise and care for their orphaned son. I am a mother to him, not just his aunt.*
>
> *My poor little Choni travels now to France. I promise you, if it was my decision, I would not let him travel alone. The unfortunate circumstances dictate that I send him to you.*
>
> *My son Choni is a very sensitive boy. He's very bright; you won't be able to deceive him. You have promised us you would not reveal the truth to him, but I worry about this. My heart, a mother's heart, gives me no rest. I am afraid that you want to give to him a bit of your family. Is this right? I'm not judging anyone. I did not undergo that trauma, nor am I interested in doing so, chas v'shalom. You promised my husband Chaim that you would not reveal the truth to Choni. Chaim believes and trusts you. But mine is a mother's heart, full of fear and concern. I beg you, with tears running down my cheeks, please don't disregard the tearstains on this paper. Please don't harm*

*the child, don't disrupt **his life**. There will come a day when he will know the tragic reality, and he will recite Kaddish for his parents. He will have to learn to live with his grief. But not now. Choni is so young and sensitive, and his life is cheerful. I fear the slightest unexpected wind will disrupt everything. Please allow your grandson to have a happy childhood.*

True, you are the parents of Choni's mother. Try to consider, however, what Sarah would have wanted. Would she have wanted the bitter truth told to her young son, all alone in the world?

I took Choni in with a mother's hands. I embraced him from the age of 1 month, and he is still my pampered and spoiled child. I love Choni very much and do not want to cause him pain.

If you have decided, despite everything, to reveal the truth to him, ignoring a mother's pleas, there is still a more traumatic and a less traumatic way of telling him. You can still help him have the strength to grapple with the tragedy.

Tell it to him only after he has gotten to know you. Don't shock him while he still does not know you well.

Show him pictures of his parents. Give him a feeling of companionship, and not one of pity. Don't tell him how pitiable he is, and how deserving of sympathy he is. He is a child like all other children, who has a different life than other children. Hashem presented him with a nisayon, and he has the means to overcome it.

Remind him that he has a loving and supportive family in Eretz Yisrael, and his father and mother, who are really his uncle and aunt, love him dearly and are looking forward to his return.

Allow him to call us, and to speak his mind. Please don't tell him not to reveal to us what you've told him. We will understand your perspective even when we don't agree with you.

Allow him to be alone with himself. Don't be alarmed by his cries. It's normal for any child his age to react in such a manner. Let him manage his grief as he wishes. He may prefer to confide in someone he knows well.

Rivkah, you are a mother. You have a very special grandson. Please don't do anything to harm him. Please don't cause him to withdraw into himself. Don't give him the opportunity to ask questions that will force you to reveal the truth suddenly. Take care not to disrupt the life of your daughter's only child.

He is also my son, and my cries are a mother's cries.

We are not angry and we understand your feelings. But I want you to know that had it been up to me, I would have fought you in court for Choni. My husband Chaim is the one who prevented a legal battle from erupting between us.

Give Choni the feeling that he has a second home, because he already has a primary one, from which he will not easily be removed.

Please don't stop him from contacting us — even though it may pain you because you consider yourselves biologically closer to him. It's not true. For Choni, we are his father and mother. Understand that, and allow us to raise him as we see fit.

Kisses to my Choni.

When Choni returned home on Thursday afternoon, he was more upset than Dinah had ever seen him.

"What happened?"

"I'll show those friends of mine. Who do they think they are, anyway?"

"What happened, Choni?" Dina begged him to tell her.

"Don't worry, Ima, I'll deal with it."

"With what?"

"With Pinchas' story. You know, they insulted him today. Some friends just came up to him and said that he's…that he's…forget it, it's ridiculous."

"That he's what?" Dinah's heart pounded with fright.

"Well, Ima, it's wrong, so there's nothing to worry about. They said that he is adopted. Pinchas yelled that it's nonsense. But one of the kids said that his sister is in the same kindergarten class as Gila, Yoav's daughter, and she used that word to her friends. She must have meant a different word, because Pinchas is ours. It's so wrong. But Pinchas was hurt and started to cry. The rebbi hushed the other kids in the class and said it was not true. But they had a big fight about it in class."

Choni spoke with a determined look on his face. He planned to retaliate against the classmate who had insulted his brother. "I'll show them all what it is to speak ill of my brother. As soon as I get back from France, I'll fight all those kids. But you know what, Ima? Pinchas' close friends helped him and everything will work out."

"Of course," Dinah said quietly. She turned to the kitchen while trying to catch her breath. "Everything will work out, Choni. But where is Pinchas?" his mother asked in a weak voice. Before she received an answer she heard the door open a second time. Pinchas stood opposite her, with huge, questioning eyes.

Pinchas cried, "It's not true, Ima, right? It's not true!"

"Of course not," Dinah hugged her confused child. "You

are our child; you all are our children," she sighed, looking at Choni. "Come, I want to talk to you in the living room."

She directed them to the sofa and sat down opposite them.

"Look, young kids often have huge imaginations. Sometimes they hear things from older people that are either incorrect, or that they have misunderstood. That doesn't mean we have to believe them, does it?"

"So why did all the kids in class come up to me?" asked Pinchas, still wounded.

"Yeah, why did they come up to him?" Choni's eyes burned.

Dinah gritted her teeth. "They made a huge mistake. I am your mother — both of you, along with the rest of my children. It doesn't matter what they say." She did not look into Choni's eyes when she declared her motherhood from the depths of her pained heart.

Later, she prepared a tasty supper that she hoped would help them forget the day's adversity.

Choni disturbed the calm.

"You know, Ima, we learned a proverb that seems to apply to this situation." He bit into a piece of corn and spoke, despite Dina's disapproving look at his breach of etiquette.

"Finish chewing, Choni, and then you can tell us what saying you learned."

He wiped his lips on a napkin and sat up straight in his chair. "We learned that where there's smoke, there's fire. And I see smoke, but I don't know what the fire is. Of course Pinchas is not adopted, that's foolish to think such a thing. I mean, he looks so much like Abba! So why would they come up to him out of the blue and make such comments?"

"Because kids often don't think."

Choni answered, "All right, but I do think, and the entire business seems strange to me."

"What's strange?"

"It doesn't matter."

Choni stopped talking about it and Dinah tried to act as if she had put the entire matter out of her mind. She decided that after Choni left for France, they would reveal the big secret to Pinchas. This would help him understand all the whisperings and innuendos, and to stand up to his friends with more confidence. Most important, he will be able to relate better to Choni.

True, Pinchas should not be the punching bag to absorb the blows meant for Choni. Yet, Dinah felt a certain relief that Choni was not the object of those hurtful remarks. How would he have reacted? Would they have had to tell him the truth or to deny it? It's a good thing they did not get into any unnecessary arguments, especially before his trip.

CHAPTER TEN

Moishe Kahn was 75 years old. What was he, at his age, going to do with the young grandson who was about to suddenly appear on his doorstep? It had been quite some time since he had cared for young children.

Rivkah kept repeating, day and night, "This child is ours. We will receive him as we would a son, and not like one of our other grandchildren. We'll show him much love, and he'll respond in kind. There is no need to worry."

But Moishe Kahn, who was still badly traumatized by his daughter's death, had a bad premonition. He sat silently, thinking about Sarah and what she would have wanted. If she had been alive, he would have asked her. Would she have agreed to send a young child on a plane trip alone?

"He's not that young. He has two suitable escorts while on the plane. We are paying them good money to look after Elchanan," remarked Rivkah upon hearing his fears.

Now, due to his wife's urging, he avoided Dinah's dramatics by contacting Chaim Binder in his office on Thursday evening to verify that they were readying the child for the upcoming trip.

Moishe Kahn began dictating a few details about the flight.

"So it's like this. Please write it down, Mr. Binder. We ordered tickets with Air France, Flight 139. Are you writing this?"

"Every word," lied Chaim. He was blessed with a phenomenal memory that had brought him great acclaim as a child, and now helped him in his business dealings. He had never needed written notes for anything, and neither did he now. He memorized the details without writing anything.

"The flight will leave just before 9 o'clock in the morning. The boy should be at the airport two and a half hours beforehand. You can figure — "

"Don't worry. We are not exactly novices in air travel," Chaim interrupted.

"O.K., but don't forget," agreed Moishe. Afterward, he added that this would not be a direct flight. They would stop in Athens before arriving in Paris.

"Yehudah Schick is totally dependable," Moishe tried to convince himself even more than Chaim. He was annoyed when Chaim said, "Reb Moishe, international phone calls are very expensive. It would be better if we ended the conversation. I understand you will be waiting for him at the airport. Best of luck to you."

"We'll call you again."

"It's not necessary."

Chaim Binder nearly slammed down the phone. He was angry at that elderly couple who had disturbed his family so much.

Until now, he and Dinah were sure the only victim in this story would be Choni. This was not so. Choni was not paying

the price for being an orphan. Poor little Pinchas had been substituted in his place. And Pinchas, who was never prepared for
this, now had to deal with his tormentors.

ജ്ഞ

They began seriously packing Choni's belongings on
Thursday night. Dina bought him a new shirt for the flight. She
gave Choni more than another child would have received, and
more than his brothers and sisters. Even though Pinchas, for the
most part, did not make it difficult for her, he did occasionally
protest that certain games and toys given to Choni were too ex-
travagant. He was very jealous when he learned that his older
brothers and sisters were planning a surprise birthday party for
Choni on *Motza'ei Shabbos* before the flight. Yet, he never let
his jealousy show to his brother, understanding that there was
something concealed here, beyond his understanding.

"You're treating Choni like someone who is dangerously ill,"
Pinchas told his mother after she bought his brother a new coat
but gave him a hand-me-down from one of his older brothers.

"He's not sick. He's something else…" Dinah said sadly, and
suddenly she regretted her words. Pinchas, however, did not
ask any questions, as if he understood the situation and tried to
be supportive of her and the family.

Choni and Dinah spent a few hours packing and repacking
two suitcases. They included almost anything they could find.
Choni even insisted on taking along some books, so he would
not be bored.

"But you'll be in France, where there are lots of things to interest you," Dinah objected. But Choni refused to accept her argument.

"I don't know what I'll do there with an old uncle and aunt.
What am I supposed to talk to them about?"

"They'll take you on trips. And you must be well behaved," his mother reminded him.

On Shabbos, Choni's excitement grew. After *Havdalah*, Choni felt he could not wait until the morning. He had already spoken to Yehudah Schick, who had calmed his fears about flying. He also had had a well-mannered conversation with his uncle and aunt in Paris. The aunt spoke a great deal, promising him days filled with excitement and adventure. The uncle, on the other hand, sounded old and serious. Choni was a bit afraid of him.

Yoav and Shira were the first to arrive at the good-bye party, and the rest of the family followed. They surrounded him with so much warmth and love that seemed strange in Choni's eyes, complicated in Pinchas', and emotionally overwhelming to Dinah.

The married siblings and their children gave Choni a "preflight" present: a large photograph of the entire family, including grandchildren, smiling. It had been taken at Michael's wedding.

"If you get lonely and miss us, just look at the picture and you'll see your family, who is waiting for you and loves you even over such a long distance," his siblings wrote.

All packed and ready to go, Choni felt overwhelmed. Their father urged them all to head home. "Tomorrow Choni has to get up at 4 o'clock in the morning. Please go home so he can get a good night's sleep."

Within moments they had all departed. Choni noticed that their eyes all seemed moist and the whole farewell ritual had a certain strangeness about it. "Hey, I'm going away for a week, that's all," he reminded them. "I'll bring you all lots of presents," he told his nephews, who were thrilled.

When the last of the siblings left, Choni turned to his mother. "It feels so strange to think that tomorrow I'm flying. But the present that the kids brought me is beautiful. Do you know why?"

"Why?" asked Dinah.

"Because you are in the picture, and I'll miss you for sure." Tearfully, Choni went to his room without saying another word. Deep down, Choni wanted to cancel the trip. Speaking about a trip is one thing; actually flying is another. He was very afraid of flying without his father or mother. True, Yehudah Schick was a nice man, but still —

Choni had a hard time falling asleep that night, although he decided that if he really did not want to go on this trip, he could cancel it. What did it matter if the cancellation cost some money? It was not his responsibility to worry about such matters.

❧❀❧

"Tomorrow Elchanan is arriving," Rivkah announced with satisfaction after Moishe finished reciting *Havdalah*. He sighed as he put the *besamim* box back into the old, creaking drawer.

"I don't know what to tell you. But — "

"No buts. Tomorrow we will see our Sarah's son. Believe me, I cannot wait for tomorrow."

Moishe shook his head. "I cannot imagine what he looks like, or what sort of person he is. One thing I can tell you is that he has Sarah's personality. You know, for a 10-year-old boy to agree to fly alone overseas is really something. He should have been utterly afraid, demanding that one of the family escort him. What prompted him to agree to take this trip?"

"It's the enthusiasm of our Sarah, together with the innate curiosity of the Kahn family."

"Until I see him with my own eyes, I won't believe it."

"On the one hand, I'd prefer it to be the week after already,"

Moishe said. He knew his wife would respond harshly to that remark.

"Why are you afraid to meet your grandson? He'll come visit us for a week, and become acquainted with us. He'll have a nice time and return home. We are not kidnappers. We'll just show him photographs of his mother and — "

"His mother? Rivkah, we promised!" Moishe became perturbed.

"So? Isn't he our grandson? Doesn't he have a right to know who his mother was?" Rivkah wanted to continue, but Moishe's face showed his displeasure. She decided to wait for a more opportune moment, when her husband's unfounded worries were put to rest, and they were enjoying their grandson's presence. By then, she would persuade Moishe that she was correct. In the meantime, despite her husband's fears, Rivkah felt a strong urge to drive to the airport and receive her much-anticipated grandson with open arms.

CHAPTER ELEVEN

June 27, 1976

T he worst mistakes are committed during times of confusion. There is no fuzzier time of day than 4 o'clock in the morning.

Choni awoke with tired eyes. He looked at the clock and yawned. His mother did not allow him the luxury of delay.

"Hurry up, Choni," she urged him.

"But it's only 4 o'clock," protested the sleepy boy.

"Right, and the plane leaves before 9. We don't want you to be late for check-in."

The plane? Choni stared at her without comprehending. Pinchas' blanket started to show signs of life. Pinchas really wanted to join his brother on the flight. Their parents' adamant refusal hurt him but he wanted to get up to say his goodbyes at home.

Chaim went downstairs to check the car, and Dinah prepared a cup of hot chocolate, whose sweet smells overwhelmed Choni's senses.

He dressed quickly, feeling the growing lump in his throat. When he was ready to leave the house, his mother told him to kiss the *mezuzah* and to take a few coins to give to *tzedakah*. This way he would be considered a *"shaliach mitzvah."*

"May you go through this in peace," mumbled Dinah to herself.

"What did you say?" Choni asked.

"Nothing. Let's go, Abba is waiting."

Choni's steps suddenly became heavy and measured, as if he wanted to slow the pace of his departure. Everything was happening so fast.

Pinchas stood before him in his pajamas, his *peyos* disheveled. Barely awake, he stared at Choni. He quickly smiled and handed his brother a small gift-wrapped parcel.

"This is just from me. Open it after the plane takes off. O.K.?"

Choni wanted to thank him, to say goodbye, but his mother urged him forward. "Go downstairs, Choni, the plane won't wait for you."

When he reached the bottom of the staircase, he turned around and looked up at the porch to see Pinchas waving goodbye. Choni waved a quick farewell and got into the waiting car.

Everyone was quiet on the way to the airport. The airport compound seemed to be an island of daylight in the predawn darkness. Hundreds of people milled about, smiling, shouting, and looking busy. They entered the terminal and passed through the security checks uneventfully. Without prior planning, Choni pressed close to his father, who carried his suit-cases.

"What if I suddenly change my mind?"

"What if you what?" Chaim was concentrating on the people coming and going. He had arranged to meet Yehudah Schick at a certain spot, and was annoyed that the man had not kept to the agreed-upon schedule.

"What if I change my mind?" Choni tugged on his father's sleeve, and his teeth chattered from fear. He wanted to run away and lose himself in the huge crowd, and then dive straight into his warm blanket at home.

Dinah was not with them, as she had gone to the check-in desk to ask about luggage. Chaim crouched down to look Choni in the eye. "Look Choni, at this point, you cannot change your mind. You are a mature boy, right?" His father spoke calmly. "You have nothing to fear. But if you want to come back sooner, we'll arrange something."

"And what if I only want to be there for one day and that's all?"

"We'll bring you home. Look, you are traveling for less than a week. You won't even be there for Shabbos."

"Why did you choose me?" repeated Choni for the ump-teenth time. Chaim gave up, stood up, and bumped into an el-derly man who smiled warmly at him.

"*Shalom aleichem*, I am Yehudah Schick," said the man with a noticeable French accent.

"Is this the child we are to baby-sit?" the woman next to him kibbitzed.

Chaim relaxed. He smiled at the friendly and quite elder-ly couple, and introduced them to Choni. "Yes, his name is Elchanan, but we call him Choni. He is not especially fond of flying, but you'll be able to handle it. O.K.?"

"For sure," answered Freida Schick.

Yehudah Schick made the first critical mistake in trying to forge a relationship with the boy. He pinched his cheek so hard, Choni had to bite his lip to keep from crying out. His mother reappeared and was introduced.

"They are very nice. You'll enjoy the flight together," Dinah whispered to Choni.

"O. — K.," Choni sighed.

They did not have much time to give instructions to Yehudah Schick, because the announcement came over the PA system that Air France Flight 139 was now boarding.

"Time to say goodbye." Chaim bent down to embrace the trembling child. He placed his hand upon him and recited the *berachah* a father recites over his son. Dinah could not stand the stress of saying farewell. With tears streaming down her face, she said in a choked voice, "Choni, be a good boy — we'll miss you."

She hoped he would prove to his grandparents what a good upbringing he had received, while at the same time she despised herself for allowing him to fly abroad alone.

Forgive me, Sarah, she mumbled to herself as she watched Choni walk toward the departure gate, wearing his small backpack. *I wanted to shield your son from emotional pain, but your parents are more responsible for him than I … Forgive me…*

After Choni disappeared from sight, she burst into fresh tears. "We should never have allowed him to go," she whispered to Chaim, ignoring the stares of passersby in the terminal. "We should not have permitted this. Look, he's out of our custody."

"He'll come back, don't worry," Chaim tried to reassure her. "I believe they will be considerate and not tell him anything. It will all pass more quickly than you think."

His attempts to reassure her did not succeed, and during the return trip home, Dinah wiped away tears that flowed without respite.

"A mother's heart cannot be calmed," she cried. "Now I'll be sitting at home on pins and needles, waiting to hear that Choni arrived safely in Paris and is enjoying his visit with his grandparents."

"Why wouldn't he arrive safely? Thousands of people fly daily, so should something happen just to our Choni?" Chaim found her anxiety unwarranted. He went off to *shul*, and then to the office. He maintained it would be a difficult but tolerable week. It will all pass, the Kahns would be placated, and Choni would return to them in just a few days.

Dinah could not be appeased, and kept imaging the worst.

ळळ

At 8:59, the Air France plane taxied down the runway. Choni was one of the hundreds of passengers onboard who had fastened their seat belts at takeoff. True, when the aircraft was gathering speed on the runway he gritted his teeth and shook with fear, but when the plane leveled off, he relaxed somewhat, allowing himself to enjoy the flight in the skies over the Mediterranean.

Mr. and Mrs. Schick, as Choni politely called them, chuckled at the boy's transfixed stare. "I didn't know the sky was so beautiful," Choni remarked with excitement.

Mrs. Schick smiled, "You remind me of my grandchildren. We come to visit them in Eretz Yisrael, and every time, as soon as the plane back to France lifts off, I miss them."

"So why don't you come to live here?" asked Choni, continuing to stare out the window. He soon tired of this, so he opened his carry-on bag and started munching on the cookies his mother had packed for him.

The time went by quickly, and at 11:30 they landed in Athens. After an hour, they were airborne again, this time headed for Paris.

"We have one more landing, and then you'll feel much better," Yehudah promised the boy, whose ears and stomach had hurt when the plane descended.

"My stomach hurts a lot," complained Choni.

"It'll pass," Mrs. Schick tried to comfort him.

But Choni knew it would not pass quickly. He feared meeting the mysterious uncle and aunt in Paris, and could not figure out why he had agreed to this trip. He did not know how he would react when these unknown relatives approached him. Abba had instructed him to behave as befitted a member of the Binder family, but Choni thought this task was too much for him.

"You should rest," Mrs. Schick told him. She was right. Mr. Schick reclined Choni's seat, and told him to relax and close his eyes.

Choni Binder was on the verge of falling asleep when hysterical shouts caused him to jump. Mr. Schick immediately pushed him back into his seat, holding him down with strong arms. This hurt Choni, and the prevailing atmosphere in the aircraft confused him.

He saw some men brandishing pistols and shouting wildly. He wanted to say something to Mr. Schick about today not being Purim, so why were these guys waving around cap guns…

When Choni looked at Mr. Schick, he saw that he was afraid, something Choni found disconcerting. Mr. Schick was quite large, and had a long beard that nearly reached his waist. What could a man such as this fear?

Mrs. Schick was as white as a sheet. When she did not answer Choni's questions, he finally realized something frightful was occurring.

"Don't speak, Choni; his pistol is real," Mr. Schick managed to say. Choni clung to his seat. He did not understand what everyone was yelling about. He only knew that the men had guns and looked evil, and he had to be careful.

Soon afterward, someone spoke on the plane's PA system. Mr. Schick threw his and his wife's fork, knife, and spoon onto the floor. He instructed Choni to keep silent.

The child was trembling. He understood that something terrible had happened.

Later, the armed men began moving through the aisles, checking each passenger. As he walked past Choni, one of them smiled at Choni and said something in a language Choni did not understand. Choni smiled back. He did not remember him at all. The men stared at him coldly, and checked Choni's pockets.

After that, someone made an announcement on the PA system and Mr. Schick stood up. "I have to move to another spot. You stay close to Mrs. Schick," he said to Choni, who still did not understand what was happening.

Choni looked around the cabin for clarification. People were crying or sitting silently, and there were others walking back and forth with guns. Choni knew he had to be very careful, because Mr. Schick had told him they were real guns.

Mrs. Schick pulled Choni to sit in a different area of the plane. A few minutes later, all the passengers returned to their original seats, including Mr. Schick. "*Baruch Hashem*, we're together," muttered Mrs. Schick to her husband. "That's all we need now, to lose sight of the child."

They both looked at Choni, who was about to stand up. Yehudah Schick stopped him.

"Choni, I think you are old enough for me to explain to you what is happening here. There are some Arabs who do not like

Jews. They are making demands on the Israeli government. These Arabs have hijacked the plane, and we are now headed somewhere else."

"Not to France?" asked Choni.

"I don't think we're going to France," said Mr. Schick, looking glum.

"And they can kill us?"

"Hashem is All-Powerful. Even if they try to, Hashem will protect us," Mrs. Schick interrupted.

"So it's dangerous?" asked Choni.

"Yes, and we must *daven*."

Mr. Schick continuously recited chapters of *Tehillim*, and his wife sat and cried for most of the flight. People were scurrying back and forth throughout the small aircraft, while Choni was utterly helpless. On the one hand, he was glad he didn't have to meet that old couple in Paris. On the other hand, this game seemed altogether too scary. The men with guns were not nice at all.

He regretted getting on the plane. He felt bad for his poor mother, who would be sick with worry if she had heard about the bad people with "real guns."

My friends in cheider will never believe me, that's for sure, thought Choni to himself. He tried to fall asleep, but the stress all around him did not give him the option.

Choni found himself sitting and weeping about the situation, which Mr Schick had called a "hijacked plane."

CHAPTER TWELVE

Rivkah looked nervously at her watch. "The plane should have landed a quarter of an hour ago," she complained, this time in a loud voice. "I don't understand what's going on here."

"Be patient," said Moishe. He moved aside to make room for some boys who were pushing forward.

Both of them stared at the door. They knew that their grandson would shortly appear there. They choked up and their hands trembled with anticipation, while their hearts overflowed with joy at the prospect of meeting their grandson for the first time in years.

After half an hour, Rivkah realized she was worried. "Delays are expected; this is normal," Moishe tried to explain. "I'll ask at the desk," Moishe decided.

"Do it quickly."

But he was not quick. He stayed at the information desk, then finally turned slowly to Rivkah. His face told it all.

"What did they say?"

Rivkah was not looking at her husband. She was searching the mass of arriving passengers, hoping to find her 10-year-old grandson. Where was he?

"They will make a public announcement a little later."

She was stunned into silence. "They'll what?"

"They will make an announcement later." The girl behind the desk refused to say anything else.

"Hashem… did the plane crash?" Rivkah held her head in her hands.

"You're always assuming the worst. *Gevald*!" Moishe was more worried than she, but he did not show it outwardly. He behaved calmly until the announcement came that everyone awaiting the arrival of Air France Flight 139 from Tel Aviv should move into the adjoining meeting room.

While murmuring *Tehillim*, Moishe and a silent Rivkah entered the side room and focused on the airline representative. The representative stared at the floor, and his entire bearing showed his discomfort.

The restrained and dignified French manner was shattered as the representative kept silent.

"Tell us what is going on," a middle-aged man yelled.

"We demand to know what is going on. Are our loved ones alive?" wept another woman.

The representative silenced everyone in the room.

"Ladies and gentlemen, I have the following announcement to make." The group was suddenly quiet. "A few minutes ago, we received confirmation that one of our aircraft, Flight 139, which left Tel Aviv for Paris with a stopover in Athens, will not arrive as planned."

"An aircraft malfunction?" The listeners shouted their questions.

The rep motioned for quiet.

"The plane has been hijacked by hostile elements. The plane is presently flying to an unknown destination. Air France expresses its apologies, and sincerely hopes that the passengers will reach Paris safely. We hope that everything will work out. To this end — "

The rep was unable to continue speaking, because decorum gave way to pandemonium and cries of fear. People felt as if they had already lost their loved ones. They stood around in the meeting room shouting and crying. Others stood by helplessly in the face of the horrible news.

When they heard the announcement, the Kahns were standing near the wall. They leaned against it, not knowing what to do or where to turn.

"Choni is on that flight," Rivkah kept on repeating. "Sarah's Choni… She'll never forgive us for this… Hashem, who knows if we did the right thing…who knows…?" Her husband was unable to utter a sound.

After ten minutes, everyone realized there was no point in remaining at the airport. The media would broadcast the story in depth, and they could get any new updates at home.

The Kahns did not join the group that demanded to meet the prime minister and France's national security chiefs. Instead, they left for home in a state of shock.

Back at their house, the phone did not stop ringing. It was probably their children, who wanted the latest news.

"Don't pick it up," begged Rivkah.

"Are you trying to run away from life?"

"I'm pushing it off to when I can handle it better." Rivkah disconnected the phone. "I don't want to take any telephone calls now. We have to think."

"About what?" Moishe sat down heavily on the black sofa.

"What would you like to talk about?"

"About our Elchanan. About this poor child sitting alone on an airplane, certainly afraid... the poor child... what did I do to him?"

"You are right." Moishe lit a fat cigar that he kept for times of crises. "I was ready to forgo the whole thing. But you were so stubborn about seeing Choni and disturbing his calm existence. Well, you definitely disturbed his life."

Rivkah allowed herself to weep openly. She felt guilty for the threatening situation that now engulfed them. She wanted to serve Moishe a cup of tea, but she suddenly stopped in her tracks.

"Moishe, we forgot something important."

Moishe looked at her with tired, wondering eyes. *He did not look well,* thought Rivkah. *The hijacking has really affected him. Tough times are upon us.*

"What did we forget?"

"We have to tell his parents about the hijacking." she said with trepidation. "*Oy,* Moishe, I don't have the strength to talk to them. You call."

"You had the strength to force them to send the boy!" said Moishe. "Who needed this kind of trouble?"

"Don't make it worse for me than it already is," Rivkah said.

"I'm not calling; you do it," Moishe told his wife.

Rivkah collapsed on the sofa. The phone was disconnected, and Moishe refused to call the Binders. Rivkah seemed close to a nervous breakdown. She knew that all the requests for forgiveness would not help — even if she prostrated herself before Dinah Binder. Nothing would help.

Her daughter Sarah's only son was in serious danger.

Rivkah suddenly turned to her husband, who was sitting with his eyes closed, trying to make sense of the horrendous news. "I'm not connecting the telephone now. I don't want to speak to anyone. They will find out everything on their own. I just don't have the strength for it."

She left the living room sobbing and went to her bastion — the kitchen. Her weeping could still be heard hours later. Moishe listened with half-closed eyes, unable to find the words to comfort her.

꧁✿꧂

That afternoon, Dinah called Chaim. She was more nervous than she had ever been, and even Pinchas could not cheer her up by describing some classroom antic that had happened that day in school.

"Chaim, I'm worried."

"Why?"

"Chaim, why aren't they calling to tell us everything is okay?"

"Calling?" His voice sounded far off and unclear. "Hmm… they must be busy."

"Busy? I sent them my child, and they are too busy to tell me that everything is all right? What's going on? Am I not allowed to say hello to my son? Has he already become their son? Maybe they've driven him against us! Perhaps they've already persuaded him to remain with them in Paris, with the rest of them. What do I know?"

Dinah sounded agitated and Chaim could not calm her, even though she did not yet know of the news he had heard on the radio. Up to this point, the media merely reported that the plane was hijacked. There were no details yet, just guesses as to the hijackers' identity.

Dinah would be furious that he had withheld the news from her. Chaim wanted to spare her the horror, even if only for a few hours.

"Dinah, I'll call them and find out exactly what's going on. Don't worry. I'll get back to you when I have an answer," he said in a soothing voice.

She had not the slightest idea of what she really ought to be worrying about. She was only thinking about the family feud. The situation was much more critical than that, and there was a severe lack of information about the condition of the hijacked passengers.

Chaim thought that in France there would be more information than in Israel. He decided to call the Kahns. He was surprised that there was no answer. He tried unsuccessfully a number of times to reach them, until he finally realized that their line was not connected, or that they were on the phone already, perhaps trying to call him.

Chaim closed himself in his office. He was incredibly nervous, and even his secretary did not dare approach his office when he was in such a state.

Chaim kept on trying to call the Kahns, without success. He slammed down the phone while mumbling to himself, "What a bunch of cowards, to leave me in the lurch at a time like this."

He took his briefcase and left the office.

"Clients are waiting for you, Mr. Binder," the secretary tried to convey the urgency to him.

"Let them wait. I'm not working today. Cancel all my appointments," he snapped.

"Mr. Cohen will be annoyed."

"Let him be annoyed. I'm annoyed too. Turn off the lights and lock up the office," he barked in response.

When he saw the tears in her eyes, he said, "Sorry. You heard about the hijacked plane? My son is on it."

The secretary stood in her place open mouthed while Chaim walked out. He hoped that no one would tell his wife about the hijacked aircraft.

That faint hope still held fast as he drove his car through the streets of Ramat Gan. His hopes were dashed when he arrived home. Dinah approached him with bloodshot eyes.

"What's going on?" he asked.

She looked at him with a fierce, pained stare.

"Yoav called. I know everything." She remained standing where she was, dry eyed, as if cast in stone. Chaim could not look at her overwhelming pain.

"I already know everything, Chaim. And I also know that I am responsible. It was me and only me. I should have held onto Choni and not allowed him to go. I should have hidden him. I should have plugged my ears and not listened to your arguments to persuade me. I should have fought Sarah's battle. Now Choni is alone in the hijacked plane full of cruel terrorists. Where are the Kahns? Why haven't they called? Why? Now they are keeping quiet. Now they are afraid. They don't even have the guts to tell us… This is how they've abandoned their grandson…"

Her outburst was inevitable, and despite the natural impulse to soothe her, Chaim was unable to reach her through the pain and fury that overwhelmed her. It was a mother's anguish.

CHAPTER THIRTEEN

The heat was already unbearable. Even the fan blew only warm air, as if mocking those who were staying indoors because of the heat wave.

Miri, Shimon Kahn's youngest daughter, looked at her father sitting in the kitchen, stirring the soup in his bowl.

"The soup is cold," she said after watching him stir for ten minutes.

"What?" Her father shot an uncomprehending look at her.

Miri decided to change the subject. She realized that something was going on in the house. When she asked what was the matter, they answered that she was too young. She thought 10 years old was mature enough. She decided to approach the issue from another angle. "Why don't you go lie down for a bit?"

"I'm waiting," Shimon said simply.

"Waiting for what?" Miri asked.

"For Saba and Savta to call. I want to hear how they met...
the — " He stopped short and took a close look at his daughter.
"Why don't you go do your homework?" he suggested. Sunday
there was no school, and just on this unusually hot day, this
young, unknown nephew had to show up.

Miri left the kitchen, trying without luck to figure out what
was going on.

Shimon refused to allow anyone to use the telephone. He had
arranged with his parents that they would contact him as soon
as they met the boy. But they had not yet called. Shimon cast
a nervous glance at the clock. It was late in the afternoon. The
plane should have landed already. What was going on?

He lit a cigar and opened the window. As if on cue, Miri appeared before him saying, "Ima doesn't allow smoking unless
you are very worried."

Shimon exhaled smoke. "I *am* very worried. Go do your
homework."

*Maybe the child is crying? Maybe he is afraid? Maybe they
could not find him?*

Shimon was afraid that his emotional mother would blurt
out the sensitive information on the spot, which might cause
a rift between the boy and their family. Would Choni go into
shock? He took out another cigar. He decided his mother was
too sensible to do something so rash.

After another half-hour had gone by, Shimon tried to call his
parents' house. The airport was only a half-hour drive from
their house. They should have been home already. He waited
impatiently for one of his parents to pick up the phone. He
eventually realized that their phone was unplugged.

This was too much. *You are always assuming the worst,*
Shimon reprimanded himself. *You are a hopeless pessimist.
Maybe the child is just so attached to my parents that they are*

trying to have the lengthy discussions they had missed over the years.

Shimon almost absent-mindedly switched on the radio. He barely paid attention to the reporter. *The heat wave must be affecting me, too*, thought Shimon, and stood up to turn the radio off. Before he turned the knob, the reporter calmly related a news item about a hijacked French airliner that had taken off from Israel, Flight 139.

Shimon grabbed his head with both hands and exclaimed, "That was Elchanan's plane. It's his plane. Hashem!" He grabbed the car keys and rushed out of the house.

"Where are you going?" Miri asked.

He did not answer her. He pulled out of the parking space with a roar of the car's engine. Miri was left behind in a gray tail of hot dust and engine exhaust that added to the general heat of the day.

Shimon drove with uncharacteristic wildness. The other drivers made disparaging remarks as he weaved through traffic but Shimon was deep in thought. The delayed phone call, the disconnected phone — all was now clarified. He was driving to his parents' house, although he was not even sure if they were at home.

Arriving at his parents' home, Shimon cast a glance at the front window, which was usually open. Now it was closed, possibly to keep out the oppressive heat.

Shimon nearly flew up the steps of the house, but when he reached the front door, he stood up straight and knocked calmly and gently.

"Who is it?" his father asked. So they were home after all.

"Shimon."

When he got inside, Shimon was stunned. His father appeared to have aged 50 years since the last time he had seen him. Moishe always had a blazing flint in his eyes, but now his eyes looked tired and lacked that ever-present liveliness.

"What's going on?"

"Much has happened. Believe me."

Shimon waited for his father to sit down on the sofa. "You don't have to tell me. I already know," he said gently.

"How do you know?"

"They just announced it on the radio."

His father looked up. "What did they say?"

"Nothing really. They didn't release any details."

After a short silence, Shimon said, "In Israel, they've surely called in their intelligence services. We ought to call there to find out information."

"No!" Moishe shouted immediately.

Shimon folded his hands. He could not figure out what his parents were trying to achieve. He tried to change the subject. "Did you know that your telephone isn't working? I tried calling several times and you didn't answer. Should I check what is wrong and try to fix it?"

"It's not necessary," Moishe said forcefully. "We disconnected the phone. We don't want to talk to the Binders right now."

Moishe Kahn's answer contained unspoken statements: *We blame ourselves for this. Had we not been so stubborn, the boy would be safe with his family in Eretz Yisrael*; and some others about which Shimon did not even want to think.

"The Binders must be worried," whispered Shimon.

"So are we."

"But you have to tell them. You have to — "

Moishe Kahn banged on the nearby table.

"If you are worried about them, you can leave," hissed his father. "And if you are concerned for us, please stay and be quiet."

Shimon barely recognized his father's tone and demeanor. His father, a Jew who had withstood Paris' darkest days, usually said that everything was *min haShamayim*, and that the whole story would resolve itself in an acceptably positive way. But Moishe's conscience was apparently causing him to act out of character.

"Where is Ima?" asked Shimon.

"In the kitchen. Do not disturb her."

Shimon ignored the last piece of advice and went into the kitchen. The familiar aromas that he enjoyed so much did not greet him, because the entire house had changed. His mother was sitting in the kitchen with her head in her hands.

"Ima — " he spoke hesitantly. He became angry with himself for having entered without permission. "I know you are terribly upset. Try not to worry. Hashem will help. Maybe the Israelis will do something. They won't let hostages die."

His mother stayed quiet. Shimon softened his voice. "Ima, I know that you blame yourself for this. But it's not true. You are just overwhelmed by the terrible situation. I'm sure you realize you are not guilty of anything — "

Rivkah suddenly looked up, surprising Shimon with her tears.

"Stop talking foolishness, Shimon," she scolded as she tried to stop crying. "We are not blaming ourselves for what happened now. But originally, I cried wondering if I would ever see my grandchild. Things simply changed, Shimon, they changed.

"I'm not blaming myself or your father. I'm blaming the Binders. Who asked them to move to Eretz Yisrael and to take my grandson from me? Who? Had they not broken their promise, I have no doubt that this would never have happened. Now look what kind of a mess we are in."

This entire speech shocked Shimon. Apparently the unbearable pain had gotten the better of his parents. Then he regretted that thought. *After all, they are my parents. What do I want from bereaved parents? Their conscience works overtime.*

"Ima, Hashem will help. We'll get out of this."

"With Hashem's help," his mother said. "But the first thing we're going to do after this fiasco is over will be to bring Choni back to our family."

Shimon chose his words carefully. "Ima, I'm not sure you are thinking straight. Of course, right now, we have to see that everything is done for Choni's benefit." He really meant: We have to worry that there will be someone to bring back.

He kept his thoughts to himself, however, and decided to go home. There was nothing to do in his parents' house anyway. The unexpected turn of events had left them even more broken than he had imagined. The shock certainly had a strong impact on them. Without a doubt, among all the dark thoughts and lost sleep they had had before Choni's flight, they never dreamed of a hijacked plane.

Before Shimon left the house, he asked his parents to reconnect the telephone. "Not to talk to Binder — just so you can be notified about any news."

⁂

"Where are we?" asked Choni quietly. They were about to land as the blue sea glistened beneath them.

"On the way to Libya. Do you know where that is? Or were you perhaps not listening in class?" Yehudah Schick tried to break the tension.

"I don't remember." Choni was trembling all over. Mr. Schick patted him reassuringly on the shoulder, but it didn't help. The passengers were worried, including Mr. Schick.

Upon landing, the hijackers collected all the passengers'

passports. The hijackers' faces were cold and brutal, and Choni feared they would do something terrible to the passengers.

After a few hours of waiting, Choni realized that he was hungry, and the cookies his mother had put into his carry-on bag were nearly finished. Some of the airline stewardesses distributed food to the passengers.

"It's not kosher," Mr. Schick explained to Choni as he refused to take anything from the tray.

"They will bring something for you right away," the stewardess said pleasantly.

They then brought trays of kosher fish patties, and the Schicks and Choni helped themselves.

Mr. and Mrs. Schick made a huge effort to behave pleasantly and calmly to help Choni relax. The adults spoke in French a great deal, and Mrs. Schick was often choked up, wiping away a tear from her eye. Toward Choni, however, she always showed a smiling face and spoke in reassuring tones.

The feeling of foreboding returned when, after refueling and letting a hostage go, the plane took off again, seven hours later.

"Where to now?" Choni asked Mr. Schick.

Yehudah Schick replied, "I don't know."

Adults are supposed to know everything, so why doesn't Mr. Schick know where we are going? Choni wondered as he closed his eyes, but then, in the darkness, he saw his mother's face. He sorely missed her. *She must be worrying about me, and I can't reassure her.*

CHAPTER FOURTEEN

Choni opened his tired eyes and glanced outside. The plane was taxiing in an unidentified airport. He yawned. "Where are we?"

"In Entebbe," Mr. Schick answered right away.

"Where?" Choni woke more fully from his dreamless sleep. "Where is Entebbe?" he demanded to know. But even before he received an answer, he complained, "It's so hot in here." He would have continued with his litany of complaints, had it not been for the swarthy, distinguished-looking man who entered the plane. Choni silently listened to the man's speech in a language he could not understand. The passengers applauded him. Choni noticed that Mrs. Shick also clapped.

"Who is that?"

"Idi Amin, the president of Uganda. He said that he will help us," said Mr. Schick. "I think you should go back to sleep. We're going to wait here a long time."

"It's hot in the plane," complained Choni. "Why can't we get out?"

"Entebbe is in Uganda," said Mr. Schick, ignoring Choni's complaints. "And I don't know where it's better for us, in the plane or on the ground. In any case, Choni, it's best for you to rest and retain your strength."

Later, the couple started talking, and Choni understood that he should not complain about anything. They had agreed to do his parents a favor. Now, they were worried for their own lives, and they had to take care of him as well. Choni grew silent. He checked his carry-on bag and saw that the food he had brought along for the flight was nearly gone.

Choni tried to keep busy by counting the passengers in the plane, but quickly gave up. There were a few children in the plane, but Choni was unable to communicate with them. Some spoke French, some were not Jewish, and others were older than he was. The passengers tried not to mill about in the aisles, keeping them clear for those who needed to move around. Choni sat down, folded his legs, pressed his face to the window, and stared out. The oppressive heat tormented him, but he clenched his teeth and did not complain.

Pinchas would not have been able to endure such heat; he would have broken the window, thought Choni, and then thought of his mother and father. *What were they doing just then? His mother might hire a plane to rescue him.*

After a few hours, the Ugandans brought some food to the hostages. "It's not kosher, but you are allowed to eat. You are a child," said Mr. Schick, although he was not completely sure this was so.

"I'll eat what you eat." Choni said maturely.

They drank the water and took some dried foods that were served out of unsanitary containers. At one point, Mrs. Schick started to cry, and Choni thought that her husband must be getting tired of reassuring her. Although he was frightened and confused, he kept quiet and kept his thoughts to himself.

The boredom led Choni to burrow more deeply into his carry-on bag, placing its contents on the folding table in front of him. Suddenly, his fingers touched something that made him tremble with excitement.

❧❀❀❧

At first Dinah Binder stumbled about her house like a woman possessed. "What's going on? Why isn't Israel doing anything? Why? Where are the French?" she frantically asked Chaim.

Now that the news had broken, and the media was continually broadcasting details of the hijacking, Dinah became somewhat more relaxed and reasonable. She decided that the Kahns had evidently adopted an ostrichlike strategy.

"If they would at least call and give us an update — "

"The French have less information than the Israelis," Chaim pointed out to her. "Don't fool yourself. The French don't care much about this."

"But maybe they have gathered some important details. Maybe…" Dinah, feeling helpless, pounded the small table in the living room. "Chaim, I can't … I just can't," she said. "I'm losing my mind from worry about Choni. I don't know about you, but I …"

Chaim stood near the window, holding a cup of black coffee. "This may not be the most appropriate time to mention this, but it seems to me that at some point, there is a moral obligation that needs to be rectified.

"I'm at fault, Dinah. And in *Shamayim*, I'm sure there is a couple who blame me for abandoning their son. I can see my brother Yaakov standing before me with accusing eyes. He always used to say I was too sure of myself. I would prove to him countless times that I was right, yet Yaakov would say that I sounded too cocky with my arrogant manner. Now Choni is paying the price for my overconfidence. I should have listened to you and not relied on the Kahns, who seem to have disappeared."

Dinah listened with surprise to Chaim's admission. She had never had the courage to point out this blatant flaw in her husband's personality. It was a flaw that often caused her great distress. Now, though, listening to Chaim reprimanding himself, using such strong language, was nearly unbearable.

"No one is guilty, Chaim. Surely not you. It is Hashem Who decrees everything. The only thing that matters now is what is happening to Choni at this moment."

Chaim stretched out his hands. "At first I thought of flying to France, but I've changed my mind. From what I hear, France isn't really involved in the practical details of the hijacking. It seems there is nothing we can do."

"So let's arrange a meeting with the prime minister. Surely the families of the hostages must be organizing something!" Dinah exclaimed.

"You're probably right. I'll check into it."

Through the window, Dinah could see a spectacular sunset. "Aren't you going to work this evening?" she suddenly remembered to ask.

"No way. I'll have another cup of coffee, and then I'll head over to the Foreign Ministry to see what the government has to say to its worried citizens. How could you even think about work at a time like this, Dinah?"

Dinah was pleased with her husband's answer. She had always felt that Chaim had a certain reticence regarding Choni, while the boy also seemed to treat Chaim with reserve and had never managed to develop a close relationship with his father. There had to be a very good reason for Chaim not to go to work. Chaim's reaction to today's events proved that Choni was indeed important to Chaim. How unfortunate it was that the truth was discovered only under such difficult circumstances.

"Pinchas is due home shortly. I think we should tell him," Chaim announced.

"Everything? Are you sure?"

"Everything," he answered definitively. "I think that Choni will know everything by the time we are, *im yirtzeh Hashem*, reunited with him. We will need to explain why it was so important to send him off on such an adventure. His life has already been changed, Dinah. All of our lives have changed because of this hijacking. We have moved up to a level of fear that the average family does not normally experience. You should acknowledge this as quickly as possible. If you try to act as if it's business as usual, you're mistaken."

"I agree," she said with lowered eyes.

"Our children are worried. Why don't you want to speak to them?"

"I just don't have the strength for it."

Chaim stared at her accusingly. "They're worried. Do you know that?"

"Of course."

Chaim took the car keys and abruptly left the house.

As if out of spite, the phone suddenly rang. Dinah picked up the handset.

"Reb Chaim Binder, please," she heard a French-sounding voice say.

"He's not here now. Who's calling?"

"When will he be in?" the caller asked, ignoring Dinah's request for him to identify himself.

"Later. Who is this?"

There was a brief pause before the speaker said, "This is Shimon Kahn." After a moment's hesitation, he added, "The son of Moishe Kahn."

"Finally, you are showing signs of life." Dinah could not restrain herself from voicing some criticism. "Where are your parents? What are they saying in France about the hijacking?"

The last thing Shimon wanted was to speak with a nervous woman asking a thousand and one questions.

"My parents cannot talk right now. In France they aren't saying anything," he answered in a monotone. "The French are relying on Israel for information."

"What else?" Dinah felt silly, but thought that she could press him for more information.

"There was a fatal train collision at 5 o'clock. The media is reporting this, too, so the main focus now is on this and not on the hijacked plane."

"I see. Why did you call?"

"I wanted you to know that — "

"That what?"

"That we are not indifferent to what's happening. My parents don't know how to handle it," Shimon said rapidly. "That's all. Please tell Mr. Binder that I called. If there is any news, I'll get in touch with you."

He hung up.

As Dinah sat down to think about the phone call, Pinchas came home, flung his bookbag onto the sofa, and approached her excitedly.

"Did you hear what happened, Ima? Terrorists hijacked a plane and kids are saying that it was Choni's plane... For sure it wasn't, right, Ima?" He stared at her hopefully.

"First of all, calm down. Come into the kitchen, have a drink, and we'll talk about everything."

Pinchas was stubborn. "Absolutely not. I want to know what is happening to Choni."

"You can't know, because we don't know either. Choni is right now in — " Dinah paused and took a deep breath. "He was on the hijacked plane. That's all we know, Pinchas. Now, what you have to do is to *daven* a great deal to Hashem."

"I don't believe it," Pinchas whispered. "I don't believe it. Is he really there?"

When Dinah did not respond, Pinchas left the living room and started up the stairs to his room.

She ran after him. "Pinchas, don't worry, with Hashem's help, everything will be — "

Pinchas turned to her with a stony face.

"You wanted him to go. You sent him to visit some obscure relatives. Why did you do it?" he began to cry. "Why did you send him alone to France? I knew it was going to be dangerous. Choni also was afraid, but you forced him. Who are these relatives anyway? He didn't even want to go. I won't forgive those relatives who invited him. I won't forgive you for making him go. I'm very worried about Choni. I heard they have started killing hostages. They said — "

Dinah grabbed Pinchas' hands.

"Calm down," she insisted. "You have to listen to what I'm telling you."

"In the first place, they are not killing anyone. Besides, the government is in contact with all the pertinent parties…" She realized that she was repeating the words used on the news broadcasts, but she did not care — as long as Pinchas listened to her.

"Anyway, we did not send Choni for nothing. They insisted that we send him. Don't be angry, Pinchas, they forced us."

"Who?" The question burned brightly in Pinchas' eyes.

"The relatives — the people to whom we sent Choni."

"Why?" he shouted.

Pinchas was a mature child whose question dismayed Dinah, reinforcing her fears that they had made the greatest mistake of their lives. Was Choni thinking the exact same arguments as Pinchas?

CHAPTER FIFTEEN

The telephone rang incessantly at the Binder home, but Dinah could not answer it. She was preoccupied with trying to calm Pinchas, who refused to speak to her and was totally overwrought. She heard the phone ringing; someone wanted to speak to her, to learn additional details, or perhaps to calm her or to be comforted by her. She disconnected the telephone, like the Kahns in Paris had done.

For the moment, the distracting phone calls ceased. While Pinchas was in his room, Dinah hurried to find the old photo album in her closet. She looked through it, then went to Pinchas' room with the album in hand. She knocked on the door.

"I can't now," she heard Pinchas' choked voice reply.

"You must." She opened the door. "Pinchas, you have to listen to me."

He stared at her with pained eyes. "Ima, you cannot know what those terrorists will do to the hostages. Who knows what's happening to Choni? I can't bear to think of it. How do you expect me to talk now?"

"*Because* Choni is not at home, now is my chance to speak to you. Before he returns, *b'ezras Hashem*." She said as she did not wait for her son to agree. She sat down next to him.

"Listen to me, Pinchas," she said as she moved closer and asked for his attention. He was still not looking at her, and his pain was clear. Dinah opened the album and removed an old photograph. Her hands trembled as she held it out for him to see.

"What do you see in this picture, Pinchas? What do you see here?" she asked. He glanced at the photograph. In it, there was a couple holding a tiny infant. The couple smiled for the camera, while the baby was enveloped in his mother's loving embrace. The photograph undeniably radiated a great deal of contentment.

"Answer me," Dina insisted.

Pinchas' eyes scanned the image. "I see a father, mother, and baby. That's it. Who cares?"

Dinah pointed to the man in the photo. "Correct, Pinchas. You see a father, but you don't know who he is." Trying to stimulate the boy's curiosity, she asked, "Do you remember Abba had a brother Yaakov?"

"Yes, the brother who was killed in a car accident along with his wife," Pinchas remembered. "Abba doesn't like to talk about that brother. What does this have to do with poor Choni right now?" His curiosity faded and he went back to agonizing over Choni's fate.

"It has a great deal to do with him," Dinah spoke slowly. She moved the picture closer to Pinchas. "This is Yaakov. Next to him is his wife Sarah. She is holding their baby in her arms."

"A baby? I never knew that Abba's brother had children."

"One child," Dinah corrected him, and her eyes flooded with tears. "Look carefully at this infant, Pinchas. Look very closely at this baby."

Pinchas asked, "Did the baby die in the accident too?"

"No, Pinchas, this baby did not die. He's alive."

Pinchas sat up, all disheveled. This latest disclosure caught him off guard. "So I have a cousin who lives in France, because his parents lived in France. Is that what you want to tell me, Ima? And this cousin will help us now — he will — " The boy's wild imagination grew more excited.

"Just a minute, Pinchas. Slow down. He does not live in France. This baby is only a bit younger than you."

Pinchas stared at his mother. "So why didn't I ever hear about him before?" he demanded to know.

Dinah took a deep breath. The decisive moment was at hand.

She softened her voice. "We had made a deliberate decision not to tell you about this. You do know this cousin. You're a very good friend of his. You're almost like his brother. Don't look at me like that, Pinchas. Let me tell the story from the beginning.

"When Yaakov and Sarah died, they left a helpless infant. Abba and I decided we would take this newborn baby as our child, our son. This child was called Elchanan. He's very sweet. Look at the picture. Isn't he cute?"

Dinah's voice slowly trailed off. Facing her, Pinchas blinked in disbelief. "Ima, Choni is short for Elchanan, right?"

"Correct."

"So Choni is — him — you are not even his real parents." Pinchas was finding it difficult to absorb this shocking revelation. He lay down on the bed, covering his head with his blanket.

"Why didn't you tell me sooner?" Dinah heard him ask through the blanket.

"Because we thought this knowledge would not be beneficial for you or for Choni."

"But all this time we have been living a lie!" he cried.

"It wasn't a lie. It was a difficult reality that — for various reasons — we could not tell you," Dinah explained.

She got up from the chair near the bed. "Pinchas, you are our youngest child," she continued. "You are a smart child, and so I expect you to maturely accept what I have just told you."

"I'm trying." His voice sounded faint.

"You're not trying. You're hiding under the blanket and imagining that you understand everything." She was afraid that if she was too soft on Pinchas, it would only make things more difficult later on. Pinchas had to face the facts.

"You are right, Ima," said Pinchas as he lowered his blanket a bit. He was apologetic and confused. "I will try to act mature. But — " his voice became accusatory, "I still don't understand why you sent Choni to France. Did you not care what happened to him because he is not your son? Why did he have to go there?"

His mother corrected him, "The question ought to be: Why did we decide to send him to France? Because Sarah's parents live in France. They actually wanted to raise Choni, but they were too old, and they ultimately gave him to us. For various reasons, Sarah's brothers and sisters could not take him in. They accepted our heartfelt offer to raise him. Shortly afterward we made *aliyah* to Eretz Yisrael as a family.

"Now Choni's grandparents want to see him. They demanded that we send him to France. We didn't want to get into a legal fight, so we sent Choni. We did not even tell him who they were. All we wanted was for them to visit briefly with Choni, and send him back home to us. Obviously, in *Shamayim*, different plans have been set into motion. Now you understand us, Pinchas."

She imagined his anger softening while she spoke. When she finished, however, Pinchas looked around with angry eyes, and in a voice that masked a child's cry he announced: "I don't understand. Not at all." Now he was yelling. "Why did *that* Saba and Savta not come *here* to visit? Why did Choni have to travel there alone? Why did he have to put himself in such danger? Why couldn't they let him live a calm, quiet life?"

Dinah held her son's hands. "Lower your voice, Pinchas." She begged him to remain calm. "You are right. I asked the same questions you just asked. There were difficult circumstances, and there are reasons that I cannot share with you right now. That's why Choni made the trip. Now, all that's left for us to do is to *daven*."

With a sigh, Dinah stood up and left the room. She reconnected the telephone, and sure enough, within a few seconds, it rang. With a sigh of resignation, she answered it. It was Yoav, who sought more detailed information on the hijacking.

"Don't disconnect the phone, Ima. We are worried enough as it is," he begged her.

The evening was taken up with feverish conversations. Dinah spoke with her children, but her mind was with Chaim.

Later in the evening, Chaim arrived home, exhausted and worried. Dinah and Pinchas followed him silently. He looked at Pinchas, then questioned Dinah with a glance.

He knows already, Dinah signaled with a nod. "So, what are they saying? What is the situation regarding the plane?"

"They landed the plane in Entebbe," Chaim informed her. "It is being reported in the news. Some relatives of the hostages have banded together. I hope that we will have a meeting with the prime minister tomorrow."

"That's it? Have they harmed the hostages?"

"It's not known," he said tiredly. "We have to *daven*. That's certain." Chaim shot a serious look at Pinchas. "Did you recite some *Tehillim*?"

"Of course I did."

"Very good. And how do you feel?"

"*Baruch Hashem*."

He instructed his son to get ready for bed.

"I won't be able to fall asleep," said Pinchas. He looked at his father, and then stunned both his parents with a bombshell.

"Abba, why have you always acted so coldly toward Choni? Was it because he is only your nephew and not an adopted son? Is that why you always yelled at him so much? Was it because you didn't have the strength to deal with him?"

The terrible accusation burst forth almost involuntarily, and Pinchas could not take it back.

ॐॐॐ

Choni completely forgot about the heat as he triumphantly pulled out the envelope that his mother had sent to the uncle and aunt in Paris. He missed his mother so very much that just seeing her handwriting filled him with delight. The envelope was addressed, in Hebrew, to Mr. and Mrs. Kahn. So, their name was Kahn. The sealed envelope tempted Choni. Open it? Don't open it? He hesitated and deliberated for a long time.

Mr. Schick looked at him out of the corner of his eye. "What's that in your hand?" he asked.

"You mean this?" Choni stuttered. "It's nothing. Just an envelope my parents asked me to give to my uncle and aunt."

"Well, it's a good idea for me to keep it safe for you," Mr. Schick decided and reached over to take it. "You never know what these hijackers will do with our bags and things. It's a good idea for that envelope to be in secure hands. Maybe it contains money or something else of importance."

Yehudah Schick thought for a moment, and asked, "Do you have anything else of value that I should hold for you?"

Choni shook his head. He was so stunned by the loss of the envelope, he could not say a word. His mother's handwriting was no longer in his possession. It had been taken from him, along with the pleasant feeling it gave him. His face showed resentment. In a moment of childish chutzpah, he considered demanding the envelope back from Mr. Schick. Before he had a chance to say anything, one of the terrorists entered the plane cabin. He spoke briefly, and all the passengers sat up in their seats.

"Get up!" Mr. Schick was more insistent than usual. "We're leaving the plane. Let's go. They said we have to go quickly. It's best if you run, Choni."

Mr. Schick and his wife walked quickly. They both held Choni's hands, clutching their carry-on bags in their other hands. Before them were dark-skinned soldiers, standing with their rifles at the ready. Mrs. Schick wept softly until they reached the terminal.

Up until that day, Choni had thought that adults did not know how to cry. Now he saw that he had been mistaken. When they reached the terminal building and the soldiers distributed blankets, Choni was still angry at Mr. Schick for taking away the envelope without permission.

CHAPTER SIXTEEN

"What did you say?" Chaim stepped closer to Pinchas after his rash remark. "Repeat what you just said," Chaim insisted.

"I … said that it always seemed to me that you…that you don't love … I mean, you don't … " Pinchas, who was now extremely regretful, found it difficult to speak. Too late, he realized that he had committed a major mistake. He had just revealed another hidden truth, and Chaim was now very tense.

Chaim bent down and stared into his son's eyes, then gently caressed his cheek.

"Pinchas, I thought I had such a clever son. You are so wrong about what you said."

When the boy saw that his father was not angry with him, he decided to continue the conversation.

"Abba, don't you remember? Don't you remember when

Choni brought home a test, he got the highest grade in the class, 93. And you said to him that he could have tried harder and gotten closer to 100.

"And when poor Choni told you that it was the highest grade in the class, you told him that you didn't care what grade the others get, just what he gets. And he could get a higher grade."

"I still feel that way," his father interrupted. "I know that Choni is capable of more. He's a very intelligent boy."

"And what about me, Abba? Am I not capable of more? Two days later, I came home with an 82. Abba, you hugged me in front of Choni and announced that I will grow up to be a *lamdan* and a *tzaddik*. How do you think Choni felt when he heard that?"

As he spoke, Pinchas felt a swell of bravery in his heart. He believed that his younger brother had not been treated properly. To him, Choni was a brother, not an adopted cousin. He would forever remain his younger brother. Pinchas boldly lectured his father, who stared in astonishment.

"There is much more, Abba. I don't remember everything. However, there were so many times when Choni was made to stand out, sometimes as a victim, and he often just hid in a corner. Maybe you never really wanted to take him in," Pinchas shouted.

Chaim grabbed him by the arms, shook him gently, and insisted that he stop. "You may not speak with chutzpah in my house. If you think there is something you are allowed to say, do so with respect. Shouting is a total lack of decorum. Now that I've heard what you think, please go to your room and reconsider what you've said to me. We'll talk about it in the morning."

"May I stay home tomorrow from *cheider*?" Pinchas was too embarrassed to look his father in the eye. The words came tumbling out of his mouth without any prior thought.

"Why shouldn't you go?"

"Because all the kids are constantly asking me about Choni. Besides, I can't learn when I'm under such pressure, anyway."

"All right, you can stay home tomorrow, as long as Ima is not disturbed."

Pinchas went to his room and started playing records. His parents remained in the living room, not making a sound. They were trying to digest what had been said during the last hour. "You probably agree with Pinchas, eh?" Chaim broke the silence with a question that was more like a statement.

"To tell you the truth, I don't know what to think. I'm worried about Choni. I'm thinking about him constantly. Let's leave the regrets for after Choni's return."

But Chaim insisted childishly, "I *do* want to speak about it now, Dinah. It's very important to me. Do you agree with Pinchas?"

"What's the difference what I think?" she responded. "What is important is knowing what you thought when you treated him like that."

"I…what's the difference what I thought?" Chaim collapsed into the armchair and lit a cigarette.

After finishing the first cigarette, he leaned back in the chair and closed his eyes.

"I always see Yaakov standing before me," Chaim began with a heavy sigh. "They are alike, Yaakov and Choni. Even their facial features. I could almost say they were identical twins, except for the age difference."

Dinah kept silent. She couldn't connect his pronouncements with his tough treatment of Choni.

Chaim continued in a quiet tone, "In my heart, I know at all times that Choni is an orphan, and that he's not my son, but he is so much more than a regular child. Believe me, Dinah, and I know you won't be angry with me when I say this. I love Choni with all my heart, even more than my other children. I'm not saying this simply to appease my conscience."

Chaim stood up from the armchair. He was flustered at all the excitement this conversation had generated. "I thought it would be better to raise Choni like that. Because I knew that one day he would be told the truth, and I wanted him to be prepared, immunized, not feeling how much I love him. I wanted him to be a regular kid like everyone else, with ideas, aspirations, independence, and not to be a victim of my mercy toward him.

"I suppose I was wrong," Chaim concluded in a surprisingly upbeat tone.

Dinah understood that her husband was not motivated by malice. Nevertheless, she felt that Chaim's mistake was more serious than he could imagine — perhaps even critically so.

Dinah did not want to discuss the issue further, so instead of speaking about the past, she decided to focus on the cloudy future.

"Shimon, the son of Moishe Kahn, called."

A tiny spark glinted in Chaim's eyes. "What did he say?"

"That his parents are taking it very hard, and are on the verge of a total breakdown. They disconnected their telephone, and are not interested in speaking to anyone. Those two will not be of much help."

"Cowards," Chaim snorted.

"I don't think the Kahns are such cowards, as much as I think they feel helpless," Dinah said. "They can't deal with the situation. They probably blame themselves and — "

"I feel sorry for them, and I even understand them. But in my eyes, they are not so innocent. I'm afraid there will be many more fights with them in the future," Chaim said.

"Fights?" Dinah was shaken.

"Call it misunderstandings, I don't know. I have a bad feeling about them," Chaim said bitterly.

❧❀❧

"Shimon, can you come over?"

"It's 10 o'clock at night, Abba." Shimon was stunned. He looked at his watch and at the telephone handset. His parents always got a good night's sleep, beginning at 9 o'clock in the evening. For family *simchos*, they adjusted their schedules months in advance. This phone call, at such an unusual hour, concerned Shimon.

"What happened, Abba?"

"Nothing, aside from the fact that our grandson has been kidnapped and is being held hostage by some miserable people," said Moishe with sarcasm.

"Abba," Shimon could not contain himself. "You cannot do anything, Abba. He is one of more than a hundred Jewish hostages. Go to sleep, you will feel better in the morning. Aggravating yourselves with useless thoughts will not help anything."

Moishe responded, "There is something that we have decided to involve only you in, Shimon. It would be a good idea for you to come over right now."

"What about?"

"Come and you'll find out," Moishe said, and handed the phone to his wife.

"Shimon," she said, "tell your brothers and sisters not to call here. It's too hard to deal with telephone calls, at least for the time being. You will be our spokesman, O.K.?"

"It's fine," he replied, slightly confused. After the conversation ended, Shimon picked up the phone and called one of his brothers, asking him to relay the message to the rest of their siblings. He then drove over to his parents' house.

With a smile on his face, he entered. The first sentence he spoke was, "Israel has not abandoned its citizens."

"Israel has announced that responsibility for the hostages' welfare lies solely with France. France, at least for the moment, is not planning to do anything," Moishe answered.

Shimon sat down on the worn couch. "So why did you call me?" This was not the cheerful house he knew so well. The atmosphere now was tense and somewhat bitter.

"We've decided to take certain steps. And we need your help." His mother stood before him, appearing very strong despite her 75 years. Shimon could not believe she was speaking in such a tough manner.

"What kind of steps?" Shimon asked delicately. "We are all *davening* for all the hostages to be returned in good shape. What would you like me to do? Hire a plane, fly over there, and rescue Choni? Negotiate with the terrorists? Maybe rescue all the other hostages as well? Offer myself as a hostage instead of Choni?"

"You have not understood me correctly," Rivkah said, ignoring his sarcastic tone. "We want Elchanan to return to us. Permanently."

He was in total shock. "You've decided that you want to raise him? Don't we first have to worry about him surviving this ordeal? Don't we first have to worry about his safety?"

Moishe was annoyed by his son's incomprehension. "We just don't want him returning to the Binder family. If he goes back to them, they will fill his head with malicious stories to turn him against us, simply to explain their own abysmal behavior that allowed him to fall into this terrible trap in the first place. Elchanan Binder cannot live with a family that speaks against us. We want the boy to be in our custody from the moment he is freed. We will need legal counsel, because it will have to come to court." Moishe kept on talking, rambling about all the details of obtaining custody over their grandson.

"Abba," Shimon rubbed his eyes. He felt like he was in a nightmare, yet it was all too real, worse than anything he could have imagined. "Abba, you are not seriously considering this, are you?"

"We are totally serious. Aren't you interested in helping your parents?" asked Moishe accusingly.

"I very much want to help you," responded Shimon. "But in my opinion, this is not the ideal way to deal with the situation. There are conflicting reports in the media about the hostages. Our first priority has to be Choni's well-being. We have to *daven* for him. First see him back home safe and sound, and afterward launch a custody battle over him."

Receiving no response to his suggestion, Shimon collapsed onto the sofa. "All right, what do you want me to do?" he asked, resigning himself to the inevitable. *Who ever said honoring ones' parents was an easy mitzvah,* he thought to himself, *fulfilling it not only on the physical level, but on the emotional one as well.*

"Find a good lawyer for us. We want to consult with him."

"How will you pay him?"

"We have savings."

After receiving additional instructions from his parents, Shimon turned to leave their house. "Go to sleep," he implored his parents. "You're going to need a great deal of strength for what is coming up. Not one of the hostages' families knows what to expect tomorrow morning, and what fate awaits their loved ones. Let us hope and pray for the best."

He quickly left the house, and arrived home a few minutes later. His wife was waiting for him at the top of the stairs with a surprised look on her face.

"Where were you at such an hour?"

"I was at my parents' house," Shimon answered, trying to conceal his tears. "I think the hijacking has had a bad effect on them. These are not the parents I knew."

A moment later, he added, "But I'll fulfill their wishes. You must understand that they are my parents. I will do what they have asked. They are bereaved parents, and I am obligated to honor them."

CHAPTER SEVENTEEN

Later that night, Dinah closed her eyes, allowing her memories to flood her mind again. She missed Choni very badly, and was consumed with worry about his well-being. At the same time she was experiencing a contrary sensation that Choni was well and uninjured in Uganda. These conflicting notions ate away at her.

Maybe her Choni had been thrown into a dark cell and was hungry and cold. Or perhaps they had decided to treat the children with civility? *Nonsense,* Dinah upbraided herself. *Hijackers don't care about age differences.* For them, young and old, infant and adult, are all the same. Choni will share the fate of all the other hostages.

At 7 o'clock in the morning, after she had finished *davening,* the telephone rang. She first thought the call would tell her that all the hostages, including Choni, had been murdered.

She was nearly right.

"This is Shimon Kahn." His voice was heavy.

"Good morning, what news do you have for us?" She closed her eyes, as if that would avert the bad tidings. She silently berated herself for answering the phone. She wished Chaim would have taken the call.

"So tell me, how is Choni?" she asked in an ice-laden voice.

"Ah, yes, you are concerned about Choni. I don't have any specific information about him," said Shimon. "I am calling about another matter."

Dina cleared her throat. "What matter?"

"Something not particularly pleasant, I'm afraid," admitted Shimon. "Look, last night my parents invited me to their house for a discussion. I'll be straightforward with you about what we talked about. I am personally bound to fulfill my parents' requests, but I'll try to do so in a respectful manner."

"Excuse me? What did you say?" Dinah spoke harshly.

"I will explain myself, *madame, pardonnez-moi,*" Shimon stammered. "It's like this. Clearly, Choni's safety is our primary concern at this time. But my parents have decided that when, *b'ezras Hashem*, Choni is freed, they are interested in bringing him into our family. They are planning to hire a lawyer, and the process will begin soon."

"What does this mean?" Dinah's lips were dry, her face ashen.

"Within a week or two, you will receive a letter from the attorney. The Magistrates Court in Paris will handle the case, since Choni's parents were French citizens. I hope you are not angry."

"Not angry?" she hissed. "We don't know if Choni is alive or dead, and you are talking about lawyers and magistrates?"

"Hmm… I do understand how you feel, but I ask you to consider my parents' viewpoint as well. Their daughter was dearly loved, and they would like to see some *nachas* from her son Elchanan. You have had him for ten years, and this division seems reasonable, *non*?"

"I did not know that a child is divisible. You are showing me an entirely new method of child-rearing," Dinah responded coldly.

"I don't know what to answer you. It is not my decision." Shimon was bewildered. "I am obligated to my parents, *madame*. I ask you to behave with nobility and largesse, and carry out the next step."

"What's that?" Dina shouted. She had never been so angry in her life.

"To send Elchanan to France."

"Is he in my hands? You tell me, Mr. Kahn," she lambasted him. "The child is somewhere in Entebbe, in Africa. We must *daven* with all our might that he returns to us in one piece. You should be *davening* that he returns walking on his own two feet, and not in a coffin. There are rumors that tomorrow the hijackers will start executing a hostage every two hours if their demands are not met. Who can guarantee that Choni won't be among those murdered?"

She could not restrain herself any longer. "We are fearful and worried parents. Somewhat more worried than your parents, who are only thinking about themselves."

Shimon was stunned. "Maybe it's just a way for my parents to avoid facing the present situation."

"Perhaps. But I can't share what little strength I have left. I need every ounce of it for myself. Don't bother us now with foolish arguments about where the boy will live after he returns. We should *daven* that he returns altogether."

"That we will do, *madame*."

Dinah slammed down the phone. Embittered, she walked

into the living room and saw Chaim getting ready to leave for *shul*.

"Who was on the phone who aggravated you so?" he asked her.

"Did you listen to our conversation?"

He shook his head, "No, but I heard your raised voice. It must have been someone very irritating."

"Shimon Kahn called. Their son," she told him as she dropped onto the sofa.

"What do they want?" Chaim wrinkled his forehead.

"They want to transfer Choni to their legal custody, for adoption. First, they put him into this miserable situation, and now they're not even waiting to see what condition he's in when he returns — if he even returns alive. They're ready for the next step, which is even worse than the first. Chaim, what are we going to do?" She looked at him with tired eyes.

"Did Kahn's son leave you his phone number?"

"No." Dinah was disappointed. "It would have been better if you'd spoken with him. I just became emotional and irritated."

"You're allowed. You're his mother," Chaim responded with compassion. "I'll try to have a different sort of conversation with him. It's interesting that they are so sure that Choni will come out of this alive. I think they're ignoring the main problem."

Dinah added, "Take into account that in another week or two, we will receive a summons to Magistrates Court in Paris. We'll need a lawyer."

"We're not doing anything till we ask Rav Katz," Chaim concluded. "I'm going first to *daven*."

"And then?"

Chaim averted his eyes. "I'll go to the office. I haven't been there for too long. I can't help Choni by sitting around with my arms folded."

Dinah ignored his last sentence and asked, "Aren't the hostages' families organizing a committee?"

"According to what I heard, there is nothing serious being done. I'm keeping up with the latest developments, don't worry."

"But I'm so nervous. When will you go to Rav Katz?"

"He is home in the evening. I will go speak to him later, *b'ezras Hashem*. Have a good day."

She found it difficult to answer. How could she have a good day, how could things be normal when Choni was not here? How could the sky be blue? How was it that the birds were chirping in the trees? They should be crying for Choni.

The Almighty knew how much strength Chaim Binder needed that morning to skip work and drive to Netanya, where Rav Katz lived. He had formed an attachment to Rav Katz when the Binders had first arrived in Eretz Yisrael. They were alone in the country, and along came Rav Katz, whom they met almost by accident, when they sought to rent an apartment in Netanya. Chaim had come to evaluate the neighborhood when he noticed several religious Jews walking in the same direction.

"Where are you going?" he had asked in broken Yiddish.

"To Rav Katz, to receive his *berachah*. Why don't you come along? You appear to need one also." He had joined them and, from that moment on, became one of the Rav's ardent followers. He was a humble, honest man, a brilliant *talmid chacham*, and a provider of sagacious advice. He did not head a *shul* or a yeshivah, but preferred to dwell at the edge of the city, studying Torah. He never refused admission to anyone, but did not encourage it either. Whoever came was witness to his goodness and honesty, and kept on returning.

Rav Katz respected those who came to ask his advice. He invested much thought and *davened* for the correct answer before replying to anyone's query.

One of the first pieces of advice that Rav Katz offered to Chaim was that he not live in Netanya. He continued to help him throughout the difficult absorption period, and Chaim thought of him as a father who cared for all his needs. Rav Katz knew about Choni, always telling Chaim that in the *zechus* of raising this orphan, Hashem would bless him with abundant goodness.

Chaim could not forget the incident that had occurred about two and a half years ago. Coming with Chaim to see Rav Katz, Choni had entered the Rav's room, where the Rav spoke to him. Afterward, the Rav had indicated that he could leave. Choni had not understood the hint, possibly because he was distracted by something. Chaim had urged him out with a gentle push, saying, "The Rav said to wait outside." Choni then exited without uttering a word, and Rav Katz stared at Chaim with a severe look. "Don't harden your heart toward the orphan. Pretend he is your only son." Chaim's face had reddened with shame. Since then he had not brought Choni to visit the Rav.

The memory of that episode came back to him while he was driving to the Rav's house. He imagined an accusing finger counting the many instances when he had treated Choni harshly, not only at Rav Katz's house, but all the other times that Choni had deserved to be treated with respect, trust, and love, but wasn't.

The previous year, there had been a PTA meeting, and Chaim went first to see Choni's rebbi, and afterward to Pinchas'. He

entered Choni's classroom expecting to find a very satisfied teacher.

"You are fortunate, your son is destined for great things," said the rebbi as he searched Chaim's face for an indication of nachas. Nothing. Chaim remained blasé, while absorbing what the rebbi said. "He is gifted with a quick grasp, asks brilliant questions, and is well liked by his classmates," continued the rebbi. "I would recommend giving him additional lessons in the evenings. Occasionally, he gets bored during the lesson, but this is natural. I have to repeat some sections for the weaker boys, and when I do Elchanan finds it difficult to control himself. He might talk to other boys in the classroom, and sometimes even clown around in class. You ought to speak to him about it," requested the rebbi. "Personally, I don't think we can demand so much from a young child, but let's try to control it."

Afterwards, Chaim sat with Pinchas' rebbi.

"He's a gentle child, not totally integrated into the class structure. It would be good to encourage him to make more friends. He tries hard to succeed in his studies. Basically he's a good boy."

This was the report he'd expected, but the comparison between the two boys left a bitter taste in Chaim's mouth. Both he and Dinah knew that Pinchas was "a good boy," not more. Choni, on the other hand, was a gifted child. Aside from his academic talents, he had certain traits that naturally attracted many friends.

While Chaim fought a rearguard action against Choni for Pinchas' sake, Dinah rejoiced in her nephew's successes. "They had one child, we have many. Some are more talented, others less so. Baruch Hashem, they are all good children. But Sarah had only one son. Baruch Hashem he is talented and gifted in so many ways," she often said, genuinely proud of her nephew's accomplishments.

Chaim was different. When he and Yaakov were small there was always an intense competitive feeling lurking beneath the surface. Yaakov was the younger brother, the talented one, the smart one, the one who drew friends to him like a magnet. All the while Chaim, who was no less brilliant, was somehow unable to effectively exploit it. Before reaching his 30's, he was at best a colorless person. Only after he moved to Eretz Yisrael did he blossom into a success.

The competition between the brothers was consistent. Although Chaim was older, his brother Yaakov surpassed him in everything. When Chaim married, he thought the competition was finally over, but he was mistaken. Not only did it not diminish, it intensified.

As long as it was between Yaakov and Chaim, it was bearable. However, it moved forward a generation, and now there was competition between Choni and his own child, his youngest son Pinchas. This was insufferable, and needed extraordinary effort to keep under control.

Naturally, Choni won this contest. He was nearly a carbon copy of his father.

When Chaim had returned home after the PTA meeting that night, he was especially nice to Pinchas, who met him at the door. "Pinchas, you are doing wonderfully; your teachers are very pleased with you. You are progressing in your learning, listening to the shiur, trying to participate. Wonderful! Baruch Hashem that we have such a son."

Then he turned to Choni, who was standing in the corner, smiling at Pinchas. That smile reminded him of Yaakov, who was always ready to help and nurture others. Chaim so much wanted to be like his brother, the giver, instead of *always being the recipient.*

"And you, Choni, your rebbi was very pleased with you."
Chaim did not specify any details. Instead he continued, in
a critical tone, "If you are able to grasp the material because
Hashem has granted you great ability, why do you prevent
the other children from learning?" At this point, Chaim
delivered a searing lecture to the humiliated Choni.

He concentrated on the ostensibly terrible sin of
misbehaving in class, but did not relate the rebbi's praise.

Even then Chaim knew that he had wronged the child.
Dinah tried to compensate by soothing Choni, offering him
a cup of ice-cold cola. But Choni did not hear any comforting
words from Chaim, or even any praise for his efforts and
accomplishments in school.

Now, while on the way to see Rav Katz, Chaim trembled with
fear. Will the Rav reveal the entire litany of his mistreatment of
Choni? What will he say? Will he throw him out of the house?

He arrived in Netanya after an hour's drive, and parked his
car outside the Rav's house.

CHAPTER EIGHTEEN

"**R**av Katz, I need your help," Chaim stumbled into the rabbi's study, and the elderly man gazed at him with gentle eyes.

"*Shalom aleichem*, Reb Chaim. Please come in." The Rav replaced his bookmark and closed his Gemara gently.

Chaim entered, slightly embarrassed at the indulgent welcome.

"You seem very troubled," Rav Katz noted, and poured his guest a cold drink. "Here, in Netanya it's hot. You must be thirsty."

"Thanks, I'm not — " Chaim was aghast that the Rav was serving him, but the rabbi dismissed his concern with a smile. "What's the matter? May a Jew not serve some water to another?"

Chaim sipped some water, and Rav Katz beamed with approval. "Isn't that refreshing?"

Chaim nodded.

"How is the family?"

"That's the reason I'm here," Chaim explained. "The Rav surely heard about the plane hijacking."

"Unfortunate people. Hashem will speedily redeem them."

Chaim tried to control himself, but the words came tumbling out frantically. "Choni, my son, Elchanan, my adopted son, is among those awaiting deliverance."

"Elchanan was on that plane?"

"Yes." Chaim lowered his eyes.

"And what does a young child have to do in France?" inquired Rav Katz.

"His grandparents demanded to see him — " Chaim's fingers twitched nervously over the embroidered tablecloth. "I know I made a serious mistake by sending him without asking the Rav," he admitted. "But please understand that they put tremendous pressure on me. I had no choice — I mean — I don't know what to do about the child — "

"What do you mean?" Rav Katz suddenly sat up straight and gazed at Chaim. "Explain what you mean by tremendous pressure. Regarding what exactly?"

"They want to adopt the child."

"Who are 'they'?"

"The grandparents. Today they informed us, even before he has been released, that they have hired a lawyer and want to take custody of Choni. I'm very worried." Chaim spoke quickly in jumbled sentences, so unlike his usual confident manner.

The Rav continued to stare at him. "What are you afraid of, Reb Chaim?"

Chaim's shivered, despite the room being pleasant and warm. "I'm afraid Choni will agree to stay there with them," he admitted in a low voice.

"And on what is your fear based? After all, you and your wife are his parents. Why would a child willingly separate from his parents, even if he finds out that they are not his biological parents?"

Chaim paled. He answered weakly, "O.K., I'll have to tell the Rav the entire story, the whole truth." He smiled a weak, sad smile.

"I don't know if the Rav ever noticed, but I have not always treated Choni as a father should treat his son. I mean, I always cared for him and never neglected him. But I have not been able to love him as I love my own children. And the reason is quite simple." Chaim took a deep breath. "I love him even more than my own children. However, I never showed him that love openly, so that they would not become jealous. But — "

"How did this express itself?" The Rav knew how to cut to the heart of a matter.

Chaim took another deep breath. "I treated him harshly. I could never cut him any slack, I could never give him the benefit of the doubt. He is a very successful child who reminds me so much of my brother Yaakov, *a"h*. Sometimes I want to debate him, just as I used to argue with my brother. Sometimes I agonize that if Yaakov would be alive, he would do a much better job raising him than I have."

Chaim stopped the torrent of words and sat quietly. He refused to continue, as if a bone was caught in his throat. To his dismay, he heard Rav Katz ask the question that he feared the most.

"Tell me, Chaim, how was your relationship with your late brother, Yaakov, *a"h*?"

There was no way out. Chaim closed his eyes, buried his head in his hands, and begged Hashem to open a chasm in the earth that would swallow him. He would do anything not to have to travel back to the past.

A few years back in the time tunnel would bring him back to the big confrontation he had had with his brother Yaakov. This was the argument that had forever ruined the close bond they'd had between them. It had happened on the night before Yaakov moved to Eretz Yisrael.

⊱✿✿⊰

Yaakov came to their house to take leave of Chaim and his family. The two wives prepared a light supper while Yaakov and Chaim went outside to sit on the porch.

"You're making a mistake," Chaim said in a hoarse voice. "Abba and Ima would want us to remain together, near them, in France."

"So you come too, and we'll be together." It was dark outside, and Chaim could not see Yaakov's sarcastic smile, although he could hear it in the tone of his voice. "Come on, I'm inviting you to Eretz Yisrael, and you can live near us and — "

"You know it's impossible."

"Why?"

Chaim became angry. Yaakov succeeded in irritating him with his amazingly calm yet infuriating manner.

"I'm not like you, Yaakov. I do not have the connections you have. I'd be lost in Eretz Yisrael."

"I'll help you." Yaakov's promise infuriated Chaim. The thought of being dependent on his younger brother was too much to bear. He had built a comfortable life in Paris, and did not have the slightest desire to start over again. He also openly indicated his displeasure at his only brother's move to Eretz Yisrael.

"You are splitting the family."

"Maybe you are?" asked Yaakov quietly.

Chaim was going to give a caustic reply, but at that moment, Yaakov's wife Sarah announced that dinner was ready. The two brothers entered the house in silence.

A short while later, the tragic accident occurred.

After that, Chaim eventually moved to Eretz Yisrael.

❧❧❧

Chaim grasped his head in his hands as the painful memories buffeted him.

"You don't have to answer," Rav Katz's voice sounded in the background. "But I'm trying to get to the source of the problem."

Chaim opened his eyes, now red, and looked around the room. "Yes, I am trying to help, too," he said. He was confounded. "But it is difficult for me to answer the Rav's question about Yaakov. I haven't figured out our relationship." He found it difficult to continue speaking. After a pause he said, "We had true brotherly love for each other. At the same time, we were so different, and I — I really don't know how to describe it."

As an afterthought, Chaim added, "Why did he travel to Eretz Yisrael alone? We were the only family he had."

Rav Katz listened quietly. Chaim spoke more to himself than to the Rav, but the Rav nevertheless absorbed every word Chaim said.

"We'll talk about this some other time. Right now there are more pressing problems." The Rav attempted to redirect the conversation.

"Yes, there are problems," Chaim said wearily, and then added, "But I don't want to waste the Rav's time — "

"It's all right."

Chaim calmed himself. "Okay, they hired an attorney.

Elchanan's grandparents want legal custody over him."

"Why are they now suddenly thinking about it?"

Chaim shrugged his shoulders. "It's not clear to me either. Maybe raising a very young child would have been too difficult. Now that he's older, he can manage certain things on his own. Who knows?"

"Why does it disturb you that they want Elchanan to live with them?" asked the Rav innocently. He was pretty certain of the answer, but was surprised at the vehemence with which Chaim expressed it.

"No!" Chaim pounded the table. "I refuse to relinquish Choni!" Despite all his attempts to withhold them, his tears cascaded down his cheeks.

⁂

"Take your carry-on bag."

"What should I do?"

"Take your bag and get ready to move," Mr. Schick said dryly. He then spoke to his wife in French. Mrs. Schick sobbed without a letup, and Choni was shocked. He never thought that adults were capable of crying so much.

Five minutes earlier, two Ugandan soldiers had smashed a hole through the thin wall of the room. They turned the opening into a doorway. In front of the doorway, the Ugandans constructed a crossbar. They put this there so that the Jews would have to bow before entering their new room.

"I didn't know there was another room there," Choni remarked aloud. But Mr. Schick immediately hushed him with a severe look. For the past few hours, Choni had been feeling as if he were a burden to the Schicks. True, they treated him well and spoke patiently and calmly to him. Yet, on the other hand, it was clear that they did not know what to do with him.

After they widened the hole enough to reveal the other room, one of the hijackers began shouting loudly. A woman standing near him tried to silence the hostages.

"What is he saying?" asked Choni.

Mr. Schick did not answer, and Choni did not want to ask the question again, despite his curiosity. He heard the hijacker call out a name from a list. There was the sound of someone crying, and then one hostage moved from the room they were all occupying into the "new" room.

Another name, and an elderly couple moved through the hole in the wall. Another name and a woman was heard shrieking, "*Aktziah, aktziah* — " People began yelling and wailing. Choni did not understand a word. He merely heard the woman shout, and everyone became silent. Then, in the midst of this hubbub, Mr. Schick reminded him to hold on to his carry-on bag.

"But why?" Choni asked. "How do you know they're going to call us?"

Yehudah Schick bent down and whispered to Choni. When he brought his face close to his ear, Choni felt that Mr. Schick was really concerned for his well-being. "You are a big boy, Choni; I know I can rely on you. See, your parents sent you to France by yourself. Right?"

"Right," said Choni.

"Soon they are going to call my name and my wife's. We will go together. Listen carefully now. As soon as they call your name, go right away to the entrance of the room. I'll wait for you there near the hole. If they call you first, wait for me at the entrance. Don't run, and don't speak to anyone. You're not afraid, are you?"

He was terribly frightened, but he nodded to Mr. Schick and put on a brave face.

"Don't leave anything here."

A few minutes later, one of the terrorists called his name. He did not realize that they were referring to him, until Mr. Schick pushed him, instantly reminding him where he was.

"Elchanan Binder." The terrorist sounded impatient, but the way he pronounced his name almost made Choni laugh. He restrained himself from smiling and walked by himself through the hole in the wall, slipping quickly into the adjoining room. Several pairs of approving eyes greeted him, and one man extended his hand to help him pass through the jagged opening.

Following Mr. Schick's instructions, he did not talk to the other hostages, but waited in the corner. When he saw Mr. Schick struggling to get through, he moved forward to help him. He took his belongings, and then extended his hand. He did the same for Mrs. Schick, who was still weeping.

"Why is she so sad? It's better here," Choni whispered to Mr. Schick. "It looks like they're all Jews here. There is not one Frenchman in this room."

"You are right. You have good powers of observation," Mr. Schick complimented him with a touch of irony in his voice.

A short while later, when all the Jewish hostages were separated from the other passengers, they were locked into the second room. Suddenly, they heard rousing applause from the other room, the one they had just left. At the entrance to their room, the Jewish hostages saw the Airbus' pilots and the stewardesses, who had voluntarily decided to join the segregated Jews.

"Why are they applauding?" Choni was amazed.

"Because they have come to be with us," explained Mr. Schick. A moment later he added, "They must be among the Righteous of the Nations." Choni still did not understand. He wanted to ask what that meant, but suddenly remembered something important. Fear seized him.

"Mr. Schick," He pulled at his sleeve. "I hope you didn't forget to take the envelope from my mother, did you?" Choni was extremely concerned.

"I didn't forget. It's right here," Mr. Schick answered impatiently as he patted his pocket. Choni could see the envelope.

When Mr. Schick left him to speak to the other people in the room, Choni was trying to figure out a way to get that envelope, the only memento he had from his mother, back into his hands.

CHAPTER NINETEEN

inah heard light knocking at the door, and the sound of it opening. She rose with difficulty from the chair, trying to hide her red eyes.

"Yoav? Is that you?"

"It's me." Yoav walked into the room and, looking at her, felt uncomfortable. True, it was unnecessary to explain her tears. Her son had been taken hostage, and the outcome was murky at best. Tears were no surprise at all. Neighbors came at will, bringing food, trying to say something that would calm Dinah, or asking for details or new information they did not have.

Yoav asked, "So what's new, Ima?"

"There's no news."

"All right, but still, maybe share what you know?"

She appreciated Yoav's sixth sense that almost never erred, and this time was no exception. He obviously sensed something, but Dinah just shrugged her shoulders, refusing to speak.

"O.K., I really just came by to say hello. I'll head over to Abba's office."

"Don't go," she said, although she immediately regretted it.

Yoav came back, sat down on one of the kitchen chairs, and asked simply, "Why shouldn't I go?"

"Because Abba is not there."

"Where is he?"

She most desperately did not want to involve Yoav. Not because she did not need any support, but because she wanted to protect Chaim's honor. Now, though, everything was falling apart, and she wept uncontrollably.

"Abba — is in bed — he's sleeping."

"He's not feeling well?"

Dinah wiped her face. "I don't know, Yoav. In the morning he said he was going to work, and at about 11 o'clock he was back home. He went to bed saying his head hurt. Afterward — afterward — " She forced herself to stop crying. "Abba is now shattered. There is no one with whom to speak. I think we are the only ones left to fight this battle that may already be lost."

Yoav bit his lip. He did not understand what Dinah was trying to say.

"I'm going to talk to Abba," he declared.

"No, you will not. He just fell asleep. Let him rest a bit."

Yoav decided to call his father's office. He heard the secretary's voice answer the phone.

"This is Yoav, Chaim Binder's son. Could you connect us, please?"

"I'm sorry, he's not in the office today."

Yoav continued talking in a normal tone of voice. "Ah, he did not come to the office today?"

"No, but he said that he'll be coming in the evening. Didn't he say anything to you?"

"It's O.K. I'm sure he's at home. It's just that I usually call him at the office. Thanks very much. Goodbye." He put down the telephone and turned to his mother, a bit weary. "Abba wasn't at the office today."

"No?" Dinah's eyes opened wide.

"We'd better check where he went."

As they spoke, Pinchas walked in. He looked stressed. He glanced at Yoav and asked, "Anything new, Ima?"

"Not yet, sweetie. Come eat," she offered him. She then remembered Yoav. "Have you eaten today? Come on, both of you, I'll prepare something that will help you cope with our troubles."

Since their ordeal had begun, Dinah's dedicated neighbors had been sending over cooked meals. She warmed up the food on the stove, and prepared two plates. She indicated to Yoav not to speak in front of Pinchas.

"But he's already grown up," he whispered to her. "You can't conceal from him forever what is happening."

"Leave him alone, Yoav. He's a little boy — let him grow at his own pace."

Yoav shrugged his shoulders. He washed his hands and sat down to eat. After the second bite, he heard the door of the bedroom open.

"Abba woke up. I'm going to talk to him." Before Dinah could respond, Yoav stood in front of his father.

The confrontation seemed unavoidable.

❧❦❧

A young boy with curly hair, wearing a T-shirt and shorts, came up to Choni.

"What's your name?" he asked in correct though not fluent Hebrew.

Choni wondered when all the hostages had become one big family. He looked over with hesitation at Yehudah Schick. When he saw that he was speaking animatedly to a group of the hostages, he decided not to interrupt him. Turning to the boy he answered, "Choni Binder. What's yours?"

"Michel Braun." His French accent was noticeable.

Choni suddenly had the feeling that his opportunity to perform a *Kiddush Hashem* was at hand. "Are you Jewish?" Choni asked.

"Sure, everyone in this room is Jewish. It's not easy being Jewish," answered the boy.

"We can't know what will happen, but we all have to Whom to pray." Choni showed Michel a *siddur*.

They spoke openly, sometimes bluntly, always comfortable with each other. The simplicity of youth, along with their common destiny, bonded them together as friends.

They continued talking and were nearly inseparable after their initial conversation.

Mr. Schick looked over at the boys with a critical eye. "Choni, come here," he said as he pulled his sleeve. "I see you have found some friends," he said quietly.

"One friend," Choni corrected him.

"Listen," Mr. Schick said as he tugged at his beard, not quite knowing what to say. "I realize I'm not your father, but my responsibility is to watch over you. I'm not sure your father would approve of this new friendship."

"We're not really friends, just acquaintances," Choni claimed, and defended his new companion. "They keep Shabbos, but they're not exactly religious. And it's so boring here. What should I do? Sit and stare at the guards?"

"All right, I see you really don't have what to do here," Mr. Schick said. "But honestly, I don't know if your parents would approve."

"I'll be careful. The moment he says something wrong, I'll leave him," Choni said. "If you want, you can listen in on our conversation."

"Allow me to forgo that pleasure, Choni." Mr. Schick smiled and turned away. Choni returned quickly to Michel, who was watching him impatiently.

"What did that baby-sitter want?"

"Don't speak about him like that. He's an older person." Choni has assumed the role of teacher, even though Michel was older.

"O.K., he's older. What did he want?"

"He was worried if our friendship was proper."

"And the decision?" laughed Michel.

"I don't know. But these are pretty unusual circumstances. And I cannot sit around forever in the company of adults."

"Me neither," declared Michel.

"Your parents aren't here?"

"Only my brother."

"Which one is he?" Choni asked.

Michel pointed to a young man of about 20 who looked like some underworld gangster.

"Tell me the truth, aren't you afraid to be around him?" Choni was only joking, but Michel looked around nervously. The crowded conditions and the stifling heat all had an effect on him. Michel opened up to Choni.

"Sometimes I really am afraid. But don't tell anyone."

"Are you really afraid of your brother?"

"Sometimes," Michel nodded, his curls bobbing in agreement.

Choni looked at him in disbelief. "Why? Because his clothes are so scary?"

"No, not exactly. I'm not afraid of his clothes. I'm afraid of how he talks. Once I came to his house unannounced, and I saw all types of characters there. Obviously, in France, not everyone is Jewish. So my brother did not exactly spend his days among Jews."

Choni's curiosity grew. "Did you hear what they spoke about?" he asked.

Shifting the conversation somewhat, Michel said, "My parents sent my brother on a tour of Israel, hoping to connect him to his Jewish roots. They sent me along as well. I was afraid to travel with him — "

"Why?"

"Because — " Michel glanced at his brother and then looked at Choni. "Believe me, you don't want to know, Choni. I myself regret finding out."

"So you see that it's better when you are religious. Look what kind of trouble you have when you're not," Choni said with the assertiveness of a child who had just had his lifestyle validated.

Michel gaped at him.

They spent the rest of the day at each other's side, sharing the nightmarish experience of the hijacking. Michel's brother did not once look in their direction. He sat alone, thinking, and responding angrily to anyone who dared talk to him.

"Do you think they're going to kill us?" Michel asked.

"I don't know, but it's a possibility."

They discussed death with the same equanimity and resignation as one discusses life.

"If they kill us, we won't have had a lot of time to be friends," Michel continued.

Choni was concerned about something else. "Look, I have an ethical question to ask you. Do you know what ethics are?"

"Sure, I'm the most ethical kid in my school. That's what my teachers say. That the Jews are an ethical people, and that's why they're stupid."

"Forget your teachers." Choni was impatient. "Opening an envelope that someone asked me to deliver: Is it ethical or not?"

"It's very unethical."

"Are you sure?" Choni begged with desperation.

"A thousand percent." Michel's expression made Choni laugh.

"But listen to what's in this letter. My mother sent it to my aunt and uncle. It's the only memento I have of my mother. I mean, let's say I never see her again. Don't I have a right to open her letter? Believe me, I miss her terribly."

"I also miss my parents. I didn't dream I'd be away from them for such a long time," Michel's voice drifted off as if in a trance. Afterward, he said, "But you know something? If I had an envelope from my mother, and I thought I would never see her again, even if she didn't mean it for me, maybe I would open it."

"But it's not ethical," Choni reminded him.

As they spoke, they noticed a few Ugandan soldiers dragging one of the hostages to the other room. The young man was suspected of being an Israeli Army conscript, and was returned to the group badly beaten and bruised. His interrogators had also managed to inflict a severe gash to his forehead.

This frightened the hostages and caused a commotion among them.

Michel's eyes widened. "I'm certain they are going to kill us," he cried out in a panicked voice. "When you're facing death, you don't have to worry about niceties. You're not going to see your mother in heaven, right? You're going there alone, and she's still down here. Here's your chance to read her greetings in the letter. Open it, read it, and be done with it."

Choni was still undecided. That night, he had trouble falling asleep, and it was not because of the noisy footsteps of the soldiers surrounding the hostages.

CHAPTER TWENTY

Wednesday morning found the two friends yawning. The days at Entebbe were passing slowly, filled with endless fear and terrible boredom.

Even Mrs. Schick did not greet Choni with her usual, "Good morning." It was ironic to look for anything good about the dank transit hall, with the dark-skinned Ugandans distributing meager food to the hostages. Under normal circumstances, Choni was an extremely fussy eater. But in Entebbe, he did not have the luxury of being as finicky as usual. He chose a hard-boiled egg and a few slices of bread. Michel, on the other hand, ravenously ate whatever they served.

"I'm not sure it's kosher," Choni pointed out.

"It's fine," said Michel with a mouth full of food. He did not wait for an answer. Instead he continued, "So, did you get that envelope from your baby-sitter?"

"Not yet," Choni said as he dropped down onto the badly

crumpled mattress. The room was filled with old cushions, pillows, mattresses, and several rickety chairs. Most people sat either on the mattresses or on the floor.

"What are you waiting for?" Michel demanded to know.

Choni motioned, and looked through the opening in the wall at the non-Jewish passengers. Their suitcases were stacked neatly along one wall. One group had already been freed and was on their way home. The remaining hostages seemed calm and behaved as if they were enjoying themselves. They were playing a card game that Michel called Bridge. They smiled, laughed, argued, and in general gave the impression that they were vacationing tourists.

Choni continued staring at them. They did not seem concerned about anything. They did not even glance at the Jewish-Israeli group in the nearby room.

Michel followed Choni's stare. "You see, those people have it good. They have nothing to worry about."

"Who put such foolish ideas in your head?" Choni retorted in a sudden fit of irritation.

Michel backed off. "That's what my brother said when he saw the French hostages being released. He said that we'd be killed, and they'd send the others home to tell stories about their experiences."

"Your brother is wrong. Don't listen to him." Choni was serious and emphatic.

"I have to tell you something important about my brother," said Michel. "Are you listening to me, Choni?"

"No, I can't talk to you right now. We'll get together again in an hour."

"Where are you going?"

"To pray."

Michel's demeanor was one of respect, and he stood aside

staring in wonder at Choni, who — in his opinion — was talking to himself and performing some strange movements. When he was finished, Michel called to him, "I'm your friend now. Had I seen you doing this a few days ago and not known who you were, I could have sworn you're out of your mind," Michel noted.

"You're the one who's out of his mind. I pray, you don't," Choni reminded his friend.

A fellow named Pierre was holding a guitar and invited them to join a group that was singing. They politely turned him down.

"See, they're also relaxed."

"Trying to relax," Choni corrected him.

But calm was a mirage. A few minutes after the group sat down to sing, President Idi Amin arrived. Mr. Schick quickly grabbed Choni and instructed him to stand. Everyone stood up for the Ugandan president, who seemed strange and eccentric, and had a befuddled look on his face.

"But we only stand up for *rabbanim*," Choni complained.

"And your elders," Mr. Schick reminded him.

The group of hostages listened quietly to the president's speech. Choni did not understand one word, but noticed that one phrase was used repeatedly. He wanted to know what those words meant. Michel also listened attentively, and Choni found himself looking at him with admiration. Michel was three years older than he was. He surely understood what he was hearing and would explain the words of the strange Idi Amin.

"So, what did he say?" Choni queried his friend after the president stopped speaking.

Michel sank to the dirty floor. "The situation is difficult."

"What do you mean, difficult?" Choni asked.

"Difficult. He kept on repeating that we are moving toward

the 'red line,' and the government of Israel has still not announced if they are prepared to cooperate and fulfill the hijackers' demands."

"What is the 'red line'?"

"The Line of Death."

Hearing the answer, Choni became frightened. "What does that mean?" All around him, he heard the murmuring of the hostages. The Schicks sat next to each other reciting *Tehillim*. The situation did not seem as promising as it had in the morning.

"They have designated a specific deadline for the Israeli government to respond. After that time, they are going to start executing hostages."

Choni swallowed hard. "So what do you say? How can I get that envelope out of Mr. Schick's pocket?"

"Envelope?"

"Yes, so I can see what my mother wrote," answered Choni.

Michel sat up and stared at Choni with disdain. "I'm talking to you about life and death, and you are worrying about an envelope?" Michel rebuked him. A few moments later, Michel relented, saying, "All right, I understand. You're younger than me, and I guess this envelope means a lot to you."

"So will you help me?" Choni exclaimed. He desperately wanted to escape the horrible situation. Every so often, he sat down to recite *Tehillim*. But he was distracted and did not have much patience, so he found it difficult to concentrate.

"I'll help you," said Michel. "And if I help you, you'll help me."

"What kind of help do you need?"

"Help in getting along with my brother."

Choni stared uneasily at Michel's brother, who stood alone in the corner. "O.K., as long as I get that envelope."

They deliberated for about half an hour and came up with a few possible plans. It would be Choni, however, who had to carry out the scheme. He prayed that Mr. Schick would not catch on to their plot.

He walked over to Yehudah Schick in tears, which, under the circumstances, was not particularly difficult to fake. All he had to do was to recall home, Abba, Ima, the family, and the threatening Ugandan soldiers, and the tears flowed effortlessly.

"What happened, Choni?" asked Mr. Schick.

Choni whimpered as he said, "I I miss my "

"Everyone longs for someone, child. Soon we will be home, don't worry," Mrs. Schick interrupted, with tears flooding her eyes as well.

"You know what you should do? Go say some *Tehillim* instead of gabbing with that boy," Yehudah Schick admonished.

"I already finished *Tehillim* for today," Choni told him, wiping his tears. Then he continued speaking in a low voice. "I was cleaning out my bag. And I suddenly discovered that something is missing."

"What's missing?" Mr. Schick was tired and preoccupied. He tried to speak civilly to the child.

"The envelope my mother gave me."

"Don't worry, it's in my pocket. I'm taking good care of it."

"You won't lose it?" Choni asked innocently. "Would you let me see it?"

Mr. Schick searched his pockets, and then he opened his small suitcase. "Here it is. Do you feel better now?"

Yehudah Schick fervently hoped that Choni would eventually deliver that envelope to its designated recipients. At present, of course, there did not seem to be much likelihood of that happening.

"I was afraid you might lose it. It might be better if I kept the envelope," said Choni timidly.

"If it makes you feel better, please, here you go. It doesn't seem to be anything so important. I mean there's no money or valuables inside. Just a letter." Mr. Schick handed the envelope to Choni. His voice reverberated throughout the reception hall where the hostages waited.

Just a letter.

⌘

"Abba, are you feeling all right?" Yoav scrutinized his father.

"Yes, *baruch Hashem*, I am. What is bothering you?" In an attempt to distract himself from his painful lack of self-confidence, Chaim Binder used irony and occasionally acerbic words. As a rule, however, he did not speak like that with his children. Now, though, he did. He did not want them probing his state of mind, his personal problems, and how he was solving them.

"Nothing," Yoav retreated. "I just wanted to be sure that you are feeling well. Ima said you were very perturbed today."

"I had a hard day," Chaim replied.

"At work?" Yoav asked casually.

Chaim nodded in a vague, noncommittal way.

Yoav decided to be straightforward. "Abba, I know you weren't at the office today."

"Wonderful, my son is a detective. Up to now, I thought he is a *yungerman* in *kollel*, and now he's dealing in investigations." Chaim was obviously annoyed.

Chaim's manner did not frighten Yoav. "I'm sorry, Abba, I'm not trying to be impudent," he said dryly. "But you have to realize that Ima is very worried. She does not understand what is happening to you."

"I'm glad you have someone on whom to blame your unbridled curiosity."

"Abba — "

Father and son exchanged dour smiles. Chaim resolved the issue. "Yoav, you're playing with fire. You deal with your life and its problems. Leave me to my business, and allow me to take care of my life. Do we have a deal?"

"No."

"You have gone too far," said Chaim. "This chutzpah of yours is intolerable — "

"I want to help. Choni is my brother, exactly like he is your son," Yoav implored. "You know that Ima is terribly worried. She doesn't deserve this."

Chaim stared coldly at his son. "That's enough for one day, Yoav. If I need your assistance, I'll call you. We are finished for today."

Yoav left the room sadly and bumped into his mother on the way. He sighed, "Abba is angry and edgy."

"I told you," Dinah rebuked him. "It's pointless to talk to him now. You have to wait for things to settle down."

"But he's not going to calm down as long as Choni has not returned home. You know that, Ima. And who knows when Choni will come back?"

"Don't speak like that." Dinah was trembling. She told Yoav to finish his lunch, and began to prepare Chaim's meal.

A few minutes later, Chaim joined the rest of the family. He approached Pinchas and told him firmly that he must return to his regular school schedule.

"But I can't concentrate," objected Pinchas.

"I'm sorry, Pinchas, but you have to get back to your studies. We do not know what will happen. It is a situation that will take time to resolve. It's best for you to get back to *cheider* and continue to advance in your studies. Perhaps in the merit of your

Torah learning, Choni will return soon."

"Do I have to?" Pinchas looked distressed.

"Yes, this afternoon you will go. When you come home I will want to hear what you learned. Agreed?"

Pinchas nodded. He was bewildered by his father's unusual interest in his studies, and realized that his father was going through some sort of trauma. In the beginning he did not pay too much attention to his parents' pain, because he was so engrossed in worrying about Choni. He had endured sleepless nights and great anxiety since his brother's disappearance, and his mother had been doing her best to reassure him. Now, Pinchas understood that not only was poor Choni in a terrible situation, but his parents, too, were suffering a dreadful ordeal as well.

Pinchas finished his soup, and after wiping his mouth, observed, "You know, some really bad people kidnapped Choni. But not only him; they also took Abba's heart. Right, Ima, Abba isn't the same as before?"

Dinah looked at her son and replied, "It's harder for Abba than for the rest of us. He blames himself."

"For not treating Choni better?"

"For all kinds of things. I'm not sure that he didn't treat him nicely," Dinah said, trying to support her husband.

Pinchas wanted to talk a bit more, but the mailman's knock at the door interrupted their conversation.

"A telegram from overseas."

"What do they want?" Dinah asked wearily as she signed for the message.

CHAPTER TWENTY-ONE

"**W**hat do they want?" Yoav echoed with obvious curiosity. Dinah handed the telegram to Chaim, letting him open and read it first. "It's nothing good, that's for sure," she whispered.

"That's for sure." Chaim's fingers rubbed the paper. "The Kahns did not even bother contacting us. At least they ought to have asked if Israel planned to take some action on behalf of the hostages."

"They did. Shimon called, remember?" Dinah pointed out. She did not want Pinchas to hear them criticizing Choni's relatives. It could lead to anger that Pinchas would then tell Choni. This kind of destructive family feuding could be very detrimental to Choni's well-being.

Chaim was adamant. "Shimon is a caring person. The old folks, however, are not," he said as he opened the telegram.

Dinah and Yoav waited silently as he read it. His eyebrows knitted tightly together in anger.

"What do they want?" asked Dinah.

Chaim folded the telegram as he answered briefly, "I have to get in touch with them immediately. They have one demand."

"And that is?"

"That we agree to relinquish custody over Choni." He looked past them into the empty room. "Forever."

Dinah was the first to recover her composure. "So why bother calling them?"

"Maybe they have some information about Choni from the first group of French hostages who were released. They want to share it with us."

Dinah cried out, "He's injured!" The most horrible scenes flashed through her mind.

"I don't think so," Yoav said. "If something had happened to one of the hostages, the media would have reported it. I think someone recognized Choni based on his description, and told the Kahns that he is O.K. There's really no reason to call them."

Then Yoav turned to his father. "Abba, did they write anything else?" He did not have the nerve to ask to see the telegram for himself. Even if he had asked, it was doubtful that he could have read it quickly enough. His father was not about to relinquish control of that telegram for very long.

"Yes. They wrote that the threat of legal action should be taken seriously, because from their perspective the matter is perfectly clear. It would be best if we decide quickly."

"That's it, everyone; there is really nothing more to discuss about this telegram, correct?"

"Excuse me, Abba, but I think there is something to discuss," Yoav said.

"Excuse me, Yoav?"

"Abba, Shimon probably signed the telegram. Most likely, his parents pressured him to call us, and he preferred to contact us via telegram, despite the expense."

"What are you trying to tell us?" Chaim asked.

Yoav stepped forward. "That you have to involve me in this matter. Abba, they are consulting their son. You also have a son, Abba. I can help."

Yoav stepped to the side, far from Pinchas' inquisitive ears, and whispered directly into Chaim's ear. "Let me help you, Abba. For once in my life, trust me. All my life, you've never believed in my capabilities. Now you have the opportunity."

Chaim grasped his son's hand, gently pulled him into the next room, and closed the door. The mistakes he had made with his adopted son burned in his heart. Now, with his biological son accusing him of similar behavior, he felt as if a sharp sword was being plunged into him.

"What do you mean that I haven't believed in your capabilities?" Chaim demanded in a measured voice.

"Abba, you know the truth. I don't have to explain it."

"Tell me," Chaim demanded hoarsely.

Yoav relented and began to relate various incidents but noticed that his father's face was turning white. Breaking off, he continued, "Abba, you were always at my side. We did homework together, remember? We learned Gemara. And you explained. You always explained until I understood. Your desire for me to understand was so strong that I felt that I'd never understand anything by myself. Now too, you supervise me, and it's wonderful of you. You are so concerned about me; you want everything to be right. But I'm an adult now. I don't need your help as much as I need your support and trust in me."

"Is this how you've always felt?"

Yoav feared that this outburst was excessive and poorly timed. Did his father need to think about this at such a time?

"And you didn't say anything to me," Chaim said in a soft voice. "Why didn't you say anything to me?"

"Because at the time, I didn't think it was so bad. Now, I'm telling you how it was back then. I am asking you to allow me to help, to participate. Please involve me."

Chaim Binder nodded. He had begun the long process of re-evaluating his treatment of his children. It was a deep and often painful self-criticism.

Yoav, however, misunderstood his father's nod as agreement to help prevent Choni from being sent to his grandparents. He planned to participate, but in a way in which his father would never agree.

Yoav felt satisfied and vindicated as he left his parents' house. Now, he could deal with the problem of the Kahns and their demands.

ح%৯ও

"Wake up, man, I'm talking to you." Michel shook Choni, who was in a deep sleep.

"I'm not sleeping, Michel. Leave me alone."

Michel sat down next to him and crossed his legs. "I see you are not asleep," he said. "But I'm really bored."

Choni considered telling his friend that he was not responsible for entertaining him. But he decided that would be impolite and so kept quiet.

Then he remembered, "The envelope. I have the envelope."

"Your mother's envelope?" Michel jumped up. One of the two German terrorists on duty in their area gave him a hostile look, and he sat down again.

"Why didn't you tell me right away?" he demanded.

"Because I'm thinking."

"About what?"

Choni tilted his head back slightly, and then said in a child-like voice, "I'm thinking about whether or not I should open the envelope."

They became quiet, and then Michel said, "My plan worked, right?"

"Right."

"The envelope is in your hands. So now, you have to help me, right?"

"Help you with what?"

"Help me with my brother. I told you we have some… er… problems."

"That's right. I promised."

Even though he could have gotten out of it, Choni decided to cooperate. After all, he had promised to help. Promises have to be fulfilled. That is what his parents had always taught him.

"Tell me what the problem is. I'm not certain I can help."

"But two heads are better than one, right?" Michel was optimistic. He closed his eyes, thinking how best to describe the kind of life they led. It would seem so strange to Choni.

ञ❧ॐॐ

Michel was born into an unusual family situation. His brother Gerard was always different from the others, spending his time mostly by himself. He never sat with the family on the veranda, or went fishing with them. He never spent time with his parents. He seemed to prefer being with his friends. He and his peers became a closely knit group.

From the age of 8, Michel decided to keep his distance from Gerard. His brother was then 15 years old — nearly an adult, capable of deciding things for himself. And that he did.

Gerard's friends were weird. They continually played loud, jarring music, and would glare darkly at Michel whenever he showed up. "He's not going to be part of our gang," they said one day to Gerard as they walked together on the street.

"He's not smart enough," Gerard answered them, casting a glance at his brother. Michel continued walking, a blank expression on his face, looking like he was indifferent to what they were saying. He had not the slightest interest in being part of their strange group. Besides, he was afraid of them.

At age 16, Gerard caused a humiliating flap in the family when one evening, during dinner, their father received a phone call that their son was in police custody. Their mother nearly lost her mind from worry. Their father remarked, "I knew it would come to this." Gerard was not accused of a felony, and he was a minor. He was released on his parents' recognizance.

The entire family, with tears in their eyes, went to the police station to pick him up. Gerard looked at them defiantly and declared, "I made a mistake. The next time they won't catch me."

His father slapped Gerard across the face, but he did not even flinch.

"I forbid you to associate with those hoodlums," his father ordered as they drove home in the car.

Gerard surprised everyone with his pretentious and insulting remarks. "They are not merely my friends. They are my family. I'm going to leave the house and move in with them."

His mother did not want Gerard to move out. She promised not to interfere in his affairs, as long as he remained with them. Gerard continued living at home, though he remained aloof and distant. He barely spoke to his father, although his behavior was a bit more civil to his mother.

Upon arriving home one day, their father remarked, "I found out what Gerard's gang is really up to." He gripped his chest, and his face grew pale, as if he was having a heart attack. His wife called an ambulance, but he recovered on his own. Afterward, the parents spoke for a long time, quietly and with many tears.

"He has forgotten that we're Jewish. My brother should come and — "

"Shh, Michel can hear. Speak quietly," his wife said.

Dark days descended upon their house. Their father nearly stopped eating, and would sit and stare coldly at Gerard. When the boy wasn't within earshot, he would refer to him as an enemy of Am Yisrael.

The boys' father lamented that he was to blame for Gerard's downfall, because he had abandoned his ancestors' heritage. Their mother cried that she never knew anything about Judaism, because her family's assimilation went back at least two generations.

Their father checked out his wife's family background. They all turned out to be Jewish. One grandfather had even been a rabbi. They had never actually assimilated. No one married outside of the faith, but no one kept any of the commandments.

After some time, the parents wanted to inculcate some Israeli nationalist pride in their younger son Michel, in the hope that he would not follow his older brother's example. At the table, they would sing songs about Eretz Yisrael *that his father remembered learning as a youth. His mother would light Shabbos candles.*

Gerard usually made a point not to be home at these times, so this feeble attempt to instill some Jewish awareness influenced only Michel.

Gerard's gang soon turned into a Neo-Nazi group, yet Gerard remained loyal to his friends. His parents were horrified. "They seem to enjoy having a Jew in their midst," his father once commented.

Only then did Michel realize how far Gerard had drifted. The younger brother was old enough to know about the Holocaust and the extent of Jewish suffering. It was then that he started to hate Gerard. On the surface, he maintained a façade and continued to act decently toward his brother, out of respect for his mother, who wanted Gerard to remain somewhat connected to the family. Michel did not want to travel to Israel with his brother, but finally agreed. His parents hoped to give Gerard a feeling of responsibility toward his younger brother.

Once on the plane, however, Gerard turned to Michel with a wicked smile on his face and informed him, "Don't even think about touring the country with me. I'm putting you in a dormitory for the week, and I'll be off on my own." He then added, "Don't breathe a word of this to our parents."

Michel kept quiet.

But now, with the return flight to France hijacked, all those words came back to Michel. He told them all to Choni, who was terrified of the new, frightening world which he had just learned about.

CHAPTER TWENTY-TWO

"Yoav, when are you coming home?" Nechamah's voice on the phone sounded very tired. "The baby is crying, and the older children have to shower and get to bed. I could use some help."

"I'm deeply involved in something extremely important. But I'll come home to help you," Yoav said, feeling for his wife.

"Look," she said, "if it's really important, I can manage on my own. But you're coping, right? Is everything all right?"

"*Baruch Hashem*, everything is fine."

Yoav put the phone down with a silent sigh. "We must hurry up," he told Zalman. "We have to decide on a method of action."

Zalman was Yoav's close friend. They had first become acquainted when they were in the same *shiur* in *mesivta*, and their friendship was cemented during their years in yeshivah. They remained close, always knowing they each had a friend to count on in time of need. After leaving yeshivah, Zalman became a talented writer whose every written word was a gem.

"We've got to do something. How can they get away with this?" Yoav exclaimed.

"Really, Yoav, you are losing perspective here. We are dealing with an elderly couple who lost their daughter ten years ago. What do you want? Do you want them to admit that they are about to lose their grandchild due to their own brilliant maneuver?" That was Zalman: pragmatic and logical.

"O.K., let's assume that they are unfortunate people," Yoav drummed his fingers on the table. "And let's say we are not going to take any action against them. We'll show them compassion instead. I still don't think they have the right to upset my parents the way they did."

"Listen, I have an idea for you. It will not solve the problem when your brother returns home, but it will give you a short respite." For nearly an hour, Zalman elaborated on his idea. His proposal thoroughly heartened Yoav.

"An airtight solution," Yoav exulted. A few minutes later, however, his face became somber. "My father won't like it. My mother probably won't go for it either. Let's keep this under wraps."

They decided to implement Zalman's plan on the following day, before going to the *beis midrash* at 9 o'clock in the morning.

"Where is my mother's letter? It's gone," Choni cried out bitterly, then quickly stifled his tears. He did not want to cry in front of his older friend.

"Is it really missing?" asked Michel, looking around. "Maybe one of the terrorists took it."

"Don't be ridiculous," Choni replied.

Michel burst into noisy laughter. "I think the letter was absorbed into your hand." He made a great show of pulling the letter out of Choni's hand. "I'm good at magic. Did I tell you that?"

"You forgot to mention it," Choni scowled. "Now, give me back the letter."

"Not before you promise me you'll open it."

"Why do you care?"

Michel sat on the filthy mattress and motioned for Choni to come sit down next to him.

"I'll tell you why I care. As long as it is in your hands, all you can think about is your mother's letter."

Choni angrily grabbed the letter from Michel. "Don't touch things that don't belong to you. Understand?"

At that moment. Choni decided not to continue unconditionally trusting Michel. Michel was so different from him. All of Michel's attempts at reconciliation were unsuccessful.

"A nice kid doesn't behave like this. What you did wasn't magic: It's stealing," Choni clarified for Michel.

"It was just a joke."

"Nothing is funny here, in Entebbe. Nothing." Choni was furious.

He was right. President Idi Amin had announced that the killing of hostages would begin if Israel would not agree to the hijackers' terms. The terrorists were extremely hostile and the imprisoned passengers were afraid to have eye contact with them. One elderly woman did not feel well, and was taken to the hospital. Those in the know whispered that her fate was now sealed.

The second group of French passengers was preparing to fly back to Paris. As they waited to leave, they stared through the hole in the wall at the pitiful Jewish hostages in the other room.

It was clear that they were going to die.

The Schicks were unable to offer any comfort to the young boy in their charge. Choni felt he had no more strength. He refused to associate with Michel. *Yehudah Schick was right*, mused Choni. *I should never have become friendly with him in the first place. He doesn't have our values. How did he have the nerve to touch my personal letter?*

At night, while most of the hostages slept, Choni touched the envelope and thought about his mother. *Please forgive me, Ima, but I've got to open this envelope, to see your comforting handwriting. You will forgive me, Ima?* Choni thought as he stared at the letter.

With trembling, hesitant hands, he tore open the envelope and removed the letter. He looked around. No one saw him, except for one old man who was having difficulty falling asleep. He cast an unfriendly look at Choni.

"Boy, what are you doing there?"

"Trying to fall asleep."

"With papers in your hand?"

Choni hid the pages behind his back. "I'm not doing anything. I'm allowed to write."

"Don't make the terrorists suspicious," the quarrelsome old man said. "You have the face of a boy who is up to some mischief. Go to sleep."

Choni waited for the old man to finally fall asleep, then stared at the letter with excitement and strong yearning for his mother.

As soon as he saw the words on the page, Choni was thunderstruck. *How can this be?* he breathed. *Why isn't it written in Ivrit?* He checked the envelope again. *I'm sure this is not Ima's letter. Ima gave me something else. Mr. Schick fooled me. He gave me the wrong envelope.*

He stood up and furiously walked over to Yehudah Schick. He nearly awakened him, but decided not to at the last moment. He did not want to explain why it was so important in the middle of the night, and why he had dared to open the envelope in the first place.

Choni carefully put the letter back into the envelope.

The sleepless night passed. At 5 a.m., sunlight filled the hall where he and the rest of the Jewish hostages were being held. Choni felt that the sun's rays lit his soul as well. He intended to get hold of his mother's letter.

৯৩৯৯

Shimon started the car with a flourish.

"Are you ready, Abba?" he gently asked his father. "Are you up to telling it all to the lawyer?"

"Of course," Moishe Kahn looked at his son, trying to appear young at heart — or at least younger than his true age.

"O.K., because you have to tell the lawyer everything," Shimon emphasized. "Sometimes a small detail can be significant in the larger picture. And we don't want any unexpected surprises later on."

"Right."

Moishe was silent during the ride. When Shimon parked near the ornate office building, Moishe was sorry that his wife had chosen to remain at home. *Rivkah should have come,* he thought. *She could better present the story. The whole business had mushroomed because of her.*

How did she put it as they left the house? "Our Sarah wants her child to return to his roots, which is France, in our house. Yes, his uncle raised him with love and dedication. Nevertheless, for him, Choni is just another child. For us, he is all we have left from Sarah."

"So what?" Moishe remembered challenging. "They are surely doing a good job."

"We will do an even better one. Don't you see that what happened to this flight is a clear sign that everything was wrong?"

"What sign?" he had asked, feigning innocence.

"The hijacking. Look, for years airplanes have been flying without any problem. Why did they target this particular French aircraft?"

He thought of an answer, but instead had replied, "The hijackers knew Choni was on the plane?"

His wife had become annoyed. "Hashem knew that Choni was there. For us, it was a sign that we should take him into our custody — permanently."

"Perhaps it is really a different sign, Rivkah. Maybe Hashem is telling us to leave him in his uncle's home," Moishe had dared to suggest an alternate approach.

Rivkah then became angry and did not respond. After a while, she had turned to her husband and said, "Go with Shimon to the attorney and tell him the whole story."

Moishe, in fact, had had a different thought, but did not want to tell his wife. He did not even want to tell his son.

Now, however, as they approached the lawyer's office building, Moishe decided to stand up and act forcefully. As he thought about his next move, he slowed his walk. Shimon noticed the change and thought Moishe was overwhelmed. The recent events would certainly justify feeling that way.

They took the elevator to the 24th floor. "Are you all right?" Shimon asked.

"I'm trying," Moishe coughed.

When they found Room 245, Moishe said, "Wait a minute," before Shimon knocked.

He turned around and closed his eyes. He knew Rivkah

would not agree with his change of heart. He had to leave the office building immediately. Rivkah had pressured him into consulting a lawyer in the first place. He was not blaming her; after all, she was a grandmother. Her conscience had been working overtime since the hijacking. *She blames herself for the tragedy, although she won't admit it openly. In any case,* Moishe thought, *we're taking this crucial step too soon and too fast.*

At the threshold of the posh lawyer's office, he had to take a stand. He looked at his son and said, "Tell the lawyer that I'm canceling today's meeting."

"Abba, you cannot just cancel a meeting with a lawyer," said Shimon, slightly panicked. "He will charge us for his time!"

"That's fine; let him charge," mumbled Moishe. "Before we go to the lawyer, there is someone else we have to see first. Is that clear?"

"Who?" Shimon worried.

"I'll tell you outside."

Moishe quickly stepped into the elevator and pressed the lobby button firmly. *Finally, something is moving in the direction I want,* Moishe thought.

CHAPTER
TWENTY-THREE

"O.K., Abba, what's going on?" Shimon asked as he drove the car away from the lawyer's building.

Moishe Kahn felt foolish. He would have to pay for the lawyer's wasted time. In addition, he would have to give a full accounting to Rivkah, who would be upset.

At the same time, Moishe was sure he had done the right thing. "I cannot take such extreme action without consulting with the Rav of our *shul*," he said in a measured tone.

Shimon drove on silently. After a few minutes, he asked, "Do you think the Rav is going to authorize going to a lawyer to gain custody over a grandchild who has not yet been freed from Entebbe?"

"I don't know. When a Jew does not know something, he should go to his Rav, right?"

Shimon shrugged. He did not understand the need to drive his father to the lawyer's office. He thought it would be more beneficial to organize massive *Tehillim* recitations for his nephew's well-being, rather than consult with a lawyer about something completely irrelevant and in poor taste.

Only after his father got out of the car in front of the *shul* did Shimon ask the fateful question. "Why did we go there in the first place?"

Moishe hesitated, lowered his head back down into the car, and answered, "Look, Shimon, your mother is very concerned and upset about Choni. The tension has affected me too. Ima thinks we should take advantage of the situation. She is so concerned about the fate of the hostages that she is using the lawyer as a way of releasing her tension. I hate to think about what the Binders are doing right now — how they are reacting to our telegrams. They are parents, and they are suffering because of their son's situation. This battle is the *coup de grâce* that will make it the worst possible nightmare for them."

"So where are you going, Abba?"

"To the Rav. In the meantime, do not update Ima. Is that clear?"

"Totally."

Shimon started his car and left quickly. *Who said the mitzvah of honoring one's parents was easy?*

This mitzvah had become more difficult for him since his sister Sarah had died. The talk about the nephew, the entreaties, and the tears were very difficult. He had to obey his parents, to agree with them, to participate in their struggle to see their grandson. Now, he was a partner in his father's regret and withdrawal. What could he possibly tell his mother?

Shimon headed for home. He had done his share. Now he had to deal with other urgent matters that he had ignored for the past few days. As soon as he walked in the front door, his daughter Miri greeted him.

"A lot of people want to talk to you, Abba. Don't ask how many have called."

"Were they business calls?" he asked, feeling stressed.

Miri did not know the answer to his question, but she added, "There was one person who called at least five times. He wanted to talk to you. I forgot his name."

"Why didn't you write it down?"

"Because I didn't know how to spell it correctly," Miri explained.

Shimon did not have time to argue with her about the importance of writing down phone messages. She was his incessantly stubborn youngest child and thought she was always right.

He deliberately did not question Miri too closely. He didn't want to know if someone from Eretz Yisrael was trying to reach him. What could he say to them about the telegram that he had hurriedly sent to fulfill his parents' request?

He could empathize with the pain of his parents. Why should they be prevented from seeing the son of their deceased daughter? *All of the considerations in favor of the child pale in the face of my parents' well-being.* That is what Shimon thought initially. At the same time, he could also identify with the beleaguered Binder family. Personally, he was pleased that he had not taken Elchanan into his family ten years ago. It would have been too much of a hassle.

⇴

Thursday morning found Choni more irate than usual. This was their fifth day at Entebbe. Their room reeked. Just looking around at their squalid conditions and at the soldiers guarding them was enough to become nauseated. And the same boring food, day after day, along with the murky-looking water they were given to drink, was just awful. Had Choni not been so thirsty, he would have refused to drink at all.

Now he was more upset than ever. He felt that the person who had been entrusted with his well-being had deceived him.

"Are you O.K., Choni?" asked Mrs. Schick, who noticed everything.

"I'm not feeling well," he replied.

Yehudah Schick, in an attempt to lighten his mood, joked, "What's the matter? In a few hours, we will be going home. You'll miss this place."

"I know what's going on here. We're not going home in a few hours. And I'll never miss this place," Choni answered combatively. "Where is the letter you were holding for me?" he asked abruptly.

"What letter are you talking about?" Mr. Schick planned to begin *davening Shacharis* and had started putting on his *tefillin*. He seemed caught unawares by Choni's question.

"The letter. Don't you remember?"

Choni was ashamed. He had never spoken so rudely to an adult.

"I think you're having a memory problem. Choni, I gave the letter back to you. Did you lose it?" he asked.

"No. But it's not the right letter."

"It's your parents' letter. I don't have any other letter in my pocket. Would you like to check?"

Such a suggestion was awkward, and Choni — completely embarrassed — walked away. He withdrew into a corner, bemoaning the loss of the letter.

"Look, the little boy is crying," Choni heard a derisive voice call out. He looked up and saw Michel standing over him.

"What are you crying about, kid? Miss your mother again?" Michel was enjoying himself at Choni's expense.

"No!"

For the moment, Choni forgot his anger at Michel. His wrath was currently directed at Mr. Schick for hiding the letter.

"Gerard is acting strange. He doesn't talk, he doesn't smile. I can't stand being next to him," declared Michel. As an afterthought, he added, "If you aren't lonely for your mother, then why are you crying? Hey, are you grouchy about the letter?"

"Yes."

"What happened this time?"

Choni told Michel about the previous night's events. He claimed that Yehudah Schick had taken the letter from him and substituted some other letter — the wrong one — in its place. "I can't even read what's written in it," he complained.

"Why can't you read it?" wondered Michel.

"Because it's written in a foreign language. Why would my mother write a letter in another language?" Choni argued.

Michel thought for a moment. "That really is strange. Look, I've helped you out before. Do you need my help?"

"I suppose so."

"Think about it: Mr. Schick has no reason to hold your letter. Why should he? There's no money inside, right?"

"I don't think so," agreed Choni.

"So what would he do with a piece of paper? Why would he hide it?" Michel exclaimed, proud of his deductive powers.

Choni thought for a while. "What you're saying makes sense," he finally agreed. "But the letter is not mine. How do you explain that?"

"Either you are right or he is. Show me the letter and we'll check it. Let's see if the substituted letter is a good fake or not."

After thinking a few seconds, Choni agreed. He pulled out the letter from his pocket and showed it to Michel.

"You see? Look at the writing."

"It's French," Michel said simply. "The letter is addressed to the Kahn family. Know them?"

"They are my relatives. I am supposed to be visiting them in Paris," Choni replied.

Michel was very serious when he told Choni, "You owe Mr. Schick an apology. You wrongly accused him of something he did not do."

"What do you mean?"

"Your mother wrote this letter in French. You should have realized this from the outset, Choni Binder. Even in a foreign language, it's still her handwriting."

There was a moment of silence as he contemplated Michel's words. Choni then smiled tiredly. "All right, I'll ask forgiveness later. When we get home, I'm sure everyone will forgive me for my sins, including opening the letter in the first place. Honestly, I didn't realize my mother would write in French."

"If she lived there, of course she knew French."

Choni looked at Michel in surprise. "Did anyone ever tell you that you're a genius?"

"You are the first one. But maybe there'll be a few more after you."

The two of them laughed. In an instant, they became friends again.

"Please translate the letter for me," Choni begged.

Michel did not begin reading immediately. "It's not so easy for me. There is a mixture of two languages. I have a better idea. I'll write it out for you. That way, you'll be able to concentrate on it."

"How long will it take?"

"About an hour, I guess."

Michel sat down with a few sheets of paper and a pen to begin translating the French letter. He did not read the entire letter before writing, because he found the beginning quite boring. After a few sentences, however, he dropped the pen and continued reading with an open mouth. He rubbed his eyes and let out a whistle of surprise.

"Choni, come here," he called to his friend.

"Are you finished already?" Choni came over in an excited mood.

"I barely started," admitted Michel. "I don't think you ought to read this letter. Your parents will be very annoyed with you if — "

Choni's stare halted Michel.

"All right, all right," Michel retreated a bit. "But you'd better think twice before reading *this* page. I assure you that if I were in your place, I'd just forget about it and continue on with my life."

Choni looked at him angrily and said, "Do what I asked you to, and don't give me advice."

"We're friends. My advice is on target."

"I'm not interested. Translate it, and give me the paper."

Michel sighed, "Remember that I advised you not to read this letter. And don't ever tell your parents who did the translation. It'll get me into big trouble."

Michel's words served only to intensify Choni's desire to read his mother's words.

An hour and a half later, Michel passed the translated pages to Choni. With lowered eyes, he said, "I still recommend that you not read it."

"Thank you for the recommendation, and thanks even more for the translation."

"I hope you won't regret it, Choni," he said nervously.

CHAPTER TWENTY-FOUR

"You are a busy man, Reb Shimon Kahn." The language was Hebrew, fluent and clear. "Who is this, please?" he asked nervously.

"I am a journalist."

"Who?" he shouted.

"A journalist, Reb Shimon, a reporter. I don't think you are acquainted with the newspaper in Eretz Yisrael for which I write. It is a religious weekly publication. But I'm certain you would be happy to cooperate with me."

The voice was pleasant, but Shimon was frightened.

"To cooperate about what?"

"The story of Elchanan Binder, what else?"

Shimon dropped into a chair. He forgot about his workload, and broke out in a sweat.

"How do you know about Elchanan, for Heaven's sake?" Shimon shouted.

The journalist seemed amused. "Calm down, Reb Shimon. There's no reason for you to be angry. *Klal Yisrael* needs a great deal of *rachamim* in these turbulent days. As for Elchanan, well, who in Eretz Yisrael does not know about him?"

"Everyone knows?"

"Hmm…." The journalist cleared his throat. "I have not yet introduced myself. My name is Zalman Sofer, and I am a noted reporter. I have been advised that the matter of custody is about to be brought before a court of law. Can you give me any additional details?"

"No," Shimon said simply.

"Why not?" the reporter inquired.

"It's a family matter."

"Family matters are resolved within the family, Reb Shimon. Once you have gone to court, it is in the public domain. But," the voice now turned soft as melted butter, "you don't have to answer me. I can just write that the French family members declined to comment. Nevertheless, my recommendation, Reb Shimon Kahn, is not to refuse to cooperate. Most of my readers understand that someone who maintains silence probably has something to hide, and is worried about losing in court."

"We have nothing to hide. I ask you not to write about this at all."

"Why not?"

Shimon thought for a moment, then cried out with emotion and naivete, "My parents are old and weak. All this publicity will not benefit their health."

"And do they enjoy stealing a child from his parents?"

Shimon became livid, yelling, "They did not steal the child! They want to see their grandson whom they have not seen for years. Do they have to apologize to the newspaper for that?"

Yoav's friend Zalman sensed that he had gone too far. "All

right, Reb Shimon. I won't interview you. The child's family in Israel has some serious charges, and I thought that — "

"We are on the verge of canceling the complaint. So there is really no public interest in the subject at all. And I forbid you to write anything about it." Shimon thought that a tough, indisputable tone of voice would end the matter, and the conversation. The audacious Israeli reporter, however, renewed his questioning zealously.

"So you are canceling the complaint? That's news," he said firmly. "That'll be quite a scoop for my paper. Why are you canceling? Have you given up custody claims on the child?"

Zalman's questions disgusted Shimon. He shouted, "We have not yet canceled! We are considering canceling. Please don't write anything about the claims in the paper." His tone changed dramatically from moment to moment. He now sounded like a man begging for his life — a tone that apparently pleased the reporter.

"You know what?" Zalman suggested politely. "I'll call you back tomorrow. By then, you'll surely know if this is a family matter or a public matter. Just remember my compassionate gesture, because other reporters are going to call. I am reserving first rights to the story."

"O.K.," Shimon answered weakly. He hung up without saying goodbye. Miri immediately walked up to him.

"Who was that, Abba?"

"Bring me something to drink," Shimon asked in a raspy voice. She brought him a grapefruit-flavored beverage that he disliked, but he drank it without comment or hesitation.

"So, who was on the phone?" asked Miri again.

"Zalman Sofer."

"That's him," she exclaimed. "He's the one who called five times."

"I can imagine."

"Who is he?"

Shimon got up determinedly. "Miri, you are not allowed to pester Abba with nosy questions. Go play in your room, quickly. I'm going out. Tell Ima I'll be at my parents' house."

Getting into his car, Shimon sighed. He was missing too much work, and the upcoming paycheck would reflect the days he had missed at the bank.

He hurried to his parents' house, opened the gate, and rushed in.

"Abba didn't come with you?" asked his mother in surprise.

"No," Shimon responded, confused. His frenzied reaction to the phone call from the Israeli reporter led him to forget their near-meeting with the lawyer earlier that morning.

"So where did he go?" Rivkah practically leapt from her seat in fear.

"He...went...." Shimon barely remembered his promise to his father. Not one word about where Moishe had gone.

"He probably went to *daven Minchah*, and to learn, but I thought he would have come home by now. That's why I'm here."

"Ah." Rivkah was not completely mollified. "Why did you come?"

Shimon answered, "I came to tell you what just happened. I wanted you and Abba to hear about it at the same time."

Just then, as if fulfilling Shimon's wishes, the front door opened and Moishe Kahn stepped in. His face looked as if he had aged 20 years since they'd last seen him.

"Abba," Shimon trembled at the sight of his father in such a weakened condition.

But Moishe gestured, "Leave me, I'll be O.K." He lowered himself into the nearest armchair.

"What happened at the lawyer's office?" Rivkah inquired. "And why are you both as pale as ghosts?" She placed her hands on her hips as she waited for an answer.

ᡒᩞᩞᡒ

The moment Michel handed the letter to Choni, he was overcome with regret. He was three years older than Choni, and suddenly, as if in a flash, life's truth had been revealed to him. It was not easy. Michel was reeling from the story contained in the letter he had just translated. He found it nearly impossible to believe that the mother Choni missed so badly, was, in fact, not his mother. It was like a nightmare, and he found it difficult to grasp the astonishing reality that the letter revealed. He pitied Choni, and was concerned for his well-being.

As Choni's friend, he decided to spare him from the bitter truth. Choni took the translated pages with the excitement of someone stranded in the desert sighting an oasis. He barely had time to read the first word before Michel ripped the paper from his hands.

"Give it back," shouted Choni in a fit of anger.

"The paper is mine; I found the pen. So, first off, don't scream," said Michel softly. "Secondly, what kind of friend are you?"

"What do you want now?" Choni shouted at him.

"I'm helping you, but you ignore me. It's convenient for you to be friendly when I am of some benefit to you. That is not friendship, you're just using me whenever it's convenient for you. Do you agree?"

"I agree with everything you said. Just give me back the letter," he cried, devastated by the betrayal.

"Not before you help me with my brother Gerard."

Michel started chewing a fresh piece of gum. "I know that you won't help me because you're my friend. You'll do it because you want that letter, right?"

"Right." Choni was frank.

"Good, so let me tell you what is happening with my brother."

At first Choni listened because he had no choice, but he kept looking at his watch and at the letter in Michel's pocket. As the story dragged on, however, his interest and his fear grew.

"When we flew to Eretz Yisrael, Gerard told me clearly that we would not be touring together. He was not at all concerned where I went. You see — wherever I go, I take care of myself. But I needed to know where he would be staying.

"On the flight from Paris, I noticed a group of boys that Gerard glanced at, but did not talk to. I realized that they were part of his gang, even though they didn't come near him.

"When Gerard was asleep on the plane, I walked by them and they immediately quieted down. When we stood in line at passport control in Israel, they spoke quietly to one another. They didn't realize that I was nearby and was listening to them. They talked about getting rid of all the Jews in their gang after they have fulfilled their usefulness.

"I left quickly, but I think they saw me standing near them, and they were upset. I acted as if I knew nothing, but in my heart, I wished that I could have recorded that conversation. Maybe Gerard would change his mind after hearing them. And do you know what? The one who suggested killing all the Jewish members was the one who always buddied up to Gerard. Another guy kept quiet. I wouldn't be surprised if he were Jewish, too.

"Gerard took me to some kind of boarding school. I begged him not to leave me alone, but he just laughed, saying I was not a baby and I knew how to take care of myself.

"I told him that our parents will notice that there are no photographs of us together. I also told him they might even involve the police, because they were sick and tired of his uncontrollable behavior. I spoke with a lot of self-confidence, and Gerard looked worried. Afterward, I whispered that I had overheard his friends, and that he would not like what they said.

"Gerard said he did not have any friends on the plane, but I saw that he was troubled. I was frightened. Would he harm me, his own brother, for the sake of some gang?

"He actually took me on a trip one day. We took many pictures, so that he could show my parents we were together in Israel, I was very suspicious, because I knew my parents had not given him that much money. Where did he get so much money?

"And if you think we actually toured — you're wrong. We just shot pictures at the entrance to the site, but usually did not go inside. He refused to go to see the Western Wall, but I told him it would be stupid to come to Israel and not go to the Wall.

"We went, and he told me to go on but he held back. Then, I saw him go up close and stare at the stones. He even leaned his head on the Wall. If I say he cried, he'd kill me, but I saw tears on his face. He ran back to our meeting place and pretended that he had been waiting there the entire time.

"I decided that on the flight back home, I would tell him about the conversation I had overheard from the gang members. But then there was the hijacking, and now Gerard is so nervous you cannot say a word to him."

CHAPTER
TWENTY-FIVE

"**W**hat now?" Dinah asked expectantly as she opened the front door.

"*Geveret*, I'm sorry," the mailman apologized with a hint of a smile. "You have an urgent telegram."

"Again?" she asked.

"Sign here," the postman requested. "Thank you. I hope it's good news," he said as he hurried from the Binder house, leaving Dinah staring at the just-arrived message.

What do they want now? Do the Kahns want to drain me of whatever strength I still possess? thought Dinah as she sat down to open the telegram in the quiet living room. Pinchas was reading in his room, and Chaim was resting in the master bedroom. Dinah opened the telegram quickly. The words raised more questions than they answered.

It was a telegram from Shimon Kahn, of course, who had taken charge of the Choni custody struggle. More than once, Dinah had wondered why she was not hearing from any other family members. Whatever the reason, Dinah felt bad for Shimon, who seemed to be fulfilling his filial responsibilities more out of duress than free will.

"Don't announce anything yet. Nothing is final. Give us some time to think. Shimon Kahn," the telegram read.

Dinah read the baffling missive several times. Had they lost their minds, or was she simply unaware of something? She looked again at the telegram with anguish before folding it carefully and placing it near the telephone.

There was no need to wake Chaim. There was nothing he could do. The exhausting news reports constantly broadcast the hijackers' threat to begin executing hostages if their demands were not met. It was nearly one week since the hijacking. Government leaders were restrained. For the families of the captives, however, life had not returned in any way to its normal pattern. The thought that Choni was in Africa, without his parents, drove Dinah nearly to despair. He was a 10-year-old child. How was he holding up?

That day, the families of the hostages were gathering together for a meeting with Israel's prime minister. Chaim was scheduled to participate in the meeting but decided, on the advice of his neighborhood rabbi, to stay home. "Perform acts of *tzedakah* and *chesed*, and Hashem will assist you," the Rav had advised him.

Dinah usually spent her mornings visiting her grandchildren. Every day, she visited another family. She was not a guest when she came, but a member of the household. She usually brought along a homemade meal. She would baby-sit the grandchildren, freeing their parents to deal with other household affairs. It was the highlight of the week for her and her grandchildren when they got together.

Dinah had been home for almost a week. In an attempt to retain her sanity, she finally decided to resume her regular schedule. Dinah called Nechamah and asked when it would be convenient for her to come visit her grandchildren.

"Are you sure? Are you up to it?" Nechamah did not try to conceal her joy. Whenever her mother-in-law came over, it gave her a break. The children were supervised, and she had more time to deal with her household tasks. "Whenever you come, we'll be happy to have you," Nechamah said. Dinah was reassured and, for the first time in several days, even a little cheerful.

She forced herself to prepare a bag of treats for the children, then left a note for Chaim on the table. She left the house and headed for the bus stop.

No one outside seemed preoccupied with the hostages. As she walked by vegetable stands, she heard people arguing over the price of tomatoes and cucumbers. As she passed by a clothing store, she noticed a young girl deliberating between buying a skirt or a jumper. As she approached the bus stop, she heard a woman telling her daughter the latest about China.

Life goes on.

She was startled to rediscover life outside the walls of her house. People were continuing to live in a normal fashion, not worried about whether their loved ones would be executed in a few hours, minutes, or seconds.

Dinah was suddenly too impatient to wait for a bus, so she flagged a taxi and directed him to Yoav and Nechamah's house. As she stepped out of the taxicab, she could already hear the jubilant sounds of her grandchildren heralding her arrival.

She withheld her gloomy thoughts along with her tears as

she approached the excited kids. She made herself smile at each one individually.

"We thought you weren't going to come to us anymore," they said as they embraced her.

"Why would you think that?" she asked. Holding her hand, they entered the house together.

The house was swirling with activity, and Dinah noticed that Nechamah was inundated with housework. Yoav was busy on the phone; he seemed to be talking to his *Rosh Yeshivah*.

"How are you, Ima?" Yoav said as he looked up at her and covered the mouthpiece. It was as if he was saying to her: *I'm happy to see you, but are you up to this?*

"Yoav, with Hashem's help, everything will work out," she answered briefly. After he ended his phone call, she remembered to tell him about the telegram from France.

"I think that something happened to the Kahns. They sent me a very strange telegram."

Yoav became tense.

"Really? What did they say?"

"It was rambling; the words were disconnected," she began. "Something like, they want to think it over. Don't go public with it…Nothing is decided yet."

Yoav listened with a half smile on his face. "Yoav," Dinah said, "do you know what's going on?" She looked at him accusingly.

He shrugged his shoulders. "They do seem befuddled. This is not a simple matter," he tried to change the subject, but Dinah noticed.

Her grandchildren were now demanding her attention, and so she did not have time to pursue whether Yoav was acting on his own. She did, however, make a mental note to discuss the matter with Chaim. Judging from Yoav's smile, it appeared that he thought he was in charge, taking actions that they, his parents, would not necessarily have approved.

When she walked out of the living room, she saw that Yoav was again on the telephone.

"Zalman?" he whispered. When he saw his mother watching him, he lowered his voice even more. "I think it worked," he said with elation.

༄✿༅

"Your story is very interesting," Choni said, stretching his arms. "We have to think about what to do about your brother. It sounds like he is in a lot of trouble."

Michel asked, "Do you think his life is in danger?"

"I don't know."

"So what do we do?"

Choni threw a hollow glance at his friend. He thought a little while, and then suddenly demanded, "Give me my letter."

"What?" The abrupt about-face startled Michel, and Choni pulled the letter out of his hands.

"I helped you. I listened to you. Now I want what belongs to me."

Michel's eyes glowed with anger. "Did anyone ever tell you that you are not a loyal friend?"

"You are the first and the last, and I don't care."

"Give me the paper," demanded Michel.

"No. I fulfilled your conditions. Now the paper is mine."

This sudden switch confused Michel. He was mature enough to understand how traumatized Choni would be by the information in the letter. He decided to try a different tack. "Choni, you didn't help me. You just listened to me. Now, we have to make a plan of action."

"I'll think of something. You can think of something yourself.

You are older and smarter than me."

"I'm thinking," Michel yelled. "I really am and … ." A swarthy-looking soldier walked by and eyed the two boys arguing. One of the terrorists started toward them with threatening steps.

The boys became silent as he passed by them. Apparently he was looking at someone else near them.

"Keep quiet. Don't you see what's going on here? Do you think you are in France?" Choni whispered.

"I will not change my mind," Michel said in a lowered voice. "If you consider me mature, take my opinion that this letter can harm you. Listen to me, it's not worth dealing with this. Just this once listen to someone older than you."

"It's O.K. for you to read and not for me?"

"It's not anything to do with me personally. Believe me, if I were in your place, I would not want to read this letter."

"You are only making me more curious."

After a brief silence, Michel said in a hopeless voice, "Here, read it. It's your problem. From now on, I have nothing to do with you. I've fulfilled my end of the deal. From this point, you handle it on your own. *Au revoir.*"

Choni did not respond, nor did he even look at Michel. He did not think for a moment about Gerard's troubles, or about Michel or the Schicks. He did not think about anything. His mind was focused on the words in the letter. He had to squint to read Michel's handwriting, which did not flow smoothly in Hebrew. You could see it was not his mother tongue.

As he scanned the pages, Choni's initial reaction was *"Well done." You translated the entire letter. I, on the other hand, do not know even one other language besides Hebrew.*

His next thought was: *I'll have to read slowly because his writing is not clear.*

Choni cried when he read his mother's words, and sighed when she made requests from his relatives. The details Dinah had written were astonishing. When he finished reading, he relaxed his grip and the paper fluttered to the floor. He dropped his head into his hands and wept, and nearly collapsed from the revelations in the letter.

CHAPTER TWENTY-SIX

Yehudah Schick scanned the hostages' room with narrowed eyes. He hated the scenes that had become all too familiar. How long was it possible to put up with the trash on the floor? How much longer would people be able to keep themselves busy doing nothing? How long could they look at the serious expressions of the soldiers and the hijackers?

Usually, in his spare time, Yehudah recited *Tehillim* or studied from a small volume of Gemara. Now, however, despite the "free time" available, he felt he was unable to concentrate sufficiently because of the general tension and the threat to his life.

Instead, he spent a lot of his time wandering around the passenger hall. He took small steps and walked slowly, so as not to end the "tour" too quickly. Occasionally he cast a glance at Choni. Sometimes Yehudah felt that he no longer had the strength to worry about the boy. At other times, he felt grateful to Hashem for creating this situation, forcing him to rise above himself and any petty considerations, and for making it necessary to care for this child and encourage him. It enabled Yehudah to reassure himself as well.

Come to think of it, where was the boy?

Mr. Schick surveyed the area until he noticed a child who reminded him of Choni. He was sitting on the floor in the corner of the room with his head in his hands, his body trembling.

Yehudah rushed to him. "Choni?"

He did not answer.

Mr. Schick was anxious now, fearing for the child's well-being. *Did something happen? Did one of the terrorists speak to him? Threaten him? What was going on?*

Choni did not respond. He just sat there on the floor, crying. He did not raise his head or respond to Mr. Schick's frantic calls.

Yehudah stared helplessly at the child. The boy was hysterical, crying desperately for his mother.

At that point, Mrs. Schick caught up with her husband. She also tried to coax the boy into speaking, but it was useless.

"I know exactly what happened to him." From behind the Schicks came a voice speaking Hebrew with a noticeable French accent. They turned around to see a teenage boy.

You…" Yehudah muttered. "I warned him not to befriend you. What do you want from him?"

"I know what happened to him," the boy asserted. "He has a right to cry." He added quietly, "And it's my fault that he's crying."

Mr. Schick grabbed him by the collar and said, "What did you do to him? Tell me what you did."

The boy gasped, "Nothing. Leave me alone."

One of the terrorists who had joined the hijackers walked

past and stared at them. She was an evil woman, and reminded Yehudah Schick of the stories some of his friends told about the woman kapos in the camps during World War II. They were reputed to be even more brutal than the men. This terrorist was always quick to anger, and constantly shouted. The men, in contrast, seemed to be able to control themselves.

As she walked past and glared at Yehudah and Michel, the two were shaken. Yehudah released the boy from his grip. Michel backed up and kept his distance.

"If you want to find out what happened, I'm willing to tell you. Just be polite, and I'll help you."

"Talk," Mrs. Schick ordered.

The boy took a deep breath. "Well, you didn't ask my name, but I'll tell you. My name is Michel." The Schicks remained silent, perhaps because of all the other people around them. "You are Yehu — "

"Who I am is not important," Yehudah cut him off. "Tell us about Choni." He did not particularly care for this arrogant young man.

"I told Choni not to open the letter."

"Which letter?"

"The letter from his parents. You gave it to him." Michel sent him an accusatory look. Yehudah grabbed his head. "You're right...the letter...," he murmured. "It really was not meant for the child. It was foolish of me to give it to him."

"The letter was not yours," Michel reminded him gently. "You didn't give it to him. He gave it to you, remember? Anyway, Choni opened the letter, which was not even addressed to him."

Yehudah's curiosity got the better of him, despite all his efforts to restrain it. He asked in a curt manner, "And what was written there?"

Michel started speaking in French. He did not want Choni to understand what he was saying. He did not know how precise his translation was, and how much of it Choni had understood. Michel unfolded the original letter and read it verbatim to Mr. Schick.

"Unbelievable," declared Mrs. Schick.

Yehudah Schick was thunderstruck. He snatched the letter from Michel's hand. "I can't believe you had the audacity to translate such a significant letter for a young child," he reprimanded. "How did you think he would react to such information?"

"I didn't think. Choni became my friend. He asked me for a small favor. Why should I not do it for him?"

"The reason is plain for you to see," Yehudah replied dryly. The three of them glanced at Choni. He was sitting on the floor, not listening to their conversation. Even though his tears had dried up, he was not paying any attention to them.

"Choni?" Freida Schick bent down and asked quietly.

"Leave me alone," Choni whispered.

"O.K."

They moved back, staring at him. He looked so pitiful.

"Maybe now you'll know not to stick your nose into other people's affairs," the Schicks hissed at Michel. "What will we do with him now?"

"I can talk to him," Michel offered.

"Don't you dare," Yehudah threatened, and Michel turned around and left. Later on, when he noticed the Schicks conversing between themselves, he approached Choni.

"It's me, Michel. You can pick your head up."

"Go away," came the muffled answer.

Michel was offended. "I did you a big favor. I tried to stop you from reading the letter. Now you are angry at me?"

Choni lifted his head and looked at Michel with wet, red eyes.

"I see you took it pretty hard," Michel said, trying to make some conversation.

Choni ignored his remarks. "If you are my friend, you have to help me. I want to know if I understood the letter correctly."

"Ask."

"My parents. They are not my real parents, right?"

"That's how I understood it."

"My real mother's name was Sarah," Choni said with hesitation. "The letter said 'Sarah *aleha hashalom*.' That means she's not alive."

"Right."

"And my father. What about him?"

"Apparently not alive either. He's not mentioned, and if he didn't raise you...."

"And I was supposed to travel to Sarah's parents. In other words, to my grandparents."

"You have a good grasp of the situation."

Choni continued cautiously, as if putting together a *sugya* in the Gemara. He was truly a bright child who was able to work things out with only a little bit of information.

"So now, I have grandparents who demand to see me. And I'm not supposed to know that they're my grandparents. Maybe they want me to remain with them in France?"

"Maybe. You don't really know if they'll like you, though," Michel winked at him. But Choni, who was utterly serious, now turned bitter and resentful.

"I don't want them. I don't want anyone else. I have one mother, the one in Eretz Yisrael. I have a father...," he stammered, and burst into heartrending cries. "Now I understand why my father...my father is...."

Yehudah Schick saw Michel talking to Choni. He quickly strode up and pushed Michel away. "You, young man, are to stay away from Choni from now on. Is that clear?"

"What have I done?"

"I don't know. But he cries a great deal when you are around."

Michel, embittered, stepped away and started toward his brother Gerard. The older boy grabbed the hem of his brother's shirt.

"Do you know these people?" Gerard demanded, annoyed.

"No."

"They were yelling at you. What do they want?" Gerard stopped Michel from running. In truth, he had been worrying about Michel from the beginning of the hijacking. Until that point, Gerard had not attributed much significance to "family." But when they were both cast into this unpleasant adventure, he felt a certain sense of responsibility for his younger brother. He was not pleased with the way that religious couple had spoken to Michel. So perhaps due to a sense of responsibility to his brother, or possibly out of sheer boredom, he decided to deal with the Schicks.

Michel tried to tell him that there was no problem with the Schicks, and no need to meddle in his business. It was no use. Gerard was angry and, dragging his brother along, confronted Yehudah Schick, who was startled to face this tough character.

"What have you got against my brother?" Gerard spoke to Yehudah without any preliminary remarks of explanation.

"I have nothing against him," replied Yehudah, who quickly recovered his mien. "All I asked is that he not associate with the child."

"What child?" They looked at Choni in the corner. "Aha, the child," Gerard observed. "Honestly, Michel, what are you doing playing with this baby?"

"We talked a little, and then the gentleman got angry at me." Michel now reverted to French, as Gerard was not too fluent in Hebrew.

The Schicks turned away, trying to ignore the threatening fellow. Yehudah was upset that Choni had befriended Michel, against his wishes. Their relationship had produced only grief. But the boy was traumatized by the entire episode, and there was no point in aggravating him further.

Freida Schick said, "Now Choni knows, and we do too. Now, we have to deal with it."

"How?" His wife did not have any answers, and the two continued wondering how to proceed.

Gerard and Michel sat down and talked. Gerard listened silently to Michel's stirring narrative.

"That's it. That's the story of this child."

When he finished, Gerard said, "Listen, I have something to suggest. What do you think?"

And before Michel had a chance to respond, his brother walked right up to Choni.

CHAPTER TWENTY-SEVEN

"**Y**oav."

"Yes, Ima?"

"I'd like to speak to you. Could you come here?" Dinah requested. She looked at him and could barely suppress a smile.

Yoav has not changed much since he was a child. Even at a young age, when he was pulling pranks of all kinds, he would attempt to put on an innocent face. His mischievous eyes, however, usually gave him away. Now, too, Dinah could detect that sparkle of deviltry. This time, though, Yoav was an adult.

"What do you want, Ima? Do you want me to prepare dinner for you?" asked Yoav.

"Of course not," she replied. "I'm asking you again, do you have any idea what the Kahns' telegram means?"

He shrugged his shoulders. "How should I know?"

"I have a feeling that you do. Yoav, please tell me what is going on."

Yoav stood facing her. She suddenly realized that her son was no longer to be treated like a child. He was the father of three small children. Now she was in his house, trying to uncover his secret about Choni and the Kahns.

"Ima, believe me, I would never do anything detrimental to you. You'll see that everything will work out for the best."

"Right, but I would like — and I have the right — to know exactly what happened."

At that moment, the ringing telephone interrupted their conversation. Nechamah, who was preparing a vegetable salad in the kitchen, was pleased to take advantage of the interruption by answering the phone. However, the moment she picked up the phone, she called Yoav.

"It's your father," she informed him.

Yoav took the phone. "*Shalom*, Abba. Is there any news?"

"From me? No. Nothing. I heard about the telegram. It is very strange...." They continued talking. In the meantime, Dinah's grandchildren, waiting patiently at her side, tried to get her attention with their artistic creations.

"Here, Savta, why aren't you looking?" her granddaughter pouted.

She tried to force herself to pay attention to the drawings, but as the time passed, she realized she had made a mistake by leaving her house. Her entire being was bound up with Choni, held hostage far away. So why was she here, in her son's house? Choni was facing possible death! How could she have allowed herself to leave her house?

"Savta isn't feeling well today," she overheard Nechamah telling her children. She appreciated her daughter-in-law's efforts to protect her. "She is very worried about Choni. When he comes back, she'll be just like she used to be."

"When will he come back?" the children asked. But even

Nechamah, the protective mother who was supposed to have all the answers, could not provide a clear answer.

"Could he die, Ima? Are they hitting him?"

The children's innocent questions pierced Dinah's heart. She was Choni's mother. How could she have allowed him to become entangled in this struggle between Israel and her enemies, with the hijackers and terrorists? Poor little Choni — he had no idea what to make of it all.

She did not know the Schicks well. She wanted them to show Choni some warmth and caring, to protect him. Was her son hungry? Did anyone care? Was there someone to make sure that he was being given food? Had she been there, she would have been sitting at his side to protect him from danger. To make sure he did not even look at the terrorists.

But she was far away, separated against her will. Had she more forcefully opposed the idea....

No one had the right to second-guess a mother's decision. She would have preferred to battle with them in court over Choni. Now, she had to struggle on two fronts: Choni's life as a hostage, and when he returns afterward, with Hashem's help, the looming custody battle with the Kahns. Who knew what the outcome of all this would be?

Dinah forced herself out of the chair and went to the kitchen to thank Nechamah for her hospitality. "It was wonderful to see the children, but I don't think I will be able to leave the house again. Perhaps when Choni returns it'll be different."

"*Im yirtzeh Hashem,*" said Nechamah.

She listened to Yoav talking to Chaim. "Tell Abba that I'm coming home," she requested. "And Yoav...."

"What?"

"I'm not finished talking to you. Remember that."

Yoav lowered his eyes and waved goodbye to her.

Dinah rushed out of the house. She suddenly felt she did not have the strength to continue pretending everything was O.K. — because it was not. The situation was terrible.

She hailed a taxi.

"Where to, ma'am?" asked the driver in a raspy voice.

"Home," she replied absently.

"And where might that be?"

Dinah told him her address, and the driver wondered how they allowed a woman to wander the streets in such a state.

"*Geveret*, did you hear about the hostages in Entebbe?" the driver attempted some small talk with this eccentric passenger. "What do you say, should we free the terrorists from prison in exchange for the hostages, or should we."

"We should," she interrupted with tears in her eyes.

The cab driver did not talk to her for the rest of the trip. He then started to worry whether this strange woman would pay the cab fare.

She did pay, with tears in her eyes as she waited for change. He thanked her and sped away as fast as possible. *People sure were strange these days,* the driver mused to himself. *She really seemed to be normal, but you just can't know anymore. Someone can appear charming, but in his heart, he is scheming against you. Another might seem to be healthy, but is actually in urgent need of psychiatric treatment.*

Like the woman with the tears.

At the last moment, Michel grabbed Gerard before he could speak to Choni. He pulled Gerard aside and yelled, "Don't you have enough problems of your own? Why are you running to solve those of other people?"

Under normal circumstances, Michel wouldn't have dared

speak like that to his brother. His friends would never have believed he would act so boldly. But now, when both of them were being held captive together in Uganda and were in mortal danger, Michel thought Gerard's aura of danger was fading. What could Gerard do to him? It was unlikely that he would respond roughly in front of the group.

"Don't interfere in my problems."

"I'm already involved," Michel replied audaciously.

"Watch your step… Now we're stuck here, but we will be released soon. Let's see you talk to me then with such nerve."

He was right, of course. Michel backed away a little. Here, under supervision of the terrorists and the Ugandan soldiers, it was impossible to make a big commotion, even if your nerves were frayed and you wanted to scream at the ever-present soldiers. There was no choice — you had to carefully watch what you did and said. But what about after this nightmare was over?

"I just wanted to help your friend. I was wrong. I have nothing to say to him."

Michel suddenly became tense. The wretched trip his parents forced him to take with his brother had had a strong impact on him. His parents had informed him about the planned trip in a way that kept him from telling them his reservations about Gerard. His parents were stern, authoritative European types, and Michel was afraid to reveal his feelings openly. He could not tell them how he was afraid of walking beside Gerard, or of the humiliation his tough brother brought him in school, including the degrading epithets he heard from classmates and even teachers. He bitterly accepted the trip, and was not surprised when Gerard had checked him into that boarding school so he could carry out his shady schemes in the Holy Land.

Michel had not known anyone at that school. The director

barely paid any attention to him, because he had performed a huge favor for Gerard by accepting Michel. Besides, he had a large group of young people who were keeping him busy. The youths at the school likewise slighted Michel. In the dining room he sat by himself at the table. Even when there was room, no one ever sat down next to him. No one smiled at him, and no one even asked his name, except for one kind counselor who occasionally talked to him.

The other kids thought he was considering enrolling in the school, and they wanted to discourage him by making his visit as uncomfortable as possible. The well-mannered Parisian boy did not belong in the school. The next few days were a total nightmare for Michel.

When Gerard finally returned to take Michel on a brief tour, he was dour and disagreeable, and it was impossible to hold a conversation.

Perhaps that was why Michel had not told Gerard about the conversation he had overheard during the flight to Israel. Michel thought that Gerard's gang were fearful of Gerard's taking a trip to Eretz Yisrael without their supervision.

Yet, in the midst of their terrifying ordeal, Gerard was suddenly acting like a brother. Michel decided he had to tell his brother the threatening remarks he had overheard on the original flight.

He began speaking to Gerard rapidly, before fear overcame him and silenced him.

"Gerard, do you know how I know about your problems?"

"What problems?"

"I heard a few words from your friends on the flight from Paris — words that you would not be pleased to hear."

"What friends?"

"The ones on the plane."

Gerard rushed over to Michel. "Again you're talking foolishness? I told you I don't know them." But the fear in his eyes betrayed him.

Michel continued cautiously, "Maybe you don't know them, but they sure know you. I heard them mention your name. What do you say about that?"

"What did you hear?" In an instant, the tough Gerard reappeared seeming a bit alone and slightly fearful.

"Tell me what you heard," he demanded.

"Look, Gerard, I have no idea what kind of gang you belong to. Is it a crime gang? Is it some kind of ultranationalist organization, or is it just some freaky cult? Believe me, I don't know, and I don't want to know. I don't want a part in any of this. I have more interesting things to do with my life." Michel spoke with an unusual maturity that discomforted his older brother.

"It's just because you're my brother that I'm telling you these things. Maybe it's not even because I love you. Maybe it's because I care about our parents, who I know care about you. Since you are their son and my brother, I'll tell you."

Michel took a deep breath. Without Choni's advice, and without great preparation, he found himself confronting Gerard. He spoke to him more now than he had his entire life.

He started describing the friends, and even told him how he saw them notice him.

"They were always smiling at you, those guys. But what do you make of this sentence: 'I would kill that Jew'?" Michel concluded.

When he saw Gerard's face, he realized what a huge mistake he had made. The blow was too much, too humiliating for him. Gerard sank to the floor, with his eyes open and fearful. He was saying to himself, *My assessment was correct. They are dead serious.* He then grabbed Michel with both hands and said,

"Be careful. Even here, they have their moles and agents. Speak quietly."

CHAPTER TWENTY-EIGHT

"**W**ho is this?" Moishe Kahn answered the telephone abruptly. The traumatic week had totally drained him. Until now, he had always looked younger than his years, but the latest ordeal had added 30 years to his appearance. He was not the agile senior citizen he once was. Now he was embittered, upset, and consumed by his conscience.

"Who do you want?" he said with irritation. But the voice on the phone startled him.

"Hello, Reb Moishe. This is Zalman," the voice said in Yiddish.

"Who?"

"Zalman. Zalman, the journalist from Eretz Yisrael. I spoke with your son Shimon. Now I'm calling to speak to you."

"Ah, you're the reporter," he said, restraining himself from adding any further appellations.

"So what news do you have for us?"

Moishe Kahn sighed. He did not like groveling before this reporter, begging him not to go public with Choni's story.

He chose a defensive strategy.

"You know what, Zalman? I have a question for you."

"Certainly, ask. Why not?" Zalman was very cooperative.

"How did you obtain our telephone numbers?"

"It wasn't difficult," the journalist responded. "Those who are familiar with the story have a right to know what your plan of action is with regard to the boy."

"And why do they have a right?"

"To know the real justification," Zalman said smoothly. "And now, Reb Moishe, are you willing to answer my questions?" There was something threatening in his tone of voice. Moishe Kahn answered calmly, "Look, at the moment we are deferring the question of adoption until the boy is freed. Whatever we decide will be in strict accordance with *da'as Torah*, and for the child's welfare. How does that sound to you and your readers, sir?"

"Sounds great."

Zalman ended the conversation quickly, and Moishe Kahn wondered about his strange and unpleasant feeling as he hung up the phone. He concluded that not only was the reporter an unknown entity, but he also had not answered the one question Moishe had asked. He had cleverly evaded the issue.

After pondering the matter for a few minutes over yet another cup of tea, Moishe decided to drop it. There were many possible reasons for Zalman's evasion, but the most likely explanation was that the Binders gave him the telephone numbers. Newspaper publicity would benefit their cause, as public opinion would certainly support the adoptive parents.

Moishe Kahn allowed himself to close his eyes and relax briefly in the armchair. Heaven apparently had different plans.

The door squeaked open and Rivkah stumbled in, her arms loaded with grocery bags.

"I did some shopping," she stated.

He stood up and helped her take the groceries into the kitchen. She noticed his trembling hands and nearly told him how he had aged. She was always careful to say this with a smile, because Moishe was and would remain young at heart, and he was physically as strong as a 40-year-old. Now, things were different. Rivkah did not want to cause her husband any pain.

He took the milk and cheese, then shuffled slowly toward the refrigerator.

"The milk on top, Moishe," she requested.

He did as she asked. Then, he decided to tell Rivkah what had been bubbling inside him all day.

"You know...we did not go into the lawyer's office."

"You didn't?" She dropped the fruit she was holding. She bent down slowly to pick it up, putting it in its place. She then turned around and started asking questions.

"Where were you? Did you miss your appointment?"

"No, we weren't late."

"Answer me, Moishe," Rivkah said as she looked at him oddly. She could see that something was upsetting him. She felt that since her grandson's plane was hijacked, she had lost control over herself, and over what transpired around her. Yet something this odd, no one expected. What other surprises were there?

"Look, Rivkah, let's finish putting the groceries away, and then we can talk."

"One does not preclude the other, Moishe," she told him. She stooped far down to reach the bags, but her back rebelled. She straightened out slowly, clutching her left side in pain.

"It does. I'll finish with the groceries while you go rest. I'll be with you shortly."

She went to the living room and waited for him quietly. Moishe put the groceries away by himself.

Five minutes later, he came into the living room with lowered eyes. "You see, something that we could do in a minute or less when we were young now requires ten minutes. That's the way of life, Rivkah. We are changing all the time, even now."

"How have you changed, Moishe?" Rivkah was clever, and he was not surprised by her question. After 50 years he was used to her ways, and she did not disappoint him. She understood the hint.

He sat down slowly on the sofa, and then spoke in a low voice.

"I've changed my approach toward my grandson, Rivkah. I did not meet with the lawyer because I felt it was an improper move on our part. Such an important step has to be discussed with the Rav of our community."

Rivkah dropped her head and thought. "Tell me what happened," she insisted.

Moishe told her how they had arrived at the lawyer's door, but then turned around. He told her that Shimon had dropped him off at the Rav's house.

"And what did he say?" Rivkah was tense. She had no patience for a drawn-out story.

"The Rav did not rush to respond," Moishe pointed out, trying to cool down the stress level. "He sat there thinking. Believe me, if we had realized how important and far reaching our actions were, we would never have made a move without first consulting him."

Rivkah noted the veiled criticism. She said nothing, because she knew that it was true.

"I acted according to my gut feelings," Moishe said. "The Rav suggested we consult not only *rabbanim*, but experts in behavioral psychology, to learn what negative side effects could arise by keeping the child in France. He could not understand how we took unilateral action without considering all the ramifications."

Moishe blamed himself as much as he did his wife. Moishe had taken the lead and urged matters forward as long as they were relegated to the realm of talk. But when it was time for action, he had hesitated. Rivkah had taken the lead and clamored for results. Now, both of them were overwhelmed by the state of events. Their grandson was a hostage in Uganda, and they both felt guilty.

When her daughter Sarah died, Rivkah had shed a seemingly endless ocean of tears. Could it be she was now crying tears of regret?

"What are you crying about? We can always change the future." Moishe's logical, masculine words did not make much of an impression on her.

"No, Moishe, it's very difficult to change anything. First, Elchanan is so far from us. At this point, we don't even know if he is alive. In addition, we'll never succeed in straightening out our relationship with the Binder family."

"Why not?" he asked.

"That's just the way it is," she declared. In her eyes, the Binder family had taken her grandson and was exploiting the current situation to cast aspersions on them.

"But they're not blaming us …."

"Really?"

"O.K.," Moishe relented. "Maybe they are slightly annoyed with us. You forget that they are right. Ultimately, we made things complicated for their son."

"Our grandson."

"It's irrelevant. The child is theirs. Sarah's only child. We gave him to them. Anyway, they deserve better treatment than we've been giving them."

"And how do you know that the child is happy there? Maybe — ,"

Moishe, now agitated, stood up. "Enough, Rivkah. I'm not interested in attributing sinister motives on the part of the Binders, and I don't want you to do so either. I think the case is closed any way you look at it."

"So be it."

They settled into a silence that lasted until late afternoon. Shimon and his youngest daughter visited and brought some light into the gloomy house.

Miri was more cheerful than usual, and threw herself at her ashen-looking grandmother.

"You look sad," said Miri.

"I really am, Miraleh. Did you come over to ask questions, or to have some of my chocolate-chip cookies?"

The two of them laughed aloud, and Moishe breathed a sigh of relief. "You saved the day, Shimon," he told his son.

"What's going on? Shimon asked quietly. "Did you tell Ima about the — "

However, Moishe wanted to talk about the phone conversation with the reporter. "It's unbelievable; he has our telephone number, too," he said with grudging admiration.

"Did you ask him how — ?"

"Of course."

"And?"

"He cleverly evaded the question. I think it's nothing more than a ruse."

They both sat quietly for a minute, thinking. Then Shimon

said, "You know, who in the religious community would be interested in this business? After all, it's pure gossip, *lashon hara* and *rechilus*, that potentially could erupt into a huge battle. What newspaper would risk its reputation for something like this? If a secular reporter had expressed interest, I could better understand his motives. I wouldn't expect any understanding or compassion from him. For such journalists, there is no mercy, just the story, even if a hundred people are killed. I'm convinced that this was some kind of pretext." Shimon was furious. He was on the verge of exploding with outrage as he realized the trick that had been played on them. "I'll call them and — "

"You will not," warned Moishe, a stern look on his face. "You'll not call or do anything before consulting with me. I will not allow you to run a campaign behind my back. Let's empathize with their feelings of helplessness, fear, and anguish, instead of getting angry with them. That anger is incurable. They tried whatever they could. It's their right."

Shimon stared at his father. "It sounds as if you've gone over to their side."

"I guess I've changed my approach," answered Moishe. He was still confused by the Rav's words and from the conversation with his wife, which was a repetition of the dialogue he had had with himself.

He did not want Rivkah to witness their conversation, but it was too late. She sent Miri to the kitchen, while she remained and listened to them talk. She saw Moishe realize there would be no reconciliation with the Binder family.

CHAPTER TWENTY-NINE

"Eat, child, you'll get sick from aggravation," Freida Schick said roughly to Choni. She did not grasp the magnitude of his tragedy, because she did not know all the details. The trauma of the hijacking was enough for her.

All she knew was that the uncle and aunt he was going to visit were really his grandparents. How? Why? She did not have the patience to find out all the details. She was concerned about an elderly hostage who became ill and was sent off to the antiquated hospital in Entebbe. Most of the hostages realized what her fate would be, but her son repeatedly inquired after her, hoping for good news.

Mrs. Schick felt a certain responsibility for Choni, and he was refusing to eat or drink. He looked so forlorn that she took pity on him and tried everything in her power to persuade him to eat something.

"Look, Elchanan, I have some chocolate. Do you want some?"

The chocolate bar that Freida Schick had in her handbag was delectable. She had planned to give it to her grandchildren when they came to meet her. Those plans were surely shelved for the moment, and she was happy to give the chocolate to Choni.

"I don't want it. I don't want anything."

"But you'll get sick if you don't eat."

"I want to be left alone." She swallowed the insult, left the chocolate bar next to him, and stepped away.

"Leave him alone; he is in a wretched state." Yehudah Schick knew the details of Choni's problems.

Freida sighed, "For what did we need this?"

"What, the hijacking or the young hostage?" Yehudah tried to smile.

"Both," complained Freida. "What will be with us? You know, sometimes I ask myself if it's worth concerning ourselves with health and cleanliness, because in a few hours, it might all be over."

"Don't speak like that. A Jew must never talk like that."

"You're right," she conceded. "Yet our situation seems to be getting worse all the time."

She was right. The Ugandan president Idi Amin had circulated among the hostages, announcing an imminent conclusion to the crisis, that a deal with the Israeli government was in the offing. Of course, the beleaguered hostages burst into applause, voicing their appreciation. Amin left the room in a very upbeat mood, feeling very proud of himself. At other times, however, he would arrive to inform them in a sorrowful voice how Israel's stubborn position would lead to the death of her citizens within a few hours. The president's updates depended on his mood, and to whom he had been speaking.

Freida Schick, along with many others, could not bear the fluctuations between the different states of mind of President Amin. It confused and demoralized them, and sometimes prevented them from functioning rationally. It was only her ongoing responsibility for Choni that kept her sane, nothing else.

Now, they had Choni's new problem on their hands.

"Yehudah, how could you have given him the letter?"

Her husband replied with uncharacteristic remorse, "It was his letter. I just took it for safekeeping. When he asked for it back, I gave it to him. I didn't dream that it contained anything so sensitive. I tell you, I don't understand how Chaim Binder could send with his adopted son a letter that contains his life history. Did he think he would not open the letter?"

"Wasn't the letter written in French?"

"Yes, but his friend Michel translated the letter for him. I knew that boy was going to be trouble, and I tried to separate them."

"You see, it was our mistake. We let them become friends."

Yehudah Schick paused his nervous pacing for a moment. "I'm not so sure," he said. "Elchanan was bored, and I was not able to occupy him or be his friend. Remember that he is scared, just like us. I don't think we had much of a choice to let them befriend each other, even if it was just to forestall fear of the future."

"Look what it has caused," said Freida glancing briefly at Choni. The child had withdrawn again.

"He's shattered."

"He has good reason, poor child."

Although she greatly pitied him, Freida now understood that her continued efforts to get him to speak and to open up were of no use.

The hostages in the hall were splitting up into different

groups. One group played nonstop, which annoyed Yehudah no end. Another group sang songs, which grated on Freida Schick's nerves. They were a bunch of boisterous youths who decided to make merry, clearly in the wrong place — at least according to the Schicks. In an effort to keep themselves occupied, the Schicks moved around from group to group, inquiring how this one and that one were managing. Occasionally, Freida Schick recited *Tehillim*. She periodically inquired after a woman who was traveling on her own to Paris. The woman sat most of the time reciting *Tehillim*. Sometimes she spoke to Freida; other times she nibbled the bland bread supplied to the hostages. Those prisoners who could not force themselves to swallow the tasteless bread faced great hunger, because it was the only prepared food that they would allow themselves to eat.

The only one who could not deal with his grief was Choni Binder. He was full of bitterness and indescribable anguish and nervousness. He wanted to sprout wings and fly straight into his mother's arms. He imagined his mother would softly stroke his hair and say, "But Choni, where did you get such strange ideas? Of course we are your parents."

"And the letter?" he would ask her, tears in his eyes. "The letter you sent to the uncle and aunt?"

"Ah, the letter refers to someone else, my curious one." That's what his mother would say. "Your friend did not translate the words correctly. Anyway, it was sent by someone else entirely, and is not referring to you at all."

At this point, the image was so pleasant that Choni had to smile. But he immediately reentered his own little world of pain, and his face reflected it. Could the letter really be a mistake? Is it just a prank Michel dreamed up?

The possibility energized Choni. It would be simply marvelous if it turned out that Michel had been playing a joke on him, trying to lift his spirits in this boring place. The letter must contain instructions for the uncle and aunt regarding how to handle him. Michel was bored; perhaps Choni's letter was an amusing diversion to break the boredom.

Excited by the idea, Choni stood up from the filthy floor and wiped the tears from his eyes. He then noticed the chocolate Mrs. Schick had left for him. The *hechsher* on it was fine, and he was hungry. He recited the *berachah* and bit into the chocolate bar with gusto. It revitalized him. It was all just a joke. Later, Choni and Michel would be able to laugh together over his reaction. He threw a grateful glance at Mrs. Schick, who was watching him with interest and satisfaction. A few minutes later, when he felt more confident, he went over to Michel.

"Feeling better?" Michel asked him with a smile. He was sitting next to Gerard, which caused Choni to recoil slightly.

"Of course I've recovered," he said, sounding very self-confident. "Listen, Michel, you are not religious, so you may not know that it's forbidden to deceive people. Even if afterward you tell them you were only joking and — "

Choni spoke and Michel looked at him in astonishment. The only one who followed the conversation — perhaps due to his age — was Gerard. He decided he would put the religious boy in his place. "Hey, kid, you are making a big mistake," he told Choni.

This caused Choni to take yet another step back. He did not particularly care for his friend's long-haired brother. He ignored Gerard, and asked Michel to come talk to him alone.

"You can talk right here next to Gerard. We're good friends," Michel said.

"But I want to talk to you alone," Choni insisted.

"You have nothing to speak to him about," Gerard said, and Choni stared at him.

"I wasn't talking to you," Choni said weakly. "Leave me alone."

Gerard understood the direction the conversation was taking. "Michel, you don't have anything to say to this kid. He thinks you are fooling him and are making up the story."

"Who told you?" Michel was surprised. They spoke briefly in French.

"Look at his eyes, see how he behaves differently now. Only a person who has fooled himself could act like that. Did you notice how he spoke to you earlier?"

"So what should I do?"

The two brothers continued talking, and Choni found himself excluded. On the one hand, he wanted to confront Michel and force him to admit he made up the translation of his mother's letter. On the other hand, he was terribly frightened of Gerard. Or more correctly, of the stories Michel had told him.

He was just a young, frightened boy, trying to prove to himself that his life had not changed. "Michel, I'm talking to you. Come here a minute."

Gerard decided to seize the initiative. "Kid, you have nothing to talk to my brother about. If you think he's a liar, well, you're wrong. He's not like that, believe me." Gerard's Hebrew was terrible, even worse than Michel's. Nevertheless, Choni understood.

Choni, getting frustrated with the conversation, said, "And I tell you that the entire story is wrong. He just wanted to play a joke on me. Right, Michel? Admit the truth."

The hope in Choni's eyes matched the desperation in his voice. Michel would have given anything to agree with Choni's "truth," but Gerard was stronger than he was.

"That's not the truth, kid. It's too bad, life is tough, and you're just going to have to face it."

"Don't get involved," Choni cut in angrily.

Michel suddenly recovered. "Choni, don't be angry at Gerard. He's not mixing in for fun. He is trying to help you. He's right, my translation is perhaps not exact, but what I wrote was more or less the essence of the letter."

Choni turned pale, and the chocolate he had just eaten made him feel queasy.

Michel continued, "Look, Choni, I'm not an author with a creative streak. I've already told you that I'm not a good student at all, while you boasted that you study Gemara. Remember? So how could I make up such a dramatic story like this? Even a writer would have difficulty creating such an outlandish tale. Now do you believe me?"

Michel's last words convinced Choni. There was no other way. All the dreams, the hopes, the desperate wishing for a different reality — all faded away in this filthy, nerve-wracking passenger hall in the Entebbe airport.

The truth left Choni thoroughly numb.

"I thought you had already accepted all this, and you're ready now to take the next step," said Michel.

"I'm not." Choni was hysterical. "What do you mean, accept?" He started yelling, and even the slow approach of one of the terrorists did not get him to stop.

"Be quiet," Gerard said, grabbing Choni. He pushed Michel away, and covered Choni's mouth with his hand.

"Be quiet," he repeated. "You'll get us all killed."

"I don't care," Choni exclaimed, frightened of the intimidating young man who now held him. However, he was more afraid of the truth that had been confined. He burst into bitter and uncontrolled weeping.

"My mother will tell me the truth, that it's all a lie. It's one big mistake. My mother … she'll tell me …."

The terrorist who was drawing closer seemed to have evil intentions. He would surely want to know the reason for all the crying and screaming. Gerard pushed Michel even further away, while Mr. and Mrs. Schick hurried over to be close to the child in their charge.

CHAPTER THIRTY

Thursday, July 1, 1976; 11:30 p.m.

"**C**ome, Miri, we're leaving," Shimon called to his daughter.

"So soon?" she whined.

"Yes, don't you think your grandparents need to rest? Besides, we have a busy schedule for tomorrow and have to get an early start. How will you be able to get up in the morning?"

"By setting an alarm clock," Miri said in an attempt to be cute.

Shimon took his daughter's hand and walked outside, waving farewell to his parents. As soon as they left, Rivkah said, "Moishe, let's pack a bag and get to the airport."

"What?" Moishe rubbed his eyes. The past day had exhausted him. Maybe he did not hear her properly due to fatigue. Rivkah, however, was very serious and repeated herself.

"I want to fly to Israel, to be close to our Elchanan. When they free the hostages, they probably will be taken to Israel. Don't you think so?"

"I don't know, Rivkah, it's late now. Let's go to sleep now, and tomorrow we'll think it over." He tried to mollify her, but she was not calmed by his words. She had heard the conversation that had taken place earlier, and she decided to take decisive action.

A war cannot be fought long-distance. It would be better to be on the spot, in Israel, staring the Binders directly in the face. Then they would be able to settle all the outstanding issues between the two families.

"Moishe, I'm determined to fly there."

She took the telephone directory in hand, searching for nearly five minutes for a specific name and phone number. Afterward, she called a travel agent and asked him a few questions. When she finished, she turned to Moishe, who was preparing for bed. "Moishe, there is a flight to Israel at 4:30 in the morning. There are seats available. Not too many Frenchmen are interested in flying to Israel these days. I want to be on that flight."

Moishe sat up. "I do not have the strength to travel," he announced. "What would we do there?"

"We would talk to Choni's adoptive parents. We could see up close what Israel is planning to do about the hostages. We'll be closer to what is going on."

"You know what," all the exhaustion suddenly disappeared, "you go and I'll stay. It's a good idea."

"Why?"

He explained it very sensibly. "Maybe the hostages will come to France — just imagine Elchanan being alone. I'll wait for him here, and you'll wait in Israel. So whichever country he arrives in, someone will be waiting for him."

"That's a good idea." Rivkah was energized and ready to take immediate action. Moishe was more hesitant than his wife. "Are you sure you aren't rushing too quickly into this?" he asked thoughtfully.

"Not at all. I've been standing around wasting time. I have my passport, and there is money in the bank to pay for the trip. I have two hours to rest. Then I'll pack a small suitcase and go to the airport. I have to be there at least two and a half hours before takeoff."

Moishe Kahn finally stood up. He dressed quickly, grabbed his hat, and went outside.

"Where are you going?" Paris was not a friendly place at night, and Rivkah was worried about her husband walking outside in the dark.

"You were going to relax before the flight, right? I'm going to ask the Rav for a *berachah*."

"All right."

Moishe strode toward the Rav's house, caught off guard by his dynamic wife's plan. She had always had bold ideas, but this latest plan was the most extraordinary, and he had certain reservations about it. To declare at 11:30 at night that she intended to fly to Israel in a few hours seemed too outlandish — even a young person would think twice before rushing into such action. But when Rivkah spoke about their grandson, she was not thinking about her age or her energy level. She was thinking only about her goals, and the best way to achieve them.

The Rav was surprised to see an elderly man standing at his door.

"So late at night?" he asked in astonishment. "Has something happened? Please come in, Reb Moishe." He offered his guest a cold drink.

Moishe told the Rav about his wife's plan.

The ticking clock in the room marked the passing seconds and minutes, setting Moishe's nerves on edge. He hoped that the Rav would forbid the trip.

It did not happen.

Eventually, the Rav spoke. "I wish her a successful trip. I think it will contribute to bringing the families closer." He added, "Please ask your wife not to speak about adoption. Only discuss matters pertaining to the child's present situation."

"I will tell her."

He did not know how to relay this information to Rivkah. Nevertheless, as soon as she saw him return, she understood what the Rav must have told him.

"Judging from your expression, I assume the Rav gave his *berachah* to my plans."

"You're right."

It was midnight. The conversation with the Rav had been decidedly brief. Moishe looked around the room and noticed the small suitcase packed and ready.

"You managed to pack so quickly?" he asked in amazement.

"I'm an old woman, and do not need much to take along with me," Rivkah explained. "My *siddur*, *Tehillim*, and some clothing. I took money from the safe. That's all. I'm ready."

"I'll come along with you to the airport," Moishe said, even though he was half asleep already.

"Don't be silly. You'll go to sleep, Moishe," Rivkah said emphatically.

Moishe wrinkled his forehead. "Just a minute. Did you tell Shimon about your plans?"

"Of course not." She was at ease, and he looked at her with amazement.

"Why not?"

"We cannot bother Shimon so much. He's been a tremendous help, but he also has a family. I cannot ask him to get up before dawn to drive me to the airport. Don't worry: A taxicab driver will be more than happy to provide the service."

"I'm sure," Moishe said with a crooked smile. "But I'd still like to accompany you to the airport."

"It's not necessary, Moishe, really. I'll feel much better knowing that you are at home and asleep. Please...."

He looked at her, shrugged his shoulders, and decided to do her bidding.

At 1:30 in the morning, he helped her carry the light suitcase to the taxi. "Go *le'chaim u'le'shalom*. Have a good flight," he called to her as she left.

Only when he reached the bedroom did he notice how much his hands were trembling. Air travel was not safe, and he had never enjoyed it. But now, after the hijacking of the French plane, he was more concerned than usual.

What if something happened to Rivkah's plane? The nightmare scenarios were stronger than all the cool logic he could muster. He could not fall asleep. He could only hope that Rivkah would call him as soon as her feet were on the ground. Israel was always a place of terror and troubles. He was sorry he had permitted her to go.

Rivkah was also very concerned. Her concerns, however, were about different matters.

From the moment the plane's wheels lifted off French soil and folded into the wheel housings, she felt elated. She was finally doing something for her grandson's sake. She was traveling to be a partner in the terrible waiting, in order to draw closer, to understand what Choni's parents were doing, and to secure his future. Just let the hostages return safely. Please, Hashem!

She had not contacted the Binder family before setting out on her journey. She now considered that a mistake. She had no one else in Israel. What would she do upon arrival? Who would meet her? Where would she go?

She, an elderly woman, had decided to travel to Israel. In itself, this was not so unusual. She had traveled several times in the past to Eretz Yisrael, and had never made a fuss about it. Of course, she was always with Moishe or one of her children on those other trips. This time she was on her own.

The plane was not full. This was not surprising. Who would want to travel to Israel during these frightening times? Still exhausted, Rivkah fastened her seat belt. "Need any help, *grand-mère*?" asked one of the stewardesses leaning toward her.

"I'm fine," she answered without even smiling. She really was a *savta*, an elderly woman without the strength of youth. How did she dare undertake such an arduous mission?

The plane landed without the usual applause from the passengers. Rivkah quickly found herself outside, in the humid, sticky, Israeli summer air. It was early Friday morning. Although slightly dazed, she found her suitcase and brought it outside. Then she found a taxi driver who was willing to take her to Jerusalem. "A modest hotel, with a *mehadrin hechsher*," she told him in heavily accented Hebrew.

The driver, nodding in understanding, loaded her suitcase into his taxi. "Please go in, ma'am."

"*Merci.*"

She closed her eyes during the ride lengthened by a maddening traffic jam at the entrance to Jerusalem. After what seemed like an eternity, they arrived at a hotel that satisfied Rivkah's requirements: simple but pleasant. She strode up to the reception desk and requested a room.

As soon as she entered the room, she called Moishe. She

could sense his relief at hearing her voice. "Are you all right? Is everything O.K. there?"

"*Baruch Hashem*, I'm here in a wonderful hotel. I forgot to ask you for the Binders' telephone number. If you get it for me, I'll call them." He quickly gave her the number, and wished her well.

After a short rest and some refreshments, Rivkah mustered the strength to contact the Binders. Her hands trembled as she picked up the phone, but she continued dialing. She waited. There was no answer. After nearly giving up, someone answered. "Hello?"

She was stunned momentarily into silence. She did not know if it was because of passing fear, or because she could not think of the right words to say.

"Dinah? Dinah Binder?" Rivkah gradually found her tongue.

"Yes, with whom am I speaking, please?"

Rivkah swallowed hard. Only now did she grasp how difficult it would be. Since the beginning of the hijacking, the Kahns had cut off all direct contact with the Binders. Now, Rivkah was calling to inform them that she had just arrived. Wasn't this a bit too much?

"*Bonjour*, this is Rivkah speaking," trying to sound as pleasant as possible.

"Which Rivkah?"

"Rivkah Kahn."

"Oh...."

The silence was embarrassing. "Dinah, I know you are angry at me..." she switched to French. She would be able to express herself more clearly in her mother tongue. "I hope you understand that the trauma of the hijacking hit us terribly hard. We were not coping."

Dinah remained silent.

"I arrived in Israel a short while ago to be closer to Elchanan... when he, *im yirtzeh Hashem*, returns." Rivkah said in a subdued voice, trembling with emotion.

"You are in Israel?" asked Dinah in surprise.

"Yes, I'm in Israel."

Now was the telling moment: Did the Binders want peace and reconciliation or not?

CHAPTER THIRTY-ONE

"**S**he's here," a frightened Dinah told Chaim.

"Who's here?" Chaim had just returned from *shul*. He was afraid Dinah was not able to withstand the enormous pressure and had begun hallucinating. "Who's here, Dinah? The house is empty, and Pinchas is in *cheider*. Who's here?"

"Kahn. Mrs. Kahn. I mean Rivkah has arrived and she —"

"She's here in Israel?" Chaim asked excitedly. "They've arrived here in Eretz Yisrael?".

"Just her. And she asked if we would like to have her for Shabbos."

"Why did she come?" Chaim sounded quite perturbed.

"To speak with us. She said she has much to discuss. She said she wants to promote friendship between the families and to make peace before Choni returns to a family torn apart."

"Where is Choni in all of this? They can already see Choni

returning home, those two — I don't know what to do now."

Chaim felt very pressured. Usually he maintained his composure, but now, things were transpiring so quickly and so close to home, he felt himself losing control again. "She should not have come without first speaking to us. For nearly a week, they were maintaining total silence, and now suddenly they're here."

"You're right," Dinah agreed and lowered her voice. "But now, I need an answer for her. You have to understand, Chaim. She called up and told me she was in Eretz Yisrael. Automatically, she assumes that I will invite her to our house for Shabbos. We'll have to cancel the other guests. Brachi, for instance, wanted to come for Shabbos and also —"

"It doesn't matter. We first have to figure out how to deal with her. Maybe we should act tough."

"I don't think so."

Dinah remembered the trembling, hesitant voice on the other end of the line. Rivkah certainly was not at ease in this situation. On the other hand, Dinah felt relief. Choni's other family was concerned about him and making an effort on his behalf. She was not pleased that until now, everything was purely talk. However, now that Rivkah was in Eretz Yisrael and had taken a serious step, she had hinted that no matter what the difficulties, she still wanted to adopt Choni.

"There's a strange odor. Don't you smell it?" Chaim sniffed around the room.

"Oh, it's the soup." Dinah flew into the kitchen. "Yesterday, I didn't to start preparing for Shabbos as usual. Today, I remembered that I did not yet start cooking anything. What can I do, so this Shabbos there won't be so much to eat — This Shabbos — Choni won't be here with us, so it's going to be different anyway."

"Very much so."

Chaim helped her remove the soup pot from the fire. He turned off the gas, and Dinah wiped up the soup spilled on the stove.

"What did you say to Mrs. Kahn?"

"She asked that we call her Rivkah," Dinah corrected him.

"What's the difference? I see you are already friendly with her — "

"To be honest with you, I pity her. Her husband is in France, and she is here by herself. We should invite her for Shabbos."

"You invited her?"

"I told her I would talk to you, and get back to her right away. She said she understood perfectly if we don't invite her. She can stay in the hotel for Shabbos."

"O.K., that sounds very good," Chaim seemed satisfied. "Look, I told everyone at the office that we would be closed today. My secretary rescheduled my appointments to next week. By then, *im yirtzeh Hashem*, we will have good news. Today I will go see Rav Katz in Netanya."

"It's Friday, Chaim."

"I know. But he doesn't have a telephone at home. I'll leave right now. I must consult him."

Dinah understood, but she worried about the woman waiting anxiously for her phone call.

"Call me from Netanya, so I'll know what to do about Rivkah."

"I will," Chaim agreed. As an afterthought, he added, "It's strange that until now, you were her enemy. Yet suddenly everything is resolved, and you are not fighting over the child."

"At the moment, there is no child," she said, her eyes flooding with tears. "Besides, the pain and worry lead to a certain solidarity between the families. No doubt we'll fight later on.

That does not mean we cannot take advantage of a few conciliatory moments."

"Do as you think best. I'll call you as soon as I can."

Chaim left for Netanya. The drive was smooth and uneventful, and the timing was ideal: not too early and not late in the afternoon, so the usual traffic jams did not slow him down.

In just about an hour, he stood at the Rav's stairs and knocked at the door, waiting for the friendly invitation to enter. The continued silence indicated that the Rav was not home. Chaim broke into a cold sweat. Just when he needed him most, the Rav was not at home.

He suddenly decided to knock on the neighbor's door to ask as to the Rav's whereabouts. "He sometimes goes to the *shul* down the street," the neighbor said, pointing at the building.

Chaim went to the designated *shul* but did not find Rav Katz. He asked several bystanders in the street, who told him about a few other *shuls* nearby where the Rav occasionally learned. After finding the first two empty, Chaim became frantic. He hoped that he would find the Rav in the third *shul*. He entered and saw Rav Katz peering into a Gemara.

Chaim was too embarrassed to interrupt the Rav. Instead, he took a Gemara from the bookshelf. While reviewing a *sugya*, he regretted that he did not spend more time learning. Despite all his efforts, his studies were not as consistent as he wanted. He recalled his father's exhortation, "The pleasure of learning is something you have to acquire. It would be a shame to lose it." Yet the economic pressures distracted him too much. He resolved to adjust his schedule to allow more time for learning.

He waited patiently for Rav Katz. When the Rav finally stood up to take a *sefer* from the shelf, Chaim approached him.

The Rav received him warmly. "*Shalom aleichem*, what brings you to Netanya?"

"I came to meet you. Something unusual has come up."

"I understand. It must be very important."

"Very," he answered.

"In that case, please wait five minutes. We'll go to the house then."

Chaim Binder nodded. Within five minutes, he escorted the Rav home.

"Please go in," the Rav said. Chaim entered and sat down on a chair. He tried to refuse the cold drink the Rav offered him, but Rav Katz was adamant.

"Generally, people come in the evening," said the Rav quietly. "I guess your problem could not wait until after Shabbos."

"I don't know," said Chaim, suddenly confused. He regretted disturbing Rav Katz from his studies.

"It's O.K. Elchanan is among the hostages. Is there no news on their situation?" the Rav said, reminding Chaim that he had visited just a few days ago. Now he felt foolish, bothering him again so soon.

"Only *tefillos* will help, Reb Chaim. *B'ezras Hashem*, Choni will return home safely."

"*Amen.*" Chaim hung on to the Rav's *berachah*. But immediately, he blanched. "There is a new problem. The boy's mother's family wants to see him. It turns out that they are interested in adopting him. Even during the adoption period, they — "

"Without *lashon hara*," the Rav interrupted pleasantly but emphatically.

"O.K. I'll skip that part. Since the hijacking, they did not call. They did, however, tell us that they're hiring a lawyer. Now Mrs. Kahn has traveled to Eretz Yisrael. She called us about two hours ago to say that she has arrived. I don't know what to do. Should I — ?"

"What would you do if a member of your family came to

Eretz Yisrael?" the Rav interrupted him.

"I'd invite them to my house for Shabbos."

"So there's your answer. I don't see any difference. I think we should move backward a few steps."

"Backward?"

"Yes. Where did we leave off in our last conversation? Ah, your relationship with your deceased brother and with his son. So, Reb Chaim, I think that, first of all, we should put matters in order."

"I don't understand."

"When Choni returns, *im yirtzeh Hashem*, ask him whom he thought about while he was in captivity."

"No doubt he thought, and continues to think, about his mother. In other words, my wife," Chaim answered.

"Good. And why not about his father?"

Chaim shifted uncomfortably. "There were many misunderstandings between us. I've already mentioned this to the Rav."

"Misunderstandings occur between parents and children, or between teachers and students. Yet despite the misunderstandings, children still love their parents, and parents still love their children. Right?"

"Correct. Should I understand that Choni does not miss me?" asked Chaim. "Will he prefer to be with his new relatives?" His voice was hoarse and emotional.

"I don't know," replied Rav Katz. "You should be prepared for any eventuality. Personally, I do not think he will leave his adoptive mother. Every child wants roots, and every child has a right to roots. But you — you only want what is best for the boy."

"Is there something wrong with that?"

"It's wonderful. But you have to know what is considered good for the boy, from his perspective."

Those last words seared Chaim's soul. There was a great deal of rebuke and it was hitting Chaim all at once without warning. Despite the humiliation, he accepted the Rav's words that were free from any egoism or selfishness.

"You don't understand, Reb Chaim — and I'm not surprised," Rav Katz said quietly. He grasped Chaim's hands. "If you had been closely in touch with the child's needs, you would not be here now, on an *erev Shabbos*, so perturbed, asking advice. You would realize what to do. The child is yours, but he is also related to the Kahns. Nothing could be more important for him than harmony between the families. This is the only family he has. How will he feel if he knows that his roots are fighting among themselves? To whom can he turn? To his deceased mother's family, or to his father's relatives? There is nothing crueler than putting a young child into such a difficult situation. Do you understand me, Reb Chaim?"

"I'm starting to," Chaim said, quite embarrassed.

"So, I'm telling you, Reb Chaim, that you have not yet made any changes in your personality. You want what is good for the child, but you never considered what *is* that good, not in his eyes, and not in yours. True, you wanted to raise him as your own child and build his emotional fortitude, and only later on reveal to him the true circumstances of his birth. Now, however, the situation requires a different approach. It will be good for Elchanan if the two families can live in peace, and can arrive at a reasonable compromise through harmonious negotiation. Do nothing that would harm this young child. He needs as much loving support and encouragement as possible." Rav Katz spoke quietly, but his words reverberated.

"You came here to discuss your relationship with Choni," the Rav continued in the same gentle tone of voice. "I think you know at this point in what direction things should move. Delve into yourself, Reb Chaim, into your personality. Learn to think about others, and you will see that others are thinking about you too. Suddenly, you will be surrounded with friends, just like your brother Yaakov, *a"h,* had, and like you always wanted. You had a brother who thought about others, who enjoyed seeing them happy and successful."

Then Rav Katz added some surprising words. "The son of Yaakov Binder is very much like his father. You sensed it. See, I have shown you the secret of them both. Now, you should be on your way — you should hurry — Elchanan will return soon, *b'ezras Hashem.* Till then, you must build the bridge between his family and yours."

Chaim took leave of the Rav, and when he stepped outside, he was sweating profusely. He felt as if he was facing a mirror and what he saw reflected was the plain truth.

As he drove down the highway, he remembered that Dinah was at home, waiting for his answer. He sighed; the Rav's stinging rebuke was still echoing in his mind, giving him no rest. He would have to find a pay telephone at the nearest gas station. It was noon, and the traffic was already heavy. Precisely at that point, he heard the news blaring from an adjacent car radio. He listened and his face froze. Only the honking of the vehicles behind him roused him from his fear-induced stupor, urging him to continue driving.

CHAPTER THIRTY-TWO

"**H**ello, I'd like to speak to Mrs. Rivkah Kahn in Room 322," Dinah requested.

After a lengthy delay, Rivkah came to the phone.

"This is Dinah Binder speaking," she said. "My husband and I are inviting you for Shabbos. Is that all right with you?"

A brief silence followed, after which she heard Rivkah's voice say, "That's fine. Thank you very much. I will come by later, say about 4 o'clock."

Dinah immediately told her, "Chaim will pick you up." She thought she heard Rivkah sigh in relief.

The phone conversation ended on a positive note, causing Dinah to wonder anew why Chaim was so emotional and angry. He had called her moments ago from a pay phone at a service station. He sounded upset.

"Invite her, Dinah," he told her in an icy voice. "And tell her that I'll come get her. She should not have to call a taxi."

"Is that what the Rav said?"

"That's what I understood from his words. The news is not saying much about the hostages in Entebbe. I've just been hearing some worthless speculation. That's all."

"Tell me what the Rav said," requested Dinah.

"The Rav said that *b'ezras Hashem*, Choni will return. But we have to mount a massive *tefillah* effort."

"You're right. How is the — "

The call was cut off, probably because the prepaid amount had run out. Dinah knew that Chaim was on his way home, so she speeded up her Shabbos preparations. She quickly jotted down a grocery list. As soon as Pinchas came home, she would send him to the fish store, the fruit store, and the butcher.

She looked at her watch and worried: She had hours of Shabbos preparations still before her. In normal times, the delectable odor of cooking foods would already be wafting through the house. How could she have forgotten to start preparing yesterday?

Indeed, the first thing to do was to prepare the guest room. Of course, it was not a real guest room, as Israeli apartments are not spacious. Dinah put fresh linens on the bed and checked that there was space in the closet. She put out some refreshments and some other items that would make her visitor's stay pleasant.

Moving to the kitchen, Dinah decided that she would omit certain foods and dishes that she would have liked to prepare. Since she was missing many required items, she decided to start cooking with the ingredients at hand.

At 12:15, Pinchas burst through the front door, blurting, "Well, is there any news?"

"Yes, but not connected to Choni," Dinah quickly replied.

She noticed the tense look on his face. "Actually, it does have something to do with him. Choni's grandmother flew in from France. She will be with us for Shabbos. Do you think you could give me some extra help this afternoon?"

"Choni's *savta*?" he murmured, not quite comprehending the confusing family lines. Until a few days ago, Choni was his brother. Now, a strange woman was coming to visit them, claiming to be his brother's grandmother.

"Yes. You have nothing to worry about. She's very nice."

"She must be like Choni," he guessed.

"That's not what I said," Dinah replied. "Anyway, you have some shopping to do. I'm sure you will do a good job quickly. I've already left the money on the counter for you. I'm more pressured than usual today, Pinchas. I haven't even started preparing anything but the soup."

"You haven't started yet? O.K., where do I start?"

"I think it's best for you to buy the fruits and vegetables. Then get the fish, and after that, the meat. I won't be able to prepare as much as I'd have liked, but it's O.K., Pinchas."

"O.K.," he replied obediently.

He bounded down the stairs and grabbed his bicycle, then set out to fulfill his mother's requests.

Within a quarter of an hour, Dinah was working at full speed. Time seemed to be speeding by. When she saw Chaim standing near her, she felt her knees tremble.

"What time is it?"

"1:30. I see you are managing."

"I hope so."

He surprised her by putting a kugel on the table. "Nechamah sent it over. I spoke briefly to Yoav, and she contributed their kugel to the occasion. She said she'll have time to prepare another one, because everything else is ready for Shabbos."

"That was so special of her," observed Dinah.

At 3:30, the soup was ready, the *cholent* was cooking on the stove, and the house had taken on a Shabbos appearance. Yoav went along with his father to bring Mrs. Kahn over to their house. He planned to take advantage of their time alone to talk to his father.

At 4:15, Dinah stood up to greet her Shabbos guest. She had imagined an elderly woman with a formidable expression, but Rivkah seemed sweet, with eyes that reflected pain and a great deal of hesitation. She carried her small, black suitcase by herself.

They greeted each other stiffly.

"Welcome. Come, I'll show you to your room." Dinah took the suitcase from Rivkah's hand, despite her objections. She led her to her room.

If Rivkah felt uncomfortable, she did not let on whatsoever to her hosts. She felt grateful that she was able to contact her husband in Paris before leaving to the Binder residence. Moishe was terribly worried about her, and was relieved to learn of the Binders' invitation for Shabbos.

"I'm happy they are being considerate. I'm sure you'll have a nice Shabbos at their house," he said with relief. "I did not like the idea of you spending Shabbos alone in a hotel."

So now she was here in the Binders' home, but somehow she felt even more alone than before. The parents' eyes reflected their pain — the pain of having their child held hostage. And in their eyes, she was responsible. It was not easy to face them, even with all the pleasant behavior. All this made her feel so lonely that she almost preferred spending Shabbos alone in her hotel room. She wanted to just sit there and wait for her grandson Elchanan to arrive, *b'ezras Hashem*, and to meet him with yearning eyes.

Instead, she came out of her room, and smiled in appreciation for the refreshments platter that awaited her.

"Thank you very much. I'm still exhausted from the trip. I won't be able to taste all the marvelous cakes on the tray."

"You can rest if you like. We'll wake you for candle lighting," Dinah suggested. Rivkah gratefully drank the coffee that was offered to her, and glanced at the photographs of Dinah's grandchildren.

"The family grows, *bli ayin hara.*"

"Yes, and so fast," Dinah gushed.

Rivkah gradually found herself having a low-key conversation with Dinah. When discussing one's children, eyes light up and voices soften. Rivkah told about her grown-up grandchildren's accomplishments, while Dinah told her the witty observations her youngest grandchildren had recently made.

A pleasant breeze flowed through the house despite the summer heat. Suddenly, an hour after entering the Binder home, Rivkah felt relieved. It was evidently not such a disastrous error to drop in on them after all — the family whom they had labeled "the enemy."

Rivkah excused herself and went to her room to rest. The room assigned to her was at the end of the hall. She took leave of her hostess and quietly closed the door, something that Chaim and Yoav, who were in the adjacent room, did not notice.

The thin plaster wall that separated the two rooms did not keep sounds from traveling through it. Rivkah, lying in her bed, heard a heated discussion coming from the next room. Although it was in Hebrew, the words were loud and clear enough for her to understand.

"Will you explain to me why Zalman called Shimon Kahn?"

The young voice replied apologetically, "I told you. I was not going to lie, *chas v'shalom.* Zalman is really a journalist. So we decided to frighten them. What, only they can threaten us with letters and telegrams?"

"What did he say to Shimon?" Chaim asked.

"That the story is known all over Eretz Yisrael, and readers want to hear their response, and — that we have already commented on the matter. You could say that Shimon was alarmed."

"And then?"

"You know what happened. He called here and begged us to stop cooperating with the newspapers, because anyway they are probably changing their approach. I think we deserve the Intimidation-of-the-Year Award no less than they."

Rivkah then heard faint whisperings, a door opening, and fragmented sentences. Then she heard Chaim's voice: "He acted brilliantly. Don't you agree?"

The response was whispered before quick footsteps left the room.

Rivkah abruptly sat up in her bed. She suddenly felt as if she was in a nest of vipers, and not in the friendly house where her grandson had spent the past ten years. Now, the missing pieces of the puzzle fell into place. The complete picture was fearful. They — the Binder family — pulled a long-distance hoax on them. And it worked. Their son had sent a fake journalist to scare her son, Shimon. True, it was without the parents' knowledge, as she gathered from the conversation she overheard through the wall. She was not able to follow the rapid flow of Hebrew words, but she grasped the general idea.

She recollected Chaim's appalling answer. What did he say? "He acted brilliantly." That was what he told his son. Yoav, she could somehow forgive. But, now, to hear such words of encouragement from his father about this reckless and foolhardy act? She could not even think of the right words for this episode. In her eyes, it was a shameful, inexcusable bluff. The Kahns used permissible, though unpleasant, means. The Binders, however, had overstepped the boundaries of propriety.

Rivkah looked at the clock. There was only a half-hour until Shabbos. Not enough time to find a suitable hotel. She would have to remain in the home of her charming hosts. She was sure they would be all smiles and sweet words.

She forced herself to hold back her tears. *Grandmothers do not cry.* That is what her youngest granddaughter, Miri, once told her. She tried to live up to those expectations, but the anger and fear forced the tears out in a massive swell of sobs.

CHAPTER THIRTY-THREE

Friday morning, the sun shone bright and hot over Entebbe. Choni stretched out and got up from the two chairs on which he had spent an uncomfortable night. His shoulders drooped. Mr. Schick had offered to let him sleep on the mattress, but the foul-smelling sheet that covered it repulsed him. He had decided to try his luck on the chairs.

Thursday night was no more restful than the previous ones. He dreamed about his mother reaching for him, but he could not reach her, because someone was pulling him away from her. Slowly she disappeared from sight. Then he saw his father staring at him with a somber face, saying, "But we're not your parents." Yet Choni desperately wanted them to be his parents. After that, some shrouded figures appeared, bedecked in white. He wanted to see their faces, but was not successful. They were his real parents.

When he awoke at about 5 o'clock in the morning, he found himself still in the passenger-reception hall, filled with people fast asleep.

At 6:30, the first group of early birds woke up. Mr. Schick was one of them. "Good morning, Choni. Did you sleep well?"

He shrugged, not indicating clearly yes or no.

"Very good." Mr. Schick pitied the poor orphan boy. He did not, however, allow his feelings of compassion to completely overtake him. "Go wash your hands. Today is Friday. We have to get ready for Shabbos."

They *davened Shacharis* quietly. Fortunately, Choni had a *siddur* in his carry-on bag, so he didn't have any problems *davening*. When he finished, Mr. Schick turned to him and said in a fatherly tone, "And now, we're going to prepare for Shabbos."

"How? What do we have to do?"

"Whatever we can," replied Yehudah Schick. He removed his suit jacket and shook it vigorously. The jacket that had been clean and pressed on Sunday had become a dusty rag. Mr. Schick took his toothbrush and tried to scrub the stains.

Choni looked confusedly at his shirt.

"Rinse the collar, like this," Mr. Schick showed him how. "Don't worry, the shirt will dry faster than you think."

Choni looked at his pants and realized they were filthy. "Start washing them with water. Scrub the stain by rubbing the two parts of the fabric together. There is no soap here, and the neighbors are not willing to let us use their washing machine," Yehudah said, in a lame attempt to lighten the moment.

At 10 o'clock, Choni washed up, including rinsing his hair, in cold water. He even cleaned his shoes with a little water.

"Your Shabbos preparations are wonderful," said Yehudah Schick with satisfaction. He called to his wife, "What do you say about our getting ready for Shabbos, Freida?"

"Everything looks like new, fresh out of the box," she smiled with pleasure.

Yehudah had a small *Chumash* with him with which he reviewed the *parashah*. He promised Choni he would lend it to him when he finished. Until then, Choni was free to do what he had been doing every day at Entebbe: to think, and think some more. Now, even his thoughts were at a standstill.

This was, of course, the worst situation he had ever confronted in his life. The hijacking, the fear of the terrorists' threats, the traumatic revelation of his being an orphan, missing his adoptive parents .... It was too much turmoil for one small boy.

"What's the occasion? Why are you all spiffed up? Has there been a change in our plans?" asked Michel when he saw Choni.

"Why do you ask?"

"It looks like you met Idi Amin himself. It looks like he promised he was going to send you home right now."

Choni was confused. "I managed to clean up a bit for Shabbos. What do you want?"

"For Shabbos? Here in Entebbe. Not bad — Maybe we should set up a *beit knesset* for you, too?"

Michel's black humor wasn't funny, and Choni felt his nerves about to snap.

"I don't want a thing. I just want to go home."

"Which team is your favorite? Maccabee or — what's the other one? I don't remember."

"What are you talking about?"

"On Shabbos. Which games do you go to?"

"Not to any game," the startled child said. "So your world really is very different than ours. You know, what bothers me the most about spending Shabbos here, is for the first time I'm so far from home without a *shul*. I think about the Shabbos table

in our house. Pinchas sits on my right, next to my father — "
He paused for a moment, and then added, "I mean my uncle. I
think that from now on, he is my uncle."

"And I think that a father always remains a father. He raised
you, and treated you like a son, right?" Michel's stare demanded a reply from Choni.

Choni closed his eyes. Did his father treat him the way he
treated Pinchas? It was hard to pinpoint precisely. He thought
of the constant jealousy whenever his father directed those soft
words of encouragement to Pinchas. His father's harsh tone
was always directed toward him. His mother's beseeching face.
The unspoken reprimands. The constant demands to perform
better and better. Did he treat him like a real son?

"What are you thinking? Why aren't you answering?" Michel
was irritated. "You had a father who ran with you to the doctor
when you were sick? Yes or no?"

Choni sighed. How true it was.

*Last year, Choni caught pneumonia. His father carried
him to the car. His mother sat next to him, giving him small
sips of water to wet his lips. He shivered with cold, even
though they wrapped him in a heavy blanket. By the time
they reached the doctor, his eyes were closed from exhaustion,
but he felt his father's loving arms carrying him inside. Even
in the examination room, he was not alone. His father held
his hand, spoke softly to him, and helped him sit up, even
wiping away his tears.*

*Although the prescribed antibiotics worked well, he still
needed and received a great deal of care and attention. That*

entire period, Choni was heavily pampered and spoiled by his parents. His father would call home during the mornings and ask him how he was feeling. It was intoxicating to take the telephone in hand and listen to his father ask how he was, what did he eat today.... Naturally, his mother did the same and more, but most heartwarming was his father's behavior. The little surprises he would bring home in the evenings, especially for him, warmed his heart and excited him. One time Chaim brought a small car, and another time a cup of freshly squeezed juice. Sometimes he brought a small chocolate bar, and even a chocolate ice cream. Choni always shared whatever he received with Pinchas, continually hoping that this wonderful period would never end.

After a month, however, he fully recovered. His father's attitude reverted to what it was before: cold and demanding.

ଛଔଔଛ

"Choni, today you're even deeper in your thoughts," Michel said, shaking him out of his sweet reverie. "You were describing the Shabbos table in your house. What did you want to say about it?"

"Ah, that my place will be empty this week. And my mother, believe me, she is surely worrying about me. And on Shabbos, you know, you're not allowed to be sad."

"What does your family do at the table?" Michel was suddenly curious about religious Jews' customs. Michel realized that just as Choni had no inkling about soccer players, so too he, Michel, had no clue as to what went on in a religious home on Shabbos. It was as if they were sons of two different nations.

"My father first recites *Kiddush* over a cup of wine. In front of him are two braided *challos*. The table is set fancy, like for an important guest. After *Kiddush*, we eat fish, and sing *zemiros* for

Shabbos. We say *divrei Torah* on the weekly *parashah*. Then we have soup, then meat with something on the side, usually kugel, and dessert. They say there is nothing like French desserts. My mother makes great desserts for Shabbos. In our house, Shabbos is the best day of the week. What's it like in your house?"

"At our house, well, you know, it's the weekend, like Sunday. It's everyone's free day. So we have two free days. That's all. We go on trips or visiting. We just take it easy."

Choni shook his head. He understood the enormous difference between them and chose to keep silent.

"So why the sudden cleanup?" Michel remembered to ask.

"I forgot to tell you that on Shabbos we wear different, nicer clothes."

Choni realized that their worlds were so different, that he tried to think of something else to discuss.

"Do you think we'll get out of here before Shabbos? Will the *rabbanim* let us to fly on Shabbos because of *pikuach nefesh*? What do we do if they decide to release us on Shabbos itself?"

"That should be the worst of your problems. I think we are in a terrible situation. Personally, I think the terrorists are deciding whom to execute first," Michel immediately regretted the last sentence.

"Soon it will be Shabbos. We're not allowed to speak about it. We're not allowed to discuss sad things on Shabbos."

"Sorry," Michel blurted out. "Say, have you noticed that my brother, Gerard, has withdrawn into himself again? He doesn't say a word to me. I think he's scared."

"Of what?"

"I don't know. But he is worried. I think that he'd better vanish the moment we get back to France. His gang will not like the fact that he was singled out as a Jew."

Choni shrugged. He was not very connected to Gerard. In

fact, at that moment, he was not very connected with Michel either. He suddenly felt a deep longing for his home, his room, his bed, the Shabbos table, and his mother's delicious cooking — even his father's loud voice. Who needed this foolhardy trip that messed up everything, just because his grandparents wanted to see him? Why did they do it? Why was he the one who had to travel to them? How could they send a young child all by himself?

The homesickness hammered at him mercilessly. He left Michel and walked around the passenger-reception hall. A group of youths sat together singing songs that he did not recognize and did not like. A young man playing a guitar accompanied them. The guitar caught his interest, but he did not move any closer to them. A few people were sitting and chatting in French. Others, speaking a mixture of broken English and Hebrew, tried to join the conversation. They talked about Idi Amin and the terrorists. It was not a suitable topic for children's ears. One of them smiled at Choni and he left the group, totally confused.

Another group sat nearby playing a game called Bridge. Choni did not understand the rules, but become engrossed in the fervor of the game. When Mr. Schick walked over to him, Choni said in wonderment, "They're playing just like little children."

"Speak quietly," Yehudah reprimanded him. He handed him his pocket-sized *Chumash.*

"Here, take this. Find a quiet corner and review the *parashah.*"

Choni obeyed Mr. Schick's instructions and did not notice, all the while, clouds gathering over the airport at Entebbe. A light evening breeze. Shabbos was drawing near.

He felt a jolt of goose bumps when Mr. Schick touched his shoulder.

"Why don't you go rest a bit? It's almost Shabbos."

"I thought they would release us before Shabbos…" Choni mumbled, drying his tears.

"We'll be free soon, *b'ezras Hashem*," Yehudah comforted him.

Choni looked at his clothes. They were clean for Shabbos, relative to their present conditions. Mr. Schick was wearing his suit and hat.

The terrorists observed the unusual preparations with extra vigilance. Someone had obtained two pitas and covered them with a napkin.

In honor of the Shabbos, the less observant Jews in the group gathered in the corner. Even the secular Israelis drew close to partake of the pleasant and comforting atmosphere.

A few women tried to light some matches in lieu of Shabbos candles, and Yehudah Schick wondered if it was halachically acceptable, since they went out right away. Shortly thereafter, someone started singing *Lechah Dodi* quietly. It was a tune that Choni knew, and the sound of it made him long for his *shul* back home.

All of a sudden, all the hostages were united, murmuring, humming, or singing *Lechah Dodi*. Some people sang loudly, some more quietly.

Choni noticed Michel and Gerard approach, and he motioned for them to wait.

Ma'ariv was quick, and immediately afterward it was time for *Kiddush*.

Choni carefully watched the man who quietly recited *Kiddush* on the two pitas.

It is forbidden to cry on Shabbos, he reprimanded himself, but his eyes filled with tears. He wanted to be at home, and to hear that the whole story that he had read in the letter was nothing more than a figment of his imagination.

CHAPTER THIRTY-FOUR

Rivkah forced herself to leave her room in time for candle lighting. She turned to the candles with a serious expression, covered her face with her hands, and found herself crying again. The tears were due more to the present bitter situation than to the lofty thoughts one ought to be thinking at such a spiritual time.

There was one consolation in all this distress — the fact that Moishe did not know what she had overheard. He was still home in Paris, only aware that Choni's foster family was hosting her for Shabbos. If he knew that the Binders were friends with the journalist who had contacted him and Shimon, would he permit her to spend Shabbos with them? Perhaps the frank and outspoken Moishe would demand explanations.

Her *tefillah* at candle lighting took longer than usual. She cried that Hashem should bring Elchanan ben Sarah back, healthy in body and soul. When she finished, Dinah motioned to the sofa. "Please have a seat. I'll be with you in a moment."

"You know, I'm still tired and would like to lie down," Rivkah told her hostess. She found it difficult to sit next to Dinah in forced friendship.

"Sure, go ahead. We'll call you when it's time for *Kiddush.*" Dinah was upset and added, "It's too bad. I wanted to show you Choni's picture albums."

The temptation of the photographs overcame Rivkah's imaginary exhaustion.

"To see Choni — for that, I'll somehow find strength." Rivkah walked slowly to the couch, and took out her glasses with great anticipation. This would not be her first time seeing photographs of Choni. Over the years Dinah had sent pictures to the Kahns, though the Binders never got so much as a thank-you from the Kahns. Lately, the Binders were a bit negligent in taking and sending photographs. Choni was growing up and they did not photograph him as much as before. Now, they took pictures at less frequent intervals, such as on a trip or at some family event, so Rivkah wanted to see current pictures of her grandson as soon as possible.

With trembling hands, Rivkah took the photo album. Dinah sat down next to her, not noticing the poignancy of the moment.

The pictures were arranged in chronological order. "Here is Choni standing for the first time." Dinah pointed to a photograph of a toothless child smiling, stretching his arms out toward the camera. "Look how proud he is of himself. It was such an experience. All the other children stopped to look at him, and applauded. See?" Dinah flipped a few pages of the album.

"Here was his first haircut. He was so frightened. He thought the haircut would hurt.

"And this picture needs an explanation." Dinah always became excited when looking at the picture of Choni when he turned 4 years old. "The *melamed* told my husband that Choni was a bright child and had all the potential to be a *talmid chacham*. Choni overheard this and was very excited. He took a Gemara and *shuckled* in front of it. You cannot imagine how this affected everyone in the house. One of the girls decided to record this sweet moment and snapped a picture. Look how happy and content he looks."

They flipped through the photographs. Rivkah could not deny that things seemed very good for her grandson here. He had come into a wonderful family that accepted him with love and warmth.

It was not easy for her to listen to Dinah talk about her grandson with such motherly love. She knew that Choni was her grandchild, and that a child normally is drawn more closely to his grandparents than to his aunt. This situation was so unusual.

She looked at a picture of Choni in Dinah's embrace, as she was protecting him from the baby chickens that walked near them in the petting zoo. Another photograph showed Chaim carrying him on his shoulders. Then another picture showed Choni dancing at Yoav's wedding — just the two of them dancing together, looking, for all the world, like two brothers celebrating a joyous occasion together.

Here was a picture of him with a breathtaking background. "The cliff of Arbel. A lovely site in the hills above the Kinneret," explained Dinah. Choni appeared very serious as he faced the camera. The similarity to his father Yaakov was inescapable. It was more difficult to find any noticeable traces of Sarah. Some had said possibly his eyes were hers, but everything else was like his father.

"Look at him over here," Dinah gushed, pointing to an unusual photograph. Her excitement irritated Rivkah, who was discovering for the first time that Dinah was his mother, whereas she, Rivkah, was playing the role of a vaguely bothersome grandmother who just wants to repeatedly see pictures of her *nachas*.

They finished looking at the album. Dinah closed it with a light thwack. "Our Choni — " she said in a thoughtful voice. The word *"our"* grated on Rivkah's ears.

"He's ours too," she interrupted her hostess in a petty way. She immediately was embarrassed and turned quiet.

"Of course he's yours also," Dinah replied warmly. She continued, "This is the first Shabbos that he's so far away. We never went away to hotels or guest houses and left the children at home. They were always with us. My husband insists on this, particularly on Shabbos, when the family has time to be together. Now, Choni is not here. Who knows how he feels...."

Every word was a knife in Rivkah's side. She imagined the accusatory tone of voice, although none of Dinah's words actually criticized her. She knew that their pain was directed at her.

"This is the first time he's so alone," Dinah repeated, completely immersed in her thoughts. She did not notice her guest's rising anger.

Rivkah swallowed the insult. They haven't seen him for barely a week. How many weeks was she separated from her grandson? How long has it been since she saw him? She counted scores of *Shabbosos*, hundreds of days, thousands of hours that she was separated from her grandson.

"It is forbidden to cry on Shabbos," Dinah said softly. "I think it was a big mistake to look at the album." As she went to put it away, she wiped away her tears.

Dinah handed her guest a *siddur*, and took one for herself.

Shortly thereafter, Chaim arrived from *shul* with Pinchas. He said, *"Gut Shabbos"* to everyone in a pleasant voice.

"Gut Shabbos, Ima, and Mrs. Kahn," Pinchas said. He then continued as if to himself, *"Gut Shabbos,* Choni."

An awkward silence fell. "I think he would not be happy if we did not wish him *'Gut Shabbos,'"* Pinchas explained. "They say the heart feels even what the ears do not hear. So he must know. Right, Ima?"

"Yes," she answered as she went to bring the wine to the table. In her guest's honor, she brought out a more expensive bottle than usual. They conducted the *seudah* quietly and in a dignified manner. Their guest sat quietly, tears often appearing in her eyes. When anyone asked her a question, she responded dryly.

Mercifully, the *seudah* ended quickly. Rivkah excused herself and went to her room. There, behind the closed door, she vented her pent-up feelings. The bewildered Binder family remained at the table.

"You can go back to *shul* and start reviewing what you learned. I'll be over soon to learn with you," Chaim instructed Pinchas. Dinah cleared the table. When she finished, she brought out some cold drinks and snacks.

"Did something happen between the two of you? Mrs. Kahn seemed very different now than she was earlier in the afternoon," Chaim noted.

"I have no idea. Already at candle lighting, I noticed an angry look on her face. Maybe we have not satisfied her expectations."

"A guest's expectations?"

"I don't know," Dinah said. "There is something going on that we don't know about. I have no idea what it could be."

"What a shame," Chaim said. "Rav Katz advised me to treat

her like family. And now look what happened."

"I have nothing to add. She walked out of here in a huff without saying a word."

Chaim sipped his drink. "Did you hear what our oldest son did to us?"

"I know he did something; I don't know specifically what it was," admitted Dinah. "Did he tell you?"

"Yes. I was very angry with him, and I still think my anger was justified."

"What happened?"

Chaim took a deep breath. "Our oldest son decided to have his friend Zalman the journalist contact the Kahns in Paris. You won't believe this, but they concocted an amazingly watertight story, saying that the entire business had already been publicized in the local religious press, and Zalman was asking for their response."

"I'm astounded that they took it all so seriously."

"Very seriously. Our son has changed from a cultured, French-born child into an overconfident Israeli. Why should a straightforward Frenchman dream that someone is trying to trick him?"

"What did they do?"

"Zalman and Yoav succeeded in frightening them," Chaim said slowly, as he cracked a nut. "We know that they started to back down. They asked Zalman not to write anything in the paper. That they are reconsidering the entire matter from the beginning. There you are, at least that small consolation — "

"Chaim, I think Yoav did something really despicable," she said, shocked by the very idea.

"He certainly deserved to be scolded for that," Chaim agreed with her, but a faint smile appeared on his face. "At least he's close to the truth. He sent a real newspaperman and the story was true. I would not initiate such a scheme, but now that it's done, it worked in our favor."

"That remains to be seen. Did they say they are waiving their claim to Choni?"

"I didn't say that. They said that they are reassessing the affair. Exactly what caused it I do not know —"

For the second time that Shabbos, Dinah's eyes started tearing. "We're all fighting over the child and where he should live. In the meantime, I don't see a child at all …." She covered her face with her hands and took a deep breath to stop the upcoming sobs.

"It's *assur* to think such thoughts on Shabbos. Why are you always a pessimist? They'll be freed. Look, despite all the terrorists' threats, so far the hostages are all alive and well."

"How do you know what is happening to them right now?" Dinah cried out bitterly. "Besides, as time passes, the terrorists will become more impatient and unpredictable — and what can save them? Israel has a policy not to free convicted prisoners as ransom payment. So what if a hundred or so people will be lost? Does anyone care?"

"Surely someone does," Chaim answered her emphatically. "Regardless, we should not put our trust and hopes in the Israeli government or in the good graces of the hijackers. *Davening* will help much more. Hashem is the only place to put our trust."

"You're right," Dinah said sheepishly. She cleared the glasses and the plate of nutshells that were still on the table. "I *davened* a lot. *B'ezras Hashem*, the *tefillos* will help and Choni will return. There is just no point in fighting over him now. And I don't understand why Mrs. Kahn still thinks that we — ."

"Shh — she is our guest; it's better if she doesn't hear you."

Chaim put on his hat and left for the *shul*; he always learned with the children after the Shabbos *seudah*. Pinchas and Choni usually left the house before him, and Chaim would follow a half-hour later. Upon arrival, he would sit with the boys and learn with them.

This time, for the first time, only Pinchas would be waiting for him. And Choni? What was he doing now? What was he thinking? Was there anyone to hold his hand and alleviate his fears?

CHAPTER
THIRTY-FIVE

The worried families of the Jewish hostages from France were much worse off than their Israeli counterparts. The stricken families in Israel had banded together, pressing for government action to free their loved ones. The French government, however, had washed its hands of the affair once the last of the non-Jewish French hostages returned to France. Now, only the Israelis and Jews were being held. The whole world was watching with baited breath, wondering, without lifting a finger in assistance, what the Israelis would do.

Georges and Annette Braun were among those worried French families whose loved ones were being held in Entebbe. At the airport, they were among the first to realize something was wrong.

"I told you it was a mistake. From the beginning it was wrong," Annette said. She tried not to sound too accusatory.

Georges did not reply.

They continued waiting patiently, and when they learned about the hijacking, they left the airport in shock.

"Poor Michel. Hasn't he paid enough of a price for his wayward brother?" lamented Annette as she wiped away her tears. "I'm sure that Gerard was not even with him. During their week in Israel, he always had an excuse why Michel could not come to the phone. Only on the last day did I talk to Michel. I'm very suspicious and very worried. And now that they are hostages, Gerard is surely taking care only of himself. Poor Michel."

Georges was too angry and agitated to reply. He nearly got lost driving home. The summer heat contributed to the stress. It had been his idea to send the boys together to Israel. He'd thought that Gerard would rise to the occasion of accepting responsibility for his younger brother.

⊱✿✿⊰

"Michel can make some sacrifices for the family. This is our last chance to turn Gerard around and bring him back to a normal existence," Georges announced. He was aware of the dangers inherent in his plan. Annette strongly objected to his idea, but he played on his wife's maternal feelings.

"Remember when Gerard was such a sweet child with those big expressive eyes? Do you want that to remain just a memory? He's caught up in a weird cult that breeds hatred of Jews. Don't you understand that they are manipulating him?"

"Explain it to him," Annette interrupted.

"We caught it two years too late, when Gerard was 15. For two whole years, those hoodlums were poisoning his mind. Five years have since passed. Some things are just — " he tried to find the right words. "Too late. It's just too late to save him."

Gerard continued distancing himself from his family. He became a loyal member of his gang. When he was younger, his parents could still occasionally keep him at home for a few days at a time, but he always returned to those people, trying to show them that he was one of them, and not part of the despised Jewish people.

Georges understood that Gerard was trapped by the gang like a fly in a spider's web. As Gerard reached maturity, his parents realized he could legally leave the house. Initially, he preferred to continue living at his well-to-do parents' expense. But when they started asking too many questions, he threatened to leave home and move in with some other gang members. His mother persuaded him to stay home.

As a last resort, Georges decided to send Gerard on a tour of Eretz Yisrael. He knew his son well, and was sure that the curious and exploitative young man would not forgo such a trip, especially since his parents were paying for it.

"Go and enjoy yourselves. I trust you to take care of your brother," Georges said briefly. All of Annette's pleadings to let Michel remain at home were overruled.

"Michel is our last hope. Young men of Gerard's age will not listen to their parents. Maybe Michel will forge a normal relationship with him," Georges explained. During the drive to the airport, he noticed with sadness Gerard's treatment of his younger brother. When Georges saw that Gerard related to Michel like a stranger, Georges realized the extent of his error in sending Michel along with Gerard. But it was too late.

Nearly a week had gone by since their plane was hijacked.

The maddening days and frightening nights of their sons being held captive were taking their toll on Georges. He blamed himself for sending them.

Annette spent most of the time in bed, her fears expressing themselves in serious cardiac irregularity. Although she did not tell Georges that he was to blame, she could not keep her anguish to herself. She worried frantically about Michel, though much less so for Gerard.

Georges, however, refused to give up. He was in touch with the Israeli embassy and a few other contacts in Israel. They all told him that the Israeli government was dealing with the situation. They all asked him to have patience.

Georges was not patient. He had only two sons, both of whom were in dire straits. He insisted that the Israeli government relent on its cardinal rule of not succumbing to terrorist blackmail. Release the prisoners that are being held in Israeli jails and be done with it. He wanted his sons to return home.

Relatives and friends of the family came over to offer their support. Influential acquaintances tried using their personal connections to gain information, but they all received the same answer: Be patient.

Georges, who valiantly controlled himself and his emotions, felt himself collapsing. He was willing to do anything to bring his boys home. He discovered that his money was not so important, after all: His social standing would not save his sons.

On the first day of the hijacking, Georges scarcely understood how he survived for even an hour. Although his spirit was being crushed daily, he outwardly projected an air of strength — if for no one else but Annette, whose health was suffering from the trauma.

On Friday, when he discovered that the refrigerator was empty, he realized that the household was not functioning. He decided to do some shopping, because without healthy meals, Annette would really become ill.

Near the entrance to the supermarket, Georges recognized several young men loitering about. He narrowed his eyes as remembered that they were Gerard's friends, those weird boys he hung out with constantly. They were probably members of the gang as well.

He walked up to them and announced, in an overly confident voice, "I'm Gerard's father."

An unusually tall boy stared down at him and said, "We're thrilled to meet you."

The supermarket was packed with customers, so Georges was not concerned about a violent confrontation. He continued, "If Gerard is important to your group, maybe there's a way to free him with — "

The giant interrupted, "You don't understand: Gerard screwed up in Israel. He's been thrown out of the group. If he doesn't get killed there, he's going to die here."

The tall boy turned around again to face his friends.

"Is that how you treat your comrades?" Georges was not frightened, even though the boy's words had shocked him. Gerard botched up in Israel? He was on a mission there for the gang? Where was Michel while all this was going on?

"He's a Jew. He's served his purpose, and we don't need him anymore. Anyway, he knows too much."

Another gang member tried to silence the giant, but he paid no attention. "Everyone knows that those hostages will be executed, sooner or later. So the dirty work will be done by those people, not by us."

The gang walked away slowly, grinning while elbowing each other. Then they realized their mistake in showing their hand. A few moments later, the giant returned to Georges, who was still standing next to the supermarket's entrance, holding his head in his hands.

He stared at Georges with narrowed eyes. "If I were you, I'd make sure that our conversation doesn't make its way to anyone else's ears."

Georges entered the store and rushed between the aisles, quickly grabbing the needed items, and deftly squeezing his way toward the cashier. This earned him some annoyed glances and snide remarks from the other shoppers waiting in the check-out line.

He rushed out of the supermarket toward his car. The not unexpected sight greeted him: The car's windows were smashed, and the words "Watch out" were scrawled on the hood.

Georges drove home in a hurry. He rushed into his house, locked the doors, closed the windows, and phoned his factory. The foreman was surprised to hear his voice. "Is there good news, sir?"

"Not yet. Tell me, Henri, how many security guards are presently at the plant?"

"Five."

"Send two of them to my house immediately."

Georges's factory housed expensive industrial equipment worth millions of francs. He could not leave the premises exposed to the possibility of theft or vandalism. The cost of the security guards was, without a doubt, worth every cent.

All the tension was taking its toll on him. His hands were shaking as he opened the side door to let the two guards into the house.

"Watch my house. One of you stay inside and one of you outside. Refreshments are in the kitchen. Is that clear?"

"Yes, sir."

Georges noticed the strange looks on their faces and felt he had to explain the situation to them. "I've got some important papers relating to the factory. I don't want them to fall into the wrong hands. Some of my competitors know that the papers are in my house."

This was no lie. The previous Sunday, he had planned to transfer the documents to the factory's safe. The hijacking, however, had put his plans on hold. The papers remained at home. Now, Georges had a legitimate business reason to post company security guards in his house. After issuing detailed instructions to the guards, he went to check on Annette.

"Finally, you're back. How long does it take to get a few things at the supermarket?" she complained while putting a cool compress on her forehead. Her mother was by her side, and she handed Annette a cold drink.

"Annette, I — " He was stressed and wanted to share the cruel information the tall gang member had told him, but Annette's defeated eyes prevented him from continuing.

"You what?" she urged.

"Hmm — I think that everything will work out. We'll yet laugh over these days," he concluded to Annette's surprise. He left the room.

Georges sat down at his desk and moved the window shade aside slightly. He stared outside. Beautiful Paris, with her endless rows of houses, stood glimmering before him. Their luxurious villa was part of this shining Parisian cityscape. They lived in an upscale neighborhood with a stunning view of the city.

But what was it all worth, without his sons?

In the relative silence, he was settled enough to gather his thoughts. Gerard's life was in danger. Even if he was released from Entebbe, mortal enemies awaited him in France.

Georges thought about the situation as he lit his cigar. He puffed on it while a maelstrom of emotions swirled around him. His fury against Gerard escalated, as his feelings of compassion increased.

He was a father. Fathers have compassion for their offspring even when they really deserve their wrath. Gerard got himself into serious trouble, so he'll have to extricate himself from it. He tried to imagine if he, Georges, had ever allowed himself to behave so arrogantly toward his own father. He closed his eyes and smiled as he remembered.

Georges father had a large yarmulka on his head. When Georges rebelled, he did not flout it in his father's face. He was afraid of his father, although he never beat or humiliated him. He actually had tremendous respect for his father. He was embarrassed to show that he had lost faith, so he left the house. He married Annette, a Jewish girl from a non-observant home. The fact that she was completely ignorant of Judaism suited him perfectly.

Now, with a strange longing, or maybe some pangs of regret, Georges decided that it would have been better to have raised Gerard according to religious Judaism. At least then the boy would not have had the audacity to join a blatantly anti-Semitic gang and agree to do their dirty work for them.

CHAPTER THIRTY-SIX

"**D**o you want to come hear *Kiddush*?"

"To hear what?" barked Gerard. He was in a foul mood, but Michel did not give up.

"Listen, my friend is religious. He knows a great deal about the Sabbath and all those quaint customs. Want to see one of them?"

"Don't bother me. You go if you want."

Michel left his older brother, wondering in what way he was disturbing him. His gang was not there. Was he involved in some secret activity? How could he possibly disturb a bored hostage sitting in this smelly hall?

He saw that there were still a few minutes until *Kiddush*, and that Choni and a few others were standing to the side of the room mumbling incoherently. Michel decided to try speaking to Gerard again. Under normal circumstances, he would never talk to his brother after being warned to stay away. Now, however, Gerard was in the same, or worse, situation as Michel.

He approached and asked, "Why are you so nervous?"

"It's adult problems; not for kids." He was right. Gerard could not act his usual wild self in here, in front of the hostages. But Michel was sure he would eventually share his burden with him.

"Look, Gerard, you trusted your friends. You went all out for them. And you're terribly frightened of them. I'm just your brother, but you know, I care about your well-being. Don't you think I deserve a bit of your attention?"

Gerard stared at him. "What are you talking about?" he demanded.

"Tell me why you are like a wild bull that saw someone wave a red cape."

Gerard sighed, "You should have understood what happened. The gang was not pleased with my performance in Israel."

"What did you do there?"

"I did what they told me to do. Unfortunately, not everything was successful." Gerard did not fall for the trap and managed to keep his mission a secret.

"It's not your fault if things didn't work out."

"True. But I did something I shouldn't have."

"And that was?"

"I went to the *Kosel* and — what's the difference? You're a kid and cannot do anything to help."

"True. Just tell me this: Can they harm you?"

"They can." He tried to conceal his anxiety by using brief sentences. "My friends are capable of anything."

Michel suddenly asked, "If they are threatening you, how can they be your friends?"

"They'll always be my friends. I was part of their gang. Whether I live or die, I am forever bound to them."

"You chose this?"

"I did."

"And there's no way to — "

"There's no way to hide," Gerard interrupted. "When I get back to France — if we ever make it back — I'll be in the worst kind of trouble. In fact, you would be better off acting as if I'm not your brother."

"It's that bad?"

"Anything can happen," Gerard said somberly.

For the first time in his life, Michel pitied Gerard, his older, intimidating brother. Although he badly wanted to help, Michel had no idea how.

"Listen, you are my brother. To tell you the truth, until today I couldn't stand you, even during this trip. If Papa and Mama would know what you did to me in Israel, if I mention a peep about sleeping in some boarding school with a bunch of strange kids, you wouldn't get away with it. But you're my brother, and I think you realize you did some stupid things."

"I didn't do anything stupid. To belong to this group is an exalted privilege. It's intoxicating, it's…." Gerard had a strangely dangerous look on his face. He looked at Michel as if seeing him for the first time.

Michel replied deliberately, "It'll lead to your death."

Gerard's face changed. "Being Jewish prevents you from achieving many goals, and from opening many doors. Just look at the trouble we're in over here because we're Jewish."

"Right. It closes the door to ridiculous cults such as the one you joined. But I'll show you other doors, new horizons in Judaism."

"Such as?"

"Let's go see what the religious Jews do on Friday night. Why not? Anyway, nobody is keeping tabs on you here."

Gerard shrugged his shoulders in acceptance. Whatever thoughts came to him were horrifying. From any angle, his future looked bleak. He joined Michel and walked toward Choni.

"Choni, are you finished *davening*?"

Choni motioned for him to wait.

In a few minutes, the strains of "*Shalom aleichem malachei hashareis*" resounded throughout the room, creating an exhilarating atmosphere. It was as if the ministering angels in heaven had descended to the Entebbe airport, to shield the hostages with their wings. The Arabs, the Germans, and the other collaborators looked on in astonishment at their captives. They seemed to be transported to another world, and no one dared interrupt this peaceful interlude. After a few moments of singing, one of the men recited *Kiddush* on two pitas, broke them, and distributed the pieces to everyone present.

A bit later, a small group sat down together and sang Shabbos songs with great fervor and emotion.

Gerard and Michel stared, enchanted. It was different and strange, an interesting ceremony that perhaps even ignited the faint Jewish spark in their souls.

"Interesting," remarked Gerard after all the men had returned to their respective corners of the hall, and the improvised Shabbos table had disbanded.

Michel dragged Gerard along. "My friend will be more than happy to answer any questions."

"I don't have any questions."

"You just think you don't," Michel teased him.

Gerard wet his lips. "You've grown up, Michel. You're not a child anymore," he said suddenly. But Michel was too busy to hear him. They were on their way to speak with Choni.

An astounded Gerard did not understand how he was suddenly standing next to the boy he had promised never to speak to again.

"Tell him, tell him how you spend Shabbos. Tell him about the life you lead," Michel urged Choni.

For over an hour, Choni sat and told about his life. He talked about the Talmud Torah where he studied, and described a lifestyle alien to the French boys. Choni shared typical stories about honesty, decency, kindness, and honoring one's parents.

"So now, you don't have to honor your parents, because they're not your true parents," Gerard argued at the end of the story.

Choni thought about that. The stories he had told about his daily life made him feel good inside. He had imagined himself at home, peaceful and secure in the warm environment he knew so well. Then that oppressive sentence, so callous, ripped apart the calm he had just built.

"I really don't know," he told Gerard. "But I'm certain that there are *halachos*, laws, about this kind of situation. I never looked into it, because I didn't think I belonged in the category of orphans...." His voice choked up and his eyes blazed, but he did not cry.

Michel spoke in a soft voice. "It's okay to cry. You don't have to be a hero in front of us."

"On Shabbos, it's forbidden to cry," Choni bit his lip. "It's forbidden to show pain and grief. Shabbos is a day of rejoicing for Jews. It's the day of rest." He recognized the words of his teachers, and the thought of them broke his heart.

What will the kids in his class say to his story? Maybe they know everything already. Maybe they all know that his name is not Choni Binder, and that he is an adopted child, a pitiable orphan.

Will his family relate to him normally after this? Do his older brothers and sisters know that he is adopted? How could they have deceived him like this? The confusing thoughts spun around in his mind.

He barely heard Michel ask, "Choni, what will your parents say? We are not religious — will they approve of our friendship?"

"My parents?" He looked at him. "Believe me, I have no idea who my parents are and what they'd allow."

"You're talking gibberish," Michel scolded him. "The parents with whom you live are your parents now."

"They're not my parents." The fury rose within him. "They lied to me my entire life! I called them Abba and Ima, when others are really my parents. Maybe they died when I was older? Maybe I would have remembered them?"

"You couldn't remember them." Suddenly, Gerard looked at the child's tragedy with different eyes. For Michel, it was an adventure to experience his friend's trauma. Gerard, however, understood that the child had woken up to a new existence, dangerous and insecure.

Gerard, too, once had a warm place called a home, and he almost lost it for a cruel gang. The choice had been his. This little boy, however, had received the shock of his life in the worst manner imaginable.

Gerard undertook the role of mediator. "Your parents are very good people. They wanted the best for you. I'm sure you will yet thank them for the beautiful world they built for you."

"It's a fake world. My brothers are not my brothers; my sisters are not my sisters."

"They are your cousins," Michel interjected.

"So they're my cousins. But they're not my brothers."

"What's the difference? They treat you like a brother; that's what counts. Look at my brother," Michel volunteered. "Do you see him? He's my brother, and I'm afraid of him, even more than you are. Would you want such a brother?"

Silence.

Gerard was insulted, though he did not show it. Choni, on the other hand, was deep in his thoughts. The traumas of hijacking and of death threats battered him to the core, while his other world, his home, was also being undermined.

Choni was organizing his thoughts. Before he could say anything, he felt a strong hand gripping his shoulder. "Elchanan, I want you to come here right away." It was Yehudah Schick.

He took the boy aside and spoke to him seriously. "I thought I could rely on a mature boy like you. You are better off not speaking to those boys. They are not religious, and I don't know if your parents would approve of such a friendship."

"They are asking questions about Torah, about Judaism. They want to hear answers," Choni replied in a low voice.

"That's wonderful. But let them ask the adults, who surely know a bit more than this little *tzaddik*," Yehudah said, squeezing Choni's arm.

Choni felt angry and rebellious, but remained silent. The good manners and *chinuch* he had received were deeply ingrained within him.

"Besides, today is Shabbos. Where is your *neshamah yeseirah*?"

Mr. Schick took Choni by the hand and walked with him to another corner. "My head hurts a lot," he said quietly to Choni. "The stress is taking its toll on my health. Elchanan, I'm going to rest, and I am asking you to stop speaking with those two boys. Is that clear?"

"But, Mr. Schick, I — "

Yehudah Schick closed his eyes and said, "Please, Elchanan, I don't have the strength right now to explain all the reasons.

It's enough for me that this boy told you information that you weren't supposed to know."

Choni's eyes filled with tears. His thoughts went to his family.

At home, his parents were sitting at the Shabbos table, eating the *seudah*. No, they've finished already in Israel. Abba and Ima were talking, while Pinchas was probably in *shul*, waiting alone for Abba to arrive. Well, Pinchas is his real son, while he, Choni, was an abject orphan whom his father had adopted out of pity. Otherwise, Chaim surely would have treated him differently. The memories and feelings inundated him again, and he fought to withhold the tears that threatened to overcome him for the second time this Shabbos.

At this exact moment, the Israeli cabinet and prime minister had just given their approval for a crack troop of commandos to board a Hercules transport plane, to fly to Entebbe. The soldiers had spent the last 48 hours constantly training and planning, leaving little time for sleeping and resting.

CHAPTER THIRTY-SEVEN

On Shabbos morning, Choni was surprised to see that Mr. Schick was still asleep.

"Will he get up for *davening*?" he asked Mrs. Schick. She shook her head.

"All night he was in terrible pain. Let him sleep a bit."

Choni was worried — the person who was supposed to be watching over him needed supervision himself.

To their relief, Yehudah Schick awoke a half-hour later. He seemed very weak, and asked Choni to help him reach the sink so that he could wash his hands before *davening*. Choni placed the *siddur* in Mr. Schick's hands, and later discovered his guardian was *davening Shemoneh Esrei* sitting down.

"I can't stand up. Sorry," Mr. Schick murmured.

A few good-hearted people came over to inquire about the sick man's situation. It was not difficult to see that Yehudah's illness was worsening. He was all flushed and his eyes were glassy. The other hostages could not do much for him, but they covered him with blankets, to make Yehudah more comfortable. Freida sat quietly near her husband. Choni looked at them.

"Do you think it's serious?" he asked Mrs. Schick.

"No, it's just a deep cough. I hope that by evening he'll feel better." She tried to sound reassuring, but Choni could see on her face that she was extremely worried.

Every half-hour, Choni brought some water to Mr. Schick, trying to help. He looked around discouraged, and saw Michel walk up to him wearing a friendly smile.

"*Gut Shabbos.* What's new?"

"*Baruch Hashem.*"

Choni did not know what to do. Had Mr. Schick been well, he would not have allowed Choni to speak to Michel. Choni knew that it was not polite to disregard Yehudah Schick's instructions, and he felt it was dishonest to take advantage of Mr. Schick's condition. But Mr. Schick was lying down with his eyes closed. He did not have the strength or the presence of mind to check on Choni's whereabouts. He was not his father, just a travel companion who had agreed to help his parents.

"You won't believe it, Choni. I have something amazing to tell you."

"What?" Choni was curious. He moved toward Mrs. Schick, who was busy taking care of her husband while reciting *Tehillim.*

"It's about Gerard. Guess what he said to me after the conversation with you last night."

Choni urged his friend impatiently, "So tell me already."

"After you left, Gerard said, 'The Jews really are unique. They are so united. They have many virtues. Even your friend — he's so different from other kids I know.'"

Michel stopped to let his words sink in. Choni forgot the

promise he had made to Mr. Schick. He was feeling excited.

"Look, you should think seriously about Judaism. You guys are Jewish, right?"

Michel smiled as he answered, "Look, Choni, people sometimes are impressed by a new idea or experience. But when it's over, and they go home, they forget about it. I believe Gerard will forget all his good intentions, if he even has any. He'll go on with his life, even if his way of thinking has changed."

Choni did not understand everything his friend was saying. Looking at Michel with trusting eyes, he said, "But you, Michel, now you know the truth. What do *you* say about being Jewish?"

"A lot of it is very interesting," Michel said evasively. "I enjoy hearing you speak about it. But frankly, if I were to pass you on the street, I wouldn't even look at you. Today, we are friends. In a few weeks, or even days, well, who knows? I have my life, my school, my friends, and a thousand and one plans. Why should I change?"

Choni was challenged by Michel's question and he thought carefully before answering. "Because it's the truth. Besides, who told you that you will have the luxury of thinking about it for years before you decide? We have to live according to the truth right now. We don't have time to waste. Maybe in an hour we'll all be dead."

"Maybe."

Suddenly, Michel's face darkened. Talking to Choni usually helped him forget the dangerous situation. Now that Choni was reminding him of their present circumstances, he tried to shake the fear of death that had taken hold of him.

Choni continued talking about different subjects that all revolved around Judaism and faith. He could not answer all of Michel's questions. He did not even understand some of them.

"I don't have answers for everything, but my father can explain it all. I promise you," was Choni's frustrated reply. He now understood why Mr. Schick had tried so hard to keep them apart. They really did live in different worlds.

Suddenly, Choni felt someone shaking his shoulder hard. He turned around and was frightened by the sight of Mr. Schick standing over him.

"Oh, I forgot to bring you water. I'm sorry."

"Be sorry for more serious problems than water."

Mr. Schick took him by the hand like an infant and led him to where he had been resting. "I promise you, Choni, it was with the greatest difficulty that I stood up. My head feels like hammers are pounding it. Your father said you are a quiet and well-behaved boy. But you have some nerve!" Yehudah Schick sounded irate. "Maybe you think that all rules are suspended because of the hijacking, but you are making a big mistake. Until the moment of death, you are going to observe the rules, the laws of the Torah. Is that clear?"

Choni nodded, upset. Although he did not understand all the fancy words, he got the message.

Mr. Schick looked at Choni and sighed, "Take care of yourself. Don't leave it in my hands to watch over you."

Finally, when Yehudah Schick was lying down again with his eyes closed, Choni decided to bargain with him. "But, Mr. Schick, they're Jews. I even talked to them about *Yiddishkeit* and they listened. Maybe they'll decide to become religious if we continue being friends."

"Maybe they will. But you are not the one to make it happen."

"Why not?"

"How will you know how to answer their questions? You're only 10!" Mr. Schick argued. Choni was astonished that Mr.

Schick seemed to know what had transpired in the conversations he had had with Michel, and did not know what to say. A moment later, Yehudah called out to him, "Don't forget, Elchanan, today is Shabbos; don't waste time with those boys."

Choni saw Michel and Gerard as *tinokos she'nishbu* — lost souls, and not rebellious sons, but still he knew that there was something to what Mr. Schick had said. In any case, Yehudah Schick was responsible for him, and was entitled to the last word concerning his actions. Choni went off to a corner and pretended to be asleep, so as not to meet up again with Michel. He was bored stiff and consumed by fear.

How will this situation ever resolve itself?

By the time Shabbos morning arrived, Rivkah felt her patience wearing thin. She could not tolerate the feigned courtesies and etiquette. The Binders had been doing everything possible to make her feel comfortable, yet she felt as if she were being confined in a den of vipers.

Their son had dared to unleash an imaginary journalist on them, using grossly unethical means to force them to back down. On top of that, she had heard how Chaim Binder viewed his son's actions. In that case, what was she doing here altogether? How could they have misled her about their real intentions?

Not only that, thought Rivkah, *but how could Moishe and I, such loving grandparents, have abandoned our grandson, Sarah's child, to the whims of such unscrupulous people?*

You, Rivkah, she told herself, *are only spending Shabbos with them. Your Elchanan was here for ten years. How did you permit this to happen?*

She decided that right after Shabbos, she would check in to the first hotel that had an available room. She was even prepared to sleep in a lobby or basement, anywhere but here. If she could have, she would have even departed on Shabbos. The Binders' smiles and courtesy annoyed her. Rivkah did not care for false, professed courtesy.

"How was your first night in Eretz Yisrael?" Dinah inquired politely as Rivkah entered the living room.

"*Baruch Hashem*. I've had more successful nights," she replied, hiding a yawn. She had fallen asleep only at about 4 o'clock in the morning. Even then, her sleep had been nightmarish and unsettled.

"How many sugars do you want in your coffee?" Dinah loyally asked, fulfilling the role of hostess.

"I'll prepare it myself," responded Rivkah coldly. At the hot-water urn, she deliberately ignored the insulted look on Dinah's face.

It grew worse as the morning wore on. Dinah tried to strike up a conversation, but Rivkah took her *siddur* in hand and spent two and a half hours *davening*.

When Chaim arrived home from *shul*, Rivkah announced that she was not feeling well, and requested that they eat the *seudah* as quickly as possible.

The Shabbos morning *seudah* was even worse than the Friday night meal had been. Rivkah sat at the table close mouthed, and barely nodded in response to questions posed to her.

"Would you like a pill for your headache?" Dinah asked with concern. She glanced at Chaim, fearing that their guest might feign some medical situation such as fainting, or even worse.

"I'm fine, thank you."

After the *seudah*, Rivkah retired triumphantly to her room. It was not a pleasant victory. After all, all she had managed to do was spend as little time as possible in the company of the Binder family.

Back in her room, she concluded that it was their duty to take Elchanan from this house, no matter what the price.

Sarah and Yaakov surely would not want their son raised in an environment where falsehood reigned. How had they, the grandparents, overlooked these blatant flaws in Chaim's personality? He had seemed so decent and good hearted. Apparently, *min haShamayim* she was destined to uncover his dark secrets.

No, Elchanan her grandson would not live here. Not any more. Who knew how much damage has already been done to that poor child's soul?

She did not leave her room until *Minchah* time. She quickly strode into the living room with her *siddur* and started *davening* before Dinah could start talking to her.

When she finished *davening Minchah*, she hastily washed her hands and ate the *seudah shelishis* in silence. Some neighbors came over to visit Dinah. None of them mentioned Choni. Dinah, too, did not speak of him. While Rivkah considered this to be slighting Choni, the neighbors' decision was very well thought out. Speaking about Choni would surely bring tears to many eyes — and crying is forbidden on Shabbos. They preferred to distract Dinah by speaking about other matters. Later, they all recited *Tehillim* together. All of them knew for whom they were reciting the *Tehillim*, although no one voiced it aloud.

Rivkah did not join the concerned neighbors, who nevertheless made every effort to be friendly and gracious to the elderly guest. She continued to treat Dinah coldly, essentially humiliating her in front of her neighbors. But her suffering heart did not allow her to care that she was hurting Dinah. Within her, a fire burned — a fire of anger and animosity.

On *Motza'ei Shabbos*, Rivkah rushed to her room and, soon afterwards, asked permission to use the telephone. Dinah agreed, of course, although Chaim had started dialing to check whether there was any news regarding the hostages.

"I didn't notice that you missed Choni on Shabbos," Rivkah inadvertently blurted out. Unfortunately, Dinah heard her and immediately reacted.

"He wasn't missed?" Dinah cried out in shock. It was a cry that shook the very walls of the house. Chaim's finger stopped in the middle of dialing the phone. Poor Pinchas stared in terror, frightened by this latest exchange.

CHAPTER THIRTY-EIGHT

All at once, the mask of politeness and civility vanished. So Mrs. Kahn really felt fine this past Shabbos — too good, in fact, compared to her advanced age. She had arrived in Israel to spend Shabbos at their house in a state of anger, full of bitterness toward the gracious hosts who took her into their home. The Binders welcomed her, knowing that she was taking legal action against them.

The shock was terrible, but the sense of betrayal was worse.

The first to find his tongue was Chaim. "Why do you think we don't care about Choni?"

Rivkah turned her face and looked aside. Finally she answered, "None of you mentioned even one word about him the entire Shabbos. If a son of mine had been taken hostage, I would not be able to prepare a regular Shabbos, as you did. But you — are not his true parents, so obviously it does not trouble you."

"You are so wrong!" Chaim clenched his teeth and signaled to Dinah not to respond. She was furious, and tears welled up in her eyes. Dinah's outburst was ready to be unleashed, but Chaim recalled Rav Katz's advice. He kept a low, calm voice and responded to the elderly woman with tact and civility, even while speaking forcefully to her.

"We made every effort to maintain a pleasant and peaceful atmosphere for the sake of our honored guest, the grandmother of our Choni. Not only that, but as far as I'm aware, on Shabbos it is forbidden to be sad and cry. I cannot promise you we have been completely successful in everything, but we have tried at least to avoid public displays of grief.

"I had expected that you would show understanding and appreciation of all this, Mrs. Kahn. Now, however, I realize that you arrived here full of anger and accusations."

"I came because I thought I would be at my grandson's house, among friends, people of *chesed*. I see that I was in error," replied Rivkah curtly. "I would like to briefly use the telephone. I thank you for the Shabbos hospitality."

She said the last words with such obvious disdain that the Binders understood that they were a mere formality.

As Dinah stood next to Chaim, they heard Rivkah reserve a room in the same hotel she had checked into on Friday. After that, she called a taxi. She spoke in ungrammatical Hebrew that under normal circumstances would have made Pinchas laugh, but not this time. The atmosphere in the house tonight was grim and dismal.

Rivkah returned to her room and packed her small suitcase. "I really do thank you for the Shabbos," she said hesitantly as she lingered for a moment in the doorway. "It will be better for me in a hotel. Shabbos was pleasant and the food excellent. It reminded me of the French cuisine to which I am accustomed.

But you have to understand that I am still angry, and — "

Her words were cut off. While Dinah, pale and offended, looked away, Chaim asked her earnestly, "Why are you angry, Mrs. Kahn?"

Perhaps it was because of the mood of the moment, Dinah's tears, and the shocked look on Pinchas' face, or maybe just because she decided that the time had come to be candid, she felt she had to tell them the truth.

"Reb Chaim Binder, I heard words that were not meant for my ears. I admit it was wrong to eavesdrop, but the words were spoken right next to me, and they are what triggered my anger. I think even you agree that I am warranted in my fury." Rivkah picked up her things and stepped out of the house in response to the taxi's beeping. This time, as he saw her out Chaim did not offer to help her or drive her, or ask her to remain with them.

He came back into the living room with a thoughtful expression.

Dinah was waiting for him there, restraining her tears. She was embarrassed to cry in front of Pinchas, who was quietly watching everything.

"Pinchas, please go to your room," Chaim instructed his son. He closed the door to the living room, and only then did Dinah release her pent-up tears.

"What did she tell you? Why is she angry?" Dinah cried. "Didn't we do everything possible for her? She didn't even appreciate the fact that we invited her even though they are busy scheming with lawyers to press charges against us."

"Mrs. Kahn claims that she heard some words that were not intended for her ears," Chaim remarked calmly. "These words infuriated her. I'm just trying to figure out what we said that so enraged her."

The two of them sat on the sofa, reviewing the details of the day's activities. There was no question that Rivkah's sudden departure from their house was a serious insult to European sensitivities. Who would have believed that a guest would simply get up in a fit of indignation and leave?

For Dinah, this was an intolerable humiliation. For Chaim, it was an interesting riddle. The truth was that he had treated his guest properly only because of Rav Katz's instructions. Personally, he thought that Rivkah had behaved tactlessly.

He tried to remember what was discussed that could have triggered such a reaction on her part.

"Dinah, try to remember at what point she began acting strange."

"From the start of Shabbos," she replied in a choked voice.

"And when she arrived at the house?"

"She was all smiles, with a pleasant manner. She went to rest, but came out of her room like a tigress spoiling for a fight. She did not start any conversations, barely responded to questions, and seemed altogether very distant."

He smiled at her accurate description.

"I see. So you're saying that she became angry with us shortly before Shabbos. What happened then?"

Dinah recalled, "Yoav came over. Don't you remember?"

"Right, Yoav came over," Chaim agreed. "And then I went with him into one of the rooms."

"Which room?"

"The room that is adjacent to the guest room. Every word spoken in that room can be clearly heard in the guest room."

Dinah asked, "You spoke to him for at least half an hour. What did you talk about?"

Chaim paled as he recollected their conversation, and stroked his beard nervously. They had just solved the mystery.

"Chaim, what happened in that room?" Dinah was demanding to know the truth, the truth that would call for eventual accountability.

"I remember that I interrupted you two and asked you to go somewhere else, so that you wouldn't disturb Mrs. Kahn's rest," Dinah continued to recount. "Yoav wanted to leave, because it was close to Shabbos. What did you two talk about when I wasn't in the room?"

"It's a long story. Now I understand what Mrs. Kahn is angry about. And she's right."

"She's right?" Dinah was aghast. What justification could there possibly be for a guest disrupting their Shabbos serenity? "Chaim, don't justify her actions for even a moment. Our child is missing, and look what that woman is doing to us. Now we have to worry about her and her needs? How could your conversation have insulted her? What could you have said?"

Chaim lowered his head. "I really did scold Yoav. But then you came into the room," he admitted quietly.

"Scold Yoav? What for?" Even at the age of 24, Dinah thought of Yoav as her little boy.

"Our son decided to help us without asking us," Chaim replied bitterly. "His good heart must have prevented him from telling us about the prank he pulled on the Kahns."

"Prank?"

"Call it a bit of mischief. Call it whatever you like. Do you remember that Shimon Kahn called us and asked us not to publicize the story about Choni, saying that he would shortly have an answer for us?"

"Yes. It was a strange phone call. How is Yoav connected to it?" Dinah asked.

She suddenly recalled Yoav smiling when she told him about Shimon's call.

Chaim explained, "Our dear Yoav decided to involve his friend Zalman in his shenanigans. His friend really is a reporter, and together they concocted a story about a newspaper article about Choni. You can imagine how much the Kahn family was shaken when they heard that we were going to publicize the story."

"And that's why they began rethinking their approach," Dinah cried out triumphantly.

"I don't know if that was the reason, although it's logical to assume that Yoav's little antic played a big part in it. Whatever the reason, on Friday he told me what he had done, and I was able to act angry, because you know that important matters cannot be settled by deception. While we were talking, you came into the room. Mrs. Kahn surely wasn't able to figure out that there were two conversations going on in the room at the time."

"So now she's angry," Dinah concluded.

"And I am too," added Chaim.

"You?"

"Yes. I disapprove of Yoav's actions. I do not tolerate such antics."

"Don't be angry. Yoav was just trying to help."

"I don't want such help," Chaim said as he stood up and lit a cigarette. "Child-rearing does not end when the child is 18, nor even when he gets married. The responsibility of *chinuch* continues even on into adulthood."

Dinah, however, defended Yoav's actions, "This still did not justify her rude behavior."

"Dinah — " Chaim was finding it hard to comprehend. "I'm not concerned with educating Mrs. Kahn. I have enough trouble worrying about my children. And besides, there's something else I have to tell you."

"And that is?"

"We must change our approach to the Kahn family," Chaim announced. "Not just for our sake, and or for the *bein adam l'chaveiro* issue, but primarily for Choni's sake. This is not something that I've decided. I am not such a *tzaddik* to lead my life on such a level on my own."

"Then who told you to do this?" asked Dinah.

"Rav Katz," came the expected answer. "He claims that our selfishness has generated the intolerance that both sides are displaying toward each other. We are too preoccupied with our own needs and gratification, and not enough with Choni's."

Dinah protested vehemently, "We don't think about Choni? If we weren't thinking about him, we would have sent him right off to France the first time they asked for him. Of course we — "

"All right, we do think about him. But also about ourselves, as parents. If Choni's feelings are truly important to you, then think about it: How do you think he would want us to treat his late mother's parents? Do you think he'd feel good about the way we are treating them?"

His compelling question caused Dinah to look away. She was indeed Choni's mother, and her maternal emotions often took precedence over her considerations for Choni.

Chaim continued in a confident voice, "I think we have to straighten out this business with the Kahns. We will go tomorrow to Rivkah and explain that we had nothing to do with Yoav's actions. Naturally, Yoav will have to ask her forgiveness for tricking them. We will continue treating her respectfully, which will foster friendly relations between our families. And believe me, this is for Choni's mental and psychological wellbeing. It is 100 percent for his sake."

This new revelation was so staggering that Dinah was unable to absorb all its implications.

"I didn't tell you all this on Friday, because we barely managed to get ready in time for Shabbos, remember? And on Shabbos, I did not want to talk too much about Choni," Chaim said softly.

They went to sleep late that night. Before Chaim fell asleep, Dinah tearfully said, "I feel horrible. If only I knew that our Choni was safe, that he's alive. I'm prepared to act politely to all the relatives. All of my *tefillos* are just that he should come back alive and healthy."

"*B'ezras Hashem.*"

"It's been a week already," Dinah continued in her tears. "A week has gone by, and we don't even know if he's alive or what is happening to him."

She cried for a while into her pillow. The ringing telephone interrupted her. On the clock on her night table it was 4 o'clock in the morning.

CHAPTER
THIRTY-NINE

Time passed slowly at the airport. The hostages' patience was completely frayed by now, and their fear was palpable. The question hanging over everyone's head was: What now? Were they destined for life or, *chalilah*, for death? The terrorists' faces were stiff and impenetrable, and they coldly eyed the hostages.

Choni wandered about in the small reception room. "Sit quietly," Mr. Schick called to him, but the boy could not obey. At this point, when he had almost completely stopped talking to Michel and Gerard, he felt more alone than ever. Choni was not even sure if his yearning for home made any sense. Exactly where was his home?

He recalled the recent dream in which his mother looked at him with amazed eyes and asked, "What are you talking about, Choni? Of course we are your real parents." How gratifying it was to cling to the memory.

On *Motza'ei Shabbos*, Choni realized that the exhausting events of the past day had taken their toll on him. He was sleepy. Most of the hostages were also exhausted, sprawled out across the floor.

Choni found a quiet spot but was not able to close his eyes.

Michel came over to him.

"What's doing, my friend?"

"*Baruch Hashem*," he answered, sounding exhausted.

"One would think you worked hard this Shabbos."

Choni shook his head in protest and smiled feebly.

Michel left with a shrug of his shoulder. Choni saw Michel turn to talk to Gerard. At least Michel had a relative with him in Entebbe. He, Choni, several years younger, was stranded there without any family.

To compensate for his loneliness, he found Mr. Schick and approached him hesitantly.

"Is everything all right?" the older man asked.

"I'll be O.K. when we get out of here," he replied curtly.

Yehudah Schick looked at him with resignation. He did not repeat the infuriating phrase, "Things will be okay." There was no point in lying to the child.

This night would mark one week since their internment in Entebbe. Only the coming days would tell if and how this affair would end.

Most of the hostages dozed lightly on the filthy blankets scattered on the floor. Silence reigned in the hall — a silence of weariness and despair.

Choni felt resigned to his fate. Just at that point, he heard some strange sounds coming from outside. What could be going on at Entebbe airport at this hour of the night?

Outside, on the tarmac, the first Hercules transport plane landed on the Entebbe runway. The Israeli soldiers inside stared at the runway lights racing past them from the windows. Ten paratroopers leapt to the ground from the open belly of the plane, and a black Mercedes with Ugandan national flags drove off the plane. The purpose of this Mercedes, which was filled with Israeli soldiers, was to distract the Ugandan soldiers, giving the commando unit extra time to enter the terminal.

Then, suddenly, without warning, gunfire could be heard from outside the terminal. Brief flashes, sounds of weapons firing, and a frightening clatter reached the reception hall where the hostages slept. The noise was terrifying, and the fear was amplified by the uncertainty of what was happening. Choni, and most of the other hostages, hid under blankets. Were they about to be massacred by the terrorists with some assistance from the Ugandan military? Had someone arrived to rescue them? Choni could not see.

To the hostages, the battle seemed long, furious, and heavily punctuated by gunfire, but it took only 30 seconds before all the terrorists in the reception hall were eliminated. "Everyone down on the ground! Everyone down on the ground!" one of the rescuers called out in Hebrew. One of the hostages clutched his red-stained shoulder. Instead of staying on the floor, he had tried to get up and an Israeli bullet hit him in the shoulder. A little girl suddenly jumped up, but the soldiers were able to recognize in time that she was not a terrorist, and they held their fire. Two other passengers who also stood up, however, were not so lucky and were badly wounded. Choni heard when one of them was hit in the shoulder.

Choni was utterly terrified. He did not have much time to think before he heard one of the soldiers shouting into a megaphone, "This is the IDF. Lie down on the floor. Don't get up."

He repeated his call both in Hebrew and in English. "We've come to take you home!"

Choni flattened himself to the floor. Once again, he regretted that he had chosen to lie down so far from the Schicks. Now, he was alone and afraid. Suddenly, he saw someone crawling toward him. It was Yehudah Schick.

"Everything is okay, *baruch Hashem*. Everything is all right. Just stay on the floor," he whispered.

Suddenly, one of the hostages got up, and after him, many others. A few remained sitting on the floor. Choni began to cry and through his tears he watched IDF medics moving among the injured hostages, administering first aid. There was still a great deal of noise and confusion as the soldiers mopped up the remaining resistance.

One team assigned to take possession of the VIP lounge in the terminal found the outside door locked. A soldier threw a grenade at the door, but it bounced off and exploded, lightly injuring one team member. They found an open door in the terminal and entered the lounge. Inside were three men. As the soldiers entered, the men stood up and began moving toward the soldiers with their hands raised. Unsure as to their intentions, the Israelis withheld their fire until one noticed a grenade belt around the waist of one of the men. After their commands to halt went unheeded, they opened fire and killed the men. As they did, one of the terrorists dropped a grenade he had secreted in his palm.

At this point, all the terrorists were dead. Only a few Ugandan soldiers stood in the way of a quick escape. Some were hiding in the tower next to the old terminal and were firing at the Israeli soldiers in the Land Rovers.

A few minutes later, the hostages were told to prepare to leave. Another soldier used a megaphone to announce that all luggage should be left behind. Choni noticed that none of the passengers obeyed. People packed their suitcases in a rush, as they did not intend to leave their possessions behind.

"It's because everything is over now. When people are in danger, they are only concerned with saving themselves. Now, people feel secure with a suitcase in their hands. They don't know what will happen next," explained Yehudah Schick, who was holding his own carry-on bag. "Take yours and stand next to the door. Let's get a move on."

Was Mr. Schick really in such a good mood, or am I just imagining it? Choni wondered. He wiped away his tears and dragged his suitcase along. With his free hand, he held onto Mr. Schick's suitcase, which made him feel safer.

IDF soldiers continued clearing the building and began evacuating the rescued hostages to one of the giant Hercules planes. They were hampered by passengers returning to the terminal to try to find lost property in the darkness. Several passengers were wandering around in a state of shock or hysteria. At the door of the terminal, the soldiers divided them into groups to lead them to the aircraft. Choni looked back at the terminal building where he saw a few wounded hostages, some IDF medical personnel, and a huge pile of blankets. He turned around and looked toward the plane.

As the hostages moved outside the terminal building, some bullets were fired in their direction. Yehudah Schick visibly tensed. A brief firefight ensued between the IDF soldiers and Ugandan Army troops; unfortunately, two of the hostages were struck and killed. After eliminating the Ugandans, the Israeli soldiers instructed the hostages to run toward the plane. The giant Hercules aircraft was making its way toward them in reverse.

Before them were a number of jeeps, and another behind them. Alongside them, IDF soldiers stood with their weapons drawn, guarding them. Everyone was quiet. To his dismay, Choni realized that they were surrounded by soldiers, even when they finally entered the plane. Since there were no seats in this plane, they sat on the floor. Mr. Schick held his hand. "Try to calm down," he implored. But it was no use. Choni continued to tremble as if stricken with a burning fever.

After being on the ground at Entebbe for only half an hour, the lead plane took off with its cargo of rescued hostages. They flew for about an hour, and then prepared to land in Nairobi.

"What's Nairobi?" asked Choni, teeth chattering.

Freida Schick explained, "It's the capital of Kenya, a friendly country. I guess they'll take care of the injured there."

Most of the hostages were frightened and sat quietly. Many of them were in shock.

One of the soldiers explained that they would refuel the planes in Nairobi, and immediately fly to Israel. This reassuring piece of news did not move the hostages. Choni, in particular, did not yet believe in a happy outcome. He was still frightened.

During the refueling, Choni overheard one soldier tell another that the commander of their rescue, a young officer named Yoni Netanyahu, had been killed by the Ugandan troops. He also mentioned they hadn't been able to rescue Dora Bloch, the sick elderly woman who'd been taken to the hospital in Kampala. The world would later learn of her death at the hands of Idi Amin's forces.

After refueling, the plane took off at 3 o'clock in the morning, headed toward Israel. Choni could not fall asleep, even with Mr. Schick's urging that he do so. It was very cold inside the plane, and Mr. Schick explained that the plane's heating system had broken down. The medical staff was giving out extra blankets to the passengers. Mr. Schick handed two blankets to Choni.

"Cover up well. We're on the way home," he said without a smile. He seemed more worried than relieved.

Choni did as he was told, even though the cold in his heart continued to pain him.

Looking around, he noticed Michel and Gerard. Michel smiled at him and made a V sign with his fingers. Gerard, on the other hand, was totally wrapped up in himself, looking very worried.

No one else on the plane smiled. There was one doctor who tried to lift the passengers' spirits. He took hold of a megaphone and announced: "This week, a new tax was levied on Israeli citizens: Value Added Tax. But for those of you who object, you have the opportunity to return to Entebbe and live in Uganda."

"Return?" Choni was taken aback.

Mr. Schick explained, "He was only joking, Choni. Don't worry."

"Mr. Schick, I want to say goodbye to Michel and Gerard. After all, I won't be seeing them after this," said Choni, half begging, half demanding.

Mr. Schick let Choni go. He realized that in a few more hours, this hardship would end. Hashem knew that he had fulfilled his responsibilities under extremely difficult circumstances.

Choni walked over to Michel and sat down. "What's doing?" he asked his friend.

Michel was elated. "Did you see that performance? Wasn't it marvelous? You see? Jews don't abandon one another. I'm telling you, France would never have done a thing. They couldn't care less."

Not all the Israeli soldiers were on their plane. There were four planes, each one loaded to capacity with soldiers and equipment. Only the soldiers whose presence was necessary flew on the plane carrying the hostages. Gerard glanced at a soldier and said, "The Jews really are different from the others."

"I thought you didn't like being Jewish," Choni said. "According to what I've heard, you curse the day you were born and — "

"Not anymore," Gerard interjected. His eyes were moist with emotion. "Believe me, I am helpless. In Israel, I can manage, but I have nothing to look forward to in France. My friends have become my enemies. You cannot imagine what those devils are planning."

Choni wanted to continue their conversation, but just then he saw Yehudah Schick motioning that he should return to his spot in the plane. The older man leaned over and, in a stage whisper, said, "You asked to say goodbye to them, and I agreed. Now, I want you at my side." Yehudah was concerned about Chaim Binder's reaction to the friendship.

"All right, I'm finishing with them."

Choni returned to Michel. "They're saying we're landing in an hour. I don't know how to say goodbye but — "

Michel quietly handed him a folded piece of paper. "Here's my parents' telephone number. Call me whenever you want."

"Thanks."

Choni did not give Michel his telephone number, thinking of Mr. Schick's reaction.

Michel continued, "I wish you much strength in dealing with your new situation. You know, you have amazing parents. They'll continue taking good care of you." Choni turned away, looking down.

Everyone would be returning to their families, their parents, their brothers and sisters. But he — Suddenly everything appeared as if in a nightmare — the hijacking, the letter, the revelation of his being orphaned.

He wanted to sleep, but over the loudspeaker came the announcement that they were on the final approach to land at Tel Nof military airfield. The passengers were excited, but Choni remained in a pensive mood. All those people had a clear future. For him, another nightmare was brewing.

CHAPTER FORTY

inah had come to believe that telephones possess a fearsome ability to transmit depressing news. That notion was dispelled in the predawn hours of Sunday, the fourth of July. Her eyes were still bleary with sleep when she heard Chaim answer the bedside phone and exclaim, "Are you sure? Unbelievable!"

After a few more emotional exclamations, he hung up the phone and bounded out of bed with an exuberant jump.

"Dinah, a miracle has happened! Hashem has performed a miracle!"

"Choni?" she asked hesitantly, fearing disappointment. But the glowing expression on Chaim's face soothed her negative expectations.

"They were freed!" Chaim said the hoped-for words, bursting into tears without any warning. All the unbearable tension of the previous week was released all at once. "It was an astonishing operation. Hashem guided them to success. *Baruch Hashem.*"

Dinah was too overwhelmed to say anything. Her tears quickly joined with those of her husband. She just cried without letup, unable to speak. She, too, needed this catharsis to relieve the horrific burden that had been crushing her this past week.

She did not even bother to ask Chaim who had called with the news. Was it the government of Israel, or friends and acquaintances who had done everything in their power to help? It did not matter. Nothing else mattered right now.

When she recovered a bit, Dinah got up and went to the kitchen to boil some water. All the hubbub woke Pinchas, who ran into the kitchen.

"Do you know what time it is?" he asked in surprise.

"Yes, we do and we know something else, too! More exciting, and more joyous," his father answered as he stepped up behind Pinchas and held him tightly by the shoulders. Pinchas turned around and stared at him in surprise.

"What's going on?"

His parents told him the wonderful news. Pinchas — a bit too sleepy to fully rejoice — grinned broadly.

Dinah prepared a cup of steaming coffee for her husband with two teaspoons of sugar, in honor of Choni's liberation. She made a cup of hot chocolate for Pinchas.

As they sat down together to celebrate, Pinchas asked, "Ima, Choni doesn't know that he's adop — I mean, my cousin. When are you going to tell him?" Chaim and Dinah looked at each other as they paled.

Dinah regained her composure first. "Now we are rejoicing and thanking Hashem for the great miracle of bringing Choni back. Later, we'll figure out what to do."

"But what about his grandmother?" Pinchas insisted, spilling some of the hot chocolate. "Does she know that he's coming home?" he asked. "Did you tell her?"

Chaim sat back uneasily, explaining, "It's still too early in the morning to make any phone calls. We'll wait a bit, and then we'll call her."

"If you were his real *savta*, wouldn't you want to know immediately?" he asked his mother.

"Abba decided, and Abba knows what to do," Dinah said. "It's wrong, even dangerous, to wake up elderly people suddenly and give them this kind of news. It's better to wait. You too, Pinchas: Don't rush to call your friends. Wait for a more reasonable hour."

"And when are you going to tell Choni?" Pinchas repeated his earlier question.

Chaim sighed, "Go back to bed, sleepyhead. You'll need strength for the coming day. It's still very early in the morning."

Pinchas sighed in resignation and headed back to his room. He planned to eavesdrop on his parents' conversation in the kitchen. Instead, he fell asleep immediately and dreamt about being reunited with Choni.

In the kitchen, Pinchas' questions were discussed. "Pinchas raised a really serious issue," Chaim said. "Choni's *savta* is here in the country. She will demand to see her grandson, whatever it takes. And at the same time — "

"We cannot expose him to any additional trauma at this time. He'll need time to recover. Mrs. Kahn will have to understand that," Dinah interrupted her husband. "Under no circumstances can the child learn about his parents right now. I'll submit a complaint to the court. This time I — "

"Calm yourself. Emotional outbursts are not going to help," he gently reminded her.

He thought quietly for a few minutes. Dinah's tears disturbed him. "We can't even rejoice at Choni's homecoming," Dinah repeated several times, sobbing relentlessly. "Why did she come here? What did she want to achieve?"

"Maybe she knew that after Choni is released, we would want a break from the custody issue," Chaim suggested. "And they are determined to minimize that delay."

"I won't let them. He's my child. I invested my soul, my whole life into that child," Dinah cried.

Chaim declared, "We cannot go to a Rav for advice and then ignore him. Rav Katz told me to treat Mrs. Kahn courteously. I intend to follow his instructions. We only want what is good for the boy, right?"

"Yes, of course," she responded with difficulty.

At 6 o'clock in the morning, the phone began ringing with the first calls. The early risers who had already heard the good news hurried to call the Binder family and congratulate them. They were relatives and close friends, none of whom knew Choni's secret. They heartily rejoiced with them over their son's release.

In between receiving phone calls, Chaim and Dinah called all their children with the happy news of the freed hostages. They phoned Yoav first.

"I don't believe it." He was overcome with emotion. "This goes against all predictions. No one thought they would get out of there alive," he whispered. "I behaved optimistically for your sake, Ima. But honestly, I was sure they were finished."

The rejoicing of the siblings reinforced how much Choni was part of their family. In honor of Choni's return, Chaim allowed Pinchas to stay home from school. At 7 o'clock, Chaim went out to the car. "I'm going to *daven*. On the way back, I'll stop at Mrs. Kahn's hotel and give her the good news. I'd prefer not doing it over the telephone."

"Maybe someone already told her," Dinah suggested. "The rescue operation is not a secret. I imagine the news has already reached many countries." She found it difficult to forgive Mrs. Kahn's behavior on Shabbos, despite all Dinah's attempts at civility.

"It's all right. I'll go anyway and inform her in more detail. Do you want to send her some cake or breakfast?"

"Of course."

A sense of joy and relief enveloped Dinah and helped to mitigate the negative feelings toward Rivkah, whom she felt had been extremely impolite during Shabbos. She put a few slices of cake on a plate and included a note saying: "*Baruch Hashem*, Who has brought us to this moment. Call us if you need anything."

Chaim took the package and left for *shul*, deciding to visit Rivkah after *Shacharis*. He found it very difficult to concentrate on *davening*. All of the friends and well-wishers coming over to congratulate him did not help either. After *davening*, he made his way to Mrs. Kahn's hotel.

A courteous receptionist gave him Rivkah's room number. He went up to the third floor and knocked lightly on the door.

"Just a moment."

Two nerve-wracking minutes later, the door opened, and a red-eyed Mrs. Kahn stood in the doorway.

"Nu, *baruch Hashem*," she said before he could open his mouth. "I imagine you came to tell me the good news. My husband and children already called me. Thank you for bothering." She was confused and excited at the same time.

"It's quite all right." Chaim put the plate on the table. "If you need anything, don't hesitate to ask."

Rivkah smiled a tired smile. "I presume you plan to go to meet him at the airport. I want to come." She voiced her request in a belligerent manner, which reminded them of the unpleasant Shabbos she had spent in their midst. "I hope you understand, Reb Chaim, we are overcome with emotion. At times like this, I find the moment ripe for forgiveness and moving on."

"Of course," replied Chaim, who was, at this point, completely baffled.

"May I come over to your house?" asked Rivkah matter-of-factly.

Chaim offered to drive her over. Why should she have to call a taxi? The plane was not scheduled to land until 10 o'clock. He could bring her to the house now, and then go on to the airport. No, she was not yet ready to leave. She would have to take a taxi to the Binders' home by herself before it was time to leave for the airport.

Chaim assented, "Whatever you wish. We'll be at home," he informed her as he left her room.

❧❀❀❧

Soon after Chaim returned home, Rivkah knocked on the Binders' front door. The house was full of visitors who had come to wish the family well and to congratulate them on Choni's imminent return.

As soon as Dinah opened the door, Rivkah fell into Dinah's arms. "*Baruch Hashem* we have reached this moment," Dinah whispered as they struggled to withhold tears. All the previous anger, humiliation, and misunderstandings suddenly vanished. They were replaced by laughter, smiles, and good will.

"Look at how many people came to rejoice with you," Rivkah remarked, noticing the many eyes in the room now focused on her.

"They have come to rejoice in our joint celebration," Dinah responded.

One of the girls assumed responsibility for Rivkah, while the rest worked to tidy up the house. Dinah went to organize Choni's room, although it was perfectly clean.

When the well-wishers left, Rivkah asked, "When are we going to the airport?"

"Hmm." Shira decided to pass the question to her mother. "It would be better for you to ask my parents directly. I know that they prefer to go to the airport by themselves. We will all greet Choni here at the house."

"But I'm coming along," announced Pinchas.

"You — of course. Without you, how could Choni come back?" his sister replied with a smile.

Rivkah went over to Dinah to discuss the trip to the airport. "Are you sure you want to come along?" Dinah asked.

"This would be my first opportunity to see my grandson since he was a baby," Rivkah answered.

Dinah sighed. *We are in trouble again,* she thought. She wanted to ask, *Mrs. Kahn, why does the boy have to suffer for all our sins and mistakes?* But she controlled herself and kept quiet. She asked Rivkah to step into the guest room, where they could converse without interruption.

"Look, Mrs. Kahn. The boy doesn't know he is adopted. As far as he knows, he's returning home to his parents," Dinah began with obvious discomfort. "I think it would be shocking to drop this emotional bomb on Elchanan at the airport. Don't you think you are rushing things?"

Rivkah answered without thinking, "It's been ten years since I've seen my dear grandson. Am I made of steel? I have the opportunity to see him, and I want to do so. This is a basic right of a grandmother."

In an instant, they reverted to the starting point: mutually intolerant and impatient.

"I don't think it's a good idea to tell him in the airport, Mrs. Kahn. He has just been through a traumatic experience! We must first make sure he is emotionally stable, considering all that he has endured. After all, he's only a 10-year-old child."

Dinah tried her best not to antagonize Mrs. Kahn with harsh words. But she knew she could not back down. She had to be firm.

"Mrs. Kahn, you are welcome to wait in our house. When Choni arrives, we will introduce you as the aunt that he was supposed to meet. Please respect our wishes, and don't say a word to him about his past or future."

Dinah did not request, she instructed, which infuriated Rivkah.

CHAPTER
FORTY-ONE

A t exactly 9:43 in the morning, the Hercules plane landed at the Tel Nof airfield. Doctors, psychologists, and a table full of refreshments greeted the hostages.

Choni searched the faces in the crowd, hoping to see his parents and the rest of his family. Instead, there were strangers there to welcome him and he felt very alone and confused.

"When are we going to Abba?" he asked Mr. Schick.

"Just have a bit more patience, Choni. We've already waited such a long time. It won't be much longer," Yehudah Schick said calmly to Choni, but he was physically and emotionally drained. He only wanted to get some sleep, which was impossible with all the commotion surrounding the hostages' rescue.

General Shlomo Gazit greeted the hostages in the name of the government and the army. He explained to them, in Hebrew and in French, "You have witnessed a military operation of the

IDF. Do not share what you have seen with anyone else." He went on to explain why talking about the operation could prove detrimental to the army.

They boarded the plane again, this time headed to the international airport at Lod.

"There they'll be waiting for us for sure?" asked Choni impatiently.

Freida Schick, distracted by her husband's condition, tried to deal with Choni's needs and fears. "Yes, they'll be waiting there for you. Then you can say goodbye to us."

"Goodbye and thank you very much," Choni corrected her as he shyly looked down. He realized he had not been easy to handle, but he had allowed himself to behave as any other child his age would. Was he to blame that his parents had sent him on a trip all alone?

Freida smiled. They were not expecting a crowd of relatives at the airport. She wanted to take Yehudah straight to the doctor, and from there, home. Hopefully, a warm bed and decent food would help him recover from one of the most harrowing weeks of his life.

☙❀❀❧

While the Binders were on the way to the airport, Rivkah told the Binder girls who stayed behind that she was returning to her hotel.

"But you agreed to wait here for Choni," they protested.

"I'm going to rest a bit, and then I'll come back. I don't want to be in the middle of all the excitement," Rivkah declared.

She ordered a taxi, and agreed that one of the girls could accompany her downstairs. "Goodbye, Mrs. Kahn. Don't forget that we are expecting you back later," Shira said.

Mrs. Kahn was increasingly impressed with the girls. So sensitive and well mannered. *And among their other traits,* Rivkah thought to herself, *perhaps they are also endowed with excellent acting skills. None of them mentioned a word about what happened on Shabbos. Is it possible their mother did not tell them? Typical for this family.*

She got into the taxi and asked to go to Lod airport.

"Are you also going to meet the rescued hostages?" the driver joked. "You're not the only one. Did you know anyone who was kidnapped?" He laughed at his own joke, and then was quiet for the rest of the trip. He was pleased that he would also be present at the historic moment when the hostages returned to their families.

The huge crowd at the airport confused Rivkah. She did not know how to locate the Binders. After some hesitation, she found a place to stand that provided a decent view of the proceedings. Several journalists stood near her, but she paid no attention to them. They assumed she was just a bored old woman who had come to watch the excitement, and they did not interview her.

After fifteen minutes of searching, she found the Binders waiting off to the side.

Rivkah put on a pair of sunglasses. She knew the Binders would identify her eventually, but figured that with all the excitement and confusion, the glasses would give her a few extra moments.

While Rivkah was observing the gathering crowd that swelled as the plane landed, the Binder family's excitement grew.

As the plane touched down, Dinah's tears started flowing.

"But Ima, you haven't even seen Choni yet," Pinchas said quietly to her. "Why are you crying already?"

She did not answer, but her sobbing grew stronger. She felt that Choni was not a nephew, or an adopted child. He was her son. She was able to appreciate him, to love him and, mainly, to rejoice at his safe return.

Two soldiers turned to an elderly couple holding a huge bouquet of flowers. They asked the couple a number of questions, and finally told them to accompany them. Chaim Binder, who was watching the couple, remarked, "Looks like a relative of theirs was injured or killed. I do hope Choni is okay."

There were rumors of several casualties. Dinah closed her eyes in terror. She tried to step aside, as if to remove herself from the soldiers' line of vision.

Wiping away their tears, the old couple followed the uniformed men. Dinah cried along with them. "They didn't come up to talk to us, so we have nothing to worry about," Chaim tried to calm Dinah, although he was sufficiently worried himself. He thought, *Until I see Choni, I won't be able to relax.*

"Here's the plane," they both murmured in anticipation. The Binders watched the taxiing aircraft. The door opened, and people started descending the steps.

Excitement overcame the onlookers, who burst into loud shouts, applause, and song. The families of the hostages pushed up close to the stairs to wait for their loved ones. Within a few moments, the entire area filled with rejoicing and tears at the reunions between loved ones.

Dinah feared that the tension would completely overtake her as she waited for Choni. "Do you see Mr. Schick? Look for him," she begged Chaim and Pinchas.

"I want everyone to calm down," Chaim called out. "People are still coming out of the plane. Apparently, the Schicks are taking their time. Please, take it easy."

Another five minutes went by, and then Dinah recognized Freida Schick dragging a large bag behind her. "Here they are!" Dinah called out.

Right behind Mrs. Schick came Yehudah and Choni.

He seemed smaller, thinner than before he had left, with a fearful look in his eyes. Dinah felt her heart go out to the child.

Pinchas could not restrain himself. "Choni, Choni, we're here," he yelled. But Choni did not hear him over all the singing, clapping, and yelling that was going on all around.

Pinchas ran anxiously toward him, forgetting to ask his parents for permission. When he was a few feet away, Choni noticed him, and immediately afterward, he saw his parents. He stood frozen in place, as if in shock, staring at his mother. She smiled warmly at him and waved, tears blurring her eyes.

Choni started to cry, and Pinchas hugged him.

Choni wiped away his tears, smiled at Pinchas, and then ran straight to his parents.

"*Shalom*, my child," Dinah said, leaning toward him.

"*Shalom*, Ima," he said, and as he said these first words, he felt tears flowing down his face.

His father embraced him tightly, saying, "*Baruch Hashem*, you're back. Are you all right? Did they hurt you?"

"I need a drink," Choni said in a small voice.

Dinah went to get him a cup of cold water. "Drink up, we want you to feel good, Choni. *Baruch Hashem*, you are finally free."

The small group went to sit in a corner, so obviously pleased to be together again. Choni looked from one family member to another and saw that they were all staring at him and smiling.

"What are you looking at?" Choni asked in confusion. "It's just me."

"Of course it's you. But you have no idea how much we missed you — "

"We wanted to see you," Pinchas added. "To believe that it was really you. Was it scary over there?"

"A little. But I don't want to talk about it now."

Choni turned toward Dinah. "I thought about you the whole time," he told her. She was so overwhelmed, she nearly passed out.

"Me too, Choni, and I *davened* for you. I never stopped *davening*."

"And what did Abba do?" Choni demanded. He turned around and discovered that his father had disappeared. "Where is Abba, anyway?"

The three of them looked around until they finally found him standing with the Schicks, listening closely to what Yehudah was saying.

"What are they talking about?" Pinchas did not understand.

Choni's face darkened. No doubt, Mr. Schick was reporting the friendship with Michel and Gerard. Strangely, he did not even see the boys. Choni squinted his eyes and looked in all directions. They had vanished as soon as they had descended from the plane. Where could they have gone?

"Are you looking for someone?" Dinah asked.

"No, I'm just looking around — "

"You must want to get home already, right?" said Pinchas.

Choni was confused. His family, who missed him so much, was at his side. But for some reason instead of feeling complete, he felt a gaping hole in his soul.

"It's all right, you're allowed to be mixed up. You've experienced something terribly unpleasant," Dinah said. "Let's go to the car. It's time to be heading home." Choni liked the idea because it would give him a chance to unwind and breathe more easily. He turned around one more time in a vain search for Michel, and then walked with his mother and brother toward the exit.

"What's the matter, Choni?" wondered Pinchas. "You're acting so strange."

"No, it's — " He reddened a bit, and suddenly noticed an elderly woman wearing sunglasses looking at him. Or was she looking at the people accompanying him?

He was confused. He had not expected his return home to be like this.

"Choni, wait," he heard his father say. He stopped for a moment, but did not automatically respond with the usual words: "Yes, Abba."

He suddenly remembered that they were not his real parents, and that his brother was really a cousin. This realization, along with all the excitement of the day, made it difficult for him to express himself.

"So tell us something, Choni. It must have been frightening over there, no?" Chaim asked as he wrapped his arm around him. Such a fatherly embrace, so warm and supportive, yet Choni wanted to run away.

"We were O.K. Mr. Schick must have told you everything."

"No, he didn't tell me very much. We talked about other matters."

About Michel and Gerard, and the big secret that was uncovered? Choni's head swam just from the thought of it. If his father knows, let him be the one to mention it first. Choni was not going to say a word about his adoption. He did not have the strength to confront his parents with the truth. The matter could remain concealed forever.

"You seem lost in thought, Choni," Chaim remarked as he tried to pull Choni closer. Choni, however, remained stiff, cold, and aloof. What was wrong?

"It's all right, Choni. I understand that you need some time to unwind," Chaim tried to reassure his son, and maybe himself as well. "You don't have to be afraid now that you are back with us."

"I'm not afraid," Choni replied.

Just before he got into the car as they were leaving the airport, he spotted Michel and Gerard getting into a taxi. His eyes lit up when he saw them. After all, they had been his friends for the past week. Michel also seemed excited. Choni hesitantly raised his hand to wave goodbye, then got into the car.

The entire way home, he pretended to be asleep. He did not have any strength for more questions.

"He just doesn't know how to deal with it," he heard his mother explain to his father and to Pinchas.

CHAPTER FORTY-TWO

The moment the Binder family got into their car to go home, Rivkah rushed toward the line of taxis. Most of them were occupied, and she signaled impatiently with her hand for a free cab. *How rude to subject newly arrived tourists to this wait. Surely they could provide a few more taxis,* she thought. It took her fifteen minutes to secure a cab.

She gave her hotel's address to the driver in a weak voice, and asked him to drive as fast as possible.

"What's the rush, ma'am?" the driver mumbled more to himself than to her. "Everyone is rejoicing today because the hostages were rescued. Just you seem — " He did not know if she understood Hebrew, so he stopped talking.

They reached the hotel quickly. At the reception desk, she requested a line for an international telephone call. The desk clerk pointed to an available phone.

"Moishe, it's me," she said into the receiver.

"*Baruch Hashem.*" His voice sounded hoarse and exhausted, but relieved. The last few days had been very difficult, and both of them felt that they had aged considerably during this time.

"Rivkah, I heard they are free and back in the country. Did you see our Elchanan?"

"I saw him."

"Did you talk to him?" he asked in a yearning voice.

"Not yet."

"Why not?"

She explained that the Binders had not let her go along with them to the airport, and how she had taken a taxi there by herself. She had watched them for a while, then witnessed their reunion.

"He doesn't look happy with them," she said decisively.

"You cannot judge anything based on this meeting," Moishe said, more even handed about the matter. His mind was as clear as a 20-year-old's, particularly when dealing with such problems. "We are dealing with a child who has been through a severe trauma. He was surely emotional and his responses may be abnormal."

"You're right. He seemed to be close to Dinah, but he barely spoke to Chaim, his uncle, his father's brother."

"You see! You cannot draw any conclusions from a meeting after a week's absence, and under such dreadful conditions." Moishe exulted in his victory.

Their conversation was becoming lengthy and costly. "I've got to end now, or I'll have to pay an extra charge," Rivkah informed him.

"When will you meet him?" asked Moishe.

"When they invite me again. Really, I left their house on my own, but I'll wait for a new invitation to go back."

"Call me afterward."

"Okay. Moishe — "

"What?"

"Don't forget that he doesn't know we are his grandparents. Don't raise your expectations. He might even be angry at us."

"You're right." His voice trailed off. He sounded lonely. Rivkah was annoyed. Why wasn't Shimon or one of the others with him?

She restrained her anger and made a mental note to tell her daughters to visit their father while she was abroad. True, each of them was busy with her own family, but that did not give them license to completely ignore their father.

Her thoughts shifted to the here and now. In an hour, she would meet her grandson. The last time she had seen him, he had been a baby who barely smiled. Today, he is grown up, almost a young man. Rivkah was nearly overwhelmed by emotion.

She waited in the hotel lobby. After an hour and a half, she felt insulted. Was the Binders' family reunion so joyful that they had forgotten about the aged grandmother? Time passed by slowly, and every minute that passed intensified her rage and despondency.

ജ്ഞ

"Choni, you're so quiet. Tell us something." The atmosphere in the car could best be described as gloomy.

"Give him time to recover and get back to himself," Dinah insisted. "He's a little overwhelmed right now."

Choni smiled at his considerate mother. She knew just what he needed.

Pinchas, however, was impatient and confused. While he felt a brotherly relationship with Choni, the knowledge that he was not his real brother served to intensify his desire to protect his cousin who had no immediate family. His parents had warned him not to breathe a word to Choni about the grandmother who was presently in the country. He was also forbidden to mention the adoption issue, until his parents would decide how and when to reveal the subject to Choni.

Choni sat quietly in the backseat of the car, thinking bitter thoughts. *They are not my parents,* he kept on repeating to himself in disbelief. *This brother in the car is not my brother. They are just pretending. I'm really an orphan.*

This train of thought rapidly brought tears to his eyes.

Looking over at him, Dinah said, "It's all right to cry after enduring such a week," and she handed him some tissues. "It really was a grueling week, wasn't it?"

He nodded.

"Is there anyone at home?" he asked vaguely.

"Of course. The whole family is waiting for you, even your nieces and nephews. They're all there to see you."

Choni smiled weakly. All he really wanted to do was to crawl into bed, deep under the covers. He felt as if he had not slept in a bed in years.

"Choni, what's the first thing you're going to do when you get home?" asked Pinchas.

Chaim and Dinah waited expectantly for his answer. He thought for a moment. "I'm going straight into the shower. In our hotel in Entebbe, they forgot about that little detail." The rest of the family burst into laughter, and the mood in the car quickly changed. It became cheerful and upbeat.

Dinah pulled some candies from her purse. Handing two to Choni, she advised him to eat slowly. After a week of "dieting," it was important that he not overeat.

The sweets further lightened the atmosphere, and in that high-spirited mood, the family arrived home. They let Choni and Pinchas enter the house first. Chaim wanted to go in together with them, but Dinah signaled for him to wait.

"What are we going to do about Mrs. Kahn?" she asked.

"Is she upstairs?"

"I think so. She knows that he's scheduled to come home. What are we going to say to him?"

Chaim stopped in his tracks and sighed. His policy was to achieve a consensus with as much harmony and good will as possible. The Kahns were making this nearly impossible.

"Let's go upstairs and introduce him to the aunt he was supposed to visit in France. I'm sure that he will not be very polite."

"That's for sure," Dinah agreed. "He must hold them partially responsible for the trauma of the past week."

They headed up the stairs, but Chaim was still unsettled. "Mrs. Kahn doesn't bother me as much as Choni does. He was acting very strange. Didn't you notice?"

"Maybe it's normal after enduring such a terrifying experience," replied Dinah in a calm voice.

"Unless I'm making some huge mistake, I would say that he practically ignored me."

Dinah would not accept that. "You're imagining it. It looks like you also need to recover from this week," his wife replied.

"That I need to recuperate is certain. But I'm not usually given to fantasies. We'll see. It's not going to be easy. Choni will find it hard to return to his regular life and schedule. Sending him on this trip was a huge mistake, and he knows it."

They entered the house quietly, but the gloomy atmosphere had given way to an excitingly joyful one. For one thing, the grandmother was not there. The girls explained that she had insisted on going back to her hotel, causing Dinah to sigh in relief.

The grandchildren jumped all over Choni in excitement, while his older brothers and sisters watched with obvious delight in their eyes. Music played gently in the background and the dining-room table was laden with mouth-watering pastries and sweets.

The family surrounded Choni with love and warmth, and he began to forget some of the painful thoughts that had disturbed him on the way home. He started to feel like one of the family again.

"Are we celebrating some important occasion?" he asked with a smile. "Did you all come here for me?"

"Just wait, the real party has not yet begun," Chaim said, patting him on the shoulder. "We are going to make a big *seudas hoda'ah*. Then you'll see how we make parties." Everyone laughed in response.

All at once, Choni reminded himself about the wounded and the dead, and the elderly woman who had been left in a hospital in Entebbe. What had become of her? His face darkened. "I really do have to thank Hashem for allowing me to return unhurt. Not everyone came back," he remarked wistfully.

The family did not allow him to wallow in his memories by himself. They bombarded him with a thousand questions. How did the terrorists hijack the plane? Where were they? How did they sleep? What did they eat?

Choni enjoyed relating the really tense moments, even scaring some of his older nephews. He told them about the silence in the plane, the frightening terrorists, and the tasteless food. He also mentioned the adults who sat and played card games all day because they had nothing else to do.

He deliberately omitted any reference to his friends Michel and Gerard, but told about Yehudah Schick and his aches and pains.

"We owe the Schicks a huge debt of gratitude," Chaim suddenly recalled. "He was not well when he returned. He nearly fainted in the airport. I hope he's feeling better now."

"We should buy them a nice present, visit them, and wish him a *refuah sheleimah*," Dinah announced.

"Why buy a present?" Choni did not understand.

"For taking care of you during such a difficult time."

"I wouldn't baby-sit for you even in a calm situation," offered Yoav. They all broke into good-natured laughter.

All this talk actually reminded Choni about something else. These people weren't his parents. His aunt and uncle had agreed to take him in. Would he have to give them an expensive present one day too?

"Why are you so quiet, Choni? Tell us more," the other family members demanded. But Choni had quickly tired of all the commotion.

"I'm so tired. I really want to rest," he said in a monotone.

"He does need a great deal of rest," Chaim ruled. "Many thanks to everyone who came over for this little celebration, but it's enough for now. Choni is exhausted, and needs some quiet. Right, Choni?"

He nodded to his father in agreement, and went to talk to Dinah. The rift between Choni and his father was not apparent to everyone, yet Dinah and Pinchas noticed, and wondered about it.

Chaim was hurt, but decided not to attribute particular significance to it. He thought that the stress of being held captive under such frightening circumstances could be causing Choni to behave strangely. Give him time. Tomorrow, things would be back to normal.

Choni luxuriated in the pleasure of a hot shower after a week of not taking one. He emerged clean and refreshed, and he headed for his bedroom.

Bed? How long since had he seen his bed?

Everything in the room was clean, fresh, and polished. Choni thought he was dreaming. His mother came in bearing a bowl of hot soup. "Here's something that will help get you back on your feet, instead of just cake and chocolates. Eat up, and get some rest," Dinah suggested with concern.

"Thank you, Ima." His voice was slightly hoarse, and his eyes were full of tears. "I thought about your food when I was there."

"And you didn't think about me?" Chaim stood in the doorway, having asked the teasing question.

Choni smiled but did not reply. He finished his soup and collapsed into bed.

Everyone in the house was particularly careful not to make noise that night so as not to wake Choni. After a few hours, however, Dinah emitted a restrained cry. "Mrs. Kahn! We completely forgot Mrs. Kahn," she reminded her husband. "I'm sure she's angry at us for a change." The conflict was still unresolved, and now the real battle was about to begin.

CHAPTER FORTY-THREE

"Annette, I told you, I'm doing everything possible to get us tickets to Israel."

"I'm so worried," Annette said in a broken voice. "Gerard and Michel did not even call to tell us they're okay."

"I checked with the Foreign Ministry. Their names do not appear on the list of killed or wounded, so they must be all right."

"So why aren't they calling? Maybe they're missing."

Georges sat back in silence. He did not generally allow himself unnecessary talk on the phone. In fact, he decided to go home and tell his wife about the telephone call he had received at his office. He did not want to tell her over the phone. The line was not secure, and using it might put Gerard into even greater danger.

Gerard had thoughtfully called the office instead of home.

Georges knew about his son's dangerous relationship with the gang of murderous extremists who wanted to take revenge on him. Gerard would have to stay out of France for the next few months. It was best if his former "friends" did not know where he was living.

Georges gave a few last-minute instructions to his secretary, and left the office. Even important customers did not interest him when his sons' lives were at stake. He noticed how his attitude toward money had changed since the start of the hijacking. He had two sons, and did not plan to lose them. No way.

He pressed the accelerator and hurriedly made his way home.

"Annette," he announced, "They phoned, and they're fine."

"When did they phone? And why didn't you call me right away?"

"I wanted to tell you in person." He fibbed a bit, to protect her from the unpleasant news. No mother in the world would want to hear that a murderous gang was threatening her son. What point was there to tell her about the threats? Could she do anything about them? It was bad enough enduring the hijacking. Let Annette enjoy the knowledge that her sons were alive and well.

"So when are we flying to Israel?" Annette asked eagerly.

"I don't know. The travel agent was supposed to leave me a message either at home or at the office. Don't worry, you can rely on him to do his job."

Georges went outside to smoke a cigar. Annette could not tolerate the smell of tobacco in the house, nor did she like to see him smoking.

He noticed a folded piece of paper sticking out of the mailbox. He walked over and pulled the paper out. On it were some sloppy, handwritten words.

"Gerard was not saved. Just a temporary respite. We'll catch him. He's cooperating with the Jews. We'll avenge ourselves on him."

The words were written at a slant, in an effort to avoid identification. The paper was old and crumpled, adding an element of fear to the already threatening atmosphere.

Georges folded the incriminating note and put it in his pocket. He did not plan to show it to Annette, who was already hysterical about her sons. True, Gerard had not wanted to travel to Israel, but now he would have to remain there for the foreseeable future. Georges was secretly pleased with the developments. Gerard would finally learn the truth. Until now, he had been ashamed of his Jewishness, and had always tried to flee from it. Now, he was learning that it was impossible to run away.

Georges had already learned that lesson. He was a child of the Holocaust, and he had learned the hard way that one cannot escape his Jewishness or his Jewish fate. He survived the war along with his parents, enduring the worst imaginable conditions. They lived with false identities, using forged papers, and prayed for the end of the war. But he did not follow in his parents' footsteps. Georges grew up and grew away from his parents' way of life. The waves of anti-Semitism did not faze him, but Gerard's membership in an anti-Semitic gang did frighten him. He would have liked to return to Judaism, but it was very hard at this stage. He realized that the boys were grown up now and had their own opinions that he could not change. He realized again how right his father had been about trying to flee the inevitable Jewish fate.

Georges lit another cigar. Annette would not be pleased, but he was at his wit's end. Even in Israel, they would need assistance. Gerard would need a new identity, a place to live, and, most important, new friends.

"Georges, you have a telephone call," his wife called from the window.

He came in, and was pleased to hear the travel agent's voice. "Good news. There's a flight leaving today at 5 o'clock."

"Let's hope that security will be adequate," Georges remarked. "I don't have time to visit Entebbe."

After hanging up, he told his wife the news. Annette was thrilled and immediately began packing their suitcases. The boys would need new clothing. They surely would not be able to get to a washing machine in Israel; who knew how they looked?

She decided afterward to prepare some of the boys' favorite foods. She smiled and hummed to herself amid the delicious kitchen aroma. Georges, however, was nervous.

He must be blaming himself for this, thought Annette. *The trip was his idea. Next time, he'd be well advised to listen to a mother's intuition.*

Georges had different thoughts rushing through his head. *Poor, innocent Annette,* he thought. *You have no idea what's waiting for us. If you did, I doubt you'd be singing and smiling to yourself over the stove.*

At 2 o'clock they left the house for the airport. Georges was quiet and reflective during their drive. Annette asked a number of times where the boys were staying. Her husband replied that they would learn their address only when they arrived in Israel.

After the plane took off, Annette commented, "Strange that the boys did not call me. What would be so terrible if they spoke to a worried mother?"

"They couldn't call," Georges explained patiently. "They used up all their money, and they didn't have any friends to borrow from. Don't forget that they are alone over there."

"So where are they staying?"

Georges clenched his teeth. He would not divulge their location, even to Annette. The passengers were all Jews flying to Israel for various reasons. No French tourists would risk a trip to Israel until things settled down. Georges kept his mouth closed, just in case.

The possibility of some unexpected surprises weighed on Georges' mind. He decided that the members of Gerard's gang were too young and inexperienced to charter a plane and hire a private investigator to follow him. Come what may, he decided he would do whatever was necessary to protect his son's life.

৯৵৵৽৽৹

Rivkah sat in the hotel lobby, her eyes swollen with tears. Four hours had passed. It was late afternoon, and the sun was setting in Israel.

"Mrs. Kahn, you have a telephone call at the desk," the receptionist announced on the public address system. Maybe they finally remembered her, the aged grandmother, and her right to see her grandson.

She took the telephone, intending to be magnanimous and forgiving. And most of all — to see her grandson Elchanan face to face.

It was the first time she was disappointed to hear Moishe's voice.

"Don't I deserve to hear how the meeting with our grandson went?" he asked with a touch of reproof in his voice.

"Surely you deserve it," she replied in an attempt to assuage his feelings. "But I don't have anything to report."

"Why not? Didn't he talk to you?" Moishe sighed bitterly.

"Not at all. He didn't even see me. We didn't even meet yet."

"I don't understand," Moishe became agitated. "You had an

agreement that after they brought him home, you would be allowed to see him."

"True," Rivkah explained. "I was sure they would come calling, to bring me to their house after they prepared him for the meeting. I thought the obliging Binder family would remember me. I guess they didn't. Looking back, I'm just surprised I ever expected it in the first place."

"So you're just sitting around?" Her husband began to get angry.

"Sitting…" She held back her tears. Of what use were tears when Moishe was abroad, unable to help? "I must see them interacting as a family. I want to see up close how Chaim treats Choni. I already mentioned that I suspect — "

"Do you want me to come to Israel?"

"Let's wait a bit." In fact, she liked the idea. Yes, she definitely would like him to come here. It would give her moral support. But she did not want to pressure him. First, let her see Choni, talk to him a bit. Then she would decide what to do.

"Call me when you've met him."

"*Im yirtzeh Hashem.*"

She went slowly back up to her room. It had been a long conversation. Most of their savings would be spent on Sarah's son. He deserved it.

Two hours later, a knock came at the door.

"Who is it, please?"

"Dinah Binder," came the voice from the other side.

She opened the door, trembling slightly. She thought that Dinah had brought Elchanan along, which caused her to smile and put her in a forgiving mood. She was bitterly disappointed to see Dinah enter the room alone.

"How are you, Mrs. Kahn?"

"*Baruch Hashem.* What do you want?" Her change in mood

was reflected in the tone of her voice.

"I came to tell you that Choni arrived utterly exhausted. He talked a little, ate a little, and went right to sleep. We thought he would wake up after a few hours, but it appears that he's asleep for the night. As you surely realize, the stress of the past week has taken its toll."

"You're right. But, he must have been awake for a few hours, because the whole family was there," Rivkah asserted combatively. There was a limit to telling lies.

Dinah blinked uncomfortably. "I'm sorry, Mrs. Kahn, I thought you would be in our house when we arrived, so that there wouldn't be any problems. We were surprised to find out that you had left. In any case, the time with Choni flew by very quickly. By the time we noticed, he was just too tired to talk anymore. Besides, I don't think he was in the right mood to meet new relatives."

"I'm his grandmother," she reminded her.

"Of course," Dinah acknowledged. She added, "I came to tell you that our home is open to you, and you are welcome to stay in our guest room. In the morning, you can meet Choni when he is fresh and attentive. We really would like you to come, Mrs. Kahn."

Rivkah deliberated. She did not look forward to sleeping alone in a hotel room, in a strange place. On the other hand, the Binder home was a source of some stinging memories.

"We really would like you to come," Dinah repeated, playing upon Rivkah's hesitation.

The feelings of bitterness and anger made Rivkah decide, "No, thank you. I prefer to stay here. When he wakes up, I'll be very grateful if you would bring him here."

"Wouldn't it be better to come to our house?" Dinah tried gently.

"No."

Rivkah felt that the war was not yet over. It would be in poor taste to clash with the family that had shown her such hospitality, but she wanted to see if they would keep their word and bring Choni to her.

She managed to get through a very bleak and unpleasant night. By 6 o'clock in the morning she was awake. Then she remembered that Elchanan would probably not awaken before 7 o'clock. Even then, it was likely he would still be tired and would want to sleep a few more hours. The poor child had not slept normally for an entire week.

She *davened* and descended to the dining room for a simple breakfast. She went back up to her room afterward and opened the window, staring down at the noisy street below. When would Chaim Binder's blue car arrive?

She spent an hour out on the balcony, and finally decided to head down to the lobby again. Another elderly woman tried to strike up a conversation with her, but she could barely understand a word of what she was saying. The woman was mumbling, and anyway, Rivkah was not in the mood for small talk.

It was 11 o'clock, and they were taking their time. How long would they continue to torment her?

At 11:30, Chaim Binder finally arrived, out of breath.

"Choni refuses to leave the house. Please come with me," he said courteously. She did not know if this was a ruse or not, but she did not hesitate to join him. What choice did she have?

A moment before climbing up the stairs to the Binders' apartment, her heart began to pound wildly. In a few seconds, she would see Elchanan. It would be like greeting Sarah again, the past, the future. She began to cry.

CHAPTER FORTY-FOUR

t took them until 9:30 to awaken Choni. Even then, he was groggy and disoriented. In a hoarse voice, he asked if they had come to rescue him.

"You're already home, sweetie," Dinah calmed him. "You have to *daven* and eat something. Then you can go back to sleep."

He stretched his arms. "I can't believe I'm home," he called out excitedly. "I was just next to all of them. Next to Mich — " He stopped himself.

Dinah did not notice his slip of the tongue. She was just pleased to see that he was in a happy mood. "Wash your hands and get dressed," she told him. "I'll have breakfast waiting for you after *shul*, including your favorite cornflakes."

The morning started in a jovial manner. For a change, his father was home. Choni went off to *daven Shacharis* at the last *minyan* in the *shul* nearby. His appearance there caused a great stir, and all the men present congratulated him on his safe return.

By the time he got home and sat down to breakfast, the telephone calls had begun. He spoke to the principal of the *cheider*, who described in glowing terms how all the boys had *davened* for his well-being. He talked to his teacher, and even to a few of his classmates.

Suddenly, without warning, it happened. No one knew exactly how or why. One minute Choni was describing the fear they all had experienced at Entebbe, the terrible food, and the uncomfortable mattresses, and then all at once — silence. His eyes glazed over with a bitter memory, and he withdrew from everyone around him.

Chaim and Dinah immediately noticed the mood change. They interpreted it as part of Choni's very natural need to recuperate from the most frightening experience of his young life.

"But what about the grandmother?" Dinah whispered to Chaim. "We have again forgotten about her."

"Maybe he'll agree to come along with me to visit her," Chaim replied. "On second thought, I don't think he'll agree," he concluded.

Choni's response was unequivocal. "I'm not going anywhere right now. I don't want to meet any aunts, no matter how old."

"It's a mitzvah and a *chesed*," Chaim explained patiently. "Your aunt was extremely worried about you and even felt guilty about having invited you to France. She wants to see that you are O.K. Yesterday, she wanted to come over here to visit you. We cannot turn down her request again today."

Choni dug in his heels and refused to budge.

"All right," Chaim said as he got off the sofa, "you don't have to come with me to the hotel. I am going to bring her over here to the house. She's coming to visit you, and I expect you to behave like a mature boy."

Choni went into his room, while Dinah used the few remaining minutes to straighten up the living room. Something was bothering her. It was Choni's behavior — his frightened eyes and strange expressions. It seemed as if he was in the midst of some emotional storm. "That's how children in distress behave," she once had heard a psychologist explain. Choni was showing all the appropriate signs.

She thought Choni blamed the Kahns for the hijacking, so they would find it very difficult to communicate with him. On one hand, she felt sorry for them, yet on the other, she felt a sense of relief. Now the grandparents would realize where things stood, and would leave things as they were.

Fifteen minutes later, Chaim opened the front door and cheerily greeted everyone. "Choni, where are you? Come greet your aunt," he called.

Pinchas, who had also stayed at home that day, looked curiously at the elderly "aunt" he recognized. Choni came out of his room and glanced at the flustered woman. "*Shalom*," he said calmly, and promptly headed into the kitchen.

Surprised, Mrs. Kahn swallowed hard and searched vainly for something to say.

Chaim, embarrassed, followed him into the kitchen and said sternly, "Your aunt wants to speak with you. Come here."

Choni looked blankly at the woman and muttered, "She's Pinchas' aunt, too. He can talk to her — "

"You're right, he is. But we're talking about you now. And I will not permit such inappropriate behavior in our house. Bring out the cake platter, go over to her immediately, and speak to her respectfully."

Dinah cast a warning glance at Chaim as she stepped into

the kitchen. It was unusual to have to force a child to talk to his aunt. In any case, this was the wrong time for this meeting to be taking place. Choni had to settle down and return to normal. In the meantime, Mrs. Kahn would have to wait patiently.

"Ima, what should I bring her?" Choni was behaving strangely. He was acting to fulfill his father's bidding, but he seemed to be angry with him. He would speak only to his mother, ignoring Chaim as he did.

"Here is a tray with glasses and cold drinks. Ask her if she would like coffee, instead." Dinah hurriedly cut the cakes she had prepared.

Choni walked out of the kitchen with the tray and found the elderly woman sitting in an armchair, looking confused.

"Would you like a cup of coffee?"

"No," she said, smiling faintly at him. "Thank you for offering. Actually, I would like to talk to you. Come sit down a little," she said, pointing to the armchair near hers.

As he sat on the chair, he began swaying nervously. The information he had learned while in Entebbe had seemed terrible. The present reality, however, seemed much worse.

He knew this woman was his grandmother, his mother's mother. She was his closest living relative. But she was so old, so foreign, and so aloof. And anyway, he did not know her. Nor was he interested in knowing her. He wanted to turn the clock all the way back to the way things used to be.

His father, standing at his side, whispered to him, "Speak to her."

Choni became irritated. This man was not his father, he was just an uncle who was pretending to be his father. They were all lying to him, but he knew the truth.

"How are you feeling?" he asked Mrs. Kahn politely.

"I'm very excited to see you, Elchanan," she said with a

distinct French accent. "The last time I saw you, you were a baby."

"And Pinchas?" He deliberately steered the conversation toward Pinchas. He pretended that everything was as he had previously known it to be.

"Pinchas, too — " she replied slowly. "We missed you very much. We wanted to see you. When your plane was hijacked, we were terribly worried about you."

"Because you were afraid you wouldn't get to see me?" Choni was trying to understand.

"Because we thought that — it doesn't matter — ," the elderly woman said as she poured herself something to drink.

"All right, so now I will not be traveling to France. I don't think I'll ever fly again. Please say hello to my uncle for me." He ended the conversation impudently. He was not interested in charades.

"Just a minute, Elchanan. Don't go." She fished in her pocket. "I wanted to give you a little present, but I seem to have forgotten it at the hotel," she muttered.

"I'm too old for presents," he glowered at her. "And if you do find it, you can give it to Pinchas. He is your nephew just as much as I am. He also deserves something."

"Choni!" Chaim shouted.

Choni was startled. Usually, such an outburst was followed by a slap. Would Abba do that in front of his purported grandmother? But suddenly his mother appeared at his side and explained, "Choni is still disoriented from the trauma of the hijacking, and all the flying. He is really a gentle, good-natured child. But right now, things are still difficult for him. Right, Choni?"

His mother's words were so warm and calming. She had discipline written all over her face, but her manner was soft and loving. Not like Chaim's outcry.

Choni nodded in agreement, somewhat embarrassed. "I'm very tired. I'd like to go rest now."

"Have you already eaten?" Mrs. Kahn was worried about him.

"Yes."

"Maybe there is something bothering you?" the aunt continued.

"You — " He wanted to blame her, but held back after he saw his father's expression.

Choni sauntered out of the living room while his mother stayed behind to chat with Choni's "aunt." His father followed him into the bedroom and closed the door. Choni stepped back, anticipating what was to come. He was not happy to be alone in a closed room with his father, or uncle, or anyone else.

"Would you like to tell me what that was all about?" Chaim asked sternly.

"I'm very tired. I want to sleep."

"Your conduct was absolutely unacceptable, even if you did just have a difficult experience," Chaim continued. "I expect to see a serious improvement in your behavior."

"All right."

Choni's laid-back attitude bothered Chaim. "You know what your aunt must be thinking? That you are an undisciplined child, lacking *chinuch*."

"So?"

"What do you mean 'so'?"

"She doesn't matter to me." Choni exuded an air of nonchalance, but his heart was pounding. Perhaps now his father would tell him that she is really his grandmother. If he does not, then maybe it was all made up, including the letter and Michel, who was rapidly fading from his memory. Maybe it was all false, and he could continue living his life as it was before his trip. Maybe the entire story was made up.

Suddenly, all of Michel's stories seemed unreliable. Why should he accept the word of a stranger? Who knows if he told the truth?

"Choni," his father said harshly, "what kind of talk is this? An elderly aunt comes from France to visit you, and you ignore her. She was extremely worried about you, you know — "

"Why did she remember me only now?"

"Because now we had decided that one of you should go visit her."

"Why not Pinchas?"

"Because they especially liked you as a baby. That's how aunts are sometimes."

So many explanations that sounded plausible. Choni stared silently at his father, wishing he could tell him about the letter. He wanted his father to reassure him and tell him it was all not true. Let him burst out laughing that those people managed to completely fool him.

But his father's nervous movements delivered a completely different message, and Choni was afraid that his father would bend down and explain that it was all true after all. At that moment, Chaim would cease being his father, and his mother would become his aunt. And he would have to go live with his estranged grandparents in France.

Hot tears flooded his eyes at the thought of all that could happen.

"Why are you crying, Choni?" his father asked in a soft voice, though not quite as soft as his mother's. "You know, you really do need some rest. I think you should stay here in your room and get some sleep."

"O.K."

Chaim left the room, leaving Choni to bury his face in his pillow and cry.

It was simply impossible that an aunt from France would come all this way just to visit him. It was also impossible that they would just send him there to live. Someone was lying to him. This was the real thing. Michel was telling the truth.

He stifled his cries, hoping that no one heard him. He could hear his mother's voice as she spoke to his "aunt." After he calmed down, he tried to listen to their conversation. They were speaking rapidly in French. Choni could understand a few words, and he listened silently, trying to decipher what they were saying.

His mother was insisting that he had to recuperate from the traumatic trip. The elderly "aunt" did not understand from what he needed to recover. In fact, she said, an entire day had gone by, and Choni still seemed very unsettled. And what kind of *chinuch* was this, what kind of behavior?

His mother apologized. She switched to Hebrew, to slow down the pace of the conversation, explaining to Mrs. Kahn that Choni was normally such a well-behaved boy, and she must be patient and understanding of his feelings.

Mrs. Kahn was angry, and she interrupted Dinah with a rapid string of French words that Choni did not understand.

Finally, the woman left the house, slamming the door behind her. Choni remained in his bed.

He was now certain that Michel was right, but he preferred not to acknowledge it. He would rather be in this house, even with his tough father. Let his "aunt" find other grandchildren!

CHAPTER
FORTY-FIVE

"Moishe, the news isn't good," Rivkah said to her husband over the phone.

"Did you see the child?" he asked fearfully. "You mean you haven't seen him yet? It's been an entire day and — "

"I saw him. That's why I don't have anything good to report." She started crying again, and Moishe was appalled. How could he have let her travel to Israel to confront those people? How did he ever permit such a family to take in his grandson?

"What happened, Rivkah? You must tell me everything, slowly and clearly," he urged her.

She told the entire story, omitting her feelings of humiliation when the boy spoke to her impudently, though Moishe read between the lines. "It seemed as if they thanked him for his rude behavior, and then they went through the motions of rebuking him. You should have seen how calm the mother was when she scolded him."

"Just a minute. That's something you don't have to be angry about. The boy endured a hijacking. We cannot expect him to behave normally right away. Did you expect that he would forget the entire episode and begin smiling at once? He has to start life over again. Don't forget, he is probably having nightmares and flashbacks. Give him time."

"He is very aggressive," Rivkah complained. "A child should not behave that way, even after enduring such hardships."

Moishe sighed. He recognized his wife's stubborn streak. At home, she had been the one who had educated and disciplined the children, while he had provided comfort. With the grandchildren, however, Rivkah usually was the proud, loving grandmother, but apparently Elchanan was more than just a grandchild. She felt he was practically her child, and that was the cause of the problem.

"Do you hear me, Moishe? We must take the child out of this environment, and make him into a *mensch*."

"I hear you," he said, sounding far away. "When are you coming home?" he asked suddenly.

"When the child is in my hands. You should have seen the parents' haughtiness when they explained Choni's emotional distress. Chaim at least showed some degree of caring. But Dinah? Nothing. She defended him, and that's it. As if I counted for nothing."

As she spoke, her tears rolled down her cheeks, indicating her complete frustration at the way things had turned out. She had expected the child to fall into her arms and speak lovingly to her. She had hoped to feel a bit of her Sarah, for whom the longings had diminished but the soul still yearned.

But Elchanan was so distant, not at all the wonder grandchild she had expected to meet. Nevertheless, she was determined not to let the Binder family ruin the child.

"Do you hear, Moishe? Go back to the Rav and talk to him. Tell him about the substandard upbringing, the child's attitude. Maybe at this point, he will decide that we should initiate legal proceedings. It's unacceptable that he should be raised in such a negative environment."

"I hear you, Rivkah." His voice sounded slow and measured. This bothered his wife, but she did not react to it. "I understand your feelings, but I think we should wait. Try to control yourself, and ingratiate yourself with the family. Give them reason to invite you over more often. Buy presents for our grandson, and he will start to like you. Then, you will be able to decide if things are really as bad as you think, or if they're just a result of your frustrations."

It was simple logic, but Rivkah could not think of any excuses to approach the Binder family after the harsh words she had said to them. However, Moishe, as usual, was right. She was too impetuous.

"Rivkah, please don't go there today or tomorrow. Make an appointment to visit them in three days."

"Three days?" She sounded shocked.

"Yes." Moishe was resolute. "I agree with them that the boy needs time to recuperate. After three days, he'll calm down, and it will be possible to ascertain the whole truth. Am I clear?"

"And what should I do here for three days by myself?"

"Relax. We've gone through a difficult time."

Moishe was right. It has been an excruciating week. But to just relax alone in the hotel, drinking endless cups of coffee, seemed unreasonable.

She knew that Moishe felt just as terrible about the situation as she did. Still, he suggested waiting, which *was* good advice.

She decided to accept his suggestion, and told the Binders about it. They agreed to bring Choni to meet her in a park on Thursday evening.

Until then, she would do as Moishe instructed her. Drink coffee, nibble cake, and relax.

Woe to such rest.

ஐ❦❦ஐ

"Choni, it's 7:30. Time to get up."

Choni rolled over to the other side, turned off the alarm clock, and went back to sleep.

"Choni, don't you want to go to *cheider*?"

"I want to sleep."

Dinah nearly gave up. She had hoped Chaim would be able to regain control over their extremely pampered child. Pinchas, who had gotten up at 6:30, came home from *shul* and looked suspiciously at the closed bedroom door.

"I thought Choni was going to *cheider* today," he commented to his mother.

"It's still hard for him to get up on time."

"Well, I'm going then. Have a nice day, Ima."

"Have a good day, Pinchas. Don't forget to take your sandwich." She accompanied him to the door and watched from the porch as he disappeared down the street. She had watched her older children, and so she would watch her youngest, too.

She was relieved to hear Chaim's hearty, "Good morning," as he opened the front door.

"So, have things returned to normal yet?" Before she could reply, he continued, "Choni, *baruch Hashem*, is in *cheider*, in good hands. So everything is back to normal. In fact, the only matter left to deal with is the problem with — "

He stopped when he saw Dinah put her finger over her mouth.

"What happened?" he asked in surprise.

"Choni did not get up yet," she told him. "I think he needs some discipline. All the pampering may lead him to completely lose himself."

"Why didn't you say anything to him?"

She flashed a restrained smile. "You know that's not my area of expertise."

"Well, you can learn new techniques."

Chaim opened the door to Choni's room and walked over to the window. He opened the shutters, flooding the room with light.

"Good morning, Choni. You are late this morning. I don't think your rebbi will like this sort of a return to your studies."

Choni closed his eyes and covered his head with the thin summer blanket.

"Choni, it's time to get up." Chaim shook him.

"I want to stay home one more day," Choni mumbled through the blanket.

Chaim quickly said, "I would rather remain at home today, too. Do you know what is waiting for me at the office? Nevertheless, I got up, went to *shul*, and now I'm on my way. I have a responsibility to provide for our family. You have a responsibility to learn. I won't allow you to waste another day. Not your day, nor mine."

His words were forceful, and his tone of voice left no room for doubt. Choni got out of bed, washed his hands, and started getting ready, albeit with an angry look on his face.

After *davening Shacharis*, Choni approached Chaim and said, "They'll all ask me questions in *cheider*. I'm tired. I don't want to go."

At this point, Dinah intervened.

"You don't have to answer anyone, Choni. Besides, you can ask the rebbi to tell the boys not to ask questions."

"That's impossible, Choni," Chaim exclaimed, while indicating to Dinah not to interfere. "You just can't ask everyone not to ask any questions. It's natural for them to ask, but you can learn to deal with the answers as you choose. We can't isolate you from life and ensure that no one ever asks what happened in Entebbe. Let's decide that you respond briefly, and then change the subject. O.K.?"

This ended Choni's objections. His mother prepared his mid-morning snack to take to school. "Your favorite: hot dog in a bun. So that your return to learning should be enjoyable."

He took the bag from her, and, with a notable lack of enthusiasm, left the house.

"So on the first day, it's a little difficult to get back to the regular routine. On the second day, it will be much easier. And on the third day, it will run automatically," Chaim predicted.

"I sure hope so," sighed Dinah, "but I'm afraid this is just the beginning. Choni is unsettled. I cannot figure out what is bothering him."

"You have such fears, like all mothers," Chaim chuckled.

Dinah laughed along with him, "I have a mother's heart, don't I?"

In the afternoon, it became apparent that she was right.

A man phoned and asked to speak to Chaim. Dinah hurried to give him the telephone number at the office. A few minutes later, Chaim called home, in an obviously agitated state.

"Did Choni come home from *cheider*?"

"Not yet. What happened?" Dinah panicked.

"The rebbi called me. Some highly unusual things happened today," Chaim began. He sounded stressed as he recounted what the rebbi had told him. "Choni arrived in a very tense state. He spoke to the rebbi with chutzpah. He annoyed the other children, interrupted the class, he belched and coughed loudly. Should I go on?"

"No," Dinah was nearly in tears. "I told you something happened to him. What could it be?"

"I don't know. Maybe we really should keep him home for the rest of the week to let him recuperate from the trauma."

"What did they say in *cheider*?"

"First the rebbi spoke to me, and afterward the principal. They expressed understanding that the child went through a difficult experience. But for obvious reasons, they cannot allow him to come to school until his behavior improves. The principal thinks Choni probably needs some professional help as well. After all, he endured a terrifying experience without his parents. And I'm afraid that if his grandmother tells him the details of his personal history, he could suffer an emotional breakdown."

Dinah was helpless. "What should we do, Chaim? They don't want our child to continue learning at the *cheider*!"

"They do," Chaim said in a calming voice. After a brief pause, he continued, "I told them the truth about Choni. You know, an orphan — it's a different story. They treat him differently. The principal was stupefied to hear that Choni is our nephew. He was overwhelmed by the kindness we are doing for him, and finally decided that since we were coping with such fortitude, that they too would try to deal with this exceptional situation. They turned completely around in their attitude toward him. I had to tell, Dinah, believe me."

"I believe you."

Chaim felt relieved that she accepted his decision. He continued, "The principal could not believe that the child is not being raised in his parents' home. It seems so — ."

"But, Chaim," Dinah interrupted impatiently, "I don't understand why you seem so surprised. We are his parents. What *chesed* are we doing? He is our child, and we are doing everything for him, just like we do for the rest of our children. I don't see what all the amazement is about."

The bottom line was that Dinah just wanted to see Choni settled. "We need to make an appointment with a specialist who can deal with him. I don't see any other way past this situation," she said to Chaim. As she spoke, there was a knock at the door, and in came a noisy and famished Choni.

"Ima, what can I eat?"

She quickly ended the phone conversation with Chaim and turned to the temperamental child. "First of all, *shalom*, Choni. How are you? How was your first day back in *cheider*?"

He sat down at the kitchen table. "Not so good. I think the rebbi was angry at me."

"Why do you say that?" Dinah deliberately did not tell him what she had just heard. She wanted to first hear it from Choni's perspective.

He gulped down the soup she offered him. "I just told him the truth. And he got angry. What's wrong? Am I not allowed to say the truth?"

"It depends on what truth," she replied calmly. "And maybe you added some chutzpah into this truth."

Instead of reacting, Choni asked for another bowl of soup. Dinah desperately tried to figure out what her son was thinking.

What had he endured during that week? Who really knew?

She accidentally dropped the spoon she was holding. As she bent down to pick it up, a marvelous idea came to her. Why had neither she nor Chaim thought of it earlier? How could they have skipped this important step?

CHAPTER FORTY-SIX

The current migraine attack was unusually strong and long lasting.

"I'm not surprised," said the American-born doctor. "Stress and fear tend to aggravate these attacks. You must rest, Mr. Schick. The trauma is past. Now you have got to relax, and allow healing to take place."

Practical advice is not that easy to implement. Yehudah Shick's headache did not get any better, but in fact became worse. The concerned doctor ordered a battery of tests, which in the end were inconclusive. The doctor advised consulting a psychologist. Freida and the children, however, were thinking along different lines and were terrified that perhaps he had caught some deadly virus in Uganda.

The hijacking left its mark on the Schick family. Yehudah spent most of his time in bed at his daughter's house, evincing no interest in his surroundings. He barely spoke and seemed withdrawn. Freida was at his side constantly, and their married children expressed their fears aloud. They had not even heard the details of their parents' frightening experience, because the occasion never arose for them to talk about it. Everyone was focused only on Yehudah's severe migraine.

Freida did not let her children visit for extended periods. "Let us recuperate," she begged them repeatedly. "When everything returns to normal, then come visit. You know how much we missed you, and thought about you. But we just need our rest right now."

It was no use. It was impossible to keep the children away. Their oldest son came bearing a natural cure, the second brought advice from an expert on migraines, and the third child sent over meals, but Yehudah barely responded to any of these attempts to help. The pain wracked his head, keeping him in bed and unable to function.

Yehudah was ashamed to share his experience with anyone else. He had remained strong while he was going through the trauma. Only after it was over did he allow himself to react to the stress and the fear that buffeted them at Entebbe. Such was Yehudah Schick.

During a quiet moment in the evening, the phone rang. Initially, Freida did not answer her daughter's phone. So many people had called congratulating them on their return and wishing them well, but even more people were curious to hear about the hijacking and the rescue. At one point, Freida had disconnected the phone.

Suddenly, Freida remembered that she was waiting for one of her children to call about a certain natural cure that might help Yehudah. She picked up the ringing phone.

"Uri?" Freida asked, expecting to hear her son.

"*Shalom,*" said a woman's voice. The caller's gentle tone kept Freida from hanging up the phone.

"Is this Freida Schick?"

"Yes. How can I help you?"

"This is Dinah Binder. I wanted to tell you how grateful we are to you."

"Who are you?" asked Freida, losing patience. Surely this must be another woman trying to hear about the miracles of Entebbe.

"I'm Dinah Binder, mother of Choni, who flew with you and your husband. Am I calling at an inconvenient time?"

"No, Mrs. Binder. If it is you, then it is fine. You know, some people are so inconsiderate. How are you? How is Choni?" It was just a polite, matter-of-fact question, but Dinah's answer was startling.

"*Baruch Hashem*, we are still recuperating from the experience. We still do not fully understand what happened."

After nearly a week since the rescue, many people thought that the hostages should have recuperated and gotten back to their previous lives. Here, however, was a valiant woman, mother of a hostage, who was not embarrassed to admit the truth.

"We, too, have not fully put it behind us," Freida said with a sigh. "Yehudah is not feeling well. You saw that at the airport. He had wanted to speak to your husband."

"What about?"

Freida was not comfortable and dodged the question. "We decided to talk to you after returning home, but it is difficult for Yehudah to speak right now. When the migraine attack subsides, I think he will want to talk to you about Choni."

"That is why I called you," Dinah said worriedly. "The boy is very different than before the trip. He told us about some of his experiences, but nothing about himself. We have no idea how he fared during those frightful days."

"We were with him," Freida said. She sounded embarrassed.

"I know you were, and we are indebted to you for that. I can't think of the right words to use to thank you." Dinah paused a moment, then continued, "In any case, I wanted to know some more details about what Choni did during that week, and how he reacted to the hijacking. He has still not returned to his former self, and we are concerned about what happened to him in Entebbe."

Freida restrained her desire to tell Dinah everything. She was afraid that Dinah would be upset to learn that her son had become friendly with a pair of nonreligious boys, and that he had managed to find out a rather significant detail of his life. A detail that the Binder family had tried to conceal from Choni, and certainly from their friends and acquaintances.

Freida wanted her husband to break the bad news to the Binders, so she remained silent.

"Mrs. Schick, are you there?"

"I'm here. As soon as Yehudah recovers, we'll call back and talk."

"I'm very grateful to you. But perhaps you could tell me something right now? Call it a prelude."

"Yehudah will deal with it," Freida repeated stubbornly. "I really have to go now. In the meantime, I wish you success in overcoming the hardships that you are experiencing now. I hope they are solved as soon as possible."

"Thanks."

The conversation was over, but Dinah was as perplexed as ever. It is true that the Schicks had performed a great *chesed*, taking care of a young boy during a decidedly trying experience. Nevertheless, why did Freida behave in such a strange and uncooperative way? Why did she refuse to answer a simple question?

Was it so difficult to tell her, the mother, what had happened in Uganda? Why was Freida being so stubborn, and saying that only her husband could "deal with" the details?

The more Dinah thought about it, the more she decided Mrs. Schick's behavior was rather strange, and even annoying. She decided not to call Chaim at the office; he was behind in his work. Let him work without distraction, and in the evening, she would discuss the entire matter with him.

Yehudah Schick would have to talk to them, even though he was not feeling well. Even if they would have to pay him.

⁂

Freida Schick was beside herself. "Can you imagine the nerve of Mrs. Binder? It's not enough that we took care of their son. Now she wants to discuss the whole affair, as if we were to blame for the entire business."

"Mrs. Binder?" Yehudah asked. "Bring me a pill, please, with some water. Thank you. Who is Mrs. Binder?"

"Choni's mother."

"Ahh — " Yehudah swallowed the pill with one large gulp of water. "I think I'm feeling better. Maybe this migraine will eventually go away," he said in an encouraging voice.

"Not *maybe*: with Hashem's help, for sure," Freida was adamant. "So what do you say about Mrs. Binder?"

"She called? What did she want?"

"To know what happened to Choni during the week of captivity. The boy isn't telling them anything," she repeated. "We have to tell them the truth, as we decided, despite the unpleasantness."

"Yes, I agree we have to do it. Why didn't you hint anything to her?"

"I want you to do it. You know how hard it is for me. First, get well, and then arrange a call or meeting with the father. Tell him the truth."

Yehudah adjusted the pillow under his head. "The truth will come too late, I'm afraid. The child is suffering now. I cannot understand how I pushed off telling them for so long. This is something of the utmost importance!"

"Until now, you couldn't speak due to the pain," Freida reminded him. She did not like the idea of holding the meeting that same day. "Nothing will happen if you talk to them tomorrow or the next day. Anyway, there is nothing they can do to change the reality of the boy's life."

"It's amazing that he did not tell them what he knows," Yehudah said. His migraine seemed to dissipate the more he involved himself with the issue of Choni Binder.

"Why should he tell them? If he did, you would be accountable for allowing him to associate with those boys."

His headache suddenly returned. He would have to apologize, and explain how difficult it was to supervise Choni. Under Chaim's withering glare, he would have to explain why he had been derelict in his duty. After all, had Choni not befriended those boys, he would not have learned the story of his life.

"You know, they seem so much like his true parents. It's impossible to believe that …," Yehudah muttered as he placed a cold compress on his throbbing head.

Freida sat down on a chair next to the bed. "Yes, that's why I don't want to be the one to tell them. They're hiding Choni's adoption from everyone! I can't imagine how they will react when they hear that he knows the truth. What do you think they will say to the boy?"

"I have no idea. One thing is clear, however. We must tell them! Please bring me my telephone book. I have Chaim's office number there. I will ask him to come over tomorrow morning. We will finish this business once and for all. That will be better than dragging it on and on interminably."

Freida quietly brought him his telephone book. She watched her husband lift himself up from the bed. Maybe this was exactly what he needed to help him recuperate from the harrowing experience at Entebbe. Perhaps he just needed something to urge him out of bed. Freida could not understand how Yehudah had the strength to speak to Chaim Binder, but he was perfectly comfortable in such situations. He dialed Chaim's office number.

"*Shalom*, Mr. Binder. This is Yehudah Schick. Do you remember me?"

"Yes."

"I would like to talk to you about your son. Could you please come over to my daughter's house? I have not been feeling well since the rescue, and have been generally bedridden. I'm feeling better now, and the first thing I wanted to do was to call you."

"What is this about?" asked Chaim, growing a bit fearful.

"I have something very important to tell you. It's related to Choni. I'd rather not talk about it on the telephone. It would be a good idea for you to stop over here tomorrow morning. Your wife? I don't know. Maybe she should come too. She has to know the truth, I mean, what is going on.

"It's best if we meet tomorrow morning. But just to make sure, Reb Chaim, I will call you tonight to confirm that I'll be able to meet you."

"Are you enjoying your freedom?" asked Chaim.

"Not really. Not yet. We have not managed to enjoy the air." He added, "We will not be flying to France. That flight was my last. Why are you laughing? We'll see."

"I'll see you tomorrow, *im yirtzeh Hashem. Kol tuv.*"

Yehudah hung up the phone and sat down on the chair. "He already knows that something is wrong," he told Freida. "He even sounded annoyed that I didn't call him earlier."

"What did you tell him?"

"I explained why it was not possible to call earlier. You know how I was feeling a few days ago."

"Of course," his wife replied, in wholehearted support of her husband. "He has no right to make demands on us. We do not owe them a thing. We did them a favor."

"That's true. But — " Yehudah looked around the room, avoiding her gaze. Was a guilty conscience troubling him?

"I think we should have said something to them as soon as we landed in Israel. Who knows how many problems they have faced in the interim? This child is smart, perhaps too smart. How could he not tell them what he found out in Entebbe?"

They changed the subject to their own children. Thoughts about Choni caused them too many pangs of guilt and remorse. Feelings that were certainly justified.

CHAPTER FORTY-SEVEN

Georges Braun always had a strange feeling whenever he visited Israel. He inhaled as if he were savoring a quality cigar. "We are in the Holy Land. No skinheads or troublemakers will bother us here," he noted with satisfaction to Annette, who was slightly distraught.

"I don't understand why the boys are not here to greet us," she complained as she scanned the waiting crowd for a familiar face.

"Don't bother looking for them," Georges said calmly, turning toward the luggage carousel. "I told them not to come. We will go to them."

"Why?"

"I thought it would be better. They have to recuperate from the trauma of the hijacking. Why should they have to run around?"

What sort of strange reasoning was that? Annette restrained herself from arguing with her husband, and waited for further explanation.

Georges was tense; his movements were nervous and tentative. He lined up their suitcases, hailed a taxicab, and, as he got inside, scanned the immediate area. No, no one was following them.

Their destination was Jerusalem. When they reached the entrance to the city, Georges stopped the cab and hailed another. "What are you doing?" Annette sputtered impatiently. "Couldn't the taxi take us to the correct address?"

"I'm doing what needs to be done," Georges replied, equally upset. "Believe me, I don't have time for games. This is very necessary."

He made sure to erase any trace of their whereabouts, just in case they were being followed. Even though he was fairly certain that Gerard's former friends had forgotten about him, he did not want to give them any clues as to where they were staying, just to be safe.

A short ride brought them to the entrance of a luxury hotel. Annette looked at the front of the building. "Gerard certainly knows the fancier hotels in the city, doesn't he?" she commented. "Let's hope that we'll find them here."

Before they got out of the taxi, their two sons appeared, tall, strong, and at ease. They greeted one another warmly, and Annette's eyes filled with tears. In her heart, she decided to forgive Gerard for the problems he had caused when he was a member of the gang.

"So, what do you have to tell us, boys? How was it?" Georges was just as emotional as his wife was, but he tried to hide it by presenting a tough exterior.

"All right. The Israelis did not abandon us," Gerard said. "Anything new, father?"

Five minutes later, Michel was speaking to his mother excitedly, while Georges and Gerard were supervising the bellhop who carried their belongings.

It was the ideal time to exchange a few discreet words. "They're after you. Here is proof of the threat to your life," Georges said, handing a folded piece of paper to Gerard.

Gerard read it, smiled contemptuously, and said, "They won't be able to find me. They don't have anyone here. That's why they sent me in the first place." He became serious again and added, "No matter, we still have to be cautious."

Georges looked at his son. "I can't understand how you got involved with such people. And then, what broke the connection?"

"I didn't carry out an assignment," Gerard answered. "They were angry at me, but could not do anything to me from afar. I knew what awaited me if I returned to France."

"What kind of assignment?"

"It's not important." Gerard replied resolutely. Georges could see that his son would not discuss the subject. "That gang is history. I'm heading toward a new, different life."

"Some different gang?" his father asked sarcastically. "When are you going to grow up? You're not a child anymore, you know."

"I know."

The conversation would have continued, but the family reached the hotel room and arranged their belongings. Then they all went down to the hotel's lobby, and Georges ordered refreshments. It had been a long time since they had all sat together as a family. Gerard would generally disappear from the house, which offended the other family members.

As the boys recounted the details of the hijacking, Michel told his parents about the new friend he had made in Entebbe.

"He's religious. Do you know what that is?" he asked excitedly as he gulped down his milkshake.

Georges and Annette exchanged glances. "Yes, we know what that is. Are you thinking about becoming like him?"

"Well, a little. I was jealous watching them *daven* all the time, and ...." As Michel spoke, Georges noticed Gerard nodding in agreement. Georges needed to discuss this idea with his son. It was typical of Gerard to investigate something — Judaism, for example — and to ultimately decide to become observant.

Gerard added details about the religious captives. It was just as Georges thought: Gerard announced that he was intrigued by Judaism, and intended to seriously look into it.

"Why?"

"Maybe it will change my life."

Michel interrupted their conversation. "I'm waiting for a call from Choni. I gave him the telephone number here."

Georges was amused. "How do you know that he will call?"

"He'll do it more for himself than for me," Michel replied. "I'm telling you, his life has become very difficult."

They talked for another hour, and Georges decided he was pleased. His plan had worked. He had succeeded in severing Gerard's ties with the gang. All he had to do now was to steer him in the right direction. Of course, Gerard would not be able to return to France for several years, to give his old friends time to forget about him. Otherwise, he would be in mortal danger. It was better for Gerard to remain here in Israel. Afterward, he could return home and work in the family business.

"I don't know, Papa. I have to work out my plans and see what direction my life will take," he repeated.

Georges took a deep breath. Gerard had always been a stubborn child, but Georges knew that if he had lots of patience he would achieve his goal, and his son would follow his footsteps into the world of commerce.

Michel looked at his father. His promising expression brought a sense of satisfaction to Georges and Annette. *Michel would not disappoint them,* he decided, *even if Gerard decides on a different direction.*

❧❀❦❧

"I'm not going to *cheider* today." Choni emerged from his room fully dressed, apparently headed to *shul*.

"Why not?" Dinah asked, restraining herself from rebuking him in stronger language. She decided to treat him gently, since something seemed to be troubling him.

"There is a test this morning on what we learned in the last two weeks. I don't know that material anyway, so I might as well stay home."

"Why didn't you review those *blatt* of Gemara?"

"Because I won't do well anyway," he repeated stubbornly. "There's no point in trying when I know I'm going to fail. I'm going to *shul* to *daven*."

"And what will you do afterward?"

"We'll see."

Dinah held a huge sigh inside her. She had a very important meeting today with Chaim. They were going to visit Yehudah Schick. What will Choni do at home alone?

She decided to call Chaim and tell him about the latest development.

"Should I let him stay home or absolutely insist that he go to *cheider*?" she asked in a hesitant voice.

"I think that we are missing some information. Let him stay home today," Chaim decided after considerable deliberation. "The secretaries have not yet arrived at the office, and I'll try to finish up here as quickly as possible. I want to get to Yehudah

Schick as soon as we can. In any case, I have some appointments later with clients. You know, I cannot completely close my business."

"Of course," she agreed.

When Choni came back home from *shul,* he found his mother putting lunch into the refrigerator. "In the afternoon, heat it up for Pinchas and yourself, O.K.?"

He was surprised to learn that he had permission to miss school. Dinah noticed that he seemed frustrated and lonely.

"What will you do at home?" she asked.

"I'll ride my bicycle. Maybe I'll sleep a bit. I didn't sleep too much in Entebbe," he said, trying to arouse her sympathy.

"I would be very pleased if you would go to *cheider.*"

"Maybe...."

"At least after the test is over. Why should you miss a whole day?"

"I'll see...."

Before leaving the house, Dinah decided to go into Choni's room and confront him directly. He was lying on his bed, reading a book. "Choni," she asked, "is there something that's bothering you that we don't know about?"

"No," he declared, and continued reading. Dinah left the house frustrated, noticing that her heart was pounding unusually hard. *What would Yehudah Schick say? Ribbono shel Olam, what happened to Choni in Entebbe?*

Choni stayed in the house, feeling lonelier than ever. Now that he was back home, he was finding it difficult to return to his previous life. His friends suddenly seemed so immature. What did they know about life? Even his closest friend, who tried to cheer him with silly stories, did not interest him. Being at home didn't help the lonely feeling, as he no longer felt close to his parents. They were not his real parents, and this disturbed him.

The only one with whom he had any connection was Michel, who was not even here.

Choni hesitated for a moment, then began searching for the phone number Michel had given him at the last minute. His parents might not be happy about this friendship, but he felt a powerful urge to call him, to talk to him, and maybe even to share his feelings with him.

Choni dialed the number hesitatingly, but when no one answered, he hung up. Maybe they had not stayed in Eretz Yisrael. Then he would have no way to locate them. In any case, if someone did answer the phone, how could he ask for Michel if he did not know French?

He grew bored and restless. The sound of the phone ringing was a welcome diversion. He picked up the receiver.

"Hello. With whom do you want to speak?"

"Is this the Binder home?"

"Yes, it is."

"Who's speaking?"

"Choni."

"Elchanan, how are you?" The voice on the other end became excited. "Do you know who is calling? Your gran — the aunt you were supposed to visit in France."

"Ahh, yes...." His voice suddenly became cold and detached, as his heart pounded within his chest. She was not his aunt; she had started to say "grandmother." How should he treat her?

"It's marvelous that I have the opportunity to talk to you. How are you, Elchanan? How does it feel to be back — home?"

"Everything is fine. Abba and Ima are not home. You can call back later."

"It's actually you I want to talk to."

"O.K."

He became excited, but decided not to speak. Let his grandmother find the words. He was enjoying the situation. His parents were most likely trying to prevent this conversation from taking place, but they weren't home and here it was, the decisive moment, with all its frightening implications. He was ready to face it.

"Listen, Choni, I just wanted to tell you why we invited you to France. There is a very important reason. But just a minute, aren't you supposed to be in school now?"

Her question angered him. "No, I'm not. I'm staying home. Abba and Ima will be home later. Goodbye."

He hung up the telephone and went to his room, completely confused. He knew he had done something very rude, and his conscience bothered him for behaving in such an unacceptable manner. But it was all behind him now. He wanted to cry, but the tears would not come.

CHAPTER FORTY-EIGHT

Yehudah Schick felt the weight of his illness ebbing away slowly over the past few days. He awoke that morning, with barely a trace of a headache. Finally, he could get back to himself, forget the frightening experience of Entebbe, and enjoy his freedom.

Just as he took a deep breath and recited *Modeh Ani*, his heart sank. He remembered the scheduled meeting with Choni's parents this morning. He was sure that they would come, and he, Yehudah, would have to give an accounting of his actions. Or more accurately, his inaction.

He smelled a wondrous odor wafting in from the kitchen. Freida and her daughter were already baking cakes. With great difficulty, Yehudah pulled himself up in bed and called out, "Since when do you bake cake in the morning?"

"Since guests are scheduled to come over," Freida replied. He knew that she, too, was ill at ease. "Maybe my cinnamon coffee cake will put them in a better frame of mind." Although Freida's cakes could assuage many a bitter memory, they could not change what had happened to Choni on his ill-fated trip.

After returning from *shul*, Yehudah sat down to learn until the guests arrived. A short while later, he heard knocking at the door. Yehudah felt his heart begin to pound.

"Come in, please," he heard Freida say to the Binders.

Mrs. Schick ushered the Binders into the living room. They were obviously excited to see Yehudah. Yehudah was a gracious host and directed the Binders to the sofa. Freida came back in with a tray of baked treats.

"First of all, please have some coffee cake," she said to them. "You are also invited to the *seudas hoda'ah* that we are planning, *im yirtzeh Hashem*, next week."

Dinah politely tasted the cake and even asked Freida for the recipe, but Chaim Binder's gaze was serious and focused.

"Let the women indulge in friendly chitchat. I would prefer to get to the topic at hand," he said, looking at his watch, tapping his fingers nervously. "Reb Yehudah, my son was with you in Entebbe. He has returned home somewhat changed. I believe his experience there had an effect on him, but it is likely there is something else we do not know about. The child is restless and won't let himself recuperate. Did the terrorists threaten or harm him personally?" Chaim asked, a worried look on his face.

"Not at all," Yehudah answered, trying to calm the situation. "The terrorists paid almost no attention to the children. In any case, Choni was not harmed, unlike some of the young men whom they suspected were soldiers."

"I'd like you to tell me how Choni actually passed the time in Entebbe."

At this point, the women also became quiet. Everyone's attention was focused on Mr. Schick. Yehudah started to feel nauseous, and the headache that he thought he had recovered from started to return.

He bit his lip and wiped his forehead. He started talking, hesitantly at first, but afterward in a torrent. When he finished, he felt relieved, like someone who had just confessed to committing a crime. He picked up his head and stared straight into the shocked faces of Chaim and Dinah Binder.

The silence in the living room was deafening. Dinah spoke first after the lengthy pause and questioned Yehudah. He responded, and Freida occasionally commented as well.

Half an hour after it began, the Binders ended the meeting and went outside. Dinah's steps were tentative and halting, and Chaim did not stop blinking, which indicated that his thoughts were in a jumble.

"And now, I don't want to talk about anything else," Yehudah Schick called out to Freida as he lay down helplessly on his bed. He felt that he had ended his part in this drama, though he did not feel good about it.

❧❧❧

Chaim Binder grasped the steering wheel weakly, driving the car without paying close attention to the road. He kept on glancing at his wife. She realized that he was not driving home, but was headed toward Tel Aviv.

"Where are you going?" she asked.

"Let's go to the seashore. I need to unwind," he replied. "Do you think I can just go to work after this? Should we go home to Choni? We have to decide what we are going to say to him, and how we are going to say it."

Dinah's eyes were red from crying. Her tears just flowed without any restraint. They didn't speak again until they arrived at the seashore, which was nearly deserted.

"How did he manage to hide this information from us? How?"

Chaim folded his arms. "Just like his father," he answered. "He also used to act like that."

"He's young, Chaim. He's only 10 years old."

"But he's as smart as a 40-year-old."

After walking for a quarter of an hour on the scorching sand, talking about Choni's precociousness, Chaim lit a cigarette and asked nervously, "What do we do now?"

Dinah did not answer. Chaim had always said that they needed to tell Choni the truth. Because "at some point, he will find out. It's better for him to hear it from us." Dinah had consistently refused, to protect the child. Now they realized that Chaim's argument had proven to be correct. Now what were they to do?

Should they go home and tell the boy that they knew everything that had happened in Entebbe? Should they let him continue the charade? Deny the whole story? Verify its veracity?

"It doesn't work like this, Chaim," Dinah began. "We have to consult *da'as Torah*."

"You're right," he replied. "I'll go back to Rav Katz and ask him how we should handle this difficult situation. For now, I think that we have to overlook the problems Choni is creating in school. He must be so confused and insecure."

"Definitely. We can only imagine what he is feeling after going through such a frightening experience as a hijacking, and then finding out something so traumatic. By the way, I do not look favorably on this relationship with Michel. That is his name, right, Michel? I'm afraid Choni may try to contact him."

"He is the only one who knows about Choni's family situation. And Choni probably feels alone, as if no one understands him. Surely he will try to contact the one person who does understand. We must do everything possible to prevent that from happening. These friends sound very questionable to me." Chaim's face was serious to a frightening degree when he concluded.

They walked toward the car. The roar of the nearby waves did not calm them. In fact, it was a harbinger of the impending storm.

Choni, child of ours, how could you do this to us? How did you find out about secrets that you were not supposed to know?

The most painful part of it for Dinah was that Choni now knew that she was not his natural mother, even though she was his mother with all her heart and soul. Now she understood the strange looks he had been giving her since he returned from Uganda; those rebellious eyes, the nervousness, and the tears.

"I hope Sarah is not angry at me," she said to Chaim as they got into the car.

"Who?" He thought he had not heard correctly.

"Sarah, Choni's mother. And Yaakov too." She lowered her eyes as she said, "They must be furious over the latest developments."

"They're in the *olam ha'emes*," Chaim said forcefully. "Listen, Dinah, they know that we are doing everything for the boy's well-being. I am sure they appreciate it. Who knows, maybe something positive will result from all this?"

"Maybe."

Chaim had not yet gotten into the car. He was staring out at the ocean, watching the waves. "Stop blaming yourself," he told her. "We are doing everything possible for Choni's sake. Hashem, the Father of Orphans, will continue to guide us."

"You're right. As usual," she apologized, although her intent went beyond Chaim's last words. He was right then as well, years back, when he had insisted that Choni must be told the truth. Now, it was too late.

They arrived back home, and before Chaim could return to the office, Dinah asked the fateful question: "What should I say to Choni?"

"Nothing. For the moment, let everything continue as it has until now. I will go to Rav Katz and discuss the matter with him. Treat Choni gently. Don't make it harder for him than it is already."

She walked up to the house in a confused state, and was concerned when Choni did not answer her knocks. After a few moments, she calmed herself. Maybe he finally went to *cheider*?

Dinah found her key and unlocked the door. "Choni?" she called out.

The door to his room was closed, and she opened it quietly. Choni was stretched out in bed, fully dressed, his face partially covered with the thin blanket. She could not tell if he was asleep or not. Dinah turned off the light and silently left the room.

She headed to the kitchen. All her household chores were waiting for her. There was no respite from the family's needs, even in difficult situations. She decided to prepare supper, then deal with the laundry, but the ringing telephone interrupted her.

"Is Reb Chaim Binder home?" She heard the voice of an elderly man speaking French.

"No. Who's calling?"

"Moishe Kahn. I demand to speak to him immediately," he continued. There was no denying that tone of voice and his choice of words. He was irate.

"He's at work now, Reb Moishe. Maybe I can help you?" She felt that propriety dictated that she swallow her pride.

"We are furious, Mrs. Binder," the old man said bluntly. "My wife is alone in the country, without any close relatives. She is sitting by herself in a hotel, waiting for you to magnanimously invite her to meet our grandchild. Do you understand that he is the only son of our youngest daughter *aleha hashalom*? Apparently, you do not. My wife is trying to contact you, but you ignore her. Either you don't answer the phone, or you aren't home. You have lots of excuses, but we know the truth."

His words irked her. "What truth?"

"The bitter truth," Moishe Kahn replied smugly. "You told Choni that you are not his parents, and goaded him against us. My wife spoke to him, and told me afterward that never has a child spoken to her with such chutzpah. No one would speak with such galling impudence to their grandmother, or even to someone purported to be his aunt. The child hung up by slamming the phone down. You are provoking him against us, and we are prepared to respond accordingly."

"Why do you think we would provoke him to such behavior?" Dinah tried to calm him with rational words.

Moishe Kahn remained unconvinced. "Either you are provoking him, or he is suffering from a serious lack of *chinuch*," he announced. "And I think that either way, we have to remove the child from your custody as quickly as possible. He needs a warm home and proper upbringing. Why is the boy at home at a time when he should be in *cheider*? And if he's not well, why are his parents not at home with him?"

The accusations were serious, and Moishe Kahn's wrath was clear. Dinah was silent and finally heard the phone slammed down with angry finality.

CHAPTER FORTY-NINE

Choni had more than one reason for hiding under the blanket and ignoring his mother's questions. After the botched conversation with his grandmother, he had received another phone call.

"*Shalom*, I'd like to speak to Choni," Michel said in an important-sounding voice. Choni was unable to restrain himself and shouted in surprise, "Michel, how did you find me?"

The familiar voice triggered mixed feelings in him. On the one hand, he was overjoyed to hear from Michel. On the other hand, talking to him produced flashbacks to those days in Entebbe; the frightening terrorists, stinking mattresses, and the oppressive passenger-reception hall.

"Hey, Choni, how are you?" Michel's voice sounded warm and friendly, and it had an immediate effect on Choni. "How are you recovering from our adventure?"

"*Baruch Hashem*, still recuperating. You can tell that I'm not going to *cheider* yet. But seriously, how did you get my phone number?"

"I needed to find you, and I did." Michel did not elaborate on his efforts to find his friend's telephone number. They had searched through telephone books, and even asked the hotel receptionist for assistance. He had dialed seemingly endless strings of numbers before dialing the correct one.

"So how are you feeling now?" Michel asked. "Did you tell your parents? Did you meet your grandmother?"

"They don't know that I know," he blurted out.

"Why not?" Michel was surprised. "Why didn't you tell them?"

"I don't know. It's a little complicated."

Michel was quiet for a moment, and then changed the subject. "Look, I called you because I need something. Actually, I need to meet you urgently. My parents are here in the country."

Choni was surprised. It was easy to talk, but the truth was that Michel might not be a welcome guest in the Binder home. "What do you want?"

"Help," Michel replied simply. "We're friends, right? I need your help."

"I don't know if my parents..." Choni found it difficult to explain about some observant Jews' attitude toward nonobservant Jews. He was afraid Michel would be justifiably insulted. Besides, he did not know his parents' views on the matter, as they had not yet had his opportunity to befriend nonreligious foreigners.

"Where are you? Give me your telephone number, and I will call you back later. We'll decide where we should meet."

Michel told him the hotel phone number. "I hope to hear from you really soon," he told Choni, and hung up.

Choni remained standing at the telephone, troubled by mixed

emotions. He was extremely pleased. The conversation with Michel was good for him — he felt that he had spoken with an old friend — yet he felt guilty. Who knew how his father would react when he learned that his son was friends with a French teenager? His brother Gerard was altogether an undesirable type of person. How could he have befriended these boys?

Choni, however, had a good heart, and still had enough of a child's innocence that he decided to ask his mother if he could host Michel and his parents. He would tell his parents in the evening about the phone call from Michel, and ask their permission to meet the boy who had comforted and supported him so much during the difficult days at Entebbe. If his father asked how Michel had helped, he would answer that when Mr. Schick was not well, Michel had kept him from feeling lonely.

When Choni thought of Yehudah Schick, he felt inexplicable relief. He felt bad that Mr. Schick was unwell, but on the other hand, he was glad that his condition kept him from speaking on the phone, so Mr. Schick could not tell his father anything about Michel. This way, Choni could instruct Michel to appear in suitable attire, and no one would suspect a thing.

In the evening, his father called him into the living room. He seemed in a stubborn mood, almost combative. Choni was startled when he came into the room.

"Here's the boy who didn't want to go to *cheider* this morning," Chaim scowled.

"But I went in the afternoon," Choni protested. He was calm and well behaved then, and had left the house without an argument. Why was his father harping on this?

"Do you deserve a thank-you for that?" His father's voice was angry. "Even if there was a quiz, you could have asked me to help you make up the material you missed. I would have gladly helped. I don't know what to do with you, Choni. I tried to speak to Rav Katz, but he is not well these days, so I could not visit him. I am at my wits end."

Chaim decided to approach Choni in a very direct manner, practically like an adult.

"The Kahn family is very angry at the way you've treated them," he said in a serious tone. Choni looked at the floor. "We are also worried about your behavior. I'm asking you again, is there something you are not telling us?"

"Why should I have something to hide?" he asked, childishly shrugging his shoulders.

"I know why. Earlier this afternoon, someone named Georges called me, thanking me in French for inviting him to my house. Do you know who invited him to our house?"

Choni quickly looked down humbly, whispering, "I wanted to ask you, but I didn't manage to — "

"Is this man Jewish?" Chaim continued. "And who is your friend Michel? Is he somehow connected to this?"

"I don't know what happened," Choni said, blushing. "I told Michel that I would give him an answer in the evening, after asking your permission. So how did they manage to — ?"

He wished that his mother were at his side, but she was in the kitchen preparing supper. Would she come to save him from this horrible mess?

Chaim continued speaking, and with each additional word, the fear grew in Choni's heart that maybe Georges had told his father some more information about their family.

His father had a look of deep concentration in his eyes. But despite the angry appearance, Choni could tell that he was conflicted.

Chaim realized that the child before him was very agitated, much more than he had anticipated. He was about to deal with the third and most painful blow, but decided at the last minute to restrain himself. Choni was not ready for it. Even though he seemed adultlike, he was just a young child, so young that Chaim's heart ached at having to act tough.

"Michel and his family are coming over tomorrow afternoon to visit. You will, of course, go to *cheider*, and I expect to hear positive reports from your teachers. You don't have to be outstanding, but I do want you to try. Do you promise?"

Choni nodded in agreement.

The delectable aroma of fresh omelets spread throughout the house, causing a warm homey atmosphere to replace the stern, disciplining one.

"Supper is ready. What are you waiting for?" Dinah could not understand why no one was coming into the kitchen. Opening the door to the living room, she saw Chaim and Choni sitting quietly, looking at each other. She realized that their serious conversation had begun, although Chaim had agreed that they would talk after the meal. Why had he changed his mind? Maybe he wanted to spare her the tension that such a talk would create.

Chaim lifted an eyebrow and slightly turned his head to indicate that he had not yet told Choni the essential news. He said, "We're coming to eat. I spoke with Choni a bit. I think that from now on, he's going to change." Chaim suddenly stood up, stroked Choni's cheeks, and held his shoulders tight. "Right, Choni?" he asked.

"*B'ezras Hashem.*" Until now, Choni had accepted his father's displays of affection as something natural. But now that he knew that Chaim was only his uncle, he was confused.

"So now you can come and taste the delicious salad I prepared," Dinah said, trying to sound cheerful. "I hope that tomorrow's meal will be just as tasty. You have found some interesting guests for us, Choni?"

Choni could still not understand why Georges had called and thanked his father for the invitation. Why had Michel let him?

"Shimon, I have an urgent favor to ask of you."

"Of course, Abba."

Moishe was not happy to bother his son again, but all his other children were busy and Shimon gladly helped with whatever his parents asked. He was truly a gem of a son.

"I have to fly to Israel, urgently."

"Did something happen to Ima?" asked the worried son.

"A lot has happened to her."

"Is she okay?" Shimon asked.

Moishe quickly took hold of the situation. "She's feeling fine, but very alone. The Binders don't invite her to their home. She is neglected there, Shimon. I cannot believe that I placed my grandson in the custody of such irresponsible people."

"Maybe it just appears that way to you?" Shimon tried to blunt his father's harsh words.

"No, you should have heard how that grandchild spoke to her. With unbelievable impudence. Here in France, you would never hear a child speak like that to an older person. Maybe they urged the boy to behave rudely toward us."

"So why do you want to fly there? Why don't you ask Ima to return to France?" Shimon asked logically.

"I want to see Ima and my grandson. I want both of them here in my house. I want to see them here, so I must go get them." Moishe was unequivocal. "How soon can we arrange a plane ticket?"

"I'll call you back in half an hour and let you know. By the way, are you planning on initiating legal proceedings while you are there?"

"I haven't decided yet."

"Okay. You know what I think, Abba? That I should order two tickets."

"You're coming along?" Moishe's relief was palpable as he exhaled deeply.

"I'll check with my wife. If she agrees, I think I can forgo my regular schedule for another two or three days. Nothing terrible will happen."

"Thank you, Shimon."

All at once, a huge burden rolled off Moishe's chest. Shimon's participation would make all the difference. A helpless, elderly couple looks different when a clever and energetic young man stands at their side. He felt grateful that his son understood how much his presence was needed and appreciated.

Moishe still recalled Rivkah sobbing with disappointment and frustration. "That Sarah's child would talk to me like that," she kept on repeating. "Who would have believed such a thing was possible?"

She had been ashamed to ask Moishe for support. It would be an admission that she could not manage on her own. Besides, she was disillusioned by the struggle and by Choni's behavior. She no longer felt that they had to obtain custody of their grandson at all cost. Moishe, who originally was skeptical about the plan, was now its strongest proponent.

For half an hour, Moishe paced the floor nervously. He imagined himself arriving in Israel, speaking with his wife and grandson. The Binders would agree to transfer custody of Choni. Then they would all return joyfully to Paris. Obviously, they were too old to raise a young boy and deal with his daily needs. Maybe Shimon would agree to take Choni. Perhaps they could find some other arrangement, as long as Choni would no longer be with the Binders.

Shimon called to tell his father that he would travel with him, and that he had acquired the necessary tickets. Tomorrow at 10 o'clock in the morning, they would be on a flight to Israel. Tonight they could sleep soundly, knowing that the following day, Elchanan would be in their loving arms.

CHAPTER FIFTY

Arriving home from *cheider*, Choni opened the front door hesitantly. It was just after 12 in the afternoon. He heard French voices in the living room and knew who had come to visit.

Michel's young voice resounded in the house. Afterward, he heard the slower, more mature voice of Gerard. It seemed strange that they were having a friendly conversation. Choni snuck in and put his bookbag in its place. He went into the living room wearing a thin smile.

"Choni, it's good to see you," Michel announced, his eyes shining with excitement. Gerard also looked at him and gave a friendly nod. Choni greeted Michel's parents in a low, bashful voice. They looked him over with well-mannered curiosity.

"So now you meet again," Chaim stood at Choni's side, putting his hand on Choni's shoulder. Chaim was providing unexpected support for his son.

Choni flashed a questioning glance at his father. He thought that Chaim would not approve of this relationship. So why was he acting so friendly, while his mother was chatting vigorously with a woman who did not appear to be observant?

"So, Choni, did you manage to accomplish anything while you were in Entebbe?" asked his father.

"Me?" Choni was thunderstruck.

"Yes. Take a good look at Gerard. Do you see anything different?"

Choni took a second glance. Gerard's eyes had frightened him. He had tried to avoid him when they were in Entebbe, but here he was less frightening. And then he saw it: On the top of Gerard's curly locks, a small yarmulke rested.

"That's because I'm a Jew, and I'd like to return to the roots of our heritage," Gerard announced. His sincere and unpretentious words impressed Chaim deeply.

"It was mostly your doing, Choni. Your splendid behavior while you were in Entebbe," Chaim said as he squeezed Choni's shoulder again.

Choni was speechless. Michel took him aside and briefly outlined what happened.

"Gerard decided to return to his roots. Papa disagreed in the beginning, and Mama could not understand what he was doing. Turns out, he was distancing himself from his old friends because it was dangerous for him to return to France. He has already spoken to some rabbis, and it appears that he will stay here to learn." Michel, in his excitement, slipped occasionally into French as he spoke.

"That's good." Choni could not think of anything better to say. He sat down next to Michel on the sofa and avoided his mother's gaze. She gazed at him with approval and admiration as she continued speaking with the boys' mother.

"And what about you, Michel? If it's good for Gerard, it's good for you too," Choni suggested.

"Me? What?" Michel was confused. "I don't know. I had planned to be a scientist. Maybe I'll change my plans. Gerard and I were always different." Those words were enough for Choni, and he dropped the subject.

When they were in Entebbe, he had found it easy to talk to Michel. The tribulations they faced there brought them together. Here in Israel, however, they found it hard to communicate. Perhaps it was better this way.

Michel had no intention of remaining quiet. He told about the trips they had taken, and the places they had visited. He spoke excitedly about the interview with some newspaper reporters who had wanted him to tell them about his experiences in Entebbe. They even quoted him verbatim in their article. Choni listened politely.

A short while later, Dinah served lunch. Pleasant conversation continued around the table and the time flew by faster than they had anticipated. Georges and Chaim worked out a plan to get Gerard settled. Georges pulled out a thick wad of money from his briefcase and handed it to Chaim, requesting that he find an appropriate yeshivah and suitable housing for his son. He still did not trust his son enough to hand him such a large sum of money. If Gerard felt slighted, he did not show it.

No one dreamed that the real problem would arise at the end of their enjoyable visit. After agreeing that Gerard would seek admission to an appropriate yeshivah, and Chaim generously declared that their house would be his home in Israel, they began their goodbyes. Michel said to Chaim, "I see that Choni really is like your son, and he treats you as if you were his parents."

"What are you saying?" Choni flushed and angrily pulled Michel's sleeve.

But Michel told Choni excitedly, not paying any attention to what was happening in the room, "I was sure that you wouldn't relate to them. They are, after all, not your real parents. But, after meeting them, I see that they really are terrific parents. It would be a shame to ruin the relationship. All right, I see my folks are ready to leave, so goodbye, and let's stay in touch."

Choni's looked around nervously.

"Do you have any idea what he's talking about?" Chaim stood near Choni, stroking his hair.

"I...."

Choni was visibly upset. Then he noticed his father's calm demeanor, and suddenly realized that his father knew the truth: They knew that he knew. This revelation further distressed and disoriented him.

Georges stood in the doorway, and Annette had already started down the stairway, continuing to thank them. Michel departed too, unaware of the firestorm he had ignited. Gerard shook Chaim's hand and left as well.

Only when the door finally closed and Choni stood there trembling, hanging on to the doorknob for support, did Chaim turn to face him and begin talking to him. Dinah watched them, but in a moment of panic, ran to the kitchen, and decided not to join them.

"Well, Choni, I think it's time for us to speak openly and truthfully."

"I — don't know what the truth is anymore."

Chaim led the child into the living room, and sat him down on the sofa. He poured a glass of cold water for Choni and told him to sip some.

"You look pale. Try to relax, Choni."

"Is it true?" Choni's lips were parched, and he could not look at Chaim.

"You are our child, and we love you. That is the first truth. The second truth is — " Suddenly, Chaim was unable to look at the orphan. "Your parents were killed in an automobile accident. Your father, *alav hashalom,* was my brother. We took you, Choni, to be our son. From the moment we took you in, you were our child, just like our other children. Is that clear?"

Choni was unable to utter a sound. After a brief pause, he managed to say, "And I thought maybe Michel was lying to me."

"He was not. He told the truth. By the way, Mr. Schick told us that you knew. Michel's words did not surprise us."

"So you also know that — " Choni was confused. "And that woman is really my grandmother," he continued.

"Yes, she is your mother's mother. I think that we did you an injustice by not telling you the truth before your trip. Now, she surely feels deeply insulted by your behavior. She was very excited to see you, but you caused her a lot of grief."

"I don't know her at all," Choni declared defiantly.

Chaim forced himself to remain silent and not rebuke Choni for his insolent response. *Choni is just a child,* he reasoned, *and it was difficult for him to control himself at such a confusing moment.*

Both of them fell silent. Then Choni murmured, "I still thought it was not true."

Dinah looked in from the kitchen. Chaim nodded; he had gone through the hard part with Choni. Now he needed her to participate too.

Dinah sat down on the sofa near Choni and poured herself some cold water. She, too, was exhausted and overwrought. She asked, "How does the truth feel, Choni?"

"I don't know. I'm confused." He did not even look at her. "I have to be going back to *cheider*. It's already 3:30. Abba does not want me to be late. Right, Abba?"

"Yes, but today I think you can — "

"So I'll go rest in my room."

Chaim and Dinah watched Choni as he headed toward his bedroom. "I think he's sleeping too much. Maybe it's because of the shock of what he has just learned. Or perhaps it's because — " Dinah struggled to understand Choni's feelings.

"He needs to rest, and so do I. This has been a hard day for all of us. I hope this business is ending. Choni knows, and we know that he knows. We have quite a situation on our hands," Chaim remarked, concealing a yawn.

The telephone rang. "Maybe it's Pinchas. He went to Yoav's for lunch." Dinah ran to the phone, where she heard a low harsh voice ask for her husband.

"Who is calling?" Chaim was ready to leave the house and return to work. He had missed many days at the office and wanted to catch up on lost hours of work.

"One moment, I'm sure he'll speak to you."

Dinah gestured to Chaim to take the call. "It's a long distance call — Moishe Kahn."

When he took the phone, Chaim heard the angry voice declare, "This is not an overseas call like your wife thought. I am here in Eretz Yisrael, Reb Chaim. You had better have some convincing reasons why we should not remove Elchanan from your custody. My son Shimon is here with me. We demand to see the child."

"First of all, *shalom* and welcome, Reb Moishe," Chaim said, trying to keep his composure. He suddenly realized that the real crisis was now upon them. "I'm glad to hear that you decided to come visit. Really, it's a great idea for you to come and visit Choni. Your wife has already seen him."

"I know what my wife has seen, including some things that

were not too pleasing, like your upbringing of our grandson, and his behavior. Reb Chaim, I thank you for your devotion to my grandson, but the time has come for us to take him back to France."

"Why don't we discuss this first?" Chaim suggested cautiously. He realized that the elderly man was still exhausted from the plane flight. He heard Shimon in the background and even Rivkah's excited voice as well.

"I understand that your wife might have been insulted. But please understand, Choni has still not gotten back to himself. He is still suffering from the frightening experience of the hijacking. You must be considerate."

"We're trying. In the meantime, I want to see my grandson. When can I come over?"

"You are all invited over for dinner at 8 o'clock."

"Don't bother. We're not coming to eat," came the reply. "We just want to see our grandchild. Is that such a big request, Reb Chaim? Or are you concocting something behind our backs?"

"Of course not. We'll see you at 8 o'clock." Chaim put the phone down with a gloomy expression on his face.

"They're here in the country. He and his son," he announced darkly to Dinah. "I'm afraid they're in a combative mood. I have no idea why they are fighting over Choni, but I invited them over this evening. We have to prepare Choni for this visit."

"They're fighting for themselves, because of their longing for their daughter," Dinah explained. Even while justifying their actions, her eyes showed her sadness.

"I'll make my best cake; maybe it will help the mood. We have to explain everything to Choni, and coach him how to behave."

"I'll come home early. Let's hope everything will be okay." Chaim left the house with a splitting headache.

Dinah began baking, and then straightened up the house. Choni, however, preferred to bury his head in his pillow, falling into a restless sleep.

CHAPTER FIFTY-ONE

The Binder home had seen its share of embarrassed silence. Even now, there was an unpleasant quiet in the living room, and Choni intensified it. From the moment that everyone knew that "everyone knew" and that "there is nothing more to conceal," Dinah could not connect emotionally with her son.

Choni seemed to be the most unhappy of all. He found it hard to look his mother in the eye. When he did glance at her, he seemed to be accusing her of something. She could not tell what.

Just before his grandparents came in, she took him aside.

"Are you angry, Choni?"

"Not really. What do you want?" He was not being impudent; it was hard to control his raging, conflicting emotions.

"I want you to relax. Look, nothing has changed! We took you in as a son, and you continue to be our son. Do you understand?"

"Yes."

She wanted to elaborate, but the insistent knocking on the door cut her off. She opened the door to Shimon, whose body language indicated that he had taken charge of the affair.

"*Shalom aleichem*," Shimon said as he entered somewhat aggressively, shook Chaim's hand, and looked with curiosity at Choni.

"And this is little Elchanan," he announced festively, in broken and grammatically incorrect Hebrew. Choni and Pinchas tried to hide their amusement, but were not successful.

After him, the elderly couple entered. "*Shalom aleichem*, grandson.ated." Moishe stuck his hand out toward Choni, but the boy just nodded while remaining on the chair, as if his pants were stuck to the seat. His cold response annoyed Moishe, who could not understand why the child did not move toward him.

They all sat down in the living room, where Mrs. Kahn placed herself close to Choni and tried to persuade him to talk to her. "We are already acquainted, so you are not afraid of me, right, Elchanan?"

He smiled in response.

"Why don't you talk to us? Don't you understand us?"

"I understand. I also talk. How are you?" But the child within him rebelled at everything that was happening here against his will.

Dinah brought a plate of coffee cake to the table. "In honor of our dear guests," she said pleasantly.

She sat down at Mrs. Kahn's side and said, "We spoke candidly today with Choni about his being adopted. He is still feeling the effects of the traumas that hit him, and has not fully recovered yet. Try to understand his situation," she said.

Choni's grandmother did not exactly understand. More importantly, she did not want to. "Do you mean he only found out today?"

"It's a long story that's not for now," Dinah commented, glancing in Choni's direction.

The silence in the room became oppressive. Shimon engaged Chaim in some small talk.

Moishe Kahn wiped away some tears. "I am overwhelmed. You have no idea what it's like for me to meet my grown-up grandson. We missed you, Choni, even if we did not know you. You are part of our family."

Choni wished the visit would end at that moment. He was not affected by his grandparents' display of emotion.

Shimon tried to get the conversation onto rational ground. "It's time for children to leave the room," he tactlessly insisted. "Only Abba and Ima can stay. It was nice to meet you, kids."

Pinchas and Choni left the room, barely containing their amusement. As they left the living room, Pinchas burst out laughing. Choni laughed only outwardly. Inwardly, he wept. The mistakes in Hebrew did not amuse him. They embarrassed him, by displaying his relatives in a negative light. The very fact that they were his relatives confused him.

In the living room, the oppressive silence continued. They decided to switch to speaking French, which was easier for the Kahns.

"This cake is excellent," Shimon announced as he took a second slice, in his attempt to pay a compliment to the lady of the house. He wanted to lighten the atmosphere a bit before getting to the unpleasant part.

After they all agreed that the cake was delicious, and that Choni looked well, Shimon continued speaking, with his parents' approval. He explained how shocked his parents were at Choni's behavior. This was not how a proper Jewish child conducted himself. "Of course, we aren't blaming you," he said pointedly. "But maybe Elchanan would be better off growing up in the family that was truly closest to him."

Chaim listened quietly, but Dinah protested, "Choni has gone through a traumatic experience! You cannot judge him as he is presently. Besides, it makes no sense to uproot him from his family and his parents. Doing that would be utterly irresponsible."

Shimon ignored her remarks. "We'll decide on which course of action to take. It's true that the child has difficulty communicating with us, but we'd like to talk to him some more, perhaps without the two of you present."

At this point, Chaim interrupted. He asked, "What if Choni doesn't want to participate in these private conversations?"

Shimon seemed confused. "*B'ezras Hashem*, he will be interested. Why should you assume a negative premise?"

The conversation's harsh undertones escalated. The cake's delectable taste faded away. The coffee was not particularly sweet either.

The Kahns finally rose to leave, then found Choni to say goodbye. As Shimon offered his hand to Choni, he said, "We are in a hotel, and will be in the country for the coming week. We are sure you will come and visit your grandparents." Shimon did not leave the boy any choice. Choni nodded. He honestly did not know what to say. To his surprise, he realized that his parents were unable to help him cope with his new family. They were just as helpless as he was.

A grim stillness filled the house after the Kahns left. As Chaim announced that he had to go back to the office, Pinchas silently began straightening the living room, and Choni went into the kitchen. Dinah entered the kitchen and saw her son energetically washing the dishes.

"Well?"

"Well, what?"

She decided to continue the conversation she had started before the Kahns interrupted. "Choni, we didn't discuss your feelings. You didn't tell us what you felt when you found out about your adoption."

Choni concentrated on scouring a small plate, as if it were the most important thing in the world. "You know, I was able to figure out everything because of your letter," he said abruptly.

"That's right. I sent a letter to your grandparents," Dinah affirmed. She was excited that Choni was willing to share this aspect of his Entebbe experience.

"You wrote all sorts of things. Then I understood — but I didn't believe it was true. Things like this happen only in fairy tales."

"Not exactly. Many *sefarim* discuss things that happen in life, and precisely because they are rare occurrences, they are mentioned. See, like what happened here."

"I don't want to be a child of *sefarim*. I'm Choni, and I want to continue being the Choni I was before all this happened," he said tearfully, setting the plate down on the counter.

"Now I understand why Abba always treated me so — "

"Like what?" She was shocked.

"Treated me a little harshly. Not like Pinchas."

"What are you talking about?"

"That's how I felt. And when I got back home, I couldn't look at him, because he's not really my father. And you are not really my mother."

"But we raised you, and we *are* your family. You were a little baby when you joined our family, just as if you were our own child," she said, in an emotion-filled voice.

She suddenly thought of Sarah, Choni's mother. She remembered a conversation they had had shortly before Choni was born. "I have a dream, that one day my children will, *im yirtzeh*

Hashem, be as sensitive as Yaakov," Sarah had said.

Well, then, Sarah's child indeed took after his father. But in this case, it turned out to be detrimental. He was so sensitive that he understood what was disturbing the adults and what motivated them to do what they did.

He is a sensitive boy, Sarah, Dinah thought. *Daven for him. We are doing all we can so that everything should be good for him.*

Sarah had continued that conversation, saying, "My greatest fear is that as parents we might be unable to provide our child with everything he needs. You know, health, wealth, and so on. And I so much want my child to have everything."

Sarah, your child truly has everything; health, love of life, intelligence. He is a very talented child. But he does not have parents. We, Chaim and I, are his parents. Still, the boy is dissatisfied. And rightly so. He wanted to know his parents.

"You're crying, Ima?" Choni brought her back to the present. He said the word Ima a bit differently, and Dinah flinched.

"I'm recalling the time — "

"What time?"

"A long time ago, when I talked to your mother — "

Choni paled. This was the first time she would speak openly about him being adopted.

"You knew my mother?"

"Very well. We were close friends, and I liked her a lot."

"Am I like her?" he asked bashfully.

"No, you are really more like your father. Why do you ask?"

"You said that you liked each other a lot, so I thought — "

"I have always truly felt you were my son, because your mother and I were such good friends. I was so happy when you were born. I immediately felt close to you. But you were born in Eretz Yisrael, and we were still in France."

Choni listened to the portions of his life history that had been missing until now. He listened like an impartial observer, an outsider, not like someone who was deeply involved in the story, who was the main character in the story.

"Then why did you take me? Why didn't my grandparents?" he finally asked, after hearing all the details from his mother.

"Because they were too old, and they were broken by your mother's death," Dinah explained.

Just then, Pinchas came into the kitchen. Choni abruptly changed the subject.

As the night wore on, Dinah found it difficult to carry on with her chores. She had told her adopted son about his past, about his parents and their family. She felt a sudden bonding with Choni, a sense of dedication to his well-being. It was much stronger than anything she had felt in the past. She was thrilled at the positive change in Choni's attitude regarding the adoption. Yet she soon realized that her satisfaction was premature.

A short time later, when Choni went to his room for the night, he whispered to his mother, "I do not like that family. You promised me *you* would always be my family. They just want to take me to their house. I don't like them, and I don't want to visit them. As far as I'm concerned, they can go back to France right now. You can tell them I said that, O.K.?"

Dinah did not know how to respond. "That's not very polite, you know."

Choni was agitated and did not care. "So what? I am not going to visit them," he said firmly and left the room. Dinah remained alone in the kitchen, wondering what to do next.

CHAPTER FIFTY-TWO

"**W**hat should we do with Choni, Chaim? I'm sure that the Kahns want to take him from us. They are convinced that we are turning him away from them." Dinah was exhausted from all the fighting. "Chaim, I cannot see any way out of this. The whole thing has become so complicated," she said in despair.

"I honestly don't know what to do," Chaim said angrily. "I loved my brother. I was prepared to go through fire and water for him, despite our differences. And I love his son — our son." His poignant announcement brought tears to Dinah's eyes.

"I feel the same way toward Choni. He truly is our son."

"From an emotional standpoint. Legally, however, he may belong to the Kahns more than to us, because my parents are no longer living," Chaim interjected. "I wanted to ask Rav Katz what we should do. The irony about it is that if Choni had treated them nicely, they would have left here satisfied, knowing that he is in good hands. Choni doesn't understand that his future depends on them."

"He is too young to understand," Dinah said in Choni's defense.

"True, but we've got to explain to him how serious the situation is. He must treat his relatives properly. He has to learn to respect them, to treat them properly, and to give them what they want. Only then will they leave him, and us, alone."

It was late, nearly midnight. It was unusual for them to be sitting in the living room and talking at such an hour. The unique situation, however, demanded it.

"Choni said he is not interested in visiting them under any circumstances. So even if we take him forcibly to their hotel, what good will that do? You know what will happen. He will ignore them, making the situation worse."

"It's interesting that he's so angry at them," Chaim said.

"They are threatening his existence, his familiar routine. He's fighting back against that threat," Dinah explained.

"Not just that. There is something deeper here. Something Rav Katz explained to me."

"Rav Katz?" Dinah did not understand.

"Yes," Chaim said as he rose from his chair. "You won't believe it, but now I'm beginning to understand certain things that he told me a while ago. Things that, at the time, I actually dismissed as irrelevant."

"Such as?"

Chaim took a deep breath. "You know, the child has been ours practically from the day he was born. He is sensitive to our emotions and thoughts, and he understands that we are afraid of his family. He senses all the hidden feelings that we think we are hiding from him."

"And what are we broadcasting?" Dinah asked. She already knew the answer, but wanted to hear Chaim say it.

"We are angry at them. We do not like them. Isn't that the truth?"

"Well, maybe." She did not want to contradict him.

"And Rav Katz told me many times that I have to love Choni's family, for the child's sake. So he will also love them. It's obvious the boy would imitate our behavior. In a childlike manner, of course, because he's not mature enough to conceal his feelings toward them."

"Are you saying then, that we are guilty?" It was a painful question, but she had to ask.

Chaim concluded, "We have to change our approach, that's all."

They heard someone knocking on the living-room door. The Binders were startled. Pinchas stood in the doorway, looking frightened. Dinah was amazed at how he had matured recently.

"I think Choni is crying," Pinchas reported to them quietly. "I can hear him."

"Crying?" They were not surprised, but they were worried.

"I'll go to him," Chaim decided. He asked Dinah to keep Pinchas out of his room. Dinah hurried to the kitchen to prepare a cup of hot chocolate for him.

"It will all be solved soon. You have nothing to worry about," she promised Pinchas when she saw his worried look.

"Do you think they'll take Choni with them?"

"I hope that they will understand that his home is here, with his parents and his family."

"I really feel that he is my brother, even if he looks for more attention than any other kid in the world," Pinchas declared.

Dinah urged him to finish drinking and suddenly realized

that she needed to make a point of paying more attention to Pinchas. He was their son, also. In all the excitement, he was almost forgotten.

"Go to sleep. Tomorrow, *b'ezras Hashem,* will be another day fresh with good news," she said and hoped to have good news for Pinchas, as well as for herself.

Pinchas went to bed, and Dinah hurried to the boys' room. She was surprised to find Choni sitting up on the bed, leaning on his father, who was embracing him warmly. They were whispering together quietly, and she could scarcely hear their words. They did not notice her, and she retreated silently back to the kitchen. She did not know whether to be jealous or to rejoice.

It was an unbelievable scene. The whole family knew about the awkward encounters between Chaim and Choni over the years. Even Chaim could not deny them, and they caused Dinah endless anguish. Countless times she had begged her husband to soften his approach, to no avail. Chaim claimed that he was training the boy, strengthening him, to face life's tribulations. Choni often became angry with his father, and felt himself singled out for extra harsh treatment.

Dinah was overwhelmed with questions: What was Chaim whispering to him? Did he tell him about the pain he had felt when his brother died? Did he tell Choni how much he resembled his father? Or did he tell him how much it hurt him every time he had to discipline his brother's son, instead of watching Yaakov raise him?

What was he saying? What was Choni's reaction?

Suddenly, Dinah felt a rush of gratitude to Hashem, for granting Chaim the patience and understanding to explain it all to Choni; for the intelligence, the sensitivity, and good nature to admit the mistakes he had made. They were not malicious errors, only well-intentioned ones. Now Choni was hearing it all.

Was he old enough to understand?

Half an hour later, the two returned to the kitchen. Choni's eyes were still wet, but his face shone with an unusual serenity.

"I couldn't sleep. I was thinking about everything, and I started to cry. Suddenly, Abba came in," Choni told her as she prepared a cup of hot chocolate for him.

"Is everything O.K. now?"

"*Baruch Hashem*," he said, smiling.

Chaim went to get ready for bed at 1:30 in the morning. Choni remained with Dinah in the kitchen.

"The whole time, I thought maybe Abba doesn't like me. That I am not good enough for him, and that everything was my fault. Now, I understand everything. Abba explained to me things that I never imagined. He really does love me."

"Of course, Choni. We all love you."

He smiled and sipped the warm drink. Once again, he seemed to be a child and an adult combined into one person.

"And now, will you agree to go visit your grandparents in the hotel?"

"Yes. Abba explained that I should be happy that my family takes an interest in my well-being, and I ought to thank them for their interest. The entire time, I thought they just wanted to take me away from here," he said innocently.

Dinah nearly burst into tears.

"What will you tell them if they suggest that you come live with them in France?" she asked delicately.

"I'll tell them that I'll try to get over my fears from Entebbe, and of flying, and will come to visit them. If they miss me very much, I'll even invite them to come here. Abba said that as far as he is concerned, they are just like family. Do you also feel that way, Ima?"

Dinah closed her eyes for a moment, then said, "If Abba does, then I do."

Choni was exhausted. He finished the warm drink and put the cup in the sink. "So tomorrow I'll go visit them," he concluded. "Then they'll go back to France, and I'll go back to *cheider*, and our lives will continue as usual, without problems."

"*Im yirtzeh Hashem.* Are you anxious to get back to your regular routine already?"

"Very much."

Choni finally headed off to bed, but just before he left the room, he turned to his mother.

"Ima?" he said in a special tone of voice.

"What, sweetie?"

"You know, the moment I found out I was adopted, I felt terrible, like I was alone in the world. But Michel translated your letter word for word, and I kept hearing one sentence over and over in my head. I knew it was true. You wrote that you would always remain my mother, no matter what the circumstances. Those words — only a real, true mother could say them.

"Today, I realize that if Abba would have written that, I'd be even more relieved. Because for me, he will always be my father. I am not alone. But your words comforted me when I was there, because I knew that whatever happens, you are always my mother. I feel as if I'm your real son."

Dinah was so overwhelmed she could barely speak. "You are my real son," she barely managed to say.

Choni finally went to bed, and almost immediately his parents heard his gentle breathing as he fell asleep. Chaim returned to the kitchen in his pajamas. Now, it was his turn to have a warm drink in the kitchen.

"Why are your eyes wet?" he asked Dinah.

"Probably for the same reason yours are," she replied.

Their emotions were hard to contain. "He understood; he's such a clever child. What a shame Yaakov didn't know him," Chaim's voice nearly broke as he said those words.

"He does know him. He sees him from *Shamayim*, accompanying him wherever he goes. Sarah too...." Dinah said quietly. "I feel as if Sarah dictated those words to me in that letter. Choni was moved by the sentence saying that I would always be his mother. Do you know what? I think that Sarah will also always be his mother. She watches him from *Shamayim*, maybe takes care of him, I don't know. Sarah and Yaakov sent him to us, for us to raise as our child."

Chaim seemed lost in thought as she spoke. Then he said, "Everything is fine. The fact is that a life-changing event ended well. The question is, will the Kahns also understand this, and will Choni be able to explain it to them?" Chaim asked. "Maybe they are seeking a custody fight; they seem convinced that Choni should go to France with them."

"Maybe. But Choni will tell them about his life. You spoke to him, and he understood and agreed. He will do his best to show them what he really is, and I am certain they will understand. Look, ultimately, they are his family. They love him just as we do. They simply haven't been able to put the pain of Sarah's death behind them, and to make a distinction between Choni and his deceased parents. To distinguish between their pain and anguish, and their anger," Dinah explained.

"And if they don't?" Chaim asked.

Dinah shrugged her shoulders. "May Hashem have mercy on all of us."

The first light of dawn was already visible when Chaim and Dinah finally went to sleep. In the morning, Chaim and Choni headed toward *shul* to *daven*. After breakfast, they met with the Kahns, who were expecting their grandson. Chaim left Choni alone, while Dinah sat at home reciting *Tehillim*. She hoped and prayed that Choni's sincere words would penetrate their hearts. Her fervent prayers worked to convince the Kahns to leave Choni in their hands. Choni accepted the fact that he has another family, and that he has to respect them, to love them, and to give them some comfort because he is their beloved daughter's son.

Later on, the Binders celebrated Choni's rescue with a *seudas hoda'ah*. They invited the entire family, from Yoav the eldest, who worked so hard doing everything possible for his younger "brother," down to Pinchas the youngest. They invited the Kahns, as well as friends and teachers. They also invited Gerard, who was taking his first tentative steps toward an observant lifestyle with great courage.

"Abba, Ima, you didn't have to work so hard…" Choni told them after the *seudah*. But he knew as well as they did that as his parents, they would always do their best for him.